MOROCCONOMICS

A NOVEL

WALKER ZUPP

MONTAG

Montag Press Team:

Cover: Rick Febre
Editor: Charlie Franco
Managing Director: Charlie Franco

A Montag Press Book
www.montagpress.com
Montag Press
777 Morton Street, Unit B
San Francisco CA 94129 USA

Montag Press, the burning book with the hatchet cover, the skewed word mark and the portrayal of the long-suffering fireman mascot are trademarks of Montag Press.

Printed & Digitally Originated in the United States of America
10 9 8 7 6 5 4 3 2 1

DEDICATION

This book is dedicated to uncertainty
and the morons who try avoiding it.

ENDORSEMENTS FOR MOROCCONOMICS

"Walker Zupp's story treks through historic swaths of Morocco on a quest that explores both the beauty and banality of life. Morocconomics is a richly-told tale, layered in history."

—Charis Emanon,
author of *51 Ways to End Your World*

"You will need careful eyesight in the paranoid landscapes of Walker Zupp's *Morocconomics*. My advice would be not to drink the water and not to trust a soul, for we are all watching *someone* in this novel. Keep your panicked eyes peeled! From the tricky neologism of its title, through the tight restricting nightmares of its plot, the author leads us with verve and helps us to grow as readers. Learning about Zupp's imagined world has been an invaluable experience. I was challenged and wrenched away from my comfort zone. I enjoyed not knowing who to believe."

—David Mathew,
author of *Abandoned Dental Clinics*

Was he free? Was he happy? The question is absurd: Had anything been wrong, we should certainly have heard.

— "The Unknown Citizen"
by W.H. Auden (1939).

PROLOGUE

Outside the prison, two North African gerbils had made their peace with nature, and inside the prison were little rooms for people charged with fake crimes.

Outside, the descendants of the Neanderthal-like pebble people, who had once foraged for nuts and berries around Morocco's semi-tropical forests between 100,000 and 75,000 B.C., now carried semi-automatic weapons and politely followed orders without questioning them at all. Whether human nature had changed or was simply a mid-afternoon re-run of our most popular genocides and murders, made little difference, since our story's champion had no idea what, or who, a Neanderthal was.

Inside, Lou Baring was twenty-nine-years-old. He coughed and touched sores that had manifested as a result of poor hygiene and little washing. He had a scraggly beard and scars on his face where the guards had put out cigarettes. There were bruises on his skinny body from mid-day beatings at the hands of visitors - whom he hadn't solicited.

Suddenly, the door slammed at the end of the burnt-sienna corridor and two guards approached wearing military-green uniforms and bland military caps.

Lou struggled to stand. He looked through the barred door at the shadowy figures illuminated beyond. Keys jangled and the door to his cell screeched open.

The bigger of the two guards filled the doorway and stared dully at Lou. He made way for the smaller guard who put a hand on Lou's shoulder and guided him out of the prison cell. They walked down the corridor that had been Lou's home for so many days?…weeks?…months?…

They entered a wider corridor where equally clad guards were frog-marching similarly malnourished prisoners with bags on their heads up and down the corridor. The set-up was immense and Lou was just another tourist to be charged with crimes.

After five minutes of painful walking, Lou and his guards reached a large pair of doors which then opened and led into what had been the bustling Republican Theatre. The communists had turned it into a tribunal hall where the accused were tried and studied concurrently by the youngest, newest, and spottiest members of the party.

Lou was half-dragged, half-escorted down the fading red carpet to the stage. He shifted his eyes from the eager crowd with their electronic tablets to a wheelchair-bound woman being escorted off of the stage by the ever-helpful Dr. Zaki. The woman, deathly pale, wearing an oxygen mask, was swiftly wheeled away. Then Lou took her place onstage. He was seated on a chair and scrutinized by military-green officials smoking cigarettes at a long table that had once carried meals. The bearded and sad-eyed leading judge – who appeared to have an aura of royalty about him - observed Lou for a fleeting moment. "State your name, please," said the judge in English.

"You know my name," said Lou. He had had to state his name many times. A guard punched his frail shoulder. *"Lou Baring,"* said Lou.

"State your occupation, please."

"I am a property manager in Marrakech," he lied, trying to replace the present with the past, and staring into it, wishing he was years younger and not the current Lou.

An unhappy burbling washed through the crowd before the tribunal. Capped heads turned to other capped heads condemning Lou Baring.

"Lou Baring," repeated the judge. "You are charged with five counts of drunken and disorderly behaviour in the city of Marrakech and one count of pederasty carried out in an undisclosed location. You are also charged with the murder of the Mauritanian national and war hero, Kossi Bundhoo, who held this nation in the fondest of regards." The judge paused for breath. "How do you plead, Lou Baring?"

"Not guilty." Lou privately acknowledged his personal failures. "I did drink heavily. But I've been sober for several months now."

"In that case," interjected the secondary female judge. "The court shall be lenient, Mr. Baring."

Lou sat up straight, eyeing each official. "You're not going to kill Nina, are you?"

The audience gasped, tapping furious words into their electronic tablets, comparing the woman's name to the fall of the Almoravids: a sort of contemporary Californian time in the distant past, when medieval Berber women took charge, encouraged every vice, and weakened the Muslim commanders, who became ineffective and heedless.

The judges observed one other and nodded. They had reached a decision.

"Where's Nina going?" pleaded Lou.

"Mr. Baring - "

"Are you going to kill her?"

"This court finds you guilty on all charges," said the sad-eyed judge. He gestured to the guards. "Take him away."

The audience cheered as Lou was lifted out of his chair, dragged up the fading red carpet that had once carried Zaky Chafik at the premiere of his North African epic, *How The Northwest Was Won,* and taken beyond the doors which banged shut behind him.

Being inside had robbed Lou of his sense of time.

Outside, when the guards yanked him out under the slowly rising solar bomb, he was shocked to find it was early morning. Lou could see the Atlas Mountains in the distance, like a North African Mount Olympus, its Columbia-blues and cadet-greys gleaming dully like a line of oil trucks. Covered in snow, the ancient mountains seemed to tell Lou that he would never see them again. In the past, before the Spanish and the French came, tea and sugar had put Morocco in debt to Europe. Now, something like fate would put an end to Lou and the things that he didn't stand for.

FOUR YEARS EARLIER

MARRAKECH
APRIL 2089, 7:29 A.M.

CHAPTER ONE

Lou was twenty-five when he applied for an internship at Zaalouk Real Estate's London branch. After enjoying the happy-go-lucky existence of a trainee, Lou applied for an internally advertised position and received an interview. He was made a full-time real estate agent the following week and worked from there. The following year Lou was approached by his boss, James Oppenheimer, and was asked to become the property manager for their branch in Marrakech. Despite having to look up Marrakech – and subsequently Morocco – on a map, Lou accepted the post and packed up his apartment. When he arrived in Morocco, he was given an apartment in Marrakech. He liked the wide-open kitchen, the cool lounge, the large bedroom, and the marble-tiled lavatories. He had no idea that the name "Morocco" had been derived from the city of Marrakech, which had been built in the early eleventh century; nor that Moroccans sometimes referred to the whole country as Marrakech, when Turks traditionally referred to Morocco as Fez, which was actually a northern Moroccan city.

One, Two, Three

Hum it, Ham it, Hack it, Hayek
Hayek, now, baby, don't put that Keynes on me

I say, Hum it, Ham it, Hack it, Hayek
Hayek, now, baby, don't put that Keynes on me

You got me spending all this green like a clown
Just look at me

Lou's easy journey passed through his mind as he switched off *The Commie Bastards* on the car radio and turned off the roundabout towards the Zaalouk Real Estate branch. Staring into the rear-view mirror for a split second, he was afraid at what he witnessed: an aquiline nose with hairs poking out of the nostrils, heavy bags under his light-cornflower-blue eyes, and a drooped neck from too much slouching over. The banana-mania-coloured suit he wore was from Marks and Spencer's, along with five pairs of banana-mania-coloured trousers, white shirts, and an azure-blue necktie - doubtless, he wasn't wearing all five pairs at the same time, but there niggled at the back of Lou's mind the fact that he *owned* five pairs of banana-mania-coloured trousers which could only be worn with his banana-mania-coloured suit jacket, and nothing else.

Lou drove into the heart of Marrakech and parked outside the Zaalouk Real Estate branch office. The building was almost entirely composed of glass and featured large doors. Lou sweated interminably in his car, collecting himself and muttering resentments. He wiped his forehead. Then he went out and opened the big glass doors.

Inside, the air-conditioning was on full blast.

The managing director, Jack Bailey, greeted Lou and brought him through the chattering office towards the real director's office. He knocked and then opened the door.

Cleopatra Griffiths was a middle-aged woman with thick blonde hair, high cheekbones, and immaculate painted nails. She wore a carrot-orange pantsuit, hooped earrings, and the sharpest high heels that Lou had seen outside of Richmond.

Staring up from her computer screen, Cleopatra stood up, smiled, and greeted the new property manager, after which she dismissed Jack Bailey by flapping her hand.

"Lou," greeted Cleopatra. "It's wonderful to meet you." After shaking hands, she gestured to a carrot-orange chair. "I suppose I should be thankful you're able to talk shop."

"Huh?"

"Can you manage properties? I know you passed the interview with that lot in London. They were probably trying to get rid of you - but I want you to work hard."

"Uh."

"Well, come on." Cleopatra vaguely observed her desk.

"I've got a degree in it." He pointed to her computer. "You didn't delete my CV, did you?"

"No."

"Uh."

The director furrowed her brow. "Walk me through your average day. What are you going to be doing here?" She slapped her desk. "Hurry up, there's lots I need to get through this morning."

"I'll be setting and collecting rent and handling maintenance requests. I'll be filling vacant properties and setting budgets for the properties." Wiping his forehead, he winced at his doubt. "I'll be doing things the owners don't want to do."

But Cleopatra wasn't listening. She was staring out of her window at Lou's car.

"Is that your car?" asked Cleopatra. She and Lou both stared through the glass. "You can't drive a Lada."

"It's got four wheels."

"It doesn't - "

"It doesn't?" asked Lou, squinting through the window.

"No, it doesn't look good. That's my problem. The people we work with like to know they've got nice things going past their window."

"Who are they?"

"Well - " Cleopatra took a deep breath. "We manage all the property in Morocco."

"Huh," said Lou.

The director arched an eyebrow. Her knowledge of the history of bullfighting in ancient Morocco came in handy sometimes.

"That's nice," said Lou, fencing off the memories that crowded his mind - not shaping it, or forming it, but crowding it, and packing his brain like eels packed into saffron-coloured plastic, and shipped away. Early schooling in Bermuda. Boarding school in England. University in England. Although boarding and studying for one's degree were two very different things. Then the unaccountable internship at Acton Properties. Then Zaalouk Real Estate, where he appeared to belong - except what Lou identified as belonging, and meaning, was more like the grim satisfaction one gets after having sex with someone bumped into, or borrowed, from one's public transport. An ugly belonging bred an ugly meaning, but beauty was in the eye of the beholder, and Lou was no exception to that theory, which ignored brow specialists and pop stars.

"We have a monopoly," explained Cleopatra. "It's great for business."

Lou imagined a carrot-orange dragon breathing fire across a village. "Right," said Lou, re-entering the meeting. "I guess I have to manage it."

"You *are* the property manager." She hinted at a smile and leaned closer. "You set the rent. Then you collect the rent."

"What about maintenance?"

"We don't do maintenance, Lou." She pressed a button on her desk. "Faruk, we're going to be having lunch for three hours."

"Very good, Miss Griffiths," buzzed the reply.

Cleopatra escorted Lou out of her office. Then she locked the door, ushered Lou outside, and stepped into a melon-coloured taxi that rushed off down the boiling road.

Accursio's was a Sicilian-themed restaurant a few blocks over that sported terracotta slates on the outdoor dining area, bronzed-coloured carpeting, tables with draping white tablecloths, and booths with cedar-chest-coloured high-backed seats.

The kitchen was crammed with six chefs who worked either separately or together depending on the order, and a constant parade of apron-wearing waiters and waitresses who picked up the elegant crafted plates of food and delivered them to the right tables. The burliest chef stood in his underwear - nothing else - sprinkling parsley on his recently prepared plate. Pushing this over to another two dishes, he dinged the collection bell and watched as a waitress entered the kitchen and removed the plates.

The lunch service was busy. The waitress carried the plates past tables of businessmen, their clients, and listened to a fellow waiter's joke on the way...

Salvatore Yannucci was an old man with thick forearms that were either powerful or overweight. His dark eyebrows clashed with his shock-white hair. He also had a large stomach, tree-trunk legs that showed beneath his trousers, and a fat neck that flowed over his collar.

He was wearing a dark-liver-coloured suit, black shoes, a white shirt, and a cultured-pearl-coloured necktie. "Thank you, Layla," said Salvatore as the waitress deposited the food on the table, smiled at Salvatore, and scurried back to the kitchen.

The old man sniffed. "The only way to eat prawns." He started peeling their shells off. "You have to eat them raw. The only thing you need is olive oil and lemon juice." He chucked a few into his mouth and winced with pleasure. Then, he said, "And you?"

"Huh?" asked Lou.

Cleopatra rolled her eyes over her raisin-stuffed sardines.

"I mean - " Salvatore dabbed his chin. "Do you like Morocco?"

"It's different," said Lou, poking his pine-nut-coated aubergine.

"Good," replied Salvatore. He drank a glass of catarratto.

"More - *Italian*," added Lou.

Salvatore shot a glance of reproval towards Lou. He shuffled his girth closer to Lou and pointed at his caponata. "Sicilian," stated Salvatore matter-of-factly. Then he looked at Cleopatra and laughed heartily. "Don't forget that! But how's your food!?"

"It's nice," replied Lou.

"You know, I take an interest in this place. If there's anything we can do better, don't worry about telling me."

"It's nice."

"That's good. That makes me feel good." Then he looked at Cleopatra. "You keep bringing me these liars."

Cleopatra laughed and tapped her painted nails on the tablecloth.

"Don't worry," said Salvatore. "I'm just kidding. You know, Lou, this woman has great brains. She has been working hard. She's like a daughter to me."

Then he finished his wine and asked Lou if he knew about "the managers".

Lou looked at Cleopatra for help, but all she could do was shake her head. He looked back at Salvatore and said, "I don't know about them."

Salvatore licked the prawns out of his teeth as he extracted a list of names from his pocket, placed them on the table, and pushed them towards Lou Baring.

"If you have trouble with anything, all you do is call these people."

Lou nodded, chewing.

"So - ," Salvatore pointed to a name. "There are twelve regions in Morocco and the regions all have their own manager. I'll give you an example: let's say someone doesn't pay their rent in Dakhla - down the bottom of the country. All you have to do is call Faiz Impellizzeri. Or if there's a problem with a property in Marrakech, all you have to do is call Laura Donato. People say she's difficult - but they don't know her!"

Lou swallowed and put down his fork. "That's where I was confused. Cleopatra says we don't do maintenance. So, like, is that true?"

Cleopatra noted the lack of loyalty. Or maybe the curious quality.

"My dear," said Salvatore with a sombre tone. "You've brought me Mohammed. You have brought me a pure man - but I don't know what to do with pure men." He chuckled at Cleopatra. "I'm too old to wrestle - I can probably eat more than you, Lou!"

Lou chuckled.

Cleopatra chuckled.

Everybody chuckled.

"They're lucky," said Salvatore, folding his chili-red-coloured napkin. "When I was growing up in Sicily, we didn't have a home. We didn't always, anyway."

He ate the rest of his prawns.

"Non c'è megghiu sarsa di la fami," he stared at Lou.

"Hunger is the best sauce," he motioned for Lou to finish his caponata. "The sauce of life," added Salvatore.

Then he hailed the closest waiter and asked for more red wine.

Detective Mostafa Lazrak was squatting in a suburb of Marrakech and investigating the murder of a middle-aged Moroccan male whose tattoos were like a second skin. The detective had a wide mouth and bright eyes which were enlarged by thick glasses whose purpose was to avoid the awful sensation of sand in contact lenses. He wore a blue-sapphire-coloured suit, brown shoes, and a golden wrist bracelet which tinkled when he moved around.

Lifting an empty cartridge using a ballpoint pen, Detective Lazrak opened a plastic forensics bag, placed the cartridge inside, and pressed the two-part strip back together.

"He was going for his car," said Lazrak in Tamazight, a Berber dialect. The Berber languages had had a revival under the Scarvaggi Family. Tamazight was spoken in the north, mainly, but it had been adopted by others to express a certain Berber identity, even if they had Arab heritage. The Berber language had always had a rough relationship with the incoming Islam that had, to some extent, shaped Morocco.

Around 744 AD, Salih Bin Tarif declared himself a prophet, wrote a book influenced by the Koran but in his own Berber language, and decreed his own prayers and dietary laws, mixing Christianity, Judaism, and animism, whilst maintaining ideas of military jihad…

"But this cartridge would have fallen elsewhere if the marksman had been opposite," added Lazrak.

Sergeant Fatima Ahmed listened, her long hair cradled in a large bun, her face angular. She was standing as if she disliked her job.

"I mean, we could posit the guy was shot in the *back*," suggested Ahmed.

"Coming out of his own house?" Lazrak swiveled in his cheap brown shoes. "You mean the marksman was in the house beforehand. Alright."

"We found the footprints in there. They match some prints farther up the road." She pointed to the corpse. "They don't belong to *this* reject - "

"Alright, alright." Lazrak snapped his fingers and an officer wearing dark-goldenrod gloves handed him another forensics bag. "What do you think about that?" he asked pointing at the ground.

"About what?"

"Two kinds of cartridges," he said as he picked up the new cartridge using his pen and slipped it into the bag. "Sort of makes your theories all tangled."

He stood up and walked inside, beckoning Sergeant Ahmed to follow.

The television had been smashed and so had the laptop. Expensive speakers that had once driven the neighbors insane now had bullet holes in them.

Windows, plates, and glasses, had been smashed in the kitchen, in the corner of which was a pile of human excrement.

"Oh, dear," murmured Lazrak. "Better file this one under unsolved, sergeant."

"The poo?"

"No, the whole thing." He opened one of the cupboards and took out a child's cup.

"Well, the quota says we have to solve a case every fortnight," reminded Ahmed.

"Yea?" Lazrak replaced the child's cup and shut the cupboard. He sniffed.

Peering round the doorway he saw the coroner kneeling in the glass-covered privy. Under the smashed window, the coroner was collecting fingerprints by the toilet. "Whoever did this wanted to leave as much evidence as possible," said the coroner.

"But that doesn't make any sense," replied Ahmed. "The cartridges are major."

"Well," muttered the old and grey coroner. "There's no blood to speak of, which would suggest the victim was taken out of this property and then taken somewhere else. Now, as for why they let off a few rounds, I would say that that was to frighten the people who live on this street, so that they don't help the police."

"Alright," said Lazrak.

"We know what this means," added the coroner.

"Can we prosecute?" asked Ahmed.

"Depends," replied Lazrak. "We're entitled to investigate if this wasn't meant to happen. Sometimes soldiers don't follow orders. On the other hand - if it's your run-of-the-mill whack - then we had better keep our noses out of it." He leaned over the coroner, flushed the toilet, and smiled when that bad smell disappeared. Apart from the other smell emanating from the kitchen, which would require more vigorous cleaning skills than a simple flush.

"They usually tell us in advance," muttered Lazrak. He looked through the window at the light-cornflower-blue sky, intense with heat. "They're getting sloppy."

"I could put together some search warrants," suggested Ahmed.

Lazrak moved out of the bathroom and squatted by a floor-level kitchen cupboard. He poked a hairball using his ballpoint pen. A cat shot out of the cupboard.

"Still…"

"Still what?" asked Ahmed, frustrated.

"It still troubles me." Lazrak stood up and jingled his wrist. "Most of the time we know they're in charge - and they also know they're in charge. Do you understand?"

"Sure."

"But if they're letting that contract slip - then something must be changing." He chuckled as he removed his glasses, wiped them with a rag, and put them back on.

"Booking a holiday to Gibraltar wouldn't be a bad idea," his face darkened. "They wouldn't *dare* shut the airports. People in the north wouldn't stand for that."

"You could catch a boat," advised Ahmed.

"I'm not Libyan, am I?" He shook his head. "Clean up that shit."

A convoy of black Chevrolet suburban limousines made its way to Nina Scarvaggi's townhouse in Marrakech. Among the terraced housing that defined the street, Nina's townhouse was the least decorative, and its three stories sported black-coral paint, double-glazed windows to retain the air-conditioning, and a short staircase that led from the street into a homely foyer with potted cacti and paintings. The last suburban limousine pulled up and out stepped Salvatore Yannucci and Augustu Valverde. The latter wore a charcoal-grey-coloured suit with a white shirt and a cosmic-latte-coloured necktie. He also wore a dark-Byzantium fedora, had hollowed cheeks, hibernating eyes, and a silver skullcap of finely combed hair.

They were welcomed into the foyer by young men wearing floral-white shirts tucked into fulvous-orange trousers who took their hats and showed them up the staircase.

On the second floor, Salvatore and Augustu entered a boardroom of sorts with a parlour accessible through a pair of sliding doors. The boardroom area was defined by a long table that was covered in canapés, ashtrays, fruit, and anonymous bottled sparkling water. Near the empty seat at the head of the table, Salvatore and Augustu took their seats - Salvatore struggling into the narrow chair, and Augustu lowering himself gracefully onto his.

As for the other guests, they were from all over Morocco.

Lucio Vizzini sat next to Manfredi Mazzarrone. Manfredi was ignoring Vizzini as best as he could and tossing giant cashews into his mouth.

Antonio Maletto and Valentina Caruso discussed the impending jazz festival in Rabat and how they had every intention of keeping their western performers happy.

Sara Privitera and Rosa "Small Nose" Baracco - and yes, she had a small nose - exchanged numbers for holiday lets in Gibraltar, which were short on the ground.

At the other end of the table, Laura Donato cracked Persian pistachios with one hand, tossed the nuts into her mouth, and enjoyed the salt as it stung her receding gum line.

Around Laura were Tulumeu Mascali and Giovanni Alami-Russo. They told politically incorrect stories to Hamid "Blackish" Harrak-Costa - who disliked his nickname immensely - and would often change the subject when he started to look reddish.

Next to them, Mohammed Zaki-Vaccaro pulled viscous slices of smoked salmon off of their respective crackers, ate them leisurely, and pretended to not be listening.

Then Faiz Impellizzeri stumbled into the room. He was sweating and mopped his head with his sleeve before finding his spot at the table. Augustu gave the young man a hard look and kicked his foot underneath the table.

"Ouch," said Faiz, looking for whatever had scratched his French-blue shoe.

The sliding doors that disguised the parlour opened. Nina Scarvaggi entered the boardroom, closed the doors behind her, and sat at the head of the table.

Her thin lips sat in the middle of a sun-cracked face that had weathered many summers both in Sicily and Morocco. She had a high forehead and a sharp nose, and she wore a Falu-red blouse, a Finn-purple dress, and unpretentious flat shoes.

Briefly, the room listened to a catfight that was taking place on the street outside. When the victor "meowed" off and left the room in silence, it was broken by Nina.

"We're not making enough money from the hotels and the beaches," explained the chairwoman in a voice that would have chilled even the most efficient bean counters.

"They're going to Gibraltar," said Small Nose.

"Who is?" asked Nina.

"Moroccans want to get away during the summer because they don't like foreigners." Putting to one side the hypocrisy of her comment, she thought about the French Protectorate, the Spanish zone of influence, how Tangier had become a second home for many Europeans, and how long-dead Moroccan propagandists for European trade had simultaneously described those Europeans as "the unbelieving enemy", whereas other locals bemoaned how their nation had fallen to tea and sugar debts.

"It stinks," said Nina.

"Privilege is killing the economy," noted Augustu. They either needed more incentives for people to stay or more rules, Augustu added. The only way that they could incentivize local amenities was through price fixing, but then they would have to use the same policy the following year to clear up the fiscal mess they had created. "We could tax airlines. They'll have to raise their airfares, and that will stop Moroccans leaving."

Tulumeu Mascali said, "Some British territories stop importing vegetables, so the local farmers have a chance to sell their produce."

"We are going to shut the airports for three months," said Nina, making a note on her agenda. "That starts next month. Locals can spend money just as well as the English or the Germans - *or the Spaniards…*"

Everyone sighed.

As the meeting went on, green energy was the more pressing issue. They discussed tide power and solar panels, and they agreed that the difficulty was storing the energy. The bill that they had concocted to curtail smartphone usage had had good societal implications - but it hardly affected the cost of the minerals used in their production.

Nina reminded her colleagues that the Chinese owned a phosphate mine on the border between Morocco and Mauritania - in short, the mine was in disputed territory, and since phosphate was used in electronics - as well as animal feed, fertilizers, and cosmetics - they would be able to put the squeeze on the Chinese, whose solar panels had filled Morocco's warehouses for too many years without ever being erected. By refusing to channel the Chinese phosphate through their shipping ports, Morocco would be able to bargain down the price of the necessary batteries for the solar panels.

"Do you think you can handle that, Faiz?" asked Nina.

Faiz Impellizzeri ran the region closest to the border with Mauritania. He had a soft brain and too many appetites, but he had the benefit of being surrounded by the powerful business hub that his dead forerunner had forged in the dustbowl of Dakhla.

"Then again," added Nina, "the main problem might be refugees - if Mauritania gets worse." She noticed the din of agreement in the room. "Put them to work, Faiz."

Faiz nodded vacantly.

The meeting closed soon after, and the various "regional managers" pushed their chairs back in and then collected their coats and hats from the young men downstairs. They stepped into their respective suburban limousines and vanished down the street.

Back in the townhouse, Salvatore and Augusto had been welcomed through the sliding doors into Nina's parlour, which was filled with pictures and memorabilia.

Salvatore sat by an old lamp and drank an espresso. He watched as Augustu whispered to Nina in Sicilian on the other side of the room. Then Augustu bade farewell to both colleagues and went to collect his dark-Byzantium fedora.

Nina shuffled towards Salvatore and sat in the chair opposite. She sighed as she rested her chin on her palm and observed the old man for several moments.

"Tell me about about this limey," asked Nina in Sicilian.

"He's from Bermuda," said Salvatore, shifting in his dark-liver suit. "He drinks like a fish, but there's kindness in him. I said he was like Mohammed; that he's a pure man."

Nina thought he meant Mohammed Zaki-Vaccaro. "I had no idea Zaki-Vaccaro was pure. All I see are the expenses he claims - and those are far from pure."

"I mean the Koran guy - the prophet."

"Oh." Nina thought for a moment. "Don't look at him - or draw him."

"I think Lou is too nice. But the boy will learn."

"Yes." The old woman touched her arm. Her skin was like leather. "You remember the old boss, Salvatore? I know you remember him. That was a long time ago."

Salvatore nodded his fat head.

"I have dreams about the old man. I see his face and it's like this." She stretched out her thin lips and made a comically terrifying face. "That's how he looks there."

"What God gives us can't be lacking."

Nina scoffed. "It's not lacking - but some of it is twisted."

"God made everything straight. The Devil came and twisted it."

Pushing away an invisible hand, Nina rested her eyes on Salvatore's huge stomach. "The Devil's in everybody. Some more than others."

The two Sicilians sat in silence. Salvatore finished his coffee.

CHAPTER TWO

One of the crowning achievements of the Scarvaggi Family was the construction of their own Trans-Sahara railway, which ran through Morocco and the Western Sahara into Mauritania. It had been improved by Chinese investments over the past decade and now sported commercial lines as well as lines dedicated to transporting mineral ores.

The Western Sahara had been split between Morocco and Mauritania in 1976, but it was still a matter of contention, which bothered both sides. The founder of the Almoravid movement - which came to rule Morocco at one point - was a man called Ibn Yasin, a Berber who moved to Mauritania in the early 1050s. He founded a new town called Aratane, where he tried to turn the freethinking and more creative Moroccan Islam into something more orthodox. He decreed that all houses should be the same height, and he banned music, colourful clothing, and impure food. And the eventual failure of Ibn Yasin was on Ismail's mind as he travelled through the desert…

One night, a commercial train headed for the Mauritanian capital of Nouakchott departed Dakhla in Morocco with six carriages of passengers, most of whom were Mauritanians with relatives in Dakhla and the surrounding desert areas. One of the carriages carried a group of young men who were unshaven, unkempt, and altogether desperate-looking. They wore blast-off-bronze-coloured suits and white shirts, however, which suggested that they had tried to look their best even when their wallets and pockets were unable to keep up with their saving face. The youngest man there was named Ismail. His blast-off-bronze-coloured suit was the cleanest, and he had large bags under his eyes from sleeping on the streets, a not-unattractive monobrow that he refused to shave, and unruly hair he kept short. He was clean-shaven and the way his chin went in made him look like a child. He sat like the other men, hands in lap, watching the mysterious desert flicker by the window. Plains smothered with Martian-looking rocks traded with bumpier tracts of sand peppered with desiccated shrubs, after which hills with intelligent design would appear in the distance and get closer until they seemed to dwarf the carriage entirely. Something metallic and surrounded by searchlights appeared on the horizon.

"Phosphate mine," said the man next to Ismail. "That's diplomacy for you."

Many hours later, the train made its halfway stop. When Ismail looked out of the window, he realised why nobody could put a name to the little town. The group of men hopped off the train and walked through what could only be described as a frontier settlement. Ismail partially enjoyed the experience: he had been taught at school that all the world had been discovered - but here was somewhere new and unexplored, and he and his colleagues were walking around it as if it were the moon.

Boarded-up shops lined the street, the corner shop and coffee house illuminating the veiled beige of the sandy road that met solid darkness at the town's perimeter.

The men entered the coffee house, pooled their money, and bought a thermos of coffee. Ismail uncurled a piece of paper from his pocket and read the address he had written the previous morning. It filled him with blind hope. The group finished their coffee, walked onto the street, found the address, and observed the burnt-umber walls of the new-build house with its flimsy roof, small windows, and barred door designed to fend off thieves, raiders, and the dumb, local communists. Ismail knocked on the door and he and the others were let inside by a dark-skinned woman who gave them more coffee and cushions to sit on in the brightly lit living room. Then twenty other people arrived. They either sat, squatted, or stood in the cramped living room as the dark-skinned woman greeted them, shaking their dirty hands.

A man wearing a military-green uniform and a bland military cap entered the room through a small door. He knelt at the front of the room and thanked everyone.

"As-salamu alaikum," said the man.

"Wa-Alaikum Salaam," replied the living room.

"There is a new age upon us," said the man in Arabic. "You have to forget liberal promises about the environment, you have to forget equality for women, and you have to forget cheap houses for families where people can have equality and liberal dreams. I say this - not because I am against those things - but because there is something rotten at the core of North Africa. Something is rotten at the core of Maghrib. The managerial elite have destroyed the land of the setting sun looking for mineral ores and building parks for tourists. These are simply bureaucrats. They know nothing about governing countries because they spend money on thought control to keep our people weak and ill-informed. At one time, our gold brought wealth to Morocco and the rulers of Islamic Spain, but now we toil in the dust for dog food ingredients, where in the past we exported fruit and cereals, the cotton from the Atlantic plains, the sugar in the Sous, and the silver mines – the copper mines in the Atlas Mountains."

The man paused. Then he smiled.

"But this elite have controllers. And if we strike - then we can control them."

The men and women in the audience nodded.

"We need family," added the man. "We need soldiers. We need men and women who are willing to die for someone - not their smartphones or their expensive cars. We need people willing to die for their property - not because they have been locked into their property and cannot pay their bills or get water out of their faucets."

He spat on the cameo-pink tiles.

"Mauritania is only the beginning," promised the man. His eyes were bright. "Morocco is the end. We have some guests here tonight. They have travelled far to be with us. They know - as well as I do - that Morocco used to be a constitutional monarchy. That is where the constitutional monarch - the king or the queen - exercises their authority in accordance with the country's constitution, as protected by parliamentary delegates. The monarch cannot rule alone. They do not have absolute power." He sighed. "Morocco was like this - before the white men and women came. I wish to be clear - their whiteness is not what makes them evil. Their language mixes Latin, Greek, Arabic, Spanish, French and Catalan together to make something unique. They are a culture of many cultures." Then he squinted. "Perhaps there are too many cultures."

Gradually, he stood up.

"You are all under arrest," he added nonchalantly.

In the stunned silence that followed, a crash came from outside as police wearing copper-rose armour stormed the living room and aimed their guns at the audience. Arabic orders were shouted for people to lie on their stomachs so that they could be handcuffed, dragged outside, and thrown into the waiting cosmic-latte paddy wagons. When Ismail refused to obey orders, he was cracked across the head with a rifle butt.

The following morning, Ismail was nudged awake by a policewoman wearing the same copper-rose armour. He couldn't see as there was a bag on his head. Then the policewoman removed the bag, offered him a plastic bottle of water and, when he nodded passive-aggressively, tipped the spout towards his paper-like mouth.

"That's enough," said the officer in Arabic. She retracted the water bottle. "Do you understand what I'm saying?"

Ismail's bloodshot eyes darted round the cell.

"Where are you from?"

"Morocco," rasped Ismail.

"You're a long way from home."

"It's not my home. Not while they control us."

The officer scoffed. She whistled at the black-olive door. More policemen wearing the same warlike armour came in and unlocked the prisoner's chains.

"What part of the country is this?" asked Ismail.

They replaced the bag on his head. Then they removed him from the prison cell and took him through several corridors.

When they removed the bag, Ismail was standing in a well-lit courtroom with a bureaucratic judge sitting on a raised dais and a court typist who stubbed out his cigar.

"Name," stated the judge.

"Ismail."

"That's not your name." The judge motioned for the court bailiff to bring Ismail's wallet. The judge pulled the driver's license out of its invisible barrier and read out a typically Moroccan name. "*That* is your name," noted the judge scientifically.

"The name is yours. You keep it," Ismail said.

The judge returned the wallet to the bailiff. "This court finds you guilty of political agitation and conspiracy to commit terrorism carried out upon the sovereign nation of Mauritania. Do you have anything to say before you are taken to a place of captivity?"

"Fuck you."

"The bigger the head, the bigger the headaches," replied the judge, reciting his favourite Mauritanian proverb. Then he motioned to the bailiff, making a gesture with his pen, and said, "Get gay Che out of here."

CHAPTER THREE

Lou Baring stood in his kitchen wearing his white shirt and banana-mania-coloured trousers. He stared at the bottle of Wild Turkey he had purchased the previous evening. It called out to him from the darkened corner of the kitchen where he had secreted it, along with phone chargers and parking tickets. Lou had thirty minutes before he needed to drive to work and he was debating whether putting on his azure-blue necktie would make him sweat faster than he already was. He placed his hand on the battleship-grey countertop just below the base of the bottle of Wild Turkey - having decided against the necktie - and willed the bottle to empty itself into the drain – which it didn't. The truth was that he hated the bottle because it was lethal, but recently, death and life seemed similar.

Lou reached for a box of cornflakes, filled a buff-beige bowl with cereal, replaced the box, and looked back at the Wild Turkey. He reached for the Wild Turkey, whisked off the cap, poured a tumbler's worth over his cereal, and sat on the couch. Something like relief washed over Lou as he ate his cornflakes soaked in the burnt-orange liquid. He reached for his smartphone, dialed Morocco Energy, and aimed his atomic breath into the jaded holes.

"Hello?"

"Welcome to Morocco Energy Services: part of the Spanish Electric Company. The number you have dialed is no longer in service."

Lou hung up and found another number online.

"Hello?"

"Welcome to Morocco Energy Services: part of the Spanish Electric Company. For energy queries or for anything else, please press one."

Between the spoonsful of boozy cornflakes, Lou pressed one.

"Hello, can I please take your account number followed by your name and address, please?" asked the woman in French.

"Do you speak English?"

"I'm sorry, sir." There was a brief pause. *"Hello, can I please take your account number followed by your name and address, please?"*

"Fuck, yea."

"Is that your address?"

"Sorry, the account number is 1414948 - my name is Lou Baring - and the address is No. 5 Dar mok, Marrakesh 40000."

"Thank you. What seems to be the problem today?"

"Thanks, I moved in this month, and I've received my first bill. But you've charged me for the previous month as well."

"That is because no one was in the apartment."

"But - " Lou choked on his bourbon-soaked cereal. He observed the living room-cum-kitchen and was terrified to find that he was well-off. "Why I do have to pay?"

"That is because no one was in the apartment."

"Can I escalate this?" asked Lou.

"If you want to escalate this query then you will have to speak to one of our company representatives."

Lou received a new phone number from the woman. After hanging up, he entered the new number and waited for the automatic voice.

"Welcome to Morocco Energy Services: part of the Spanish Electric Company. The number you have dialed is no longer in service."

Lou threw his smartphone through the air.

Bouncing off the one closed window in the living room, the smartphone landed on the carmine-red runner.

Lou returned to eating his bourbon-soaked cereal.

He quietly thanked God, or Allah - or whoever might have been listening - that the window had been firmly shut.

When Lou got stuck at work that day, he was bored. He did little but note down the incoming rents in a carefully designed spreadsheet with an "NS" insignia at the top. These rents didn't pass through Zaalouk Real Estate so much as they passed by. Lou noticed that he had no control over where the money was going or who was getting it, which was another problem: all the rent money was going to the same account. As far as he could understand – which was about two inches beyond his aquiline nose – all the other work had been taken care of. He began to see himself as a benevolent caretaker - or a privileged insider - disallowed from even touching the interior of his own office.

The topic of politics wafted through Lou's mind.

All the wealthy people in Bermuda avoided politics and that was good. He had known political people at university, too, and they had been unhappy, argumentative, and annoying. All he knew was that he was going to get paid at the end of the week.

Just as Lou was starting to lose consciousness from the overweening boredom that emanated from his computer screen, somebody knocked loudly on his office door.

"WHUUUHAHHAA!" Lou wailed almost falling out of his chair.

"Hello?" someone called from the other side of the door.

"Come in, come in," said Lou as he rubbed his eyes.

The door opened and a medium-sized woman with dark hair walked in. She had an oval-shaped face with acute eyes and high cheekbones. She wore cyber-grape jeans, a white tee-shirt, and a dark-khaki aviator jacket.

"Are you Lou Baring?" asked the woman.

"That's me!" Lou stood up to shake a refused hand. "I'm sorry, I don't remember you."

"You don't know me. I'm Laura Donato."

"What can I do for - ?" Lou gawped as four strong men entered the room. They had curly hair and clean-shaven jaws with sideburns cut off just below the earlobe. They wore floral tee-shirts, chocolate-brown belts, and fulvous-orange trousers. Despite presenting poker-faces to Lou Baring, they carried a casual, non-professional air. " – you and…these guys?"

Laura pointed at a large map of Morocco on the office wall. "The empty properties in Marrakech?" asked Laura. "Tell me where they all are."

Embracing his inner salesman - or the part that resembled Cleopatra Griffiths - Lou stood up and joined Laura Donato by the colorfully shaded survey illustration.

"We've got residential and commercial properties." He smiled weakly. "Now, I think you're probably in the market for a residential. For you and – these guys…"

A young man wearing fulvous-orange trousers winked at Lou.

"This is good?" asked Laura, pointing at a house in the suburbs. "Big?"

"Well, you could have a pretty good party there," replied Lou awkwardly.

"Fantastic." Laura addressed her colleagues in Sicilian. "We've been trying to have a party for weeks."

The group of young men laughed.

"I want to see it now," said Laura in English.

"Now?"

"Yes, now, and you're going to show it to me."

Lou had a feeling that these people might be able to help him with his energy bill. Feebly, he showed them out of his office, went outside, and stepped into his brand-new dark-orchid Camaro.

Laura and her colleagues slid back the doors on a large white van, got inside, and followed Lou through stoplights, roundabouts, and the dark-sienna barrier of one of the most expensive gated communities in Marrakech.

They parked in the driveway of a mansion with several balconies, shuttered windows, and an Olympic-length pool. Beyond the back orchard was the arid wilderness, bereft of meaning in comparison to humanity's realm and its many slaves.

Lou wiped his forehead free of perspiration as he climbed out of his Camaro. He watched the strange men and Laura Donato step out of the large white van and saunter towards him, where they waited patiently for his damp hands to open the door.

The mansion was empty and smelled like bleach. The Dutch-white walls clashed cleverly with the ecru tiles and the bright white shutters. To the side of the foyer was a big staircase that led upstairs to four morbidly obese bedrooms. Meanwhile, the entrance to the living room was to their immediate right, as well as the parlour-room, the kitchen, and a pantry packed with fern-green washing machines. For the moment, Laura Donato was transfixed by the foyer. "Are you okay?" she asked carefully.

"Fine," replied Lou. "Except I'm not sure - "

He stopped talking to observe the actions of Laura's colleagues. Some of the men had gone back to the white van and returned with segments of carpeting, cleaning equipment, and yellow scrubbers. They laid down the carpeting around the foyer, making sure the edges were accurate. They took the excess carpet and the cleaning equipment and hid it in the living room, after which one of them nodded to Laura and smiled at Lou when she shrugged back.

" - what's going on," Lou finished his sentence.

"You four can stay in the living room," said Laura in Sicilian.

The men disappeared into the living room. Then Laura put her hands on Lou's shoulders and moved him so that he was *next* to the living room.

She looked out of the window by the front door. A Caribbean-green Ford pinto pulled into the driveway. Out stepped two men and one woman. One man and woman wore fulvous-orange trousers, whereas the third man was entirely different. He had dark skin and thin eyebrows. He wore a dark green beret, a military-green uniform, and steel-capped boots, and he moved with an elegant arrogance towards the door.

From inside, Lou could hear a mixture of Arabic and French. He had no idea what they were saying, but the conversation was friendly enough and put him at ease.

Suddenly, Laura produced a pistol with a silencer out of her dark-khaki aviator jacket and pressed herself against the wall so that the door frame would disguise her.

"Uh?" wondered Lou.

The door opened and the dark-skinned Mauritanian entered the foyer. Studying Lou with condescending detachment, he spoke to the others in French: "No matter where we go, there are white men wearing suits."

In a flash, the skin on his forehead cracked open and sprayed blood over Lou's banana-mania suit, the corpse collapsing onto the newly-installed fake carpeting.

The four men reappeared from the living room. They rolled the corpse within the fake carpeting so that the scene of the crime could literally be carried away. They and the two newcomers carried the doom-laden sushi roll to the white van, where it was lobbed into the plastic sheet-lined back, and covered it with a blanket so that it was hidden.

Then the men started cleaning the foyer. Specks of blood on the staircase and the walls were carefully wiped away using the bleach-soaked yellow scrubbers. These were rinsed in electric-purple buckets of water that were then poured into the street gutter.

"Huh?" moaned Lou. He had turned the same colour as Salvatore's cultured-pearl necktie.

"I'll get you a new suit," said Laura. "That's why you don't stand in the way."

"Laura...?" He gasped. "Huh...?"

"Sit down," Laura ordered, moving him into the living room. He was lowered onto some excess tiles as the new woman - Baaqa Bell – passed him a bottle of water.

"Drink," said Laura.

Lou gulped the bottled water. He thanked Baaqa for bringing it.

"Now," muttered Laura, gesturing at Baaqa to leave them alone. "This is so you know what happens," she explained, patting his shoulder. "You're not going to tell anyone about this…"

Lou stared at her blankly. Then - as she was talking about honour and death - his eyes traced the staircase that had only recently been washed clean of human blood.

"…*You had to see this.*" Laura's unshakeable voice audibly reappeared. She went into the foyer and gave orders to her soldiers. Then, she accompanied Lou into town.

There was a haberdashery complete with in-house tailors that had been the talk of Marrakech for many years. It was run by a bald man named Habib, whose pointy ears and buck teeth gave him a mouse-like appearance. He insisted on wearing suits that he had tailored himself, even during the hottest Moroccan summers, not unlike the composer, Ralph Vaughn Williams.

When Lou and Laura arrived, Habib was wearing black shoes, a cedar-chest bowtie, and a three-piece Columbia-blue suit. He and two women undressed Lou, took measurements of his entire body, and went to work adjusting an existing cadet-grey suit that had been sitting in one of their cupboards for centuries.

"*A shame about the necktie,*" muttered Habib as he replaced Lou's now-bloody azure-blue necktie with a brand-new burlywood necktie. Of course, it was a good fit.

After an hour of preparation, the new Lou Baring was presented to Laura Donato. She ignored his new appearance, told Habib to charge the clothing to her account, and delivered Lou to his own car.

"If you need any help," said Laura, "you have my number."

She walked away down the street as Lou stared into his lap. He was increasingly aware that his new suit fit like a latex glove - and was every bit as sterile.

Sitting opposite Cleopatra Griffiths in her air-conditioned office, Lou Baring leered at her carrot-orange jumpsuit. He couldn't help but connect her jumpsuit to the fulvous-orange trousers worn by Laura Donato's pragmatic colleagues. His brain was overloaded with Wild Turkey bourbon, and cold-blooded murder, and he saw no way out of the young offender institution that his brain had become through substance abuse.

"So," said Cleopatra, peeling a concerned smile. "How are you finding the job?"

Lou stared into space.

"Come on, Lou." Sipping her coffee, she snorted an intake of air through her nose. "You should understand - we have to do these things for the Scarvaggi Family."

"*Cleo,*" Lou murmured. *"I'm drunk."*

"I know."

"I wasn't - I'm not - I can't handle this stuff."

"You can't handle the situation either," she replied. And the joke that he maybe wasn't good at drinking, was wasted on Lou Baring.

"Do they own everything?" asked Lou. "Is there something they *don't* own?"

"They own all the properties. There are some people who maintain that they're still property-owners, but when they die, it all goes to the state." Ripping open a sachet of imported sugar, she stirred it into her coffee, ignorant of the economic destruction that sugar had once wrought on Morocco, before the great re-Islamification, and the Scarvaggi Family. "They don't like the word monopoly - they prefer *centralization.*"

"The banks - what about the - the banks?" Lou blathered.

"They don't own the banks." Cleopatra smiled. "But the banks have no option but to do business with them - and the politicians."

Lou's light-cornflower-blue eyes grew dim over his heavy eye-bags as he slouched deeper into the chair. "So, what are we doing here? They don't need my help - nobody needs my help - anyone who does must be crazy. *I'm fucking drunk, Cleo, my God...*"

"We give them credibility and they give us money," replied Cleopatra. "The money goes to our office in London, where they invest it, and make more money." She paused and stared into her cup as the perimeter was cleansed of sugar by the intense heat of the coffee. "Everybody's happy."

"Huh." The property manager rubbed his bloodshot eyes. "I'm just - having trouble *accepting* this."

"When you accept something, it means you're happy to do nothing. Think about what you want. How are you going to get what you want?"

"What do I want?" Lou mouthed the words. "Stability," added the depressed property manager.

"Good," replied Cleopatra. "The Scarvaggi Family wants the same thing. They believe - and I agree with them - that stability is the key to success. Whether it's longshoremen wanting more money, or supermarkets moaning about tariffs, or tenants complaining about pipes and windows, the point is that no one's going to take any risks." She nodded her explanation into the history books. "Now, that's *real* equity."

Lou turned the same shade as his cadet-grey suit. "And the police?"

"Well, they have a quota like everyone else." She said this as though it were an annoying meeting she had to attend every week. "There's a lot of money in this place. It's our priority to represent the Scarvaggi Family and their property as best as we can. *I said earlier to think about what you wanted* - but that's what we want right now. Good representation."

She followed this with the pre-approved line that any problem faced by Lou would not be solved by Lou, but by Laura Donato, who was the Captain of Marrakech.

"She's the captain of this whole region," exclaimed Cleopatra, leaning forward onto her desk. "What an amazing achievement for a woman!"

"Uh," said Lou.

"As for the booze - " Her eyes and blonde hair seemed to harden. "I don't care what you do in your own time. But if you bring the sauce in here, you'll be out on your bum."

Lou arose on wobbly legs and staggered to the door. "I won't let down you."

"*You won't let me down*, you mean?"

"Uh." Lou exited the office and shut the door behind him.

Cleopatra leaned back in her chair and grinned at the sight of Lou's dark-orchid- Camaro as it gleamed on the steaming tarmac in the harsh midday sunlight. Then she pressed the button on her desk.

"I'll be having lunch for three hours, Faruk."

"*Very good, Ms. Griffiths…*"

Morocco was a central spine of mountains, flanked by deserts and plains, where nearly all the main rivers flowed into the Atlantic Ocean, apart from the Moulouya, which flowed into the Mediterranean Sea. The rivers tended to be shallow, and unfit for transportation via boat, so goods had always been transported across plains, or mountains, and as night fell on Marrakech, the air became cooler as the result of gentle breezes that fell from the Atlas Mountains.

Apron-wearing proprietors set out tables and chairs on the streets of the club district as foreign men wearing brick-red trousers and open-necked shirts chased after women in citron-green blouses and thigh-high boots. They may have been from a wedding party, or some other such group, but all that mattered was that they had money – and it would soon reach the Scarvaggi Family.

Lou half-strolled, half-stumbled across the expensive cobblestones that the Marrakech council had laid out decades ago. His feet operated on autopilot and at best he was only half-certain that he would materialize inside another taproom.

"Masaa' al-khayr," said Lou as he waved to several women wearing bikini tops and chocolate-brown denim shorts. Ignoring him, they walked into a club blaring music.

"Good evening for some," mumbled Lou as he doddered into the nearest drinking establishment, smiled warmly to himself, and claimed a solitary booth in the name of debauchery, destruction, and beer. As time hissed past, Lou discovered a shot of bourbon sitting under his aquiline nose - and he drank the aperitif in strenuous gulps.

"Another, please," ordered Lou.

The waitress sighed and brought another shot of bourbon.

By the fourth shot of bourbon, Lou's eyes had wandered over to the crown-and-anchor table situated on the other side of the room, surrounded by people gambling. A drizzle of homesickness washed over Lou, since crown-and-anchor was a staple of Bermuda's biggest holiday, Cup Match, and the sweltering tents in which it occurred.

He drew air into his nostrils, now stuffy from the advanced drunkenness, and teetered towards the crown-and-anchor table. He brushed the back of a fat man wearing a champagne-beige suit.

"Masaa' al-khayr," greeted Lou.

The man growled back.

"Sorry," replied the sozzled property manager. He made it to the crown-and-anchor table. He asked the croupier, "Can I take part in your game – *pronto, my sucka…?*"

"Fine," replied the young woman in English. "You can play."

"No, I insist – I will play," replied Lou. Then he took a seat at the small table, placed several bets on diamonds and hearts, and found that he could not stop winning.

"That stupid tourist is cheating," complained a skinny man in Arabic.

"He'd have to work with me," the young woman assured him. "I don't have a clue who he is." Then she pressed a button under the table's edge.

"Listen, you stupid Sicilian," said the skinny man. "You're supposed to give people a chance. What rock have you been hiding under, you mongoloid goat-pussy-eater?"

"A lucky rock. Excuse me, *my sucka* - are we gonna roll again?"

Two gigantic bouncers with faces like cooked sirloin lifted Lou out of his chair. They plopped him by the bar, told the barman to water him, and answered a call to deal with a man claiming to be Umm Kalthoum's great-grandson, who was trying to sell her classic movies on old DVDs with posters that stuck out from behind the plastic covers.

"Hot, hot, hot," moaned Lou, watching glasses of water appear before him. "If you put a boat in one - " He laughed. "It's like I'm sitting by a lake. Bang, bang, *sucka…*"

The barman smiled and served a woman in a coral-pink headdress.

"Beer, *law samaht*," said Lou.

Then he fell off of the barstool. Two men and one woman helped Lou back onto his feet. "Thank you, scouts - " When he reached the bar, he found a beer waiting. "Oh, thank you, sir." Then the barman reached into Lou's jacket pocket, pulled out the winnings from crown-and-anchor, gave back some rather inaccurate change, and let him go. "You work at L.F. Wade airport?" noted Lou. Oblivious to the fact that he had been robbed, he half-staggered, half-walked along the edge of the bar, and found a poker table. A few minutes later, Lou sank his beer, and decided to show his cards.

"Look at this royal flush," said Lou.

"*Oh my God,*" muttered a short woman in Tamazight.

"Flush that down the toilet. Thar be gold down thar," said Lou.

"Who the hell is this guy?" complained another customer in Arabic.

"Yar-har-har, me hearties," chattered Lou. "Show me your toilet."

"No, get away - "

"Show me your toilet, Daddy!"

Then the sirloin-esque bouncers ripped him away from the poker table and threw him onto the street, where he staggered back to his feet.

Old Uncle Lou
Give me more, give me more, give me more
When the girls dance on the floor
They say, Old Uncle Lou, give me more

The next establishment had the air of one's neighborhood tavern. Dark-salmon signs flashed on and off in the far corners of the room, fluorescent bulbs brightening rows of bottles inside imposing fridges, and someone's father was slumped at the end of the counter. Observing the near-deceased man at the end of the bar, Lou regained his senses - since he had lost them on his way to this particular taproom - and acknowledged the lined face of the ancient Moroccan man sitting to his side, who creaked and wheezed with the breeze from the Atlas Mountains.

"Where are you going?" asked the old man in French. His face swirled in Lou's eyes. "My young friend - where are you going? What are you looking for?" Lou stared down and found a line of tequila shots standing to attention. Unaware of who had paid for the tequila, and afraid of more bills, Lou pushed himself off of the bar.

"No," muttered Lou as he fell off of his barstool. "No more, please."

He noticed that the old man was crying and banging his temples. "My young friend," said the old man in French, "what do you want?"

"What the - ?" Lou waved his hands in a threatening manner. "None here…"

I say, Hum It, Hack It, Hayek
Hayek, now, baby, don't put that Keynes on me

You got me spending all this green like a clown
Just look at me

When Lou opened his eyes, he found that he had made it to another bar. This one was smaller than the previous one and featured doddering barstools bursting at their seams. Two plastic fans waved the heat away like lazy arms, and there was a pool of drool where Lou had slept on the antique-brass counter. He raised his head and noted the relaxed-looking man at the end of the bar. He had a shaved head, a trimmed beard, and expressive eyebrows that tapered at the ends. He was also wearing an artichoke-green, double-breasted trench coat, a white shirt with a loosened apricot necktie, black shoes, and Crayola socks. He was sipping a cup of coffee, and acknowledged Lou with the vague curiosity one expected from medical secretaries, half-vegetable and grinning.

"Had a good morning?" asked the stranger.

"That song," mumbled Lou. "Turn it off."

The bearded man snapped his fingers.

The barman, emerging from the back, sucking on his first cigarette of the day, switched off the television.

"Rough on the ears?" asked the bearded man.

"Yeah," said Lou as he sat up, scratching his head. "Christ - "

"We acknowledge Christ too. But he won't be helping you here."

"Uh." Lou sniffed and squinted at the bearded the man. "I guess I owe you some money?"

"Nope."

Lou searched in vain for a clock.

"It's five in the morning," chuckled the bearded man. "I yanked you out of that last place at thirty past three. But don't worry about this place. It's safe."

"Thank you. But - " He had reached that special level of drunkenness where sobriety filtered back through pantomimes of reality and polka music. "Is Sal in charge here?"

The bearded man and the barman exchanged glances.

"Not Salvatore," answered the bearded man. "Nina Scarvaggi."

"That's funny - I thought - that was *his* name."

"Give me a cigarette," said the bearded man in Tamazight. The barman waddled over to him, offering his packet like an opened scallop. The stranger then lit a cigarette and stared

at Lou. "My name is Hassan Hacimi. I'm a detective in the
Marrakech Police Department." Prepared for objection, he
was dazed when he all got was Lou's dumb stare. "I work
the night shift - from half past seven through to five o'clock.
You see all sorts of things when you work the night shift.
But you, my friend - " He smiled. "You're either a foreigner
with a hedge fund - or a local with a death wish. When I
found you, you were complaining about the Sicilians. You
don't do that in public and live long."

"Guy in the club did."

"I wonder how he's doing this morning." He blew smoke
out of his nostrils. "Probably ran into Laura Donato."

"She's a murderer," rasped Lou.

"Objection, your honour," said Hassan to the fatigued
landlord. "We know nothing of the sort!"

"What?"

"It's a good thing you didn't run into her. Don't mix
drink with work, my friend."

"I wasn't working."

Hassan scoffed. "No such thing as holidays. When a
makhzan can intimidate people like they do, they don't
need slave labour."

He got another cigarette from the bemused barman.

"You know thirty percent of kids in this country are
stunted? Three in ten kids are underweight, my friend." He
moved over to Lou and faced him. "That frighten you?"

"Uh."

"Didn't think it would." He gestured with his cigarette. "But if you tell anyone about our little congress, you can forget about Donato - cuz I'll whack you myself."

"Morocco has a congress?"

The barman did a face-palm in the background.

"This one, you drunk," hissed Hassan.

"Well, I didn't ask for this."

"Then don't get drunk." Hassan stubbed out his cigarette on the ground. Then he walked towards the door and turned around. "I don't think you're a happy person."

"So?"

"You're close to them. If you ever see anything you don't like - just call me. We're on the right side of history here – us and that barman – even though I don't know his name." He reached into his trench coat, pulled out Lou's wallet, and threw it into his jittery hands. "But you're Lou Baring. So how about you stay out of trouble - for now." Hassan sniggered and walked out of the room as Lou swiveled on his barstool towards the bar, winced, and barfed on the countertop, sending the barman into a passion...

CHAPTER FOUR

Choum was a town in Northern Mauritania and was close to the border with the Western Sahara. In the years since the Scarvaggi Family had come to power, their influence upon the Mauritanian Government had led to the latter accepting Chinese subsidies in an effort to change Choum into the ultimate Mauritanian prison. Naturally, the Chinese owned the prison and made profits off of the phosphate mines which were staffed by the very same prisoners they had been charged with guarding. The town itself had turned into a breeding ground for prison guards and general staff, and the prison took priority when it came to new rations, which arrived on the railway. It was not unlike the early days of the Muslim invasion, when the Muslim Empire either conscripted the defeated Berbers or turned them into slaves. Meanwhile, the Berber women were highly prized in Muslim harems. So, for all its merits, the Muslim Empire was no better than the Roman one...

The prison in Choum was a rectangular building with a large square in the middle, which served as the recreation yard. On each of the four points of the prison stood turrets, from which guards on four-hour shifts watched the goings-on of the prison yard. The occasional tree, or shrub, dotted the perimeter of the prison, and sometimes trucks arrived with new lifers, but barring these, nothing ever grew or changed there.

The chief guard was a man called Rabie. He had suffered from a mixture of abuse, alopecia, and stress during his time with the armed forces of Mauritania, and was bald. His skin was dark, and he wore aviator sunglasses which were too small for his head, and he treated the prison as a private fiefdom, enjoying cell-checks and punishments.

He had first met Ismail when he had performed a random cell-check and had found that Ismail had managed to get *The Coming of Neo-Feudalism* by Joel Kotkin. What had followed was a beating that left Ismail with a busted lip and damaged ribs.

Two weeks after their first meeting, Rabie stopped him in the corridor.

"Where are you going, three-eight-three?" Rabie asked in Arabic.

Ismail was, in turn, stopped by Rabie's colleagues.

"I didn't say you could have lunch," added Rabie.

"Everyone else is going to lunch," replied Ismail.

"You will do well to put a *sir* on the end of that."

"Everyone else is eating the shitty food, sir."

"You'll get yours under my boot," said Rabie, pointing to his army boots. Then he clicked his fingers and watched the guards push Ismail down onto the floor. "Lick my boot. Get your tongue under there - lick it, boy."

Ismail said nothing.

"Alright, I'll give you a hand." Rabie put his boot directly onto Ismail's face.

Like a goldfish dying on a bathroom floor, Ismail opened and closed his mouth. Then he stuck his tongue out and licked the sole of the boot. It tasted like dirty rubber.

"That's it," whispered Rabie. "Keep going."

Ismail kept licking.

"Very good," added the chief guard. "Pick him up."

As the guards lifted Ismail to his feet, he spat out some sand.

"No food today," said Rabie as he turned and squeaked down the corridor.

"You stupid donkey!" hissed Ismail. "You bald bastard!"

"Alright, boys - that's enough." The voice came from Rabie's deputy, Papis, who wore aero-blue-rimmed glasses and a neck-warmer designed to pick up his sweat, along with the officer's garb, which was one size too big for the short deputy. Gesturing to the guards to release their hold on Ismail, he joined the convict. "All that time in the army haunts Rabie now and then. Just go and eat like everyone else."

"How do you work for him?" asked Ismail.

"I don't work for Rabie, I work for the prison." The sober deputy was glared at by several prisoners who stalked by, thinking the neck-warmer-wearing officer was weak. "Besides, you shouldn't have been reading in the first place. You need imagination."

"I'm in the minority."

"Doesn't matter, Ismail. Don't read that *Neo-Feudalism* stuff, in particular. You're asking for Rabie to drag you down memory lane."

"Then he can turn the pages," replied Ismail defiantly.

"Look," Papis said as he locked eyes with him. "You're smart. But don't push it." He cocked his thumbs into his belt. "Go have lunch. Think about what I've said."

The mess hall was a rectangular space with gantries that lined the rim of the room as well as the upper regions. Guards paraded up and down, staring in each direction.

When Ismail entered the mumbling buffet line, he was joined by two prisoners. The first prisoner was called Moussa and had long hair that touched his shoulders. He had been there the longest and wore thick glasses which he used to peruse the various smuggled volumes of anarchist literature that were brought to him by those like Papis.

The second prisoner was called Taleb and had a thick moustache. He had been educated in Paris, France, and was popular with the prison staff because he had been arrested several times in Europe for burning books. He was, to boot, a communist.

Collecting their couscous from the kitchen staff, the three "readers" vacated to the distant limits of the mess hall, claimed a table, and sat nibbling their true punishment.

"Yambo Ouologuem's alright," said Moussa in Arabic as he pushed couscous around the metal plate. "*Le Devoir De Violence* is a reasonable book, but if you want something special - and by special, I mean sensible - I would suggest reading *Le Vieux Pagne* by Ibrahima Aya - which is much better - he's not full of shit like Ouologuem."

"If we're talking about smuggled books," muttered Taleb in French, "then we can talk in French. I suppose I'm not asking too much of Choum's resident book critic."

"It's not," replied Moussa in French. "But Ismail's French is like this food."

"Well, he has to learn," replied Taleb as they embarked on a complex conversation about the geo-political situation in Morocco and the country's green energy policies.

Ismail caught one word in three and added "green energy" in his choppy French.

"The government in Germany - this is what I heard - they wanted more renewable energy, so they destroyed all the farmland and planted solar panels in the countryside," noted Moussa.

"Who'd you hear that from?"

"Wilson - the limey."

"Wilson paints his cell-walls with shit," laughed Taleb.

"He knows what happens in Europe. Maybe Papis is drip-feeding him the *Financial Times*. Now, that's what we need in this prison - some proper journalism."

"If it's true, what's the problem?" asked Taleb. "Good for Germany, I say."

"Except, it's not good. Because there's no bloody sun in Germany. They tried the same thing in Scotland. But they don't want to put them here - where all the sun is - because they would have to deal with West Africans, and Chinese, and the Russians..."

"Morocco - green power - fall down," said Ismail.

"That's one of the good things those goombahs are doing," noted Taleb academically. "They're the villains of the piece - but they've got some big ideas."

"The bigger the head - "

"The bigger the headaches," replied Ismail in Arabic.

"Someone's been through the Mauritanian court system!" roared Taleb in German.

Moussa shook his head. "It's lunch - it's not the cold war."

"Sorry," said Taleb in French. "But seriously - Morocco's got a bunch of big-idea goombahs behind the curtains."

"There are only so many ways you can recycle batteries," replied Moussa as if it were the beginning and end of the matter. "Chemical separation uses acid solutions to break down the different metals in the battery; mechanical separation uses brute force to break the batteries down; and you can smelt batteries, but all the different metals melt at different temperatures - "

"Use a flamethrower - like I did on the complete works of Dickens in Vienna."

"Taleb - "

"No, I see, I see. It's difficult."

"The problem for Morocco is that they don't have the facilities to do this stuff. They'll have to send all the defunct batteries overseas. But shipping is very expensive," concluded Moussa. Then he watched Ismail as he dug a trench through his couscous.

"They ship phosphate through Morocco easily enough," complained Taleb.

"They take a cut from the Chinese," explained Moussa.

Once again, Ismail straightened his back to speak the French he had been learning from their geo-political gossips. *"When revolution suck Morocco?"* asked Ismail.

Moussa ignored the excited facial expressions of his communist friend. "If there's going to be any kind of revolution in Morocco, it will have to come from Mauritania."

"We agree on something!" added Taleb as he patted Ismail on his shoulder. "Mauritania has defaulted on their foreign debt - " He counted on his fingers. " - and the army's throwing their weight around - and everyone is imagining an alternative."

"No communist to swim yet," interjected Ismail.

"Okay, I don't know what the fuck you're saying," replied Moussa in his most condescending French.

Before Taleb made yet another ill-advised contribution, he surveyed the rattling gantry above them which supported the slowly marching boots of two armed guards. The two bearded sentries passed a carnelian-red bottle between them and stopped to observe the Francophiles below. Then they moved onwards.

"The reason the communists have the best chance - " Taleb jigged his excited feet beneath the table and brushed imaginary dust off of the tabletop. " - is because they're the only ones with a program of reform."

"Come one," interrupted Moussa, "you just want to nationalize everything and abolish property. That just makes problems. You're also centralizing your problems."

Ismail's tired ear twigged. He had heard that word before and his not unattractive monobrow creased in industry, thickening the density of fur, making him wolfish. "But the Scarvaggi Family centralizes everything," said Ismail in refreshing Arabic. "What's the difference between them and what all us communists are wanting to do?"

"By Allah," said Moussa as he removed his thick glasses. "He sounds like an American podcaster, but the kid's got a point."

Dropping his fork, the usually confident Taleb tongued his moustache in rancour. "I don't - you don't know - we're the people, that's because - the hell with you, Ismail, you've got all that American theory dripping out of your dirty ears!"

"You mean I read?" asked Ismail politely.

"The guy's not a realist," Taleb said in German.

"What the hell did I say about speaking German?" carped Moussa as he patted Ismail on the shoulder, and said, "He's in here with us. That means he's a realist…"

Meanwhile, Rabie and Papis walked along the creaking gantry on the other side of the burbling mess hall. Looking down at the feasting prisoners - who seemed to Rabie like so many pigs feeding from the same trough - the chief guard recalled mealtimes in the army barracks, sweat pouring onto plates, and superiors gliding behind him.

He knew a little about "the black army of the Abid al-Bukhari" that had defended Morocco during the 16th Century. Unlike the Janissary Army of the Ottoman Empire, the infamous black army had been allowed to marry, and so their training was inextricably linked with an earlier rendition of the nuclear family. "It's the only way that people can really live," noted Rabie as he touched the rim of his aviator sunglasses. "Locked up - well-fed - you tire them out in the yard and send them to bed. If those fools in Nouakchott gave me the job, I'd turn this whole country into a prison." He whistled. "Can you imagine that? That's the only way you can get projects done."

"As it stands, sir - " Papis tugged at his neck-warmer. " - we can either send these men back to the mines - or we can think about my proposal with the library - "

"I'm not a fan of libraries, Papis."

"But sir - "

"I read your proposal. You want these dolts to bind books for the university in Nouakchott. Well, let me tell you something, boy - they're gonna carry on mining."

"Yes, sir."

"You worry about driving down the price of first editions. I won't bother you. In the meantime, I'll keep the Chinese stocked with the best work-flesh money can buy. They've been running out of Uighurs for years. We ought to help the yellow bastards."

Papis restrained himself and walked away down the gantry. Rabie continued to stare through his sunglasses at the prisoners below him - some of whom stared back.

Chun Gāo was a middle-aged woman with large cheeks and slight dimples, a small inward-facing chin, and shoulder-length hair that had been chained into a ponytail. Her work computer had just received an email from her editor in Beijing, which said the following,

> Zhí - Minister of Foreign Affairs - says line of Chinese Government is that they cannot endorse the current regime in Mauritania any more than they can endorse the "socialist insurgents". [Note use of "socialist" as opposed to "communist"; please relay this to all writers in newsroom, please.] I think the time has come for you to get out, Chun.

Chun rubbed her small, inward-facing chin, and looked across the office at the mattress where she had been sleeping. Two Mauritanian ministers had been assassinated by the local communists and she had been trying to run the news-office despite the growing silence around the building in which they worked in Nouakchott.

Suddenly, the layout editor burst into Chun's office. "We've got a boat arranged," said the layout editor in

Cantonese. They enjoyed speaking Cantonese outside of China. "We can go to the shipping port and it will pick us up."

"They've shut the airport?" asked Chun.

"Yep."

"Okay. Tell the others to pack their bags - "

"We're waiting for you. I almost got shot getting back here." Over the next twenty minutes, computers were unplugged, floppy discs destroyed, and paper files burnt.

Chun packed her things into a rucksack and walked into the newsroom where her five colleagues had collected to wait for further instructions. "How's it looking?"

The layout editor was peering through the blinds. "There are soldiers hiding behind the corners of buildings. There's one there - "

"Keep quiet," chided Chun. "Get away from the window."

On the street below, a "socialist insurgent" searched his person for another clip of ammo. Finding the new clip he emptied his AR-15, re-filled it, and fired another burst. The bullets flew around the corner of the building and embedded themselves in bricks, concrete, and the occasional member of the Mauritanian armed forces. Then the "socialist insurgent" made a dash across the street and was hit in the leg and the chest before collapsing onto the tarmac and sobbing in the solar flare that was the sunlight.

Inside the building, the layout editor skipped up the emergency staircase, re-entered the newsroom, and told his colleagues that the front doors had been blocked.

"Okay," said Chun, dialing her editor in Beijing. "Hello? - No, it's not going well - they've blocked the doors downstairs - there's no way that we can get out…"

Nina Scarvaggi sneezed in the dimly lit parlour room of her Marrakech townhouse. The ever-helpful Dr. Zaki observed the thermometer in his right hand as he stood over the old woman reclining in her armchair. Then he noted the time on his watch, disinfected the thermometer, and pocketed the instrument before clicking his heels together.

"Well, miss," said Dr. Zaki, "you're doing much better than I am." He wore a bedazzled-blue suit with a blanched-almond waistcoat. He had curly black hair, a clean-shaven jaw, and a sharp nose like an ecumenical gargoyle.

"You don't have to speak English with me," Nina croaked.

"I like to practice."

She sniffed. "Planning on going somewhere?"

"Not at the moment. Not when you're like this." He packed away his stethoscope and clicked his heels once more. "Lots of rest - and no more work. Apart from the antibiotics, I would also suggest that you allow Salvatore to take command briefly."

"Ogni mali nun veni pri nòciri," muttered Nina.

"I'm at a loss, Salvatore - would you care to fill me in?"

The underboss creaked across the floorboard in his dark-liver suit. "Not every pain comes to harm you," the overweight underboss translated.

"Nina, please," laughed Dr. Zaki, "I'm not trying to rob you of your job."

"Many have tried," the old woman hissed.

"Be that as it may, my dear, you need to recover. Salvatore has a steady hand."

"And a big car," replied the underboss.

All three of them laughed as Dr. Zaki edged closer to the door. Then he said goodbye and was escorted downstairs by a youngster wearing fulvous-orange trousers.

"Good. I can work now," said Nina. She snapped her wrinkled fingers.

Through the same pair of doors that Dr. Zaki had departed, there emerged two men wearing floral shirts and Laura Donato minus her dark-khaki aviator jacket. Laura's deputy, Baaqa Bell, entered behind them with total confidence. All three of them shoved the Marrakech Captain towards Nina, who studied her with cold eyes as she flattened her Finn-purple dress along the contours of her old legs. The head of the Scarvaggi Family regarded Baaqa Bell and returned her gaze to Laura Donato, who was yanking her arms away from the men with rancour.

"That's enough," said Nina in Sicilian. "She is not our teacher."

In the corner of the room, a cigarette lighter flashed. Augustu Valverde returned the lighter to his charcoal-grey pocket as he moved his dark-Byzantium fedora from the safety of his lap to the hardwood surface of a small table adjacent to his leg. The consigliere puffed on his cigarette, closed his eyes, and nodded to Nina.

"*Cummari*," began Laura. "I want to apologise - "

She was cut off by Nina snapping her fingers and hissing. Then she looked at Salvatore Yannucci, who had perched his girth on the edge of the armchair.

Salvatore said, "Laura - do you know why the *Cummari* is in charge?"

"Sure."

"You don't." He rubbed his meaty hands together. "Which means you don't know why the buck stops with Nina. Why she approves the orders we carry out."

"Get to the point, Sal - "

Baaqa slapped the Marrakech captain across her cheek.

"Oh - " Laura rubbed her face and spoke quietly. "You're gonna have to hit harder if you want my job - "

"When we kill a prick, they are no longer sisters," added Salvatore. "They are no longer brothers - they are dangerous. That's why these things have to be dealt with."

He clasped his hands together as if he were praying.

"Kossi Bundhoo."

The name was suspended in the air of the dimly lit parlour room.

Augustu, meanwhile, shook his head as he stamped out his cigarette. He folded his hands together in his lap and returned his dormant eyes to the crowd.

Salvatore continued, "Kossi Bundhoo wasn't dangerous. He was our brother - we gave him a passport to get him away from the communists in Mauritania - and you repay him like this?"

"He *was* a communist," stated Laura. "He deserved to die - "

"AND WHO GAVE YOU THAT JOB?"

Once again, the heavy silence made the room like a vacuum-sealed pack of beef.

"ANSWER!"

"He didn't want to pay his bar tab either," added Laura.

"You're a stupid girl," interrupted Nina. "You should have taken a hammer to his favourite hand. But you would rather kill people than make them spend their money. I'll tell you something else, you stupid girl - when I sanction a killing, the police are told in advance. When someone crops up dead at six in the morning, people get worried. They don't know who sanctioned the killing, they don't know what my plans are, and now they are thinking about their own interests, their own money, their own plans. I don't care about their plans. The power stays in this room — it always stays here."

"What do I have to do?" asked Laura, half-sincerely.

Salvatore inhaled the calmer half of the room. "Nothing."

"What do I have to do?" she repeated.

She would be dismissed with immediate effect, explained Nina. Her deputy, Baaqa Bell, would be promoted to Captain of Marrakech, in line with diversity quotas.

Laura looked at Augustu in the corner. "What's the consigliere think?"

"He thinks it's a good idea," replied Augustu, retrieving his fedora.

Krish Patel opened the door to Lou's office and leant in the doorway. He was the senior accounting manager and wore an amaranth-pink suit with an amber necktie. He wore battleship-grey shoes and Morocco-shaped cufflinks that gleamed over the cuffs of his baby-powder-white shirts. On the other hand, he had a sweet face with bear-like eyes and small ears and his hair was thick and well-combed. "Hello Lou, old chap," said Krish in a posh English accent. "You wouldn't fancy a slap-up lunch, would you?"

The two men caught a bitter-lemon taxi to a restaurant called *Patel's*.

Stepping out of the taxi, Krish pointed to the sign. Then he looked between the sign and Lou and smiled warmly. "You notice the name?"

"Uh-huh," said Lou.

Inside, they were shown to a table. They ordered a set lunch and prepared themselves for harira soup, brewat, beetroot salad, and zaalouka.

A mint tea came for Krish and a beer came for Lou. Halfway through the beer, Lou vomited into the glass. The waitress quickly replaced the glass with a brand-new beer.

"So, you - like your parties?" asked Krish.

"It's not a party when there's one person."

"It's hard getting to know people. My neighbor's from Pakistan."

The nuance went straight over Lou's head.

"How's your flat?" asked Krish.

"It's a flat - Christ - there's not much to it."

"Why not?" Krish smiled.

"Cuz the flat fairies were laid off - what's the point, Krish? What do you want?"

"I didn't mean to step on your toes," apologized Krish. "When I first came here, I was shocked by the poverty. I remember telling Cleopatra all about it - "

"Oh yea? What did she say?"

"She said, 'Lucky us,' which I don't disagree with. But there's an awful lot of money about, and there aren't many people spending it."

"No shit."

"Steady on, old bean! I just wanted to get to know you better. Tell you what, old chap, how about you get some of that beer down your neck, and I'll buy another one."

"You know any foreign languages?"

"Yes, I know Arabic. And French, and Portuguese. Why do you ask?"

"Because I don't speak any," sighed Lou. "We'll just have to risk it. The whole country's rigged, Krish, look around you. It's by the grace of God I can pee straight."

"It can't be worse than England," said Krish, sipping his mint tea.

"Can't be - " Lou looked around the mostly empty restaurant. "I know I'm drunk, but the way Westerners say their countries are as corrupt as these shitholes pisses me off because we're all in the muck together; standards went out with bronze age and shit. It's just bullshit, Krish; how can you even begin to compare England to this shithole?"

"Oh dear," said Krish. "I didn't know you had a drinking problem." He sighed. "Wouldn't have bought you those beers. Damn shame."

"I can handle it." Lou suppressed a powerful belch. Then he saw himself in Krish - even though he preferred his banana-mania suit - and asked about work.

"Well," began Krish as he ignored the vomit stains. "I get to oversee the financial operations of the company. I have to prepare statements, but I've got a whole team behind me who do much of the work. The locals are terrific workers, you know, and I've got every faith in them - everything's been running as smooth as backsides."

"So, you don't do anything?"

Krish welcomed the beetroot salad from the waitress, flapped out a new napkin, picked up his utensils, and smiled at Lou, who had also received his beetroot salad.

"When you work in a foreign country," explained Krish between mouthfuls, "you have to give the locals something in return. We've been giving this place credibility."

"Then why don't they have it?"

"Come on, Lou, it's North Africa - it's not Luxembourg." He munched happily on his beetroot salad and dabbed his mouth with an android-green napkin. "With money comes credibility. The more credible somewhere is, the more investment it gets. I mean, I don't have to tell you this, but look at Bermuda - "

"Yea, I'm from there."

"Sorry, old chap. But you know what I'm talking about."

"I do." Lou was half-slurring his words. "They invest in businesses, and scholarships for those businesses, but they don't build new roads."

A solitary munch from Krish halted the conversation.

"Yoghurt and cumin seeds," said Krish. "Ground cumin seeds - some crushed garlic by the looks of it - salt and pepper, malt vinegar - it tastes like - beets, baby spinach, mint leaves, and cilantro. I thought that's what the soapy flavour was. Sometimes you can never tell with herbs. Local herbs, too. Mind you, this is a mouth-watering salad."

Lou had barely touched his beetroot salad.

"If you knew something bad had happened," said Lou, poking the red flesh with his fork, "and it was close to you... what would you do?"

"My wife is happy to stay in England. She wants to raise our daughter there. So, I have an obligation to pay the bills, and the rent, and to make sure they're both safe."

Lou looked aghast.

"Eat your beetroot salad before it gets warm."

The property manager dragged his light-cornflower-blue eyes away from the senior accounting manager and stared around the empty restaurant with its prevaricating waiting staff, restless chefs wafting through the kitchen, and Clorox overpowering what should have been the suffocating odors of freshly cooked food and endemic stenches.

"You're confusing culture with economics," said Krish, polishing off his plate. "The great thing about the *makhzan* here is that they're liberals. They believe in personal freedom, private property, and limited government interference." He listed these strange things on his lithe fingers.

"But there *is* interference," replied Lou.

"But that's fine - so long as it's not written into law." He rubbed his cufflinks. "Legally, Morocco is an economically liberal country," added the senior accounting manager. "But the strange thing is that, culturally, Morocco's a protectionist country." He sighed into his plate. "It's one of the things that could destroy this place." When he snapped his fingers, the petite waitress sprung into action from the far side of the room. She sauntered over to the table, removed his plate, and started walking back to the kitchen, where it would be washed by a student who hated his life and wanted to die.

The region next to Marrakech was called Errachidia and it contained the Ziz Valley, a long canyon filled with palm trees and other assorted flora. The Scarvaggi Family had attempted to irrigate the valley and its surrounding antique-brass plains so that they could build farms that would export meat and produce directly into Europe. The area was prone to floods and desertification, however, and after three years of failed crops, farmer fatalities, and economic destruction, the plan had been abandoned, their money withdrawn from Errachidia, and its population forgotten. An over-abundance of pest-controlling chemicals sapped the life from the once-verdant Ziz Valley, turning the "green jewel" of the Northwest into a torrid canyon.

A baby-blue coach travelled through this torrid canyon carrying stragglers, migrant workers, and citizens of Marrakech, who wanted to visit their less fortunate cousins in Errachidia, with its squat, sandy buildings, and scattershot palm trees.

The burnt-umber hotel sizzled in the afternoon sunlight as the six-wheeled coach pulled alongside the baking building and deposited Laura Donato. She wore her cyber-grape jeans, white tee-shirt, and dark-khaki aviator jacket, and carried her suitcase into the hotel lobby: a dead room with a fan.

The concierge - a short, fat man - wore a damp undervest and dark jeans. As the disgraced regional captain walked to her room, the concierge examined her large bum.

Upstairs, Laura stripped down and put her toiletries in the cadmium-green bathroom. She laid on the bed and stared at the fan's blades spinning in broad circles. "Just like everything else in Morocco," thought Laura, shutting her eyes and sighing, thinking about women. Despite how Islam preached that all human beings were equal, Berber women were sent to join harems in the east, and this made Moroccans resentful of their Muslim rulers, who they believed to be hypocrites. It is said that during the 16th Century, Morocco was a very tolerant place, and Jews and women could travel the country without any harassment. By the time the Spaniards had their "zone of influence", the progressive Ibn Abd al-Karim sent women to school and allowed them to fight. When the Spanish and the French left in 1956, most women were illiterate and set about educating themselves, if their integration into the professional world in the latter 20th Century was anything to go on. By the end of the 1980s, women made up a third of judges, doctors, teachers, and university lecturers, whilst also heading 20% of Moroccan families, and composing 35% of the urban Moroccan workforce. Laura winced at the irony, however, that at the same time, Moroccan women were adopting Islamic values, and arguing that wearing veils was an individual expression of religious faith, instead of unsolicited oppression.

Putting that history out of her mind, Laura cracked open her suitcase. There was a rusted safe adjacent to the bed, and Laura packed the metal box with rolls of money that she had been saving for several years.

Moving to the cadmium-green bathroom, she scrutinized her shape. She touched her left breast, then her right breast, and poked the bags underneath her eyes. She would be more attractive than most of the prostitutes in town, she mused. Whereas the local service providers had likely never strayed, she would appear more cosmopolitan, worldly even. She got dressed, went downstairs, and confronted the troglodyte in his wet undervest.

"Five thousand dirhams," said Laura in Tamazight.

"The hotel's not for sale. This dumpster has been in my family for decades. People come in, they say, 'What fun to run a hotel!' Well, it's not fun, lady - and I won't have a tourist from Marrakech, with junk in her trunk, teaching me about my own hotel!"

"Not for the hotel - my body."

The concierge leant forward, his breasts waving left and right. "Too much."

"Four," haggled Laura.

"Two."

"Three." She looked as though she would kill him if he didn't accept. "You take twenty percent."

"Thirty," hissed the concierge.

Life could be embarrassing sometimes. "Deal."

Laura and the concierge shook hands, and she watched him dial the landline, before going up to have a shower.

Over the next two weeks, Laura watched the fan's blades spinning in broad circles as client after client mounted her, reached their end, and dismounted. The disgraced Marrakech captain never lost count of her sweating exhausted clients, and there washed over her the dispassion and half-pride held by supermarket cashiers. Past victims flashed before her eyes. Men and women. Her sexual clients sometimes melted into those unlucky people whom Nina Scarvaggi had condemned. With her remiss recall, there came further memories of murderous methods, weapons, dumping grounds, and rooms where secrets had been forged, threatened, and forgotten. Laura knew the cleanest way to kill was by using a wire to strangle the chosen target. Everything else was secondary, tertiary - messy methods used by amateurs, students, unhappy wives.

On the first morning of the third week, Laura had had enough. Her oval-shaped face was like the outline of a sun-blasted planet gently floating through a dark galaxy. As she turned over on her side to get out of bed, the planet disappeared, and the woman in her re-emerged, had a quick shower, got dressed, and packed her belongings.

"Don't go!" begged the concierge as he struggled to squeeze through the tumbledown gate that separated his world from that of his guests. "Please, Laura! We've been doing so well! Why don't we start a trust? That way, the money could be there in the future for family members! What about children – let's have children!"

"I don't want any," replied Laura, marching to the front door.

The heaving mass of the concierge followed her to the perimeter of the steps, as if he were trapped by the burnt-umber hotel that had been passed down. As he stuck his neck out to catch a final glimpse of Laura's admirable, cyber-grape-cradled behind, the concierge shook his head and lighted a cigarette. "A damn shame," he sighed sadly.

On the outskirts of Errachidia were two alloy-orange apartment blocks that bordered the Aéroport Errachidia Moulay Ali Chérif. Laura had accrued enough money for a deposit on one of the apartments, and she moved in the following week, preferring the new fuzzy-wuzzy-brown bathroom to the previous cadmium-green one.

Then she returned to the city-centre and applied for a job at the local supermarket. When she arrived for her interview, she had bruises under both eyes from her previous pursuit, and a shopping list and a wrinkled curriculum vitae in her back trouser pocket.

The manager, Kamal, an older man with thick sideburns and a thinning shrub of black hair on his head, wore flax-beige suspenders and Eton-blue trousers. Showing Laura into his air-conditioned office at the back of the supermarket, he casually gestured to the football medals behind his desk and scoffed delicately at their sentimental value, especially since he had won the medals fifty years ago.

Laura sat down and stared at Kamal.

Kamal stared back.

Gnawa music was playing in the background, quietly driving Kamal, Laura, and the young women who worked there as cashiers, insane.

"So, you want to stock my shelves?" said Kamal in Tamazight.

Laura nodded.

Lifting the resume before his yellowish eyes, Kamal sucked his teeth and returned his gaze to the prospective employee. "Couldn't find anything better, huh?"

"Nothing worse," said Laura, half-irritated and obsequious.

"You've got some big ovaries coming here." He looked at her petite, murderous hands. "You work for the Sicilians your whole life. Then when they fire you, you come to me."

"I didn't know they'd fire me - "

"Kill the wrong guy?" He leant back in his creaking chair. "Huh?" Then he leant forward and cupped his hands. "This whole land used to be green. You should've seen it in the old days. It's not the sun that killed this place. It's the chemicals you and your friends brought here." He whistled through his ancient lips. "What was God thinking when he made you?"

Laura shifted in her chair.

"Whatever, you need a job." He went on to explain how the supermarket worked. They imported vegetables from the Netherlands and Spain. They also imported chicken and beef from Poland, he added, which was taking a toll on his bank account. There were also local vegetables grown in vertical farming. He paid through the teeth for eggplants, beetroot, and tomatoes, and that was before they went out. "So much for the cozy independent supermarket," added Kamal sadly, remembering the old days.

"You'll qualify for subsidies."

"Oh yes, I know that. They were spending too much money on solar panels to see me through to next month.

But it didn't help that I wasn't in Marrakech or Tangier. I'll tell you something else…if this place closes, then Errachidia will have to get everything from Marrakech. And those aren't competitive prices, they're daylight robbery…"

Morocco's two problems were always a dependency on foreign markets and a lack of capital. The obvious solution to this was tax - but taxes and Morocco had had a chequered past. When the Muslims first invaded Morocco and saw Berbers convert to Islam, they continued taxing the Berbers as non-Muslims. What followed in 740 AD was a tax revolt led by Maysara, which defeated a Muslim army from Tunisia. Berbers argued that Muslims had betrayed Islam and demanded to be recognized as Muslims in their own right. Whether this happened or not was immaterial, however, since Morocco often broke from Sharia law. Under Sharia, there were only two forms of taxes permitted: the *zakat* on livestock, and the *ushur* on harvests. But taxes called *maks* were employed by Moroccan *makhzans* to raise capital, and *maks* were levied on commodities entering city gates - instead of gross amounts across the country - which was a clever, but blasphemous, method of raising money. Not that Laura knew this.

"You shouldn't talk like this," she threatened him.

"It's my business. I'll say what I want."

"You've got Medicare for people over thirty-five. We did that for people who live in places like this one - "

"They took Medicare away last year. Besides, the young people went to Marrakech! My cousin, Naashwan, showed me a map of where they ended Medicare. It's been shrinking every year - it's gotten so bad they only have it in north Morocco."

"*You're* in the north."

"Go ask the *makhzan* - they'll say we're in the *east*. Can't have that, can they?"

Laura stared at him.

"Don't look at me like that, Laura." Kamal leant back in his chair. "My cousin's good with maps, but he's got vices." He shrugged. "You should go back to whoring."

Laura stood up, walked out, slammed the door behind her, picked up some tampons from the pharmacy section, and strutted to the sole cashier.

Kamal stormed out of his office, rushing through aisles of fandango-pink, electric-violet, dandelion-yellow, and cotton-candy-pink cleaning and food products.

Just as the cashier told Laura Donato what she owed, the sideburn-sporting manager pointed from the vantage point of the produce aisle and put a stop to the transaction. "She doesn't owe anything," shouted Kamal. "Take what you want and leave, please."

A generous silence worried the cashier as she tapped her Eton-blue nails on the weathered cash register.

Then Laura bagged her tampons, walked out of the supermarket, and crossed the pavement that led her back to the half-comradely ease of her alloy-orange apartment.

CHAPTER FIVE

Ismail had been caught with another book, and he had been sentenced to "the asshole", which was a fenced-in square of barbed wire and fencing in the prison yard in which some prisoners were forced to sit for up to eight hours. After Ismail was forced to squat, his legs were tied into position. His wrists were bound with Barbie-pink zip-ties, and he was picked up by Rabie's guards, deposited in "the asshole", where he was tied to a grey post in the centre, and left to fry. "No food or water, my friend," said Rabie, wearing his tight sunglasses. "I wish you my very best."

The sun crawled across the sky. Ismail could feel his body stinging.

An hour must have passed when Ismail opened his eyes. He watched Rabie's head shining behind the fencing. The chief guard lifted a chilled bottle of water to his lips as they creased into a smile. "Have you ever read the Koran?" asked Rabie in Arabic.

Ismail's lips were like paper. His throat ached and scratched. It was painful to open his eyes, which made it difficult for him to stare back.

"No," Ismail lied.

"I didn't think so," said Rabie, emptying the bottle into the sand. Then he tossed the bottle over the fence and strolled back into the prison.

After another two hours, Ismail felt light-headed. The sun cooked his unruly hair and the pain kept him awake for the better part of the afternoon.

He recited the Koran:

"Among the people are those who say, 'We believe in God and in the Last Day,' but they are not believers.

"They seek to deceive God and those who believe, but they deceive none but themselves, though they are not aware.

"In their hearts is sickness, and God has increased their sickness. They will have a painful punishment because of their denial.

"And when it is said to them, 'Do not make trouble on earth,' they say, 'We are only reformers.'

"In fact, they are the troublemakers, but they are not aware.

"And when it is said to them, 'Believe as the people have believed,' they say, 'Shall we believe as the fools have believed?' In fact, it is they who are the fools, but they do not know.

"And when they come across those who believe, they say, 'We believe'; but when they are alone with their devils, they say, "We are with you; we were only ridiculing.'

"It is God who ridicules them, and leaves them bewildered in their transgression."

Then Ismail cried.

There was only salt - and the salt preserved him.

He could have sworn that the evening was really the morning. He remembered the sensation of darkness covering his body, the cool night air washing over him, and a hallucination that was really reality, even though he failed to convince himself of this.

Cold water rushed over Ismail's body like armies of Saharan silver ants. Having realised that he was in an ice-bath, the prisoner uttered a husky yell of protest. "HUH!" The guards pulled him out, took him back to his cell, and slammed the door behind him. Ismail drained what he could out of the black-olive-coloured sink, and was prepared to half-crawl, half-walk himself to bed, before he saw the plate of couscous. He scoffed the food which had been left by Papis, and then collapsed on the mattress.

The next day Ismail stumbled into the mess hall and gazed up at the metal gantries. The patrolling prison guards regarded the eye-bags and the messy monobrow of the physically exhausted communist, who slouched in line as he waited for his daily intake of dry meats and couscous. He was joined by the long-haired Moussa and the mustachioed Taleb, who helped their fellow prisoner to the furthest reaches of the mess hall. After sitting for several minutes and allowing the frazzled Ismail to regain his sense, he said with determination, "I'll get out of this place. But I don't know how."

"Thank God, you don't," replied Moussa in French.

"Come on," said Taleb, thinking of all the books he had burnt in Paris. "This is what we've been waiting for!"

"Death sentence." Moussa pretended to enjoy his dried meat as he leant over the table to address his crazy colleagues. He pointed to the guard immediately above them. "Check out his rifle." He waited patiently. "Notice anything different about the gun?"

Both Ismail and Taleb shook their heads.

"Exactly. Nothing's changed. They go through ammunition like they go through books. We'd be lucky if they took a potshot at a grass rat." He sighed, looking directly into the strained eyes of his fellow prisoners. "The desert does their killing for them. There's about as much life in that desert as an American supermarket."

"What would you rather?" asked Taleb stiffly. "The American supermarket, or the Western Sahara?"

"I'd take the supermarket."

"I'd take the desert," said Taleb proudly.

"That's the problem with communists. Why are you all so bloody stupid? There are so many brilliant conservative thinkers - but why are the communists all stupid?"

There followed an ideological argument in French. Ismail watched, catching two words in three of the verbal melee which turned into a fight.

Moussa then tossed his dried meat at Taleb.

"Not the moustache! There's meat in my moustache!" screamed Taleb, ripping the particles of flesh from his otherwise perfect moustache. "You offensive anarchist!"

Ismail tore the anarchist and the communist apart. Then he croaked and coughed violently. "Don't you see," rasped Ismail. "That's why we're stuck in here!"

"Your French is better," muttered Moussa. "But you don't have to insult me."

"We're so close to the Moroccan border."

"No, we're not. The Sahara's disputed."

"Tell that to the Scarvaggis," rasped Ismail.

"Tell that to the Mauritanians," moaned Taleb.

"Tell that to the Chinese," interrupted Moussa.

"Right." Ismail painfully embraced the gist of things. "We're close to *a* border - and once we cross it, we'll be able to get a movement going in Morocco - "

"If you're gonna escape, then focus on escaping," said Moussa.

"Look who's changed their tune." Taleb patted down his moustache. "That's why we never work with anarchists - "

"SHUT UP," interrupted Ismail and Moussa.

"Moussa *has* changed his tune." Moussa spoke in the third person because he knew it would annoy Taleb, who read too many bad novels. "He's remembered something."

There was a phosphate mine in Inal - and Papis was currently putting together a list of prisoners who would be willing to work without pay.

"A train runs through Inal," continued Moussa. "We escape the mine, hitch a train, and hop off when it reaches Morocco."

"There's one problem," said Taleb. He closely regarded the soles of the chief guard as they clanged above them. "The rape victim's supervising the work detail. Throw in shellshock for good measure, and that makes your mine-escape hazardous."

"No problem," croaked Ismail as he stared up at Rabie, strolling along the gantry. "He's not gonna be in charge out there...He knows that."

The following day Ismail, Moussa, and Taleb joined the line that stretched out of Papis's air-conditioned office, through the muggy halls of the correctional facility.

"How do you feel?" asked Moussa in Arabic.

"Underweight," replied Ismail.

The prisoners shuffled every minute as they shielded their eyes against the violent sunlight cascading through the high, karmic windows.

The office was corn-coloured and damp.

Surrounded by two cardboard boxes, Papis removed clean forms from one, and placed them, after signing, into the other.

When Ismail appeared, the deputy guard tugged at his neck warmer. Then he sniffed his finger. "There are better things for you to do, three-eight-three."

"Like what?"

"That's a trick question," Papis smiled, regarding the other prisoners. "The Chinese ran out of Uighurs because they weren't given safety equipment. I don't think your treatment's going to be much different."

"Then you better put me back in 'the asshole'."

Papis winced. Then he removed the appropriate cotton-candy forms, placed them before Ismail on the table, and offered a dark-purple pen to fill them out.

Ismail cast a glance at Papis as he entered his details in Arabic, and consigned his life to mining the expensive ingredients for western life. "What do you believe in?"

"I believe in rule of law," murmured Papis covertly. "I believe whatever the regime believes - even though that'll be changing soon."

"Why?"

"Never you mind," said Papis as he snatched the cotton-candy forms. Then he put them in the appropriate cardboard box, prepared some clean forms, and stared at Ismail with an expression that seemed to be veiled hope, or desperate desire.

Ismail said, "Those forms will never leave here. Will they?"

"Good luck," came the reply. Papis told the guards to take Ismail away, and the two men shared a parting glance that assured the other convicts in the sweating queue.

It was dusk when Lou drove his dark-orchid Camaro away from Zaalouk Real Estate, circled three roundabouts, and arrived outside his apartment building. Entering his kitchen, he tossed his keys onto the island - which apart from several dirty glasses, was barren - and ripped off his burlywood necktie, white shirt, and banana-mania trousers, and sat in his underwear on the couch. Next to the arm of the couch was an almond coffee table supporting a bottle of Wild Turkey and a semi-clean tumbler. He poured the bourbon into the tumbler and drank the lot before walking into his bathroom and enjoying a numbing shower. Another bottle of Wild Turkey was stationed by the bitter-lemon bottles of shampoo, and Lou availed himself of the half-empty bottle as he washed. Sometime later, he dried himself and stepped into his cadet-grey suit, and his burly-wood necktie, which the shamed Laura Donato had been so kind to arrange. He sauntered downstairs, sat in the Camaro, and drove straight to *Accursio's*.

He was shown to Salvatore's table in the furthermost reaches of the humming eatery, where the two men kissed each other on the cheeks, and took their respective seats. When the old man in his dark-liver suit flicked through the menu, Lou cast his light-cornflower-blue eyes over his thick arms and tried to lick away the bronze sauce in the corners of his mouth from the burger that he had scoffed an hour prior.

"Are we eating?" asked Lou apprehensively.

"We'll eat and talk," replied Sal as he dragged his fat finger down the wine list. He ordered two bottles of wine - one white, one red - as well as two snake-hipped starters.

After discussing the new developments being built in Errachidia, so as to draw young people back to that failing city with its parched ex-countryside, and droughts, Sal decided that Lou had heard enough about their plans, and changed the subject. "How's the property business?" asked Sal, knowing this meant something different entirely from what he had just discussed with the easy-going, but ignorant, estate agent.

"Fine, yea," replied Lou, forcing down the calamari and whitebait with garlic aioli, and trying to look malnourished by sucking in his stomach.

"That's a privilege," noted Sal, enjoying his fried rice balls stuffed with beef ragu, peas, and mozzarella. He finished chewing and studied Lou's neck. "How's the food?"

"It's good." Lou felt increasingly sick. "You run this place, right?"

"I take an interest in it. I take an interest in a lot of things." Then, when they finished their starters, he looked at Lou's torso. "You need fattening up."

"Huh?"

Sal apologized as he watched the waitress picking up their plates. "Can we also have the lamb ass and the pork belly for the old beggar?"

The waitress nodded, smiled, and disappeared.

(Salvatore had grown out of ordering his whole meal at the beginning. He enjoyed tacking on another order, then another, until at the very end, the extensive bill arrived.)

In no time, Salvatore was plying his mouth with crispy pork belly splashed with port and apricot jus. After swallowing painfully, he said, "There's a cinema nearby."

"Huh?"

"It's not a date, you know."

"Yea," laughed Lou, spreading balsamic and rosemary jus over his lamb rump. "Who's saying that?"

"You're just quiet. People are scared of me." He looked at his fat hands. "Dumb people. You don't think I'm a scary man, do you?"

"You're not scaring me, Sal - the meal - it's very nice." Gas was building up inside. He hoped that it would come out as a gas and not as a brown liquid, or a black solid.

"I miss the old country," Sal said, nodding thoughtfully at the past. "There used to be a small cinema in my town. You know, Nina and I grew up together on the coast - the children next to the sea are always looking beyond the shore. But I don't have to tell you that - you know what I'm talking about."

Lou downed his fourth glass of wine. "Did she beat you up?"

"All the time!" laughed Sal. "She's older than me. Her family ran the cinema back then and she used to chase me around the cinema when they played scary movies." He leant back in his chair and smiled at his empty plate. "They used to show some bad movies, but that was because they would find the free ones on YouTube and play them on the big screen. You know, they played many movies from the 1950s. They showed *Il Mostro Dei Cieli*: the giant bird was a puppet that was made by Mexicans - and they showed *Zombi* and *Quattro mosche di velluto grigio*: and the Italians make good horror movies, but the scripts never made any sense - so we didn't enjoy them like the others. I saw *The Sicilian* - the Michael Cimino movie with Christopher Lambert - and I remember the scene where Lambert shoots an old man in the face - and the heart - but it was like Robin Hood, because he robs from the landowners, and gives to the poor - "

"I guess that's what they think about the communists in Mauritania," interrupted Lou. "Maybe they're gonna have some influence over here. You know – pew, pew."

Salvatore disliked Lou's co-opting of his pleasant, cinematic memories. He said, "Don't mention that again," and ordered another bottle of red wine and two desserts.

"Faith is salvation," added the old man. "Not the wood of a ship."

"Huh?"

"How much petrol do they have? How much ammunition? Do they have water to cross the desert?"

"They gotta do what - ?" He waited for the wine bottle to be uncorked and tasted. "You're worried?"

"You're just like..." The underboss smiled. He sipped his wine and coughed. "They're not going to leave Mauritania. Don't worry about no stinking communists." He allowed himself a smile. "The people who leave don't come back. If nobody died, God would have to make another world - and then he would have to make another..." He stared into the distance. "When you see this movie...things will make sense."

"We're gonna go to your cinema?"

"It's not mine, Lou - I only take an interest in it."

The waiter returned with two plates of toffee pannacotta. He placed them on the table, asked if there was anything else, and disappeared.

"Eat your cake," said Sal as he pointed to the property manager's plate. He spoke as though he were addressing a child at a birthday party. "Eat, so you get strong."

When the plates and glasses were taken away, Lou noticed the bill never came. They got their coats and were shown out of the restaurant...

Outside, they strolled down the pavement. But there was a large man following them, wearing a white shirt, and fulvous-orange trousers.

Salvatore nodded quietly. "You see him?"

"Yea," said Lou.

"One of Baaqa's boys. He's a good man, who will look after us." When Salvatore said this, he and Lou rounded a corner, and faced an old-style cinema. Flashing carmine letters spelling *Accursio's Picture House* shone brightly over the darkened street, as the laughter of customers inside the golden interiors clashed against the poverty of the apartments and the old cars across the street. There was a large poster, next to the corn-coloured popcorn machine in the window, showing an olive-skinned man holding a wine bottle, standing over the corpses of small brown bodies, who still carried with them machine guns and flowers. "*How The Northwest Was Won,*" read Lou. He shuddered at the sight of the deceased racial stereotypes lying beneath the victorious European conqueror and began to feel nauseous. "Is this - the movie we're gonna see?"

Salvatore looked at him, confused. "You don't want to see *The Brain Suckers*?"

"Huh?"

"*The Brain Suckers.* That's what I wanted to show you." He pointed to the flamboyant poster adjacent to *How The Northwest Was Won* - which featured a dark-olive-green alien with an exposed brain, dripping mandibles and space helmet, menacing a blonde woman with the largest breasts that Lou had ever seen in his life, and the jagged title, *The Brain Suckers*, hovering over a handsome man with dimples. "It's a limey movie. I thought you might be homesick, so you might want to watch it."

"Oh."

"But you - you want to watch the western?"

"No, no, no - no, no - no, no, no - no - let's watch *The Brain Suckers.*"

The two men went inside where they bought popcorn and orange soda. Lou pointed to a brightened glass cabinet that held various sweets. "You've got Twizzlers!" he blurted out. "I haven't seen Twizzlers in forever!" The Moroccan cashier handed him a packet of Twizzlers, Salvatore waved off another bill, for the time being, and showed Lou into the screening room where *The Brain Suckers* had already started playing.

"But Professor," said the buxom blonde, "why do they want to suck out our brains?"

"Survival, my dear. They'll suck our brains out, no matter the cost to their own civilization – for their own development as a species."

A strapping male, wearing a gun-holster, put his hand on the scientist's shoulder. "We've got to fight back, Professor. Kill them all!"

"What next?" replied the scientist ironically. "Suck out their brains?"

"Don't be silly, Professor. I don't want to suck out their brains."

"Neither do I," added the buxom blonde.

"Very well." The scientist nodded. "There is some humanity left in this crazy world, after all." He opened the door. "Don't follow me."

The scientist went outside, where the aliens sucked out his brains.

"They sucked out his brains!" said the strapping male as he looked through the window at the brain-sucking and grimaced.

"It's horrible," cried the buxom blonde, "make it stop, Cliff!"

When the movie was over, Salvatore untied his cultured-pearl necktie, rolled it into a confectionary shape, and shoved it into the pocket of his dark-liver suit. Salvatore and Lou and the rest of the audience shuffled out of the screening room and gathered in the lobby where they bought coffees and talked about the movie. On the other hand, the underboss and the property manager - and to some extent, Salvatore's bodyguard - walked down the street to a bar with flashing, dark-Byzantium signs hanging outside, advertising liquors and craft ales. They went inside, bought coffees, and sat in the corner as Lou half-watched their bodyguard pacing up and down the arid street outside.

Salvatore said, "That movie about Morocco you wanted to watch instead - "

"No, no - no, no, no - I didn't - "

"Not every pain comes to harm you, Lou."

"Huh?"

"*How The Northwest Was Won* is an educational picture. We like to make them for the locals. We don't make those pictures for foreigners."

Now that he had sobered up, Lou noticed that his cravings were worse. He stirred uncommon quantities of brown sugar into his Americano.

"Was that movie about how you came here?" asked Lou.

"They used to have a king here. But he was executed during the revolution. The country was collapsing - there was no order, there were no rules, people were dying. That was when the first Sicilians came." He told this story as if it were local folklore. "They came with medicine and money. They built hospitals and schools everywhere." Touching the rings of his sweating neck, Salvatore sighed heavily and drank coffee. "That was fifty years ago, Lou - I was a young man, then."

"Libya sucks," said Lou, surprising himself. "Why didn't you go there?"

"Morocco had a reputation." The old man laughed. "A good reputation! You dress like a businessman, but you don't think like one."

There was a lull in the conversation.

"Who's Accursio?" asked Lou, picking at his cuticles in frustration.

The underboss went quiet. "The old days were tough. You had to work hard to put the fear of Allah in people." He smiled apologetically. "It's easy to find a weak spot."

"Uh-huh."

"My mother used to say, *Eat with gusto but drink in moderation.*" He leant back in the black-bean booth. "You drink too much - "

"Terrific," snarled Lou. "What's your weak spot?"

"I can't help you. My son is dead."

The property manager turned red as he searched through the aspects of the old man before him, and found little more than a few scattered memories of parenthood. "I'm sorry. I didn't know that, Sal. I'm so sorry."

"You shouldn't know these things. The way you talk sometimes - " Salvatore touched the sides of his coffee cup. Then he pushed the saucer round the table. "There were times when I used to get angry with Accursio. Now I feel like it was wasted time."

"I'm sorry," muttered Lou.

Salvatore gestured forgiveness by waving a fat hand over Lou's aquiline nose. "Now, I wanted to ask you about something urgent." He took a few laboured breaths. "It's about the local police."

Lou coughed, dabbed his mouth, and pushed his coffee away.

Salvatore pushed it back. "Do you know who Hassan Hacimi is?"

"No."

"He's a senior police officer who's a communist and a paedophile."

"Paedo-Paedo-Paedo-phile?"

"There are pictures." Salvatore frowned darkly. "A young man shouldn't see them."

"I don't - I didn't - don't want to - "

"It makes *The Brain Suckers* look like a children's story."

"What are you saying?" whispered Lou, narrowing his eyes.

"When someone knows Hassan, they are playing with fire." The underboss sipped his coffee and adjusted his overflowing behind on the black-bean cushion.

Lou pointed his finger. "Are you saying I know him?"

"Are you denying - ?"

"I'm not denying anything, Sal, because I didn't do anything."

"You shouldn't drink - you forget where you've been."

Then Lou leaned forward and stared at the old man. "Sal - " Lou had begun to lose his voice and rasped his way through his improvised lies. "I don't know Hassan."

Salvatore stared back. He brushed his trousers and buried the memories of his son.

"Okay."

The dark moon of Rabie's naked head glided through the corridors of the prison as guards opened pre-marked cells and dragged half-asleep prisoners who had signed up for the mining work into the security area, and then into the twilight of early morning. In the clinking chain-gang were Ismail, Moussa, and Taleb, who shivered and watched their breath in the moonlight as they were marched to the fluorescent-lit train station. Shortly afterwards, an alloy-orange freight train headed for Dakhla pulled into the station, and hissed to a halt. Two cattle-carriages opened, were filled with prisoners, and shut their doors before the freight train dragged itself towards Inal, where the phosphate mine would be waiting in the sun.

Through the slits of the cattle-carriage, Ismail could see a rocky landscape where red shapes formed plateaus, hills, and valleys, and where occasional palm trees cast shapes over Fennec foxes who had decided to retire from their nocturnal hunts. Otherwise, the experience in the cattle-carriage was morose, smelly, and repulsive as the heat of the morning took its tool on the prisoners' multifaceted, sweating crevices.

The train slowed its pace, and the prisoners grew thirsty and nervous. When Ismail turned around, he saw that

Taleb had squeezed his head through two pairs of shoulders. "Ismail," said Taleb in Arabic, crooking his moustache in a gesture of socialist solidarity.

Ismail simply nodded.

"You okay?" asked Taleb.

"It's hot."

"First they bake you - then they send you underground." The communist winked.

The inference was that they would *not* be underground because they would be halfway across the border, but Ismail merely glared back with defiant leadership.

Taleb blew spittle through his sweaty moustache. "Ha-ha!"

The freight train stopped at a purpose-built station in the middle of nowhere. The cattle-carriages were unlocked so that the chain-gangs of prisoners could be pulled out by Rabie's men who had travelled with them in an air-conditioned carriage. Rabie exited that carriage as the last of the prisoners were pushed into the perimeter of the phosphate mine and replaced his clenched aviators over his eyes, and walked after them, dreaming of rest and recreation after he had dropped them off.

The phosphate mine was a vast affair with sedimentary layers visible as a result of the endless wedging, lumping, and scalloping of the earth. Arctic-lime articulated haulers carried large quantities of unrefined dirt between extraction points, and slag heaps and bud-green bucket-wheel excavators scooped away entire hillsides of earth, and dumped the surplus muck in great piles towering over employees. On the perimeter of the mine was a large compound where the prisoners were taken. Cadmium-green container houses covered the dry earth with occasional water wells. A gaggle of Mauritanian guards and Chinese management marched towards the fresh chain-gangs and their self-satisfied guardians, chiefly Rabie.

Leading the mining delegation was a Chinese woman named Jing Fàn. Being the manager, she wore a burnt-sienna shirt, Congo-pink jeans, and very small timberland boots, instead of the dark-jungle-green jumpsuits of her various employees. She had a narrow face with deep-set eyes, thin lips that rested in a straight line, and she took off her aviators when she inspected the incoming prison workers.

"Unchain them," said Jing in Arabic.

Rabie and his guards did as they were told and the prisoners watched their new manager with a mixture of bemusement and strange terror, rubbing their wrists.

Staring back with indifference, Jing turned to one of her Chinese colleagues. "There are more blacks than usual," she said in Mandarin.

Her colleague shrugged.

"Is there a problem?" asked Rabie in Arabic.

Jing addressed her colleague, "Take the man inside and pay him."

She stepped before the prisoners as they were surrounded by Mauritanians and Chinese with machine guns.

"Most phosphate is extracted from the surface," explained Jing in Arabic. "But there is also a lot underground which needs to be removed. You will all be sent underground for twelve-hour shifts, after which you will be allowed a four-hour rest period. Then you will return underground to complete your work. When you must work hard, you learn how to do things more efficiently - so, the expectation is that your output will increase over time, without having to deduct time from your rest periods. We'll give you your hardhats so that you can get started."

The prisoners were led to the compound where they were given hard hats and dark-jungle-green mining uniforms.

Ismail, Moussa, and Taleb prepared collectively as other prisoners complained about the lack of breathing equipment and general safety.

"You work," said Jing, "or we shoot you."

A moment of silence was replaced by the shuffling of boots across pounded rubble as the prisoners gave in and marched in sequence towards the insignificant pithead. On the way there, Moussa stared ahead as he addressed his friends. "If we go down, we won't be coming back up." He breathed deeply. "Won't have the energy to run away."

"Just a little closer," whispered Ismail, eyeing the train. "Then we go for that."

Taleb made a dash for the station amongst exclamations in Mandarin and Arabic. He ran as fast as he could over the sand. One of the guards opened fire on Taleb. Three slits unzipped themselves on Taleb's back and he spun round in agony and collapsed on the ground as the distant crunching of machines continued.

The prisoners went berserk.

They threw hard hats at Chinese and Mauritanian alike and refused to work before there had been an inquiry.

During the confusion, Ismail and Moussa bolted for the train but changed direction when bullets scattered sand next to their booted feet. Running in the other direction, bullets destroyed their footprints until Jing Fàn stopped her guards, citing the need to conserve their ammunition. "Get back in line," the mine manager then told the prisoners. She pointed at Taleb's corpse. "That man doesn't have options, does he?"

The prisoners reformed their sequence and marched solemnly to the pithead.

Rabie sprinted out of the compound, zipping up his fly. Money was falling out of his trouser pockets and his aviators were on the other side of his head. "What the hell was that?" screamed the ex-soldier as he fixed his sunglasses and wiped his hands.

Jing pointed to the corpse. "Two got away."

"Send someone after them! If they come back to Choum - !"

"Why would they do that?" asked Jing in a flat, irritated tone. "They have the whole desert to play with." She looked at their diminishing footprints. "There's nothing that way." She returned her gaze to Rabie. "Only sand."

Satisfied, Rabie finished what he had started in the compound.

He caught the next train back to Choum. The countryside was suffused with sun and shadows marked the hills and rocky outcroppings which earlier had been depths; there was no depth anywhere now. Along the way, Rabie took a quick nap in the travel compartment. One of the guards woke him as the train pulled into Choum. Rabie ran his hand over his hard head, stepped into the vestibule, and prepared to open the door.

But by the time the train stopped, it was clear that the chief guard would have to cut through the prison employees who were desperate to get onto the train. As the door hissed open, Rabie and his colleagues failed to get further than the first step.

"What are you doing?" shouted Rabie in Arabic. "Get back to work, the lot of you!"

In the distance, the squat shape of the prison was clear.

Suddenly, one of the turrets exploded, launching metal, body parts, and melted circuits across the prison yard.

Rabie's eyes widened.

He touched a blue button and watched as the door hissed shut over the various guards and employees, who cursed the name of "Rabie".

Telling his colleagues to secure the rest of the train - though in reality he knew he might be sending them to their deaths - Rabie clanked the other way through cramped corridors wired with cyan-coloured fuse boxes and affordable deep-chestnut flooring. When he reached the cockpit, he kicked the door open to find a gun barrel in his face. "The people's revolution claims this train," said a trigger-happy woman in Arabic.

Around six in the morning, Lou woke up in his bedroom and staggered to the bathroom, where he collapsed before his new beige toilet, and vomited. He stood up and looked in the mirror. The hairs in his nostrils had grown without his noticing, the bags under his eyes were like purses, and his light-cornflower-blue eyes were bloodshot, crusted, and twitching, like confused automatic sliding doors. Most regrettable was the fact that his throat felt like a cheese grater - he poured himself a glass of water, downed it, and faced the consequences. When one drank as much as Lou did, drinking water was like drinking poison made from glutton thistle.

He shuffled into the kitchen.

A parrot was eating a donner kebab on the battleship-grey countertop. It was collecting curls of beaver-brown donner with its claws and chewing the dry faux-meat.

"Lou-Lou!" said the celeste-blue parrot.

"Who are you?" croaked Lou. Which seemed to be a good question.

The chronically hungover property manager's feet took him to the window. He parted the curtains, looked down at the street, and saw the throbbing traffic being touched by the morning's coral-pink sun. He saw the snow on the Atlas Mountains.

His phone buzzed next to the parrot on the kitchen island.

"WHUUUHAHHAA!" Lou screamed, jumping in fright.

"Lou-Lou!"

Lou moved across the room to the kitchen island, took his phone away from the squawking parrot, sat on the couch, and answered the call.

"Are you alive?" asked Hassan Hacimi.

"Uh-huh." Lou stared at his feathery flat mate. "There's a parrot."

"Don't come at me with your problems. You must have picked it up somewhere. I wanted to thank you for talking to me last night. Though we didn't have to go out - "

"Huh? We what …?"

"We went out, Lou. Went out with a vengeance. We were talking on the phone, and you said you wanted to meet in person. Then we hit the clubs. With a vengeance."

"The - the - capos," croaked Lou, the cogs of his mind submerged in cheap white wine and bourbon. "I gave you names. But I can't remember what we spoke about afterwards - I can't - you've gotta fill me in - "

"Lou-Lou!" squawked the colourful bird.

"I don't want the parrot," added Lou.

"Open the window," said Hassan. *"Let it fly home. They know better."*

"But I've gotta - " Opening the window, Lou threw pillows at the parrot.

Then he ran at the parrot, pushing it towards the windowsill. "I've gotta know what I was talking about. What's the point if I repeat myself?"

"...click...," the line went dead.

The parrot investigated the curtain with its beak, its black tongue fiddling with the seams and threads until it decided that the human being was more interesting.

"Kills the goombahs! Kill the goombahs!" the bird shouted.

Lou threw his smartphone on the couch. He grabbed the parrot, tossed it outside, and secured the window. Somebody knocked at the front door. Turning towards the dark-red corridor, Lou searched for his bathrobe, swathed himself in its soft embrace, stepped into the corridor, avoided stepping in his vomit, and opened the door.

He was greeted by the glass-enlarged eyes of Detective Mostafa Lazrak, his golden wrist bracelet tinkling as he lifted his badge into view of Lou's bloodshot eyes. "Detective Mostafa Lazrak. I won't ask to come in - it saves everybody a lot of time." The detective pushed past the property manager and was followed by Sergeant Fatima Ahmed and five policemen, who started turning over furniture and opening drawers.

"Excuse me," croaked Lou as he caught up with the jingling detective. "Do you guys have a search warrant?"

"What happens, man?" asked the detective, flashing his bright eyes. "Smells like you've had the window open. Still smells bad. But you've had the window open."

"Huh?"

"Jump through the window - that'll do the job. You trying to kill yourself?"

"Uh."

"I ask you if you're trying to kill yourself, and all you can say is 'uh'?" The detective's wrist tinkled. "You want a warrant, talk to him."

Lou dazedly watched Augustu Valverde as he entered the apartment with a cardboard tray of coffee and a bag of croissants. He put the impromptu breakfast on the kitchen island, removed his dark-Byzantium fedora, and raised his hollowed cheeks at Lou. "I brought you some coffee and breakfast - something you should know: the bakery is gluten-free, and they recycle everything - even the customers!"

Detective Lazrak sniggered as he searched under Lou's anorexic fridge.

"But the coffee is *splendido*."

Lou had never met Augustu, but he had heard about him.

"Augustu," choked Lou. "What's - going - on - this - "

"Come with me," said the consigliere as he guided Lou, his coffee, and his croissants towards the couch. Seating Lou on the couch, he perched on the chair opposite, handing out croissants, and packs of sugar. Lou watched Constable Harrak enter the apartment and mention something to Detective Lazrak.

"Not many cops in hijabs," thought Lou aloud.

"I never liked the word 'tolerant'," said Augustu as he removed the recyclable plastic top from his cappuccino. "When a man tolerates his neighbor - it means he doesn't like him - but since they live on the same street, he'll try to avoid the bastard."

Lou stared. He sipped his Americano.

"I want to apologise for this, Lou." He handed Lou an emerald croissant. "There's nothing wrong with it. I know it's green, but - it was worth a try." He stared angrily at the croissant, muttering, "Catalano would never tolerate a green croissant. The old crow." Then he stared at his cosmic-latte necktie, and added, "I know Sal's fond of you - but there are going to be some changes - about how we've been running things."

"What's going on?"

"You know that I am consigliere for the Scarvaggi Family."

"Uh-huh."

"Do you know what I do?"

"Uh."

"I advise the *Cummari* - which is Nina - how to run her business. And I resolve disputes. That's the ugly stuff - the only ugly stuff that I have to deal with. Detective?"

Detective Lazrak appeared behind the kitchen island. "Mr. Valverde?"

"Have you found a cadet-grey suit?"

"Ahmed found it in the shower. Looks like he soiled himself."

"Burn it, please." Augustu returned his quiet eyes to Lou. "You remember Laura?"

"Yea, she gave me that - "

"It was my decision to send her away." The consigliere sighed. "You spend hours searching for weak links around you. Trying to stop disputes before they happen." He tapped the plastic top against his charcoal-grey trousers. "We were too late on that occasion. But with the situation in Mauritania, we cannot afford to have weak links."

"Uh," rasped Lou.

"All the weak links were dealt with last time," added Augustu as he arranged his silver skullcap of finely combed hair. "They are much older than the rest of us. That's because, many moons ago, they purged the family - and changed the business. Sal was the only one who made the cut, as far as Nina was concerned, so he was promoted..." A slurp of lukewarm coffee ended Augustu's chilling story.

"Why?"

"The old boss - " Augustu ignored Lou's question. " - was from the old country. He missed the vineyard more than his desk - which put all of his colleagues at risk." As he levelled his eyes against Lou's bloodshot gaze, the long-suffering boozer shook. "The men wanted Nina to be the barking dog when she wanted to be the grazing ox. I can't imagine that she will go back to Sicily. She likes Morocco because the class system doesn't apply to her. She can do as she wishes. She has found freedom." Recalling the past, he shook his head again. "The old boss didn't agree."

"Why are you telling me this?" asked Lou.

The charcoal-grey body seemed to stiffen. "I'm not afraid of you. I know where you live. You're not difficult to find. I mean, we found you in - what - ten minutes?"

"Uh."

"There's something you should know. You are living in Nina's vision. She had bigger designs than running Uncle Lou's neighborhood. She has changed Morocco." The wavering tone of his voice, however, produced a question instead of a revelation. "I don't think she's done this - no, you need a revolution to change a country forever. We're just bank robbers." Then came a smile. "But there is honour amongst thieves."

With the search over, the coffee ingested, and the green croissants consigned to the rubbish tip outside, the police withdrew from the apartment. Augustu Valverde said that he would hopefully never see Lou again, after which he replaced his dark-Byzantium fedora, closed the door behind him, and left the building.

After collecting his senses, Lou phoned Zaalouk Real Estate and explained that he would be late. He shuffled towards his darkened bedroom where he sat on the bed, fell backwards, and started breathing heavily. He found himself crying, as he lamented his dark past, which was altogether character-forming but unimportant - and it was dark merely because he couldn't remember much of it, beyond childhood. With nothing he could do about his past, he looked to the future. The future was bleak.

Nuh-uh, he reasoned, *everybody says that. The future's always bleak. But thinking like that saves lives. Uh-huh.*

Uh.

Then he farted on the bed. But it was worse than a fart.

CHAPTER SIX

What stretched for miles was an atomic-tangerine distance where seemingly-architectured hills broke up the otherwise all-encompassing desert. The sight of these hills gave the strange reminder that all rocks came from mountains; and that mountains, in their turn, could not always serve as immortal markers for cartographers who struggled on through Indian sandburs, acacias, and tufts of morkba, and who resolutely died from heat exhaustion on these flatlands and sandbanks. There had been droughts in the late eighteenth century and during the years 1907 and 1931 and conversely flooding in 1935 and swarms of locusts eating harvests in 1905-1906. Otherwise, a lack of predators. No more lynx, hyenas, warthogs, ostriches or gazelles. All were butchered by the boom in blood sports: one the incoming Mauritanian communists had neglected to address in their revolutionary manifesto. But no matter. Where there were no beasts, there would be no beasts. There would be no hunt today. Merely a cornucopia of migratory birds who annually flocked over the shifting sands, and the terrible silence, silence, silence, that was occasionally broken up by sandstorms.

After thirty minutes of fevered walking, Moussa collapsed. Ismail knelt down, shaded Moussa's head using his hand, and noticed the Chinese-red stain.

"It went straight through me," said Moussa hopefully in Arabic.

"You're losing blood," replied Ismail, observing his atomic-tangerine surroundings. "Don't move, Moussa. Let's take a break - "

"No, we have to keep moving." Moussa winced as he got back to his feet. "We have to find the train line. We can try and catch hold."

Lacing his arm around Moussa's hot neck, Ismail led the expiring anarchist deeper into the silence, silence, silence of the endless distance, with its odd, architectured hills. Storm clouds gathered above them, their dark-electric-blue shapes glowering as the roasted ex-convicts struggled across the deceitfully uneven ground. Excited at the prospect of rain, the communist and the anarchist quickened their pace, but within an hour both were dehydrated beyond repair and lamented the lack of rain.

Suddenly the rain fell in great sheets.

"That's odd," said Moussa as he opened his mouth. "Someone's watching over us."

"Where are we going?" asked Ismail as he squinted in the heavy pellets of rain. "We need some direction; I don't know what the point - "

"Keep going forward." Moussa winced as the rain lashed his wound. "There's bound to be a rail line or a highway - " Except his knees gave out and he started sinking.

Ismail did his best to let Moussa down gently. When the anarchist hit the ground, he put his lips to the sand, slurped a small puddle down his dying gullet, and sighed. His long hair was soaked to the follicle, his glasses fogged up, and his mouth had blood around the edges. With a few distressing coughs, he began to laugh maniacally.

"Ain't this a bitch," chuckled Ismail.

Moussa laughed, watching the dark-electric-blue clouds. Then the laughter died away, and the anarchist was left staring happily at the sky.

"Moussa?"

Ismail put his head to Moussa's chest. Then he put his finger under his nose. *"Moussa,"* whispered Ismail as he gathered the body in his arms and held it quietly. Rocking the body back and forth, Ismail waited for the storm to disperse above him and rested Moussa on the ground, shut his eyes, and replaced his glasses.

Ismail stood up and continued his journey across the hydrated desert - except the water soon boiled and evaporated back into the jealous heavens.

Dark-goldenrod hills, chocolate-web cliffs, and carrot-orange rivulets passed Ismail by as he fought to keep moving against God's colour palette, and there appeared a rail line in yet another square mile of the endless breadth.

Soon Ismail found himself running up to the lonely track. His huffing and puffing blew sand off of the metal rods as he bent down and put his ear to the sizzling veneer. He could hear his heartbeat over the dead metal and the quiet sky and the old desert.

Then he heard something else. It was faint - but it was a train.

He jumped up, sucking the hot air into his lungs. He dug a trench next to the tracks to hide himself, and covered himself with sand, like a grave. The manufactured wheeze of the train came closer, the churning barks from its diesel engines growing louder until they had expanded to a deafening volume.

When the shadow engulfed Ismail, he leapt out of the sand and started running alongside the train. Baby-blue doors, footsteps, and rods blasted past the convict. He managed to grab hold of one of the rods and was dragged along the sand. Then his foot caught a fixed rock by the rail, his right arm was yanked out of its socket and his whole body was thrown away from the rail line into a small, sandy depression.

"NNNYYAAAA!" screamed Ismail as he squinted the hot sand out of his eyes, bawled with the bright pain in his right shoulder, and strained to control his limp arm. Rolling onto his back the communist wept as he stood up and hobbled after the train, which seemed to have triggered light-speed and had already become a distant speck.

The dead arm cast a strange shadow. It floated over the moving body like a spirit. Perhaps love was a shadow, thought Ismail. Perhaps the arm would lead him to peace.

An hour later Ismail was lying face-down in the searing sand.

After twenty minutes, a woman appeared and started to approach the comatose Ismail. Her face was masked by a blizzard-blue hijab and she also wore a canary-yellow robe that ebbed and flowed in the reverent current of air that defined the Western Sahara. On her back was a bolt action rifle, which she gingerly removed and aimed at Ismail, who lay motionless on the shifting sands. She nudged Ismail's buttocks with the butt of her rifle. She drew an invisible line on Ismail's right arm and noticed it was dislocated.

The woman replaced the rifle on her back, knelt in the sand, and began to play with the dislocated arm. She knew that the shoulder contained a shallow socket and that it would be easy to fix - even if there was a serious risk of lasting tissue damage. For all she knew, the tissues and tendons might be overstretched, or had snapped entirely. She rolled Ismail onto his back, grabbed the shoulder, and massaged the arm back into its hole. When the connection was made, he moaned.

"Water," said the woman in Tamazight.

She dragged Ismail back to her house, where the strong door guarded against the dropping temperatures as the sun lowered, allowing dusk to return to the desert.

Over the next few days, Ismail became aware that he was lying in a traditional mud house with one square window, shelves of bistre-brown foodstuffs, a cooking pot supported by a gas canister, several mats on the ground, and a heap of blue blankets - one of which covered Ismail's lower body for the spooky non-days that passed like the dark-electric-blue clouds that had thrust the communist towards the railway track.

Eating couscous on the second day, but nothing on the third, Ismail swirled down a toilet bowl of sleep that lasted somewhere between a moment and a whole lifetime.

Then he woke up.

"Ouch…"

"Young man, eat something," warned the woman in Tamazight. She scraped couscous out of a pot into a bowl, squatted next to Ismail, and began to spoon-feed him. The pebbles of sustenance graced his throat, but not before he had coughed violently.

"Where am I?" rasped Ismail.

"When you tell me what's going on in your head, I'll tell you where your feet are," said the woman, readjusting her full-length burgundy veil.

"My arm hurts."

"Don't move it then." She gestured at the recovering appendage. "I managed to shove it back in, but you won't be better for another week."

"A week - ?" His eyes traced the contours of the shabby dwelling with its old cooking equipment and unloved boxes of ammunition for the bolt action rifle. "How long have I been here?"

"About a fortnight." She shrugged. "I lose track of time here."

Ismail could feel the curls of his unruly hair pricking his ears. His not unattractive monobrow, however, felt as though it had been pressed onto the surface of a stove. "Who are you?"

"You first," came the measured reply.

"I'm Ismail." He eyed the framed photograph of the long-dead Moroccan King. "They caught me on the wrong side of the border and locked me up in Choum."

"You've come a long way, Ismail." A few seconds later, the kettle had boiled, and the young communist found himself being served mint tea in a polished ceramic mug. "My name is Latifah," added the mysterious woman. "I've been living in these parts."

"Why?"

"It's safer to keep my money out here." She watched the unshaven face. "You're better off working with me. Because the desert will make short work of you."

Propping his back against the wall and using his blanket as a kind of apron, Ismail returned the cautious smile, and said, "I gathered that." They sat in silence as Ismail drank his tea, listening to the wind whistling outside. "I'm a communist."

"Of course, you are," replied Latifah.

Ismail relayed his story. He said that he wanted to overthrow the Sicilians.

"I can't imagine what your excuse is," said the veiled nomad. "You don't remember what it was like before they came. You can't compare it with anything. Now, me, on the other hand - I'm old enough to remember what it was like before. The good king was still on his throne, nothing was stable, and everyone was grateful." Her eyes narrowed. "You think you understand hatred. You're not old enough to hate people. That takes years of practice - and I hate them more than you can understand."

"I know they rebuilt Morocco," interrupted Ismail. "I know things started well - but then they made too much money. They turned men, women, and kids, into serfs."

Latifah pointed to the framed photograph of the dead Moroccan King.

"Who is that?" she asked.

"The king."

"Do you know what happened to him?"

"Some people assassinated him."

"*Who* assassinated him?"

"I don't - " His sun-addled head stirred with resentment. "I don't know!" He pinched the bridge of his nose and lowered his inward-looking chin to the blue blanket.

The veiled nomad sighed. "The story goes that a recession destroyed Morocco. Then people rose up against the king and murdered him. But that's a pack of lies. What happened was that the Sicilians made a deal with the Green Party that they would frame the local populists and allow the Sicilians to take control of the economy. Except the Green Party doesn't run Morocco - the Sicilians run everything."

She remembered that Morocco, unlike other African ex-colonies, had not become a one-party state, because a split opponent was easier for the Sultan to control. Even the Scarvaggi Family had grown ignorant of this ancient advantage.

Outside, the atomic-tangerine nooks and crannies were packed with bronze and burly-wood sand as quickly as they were vacuumed free of those interim dunes, and Fennec foxes sprung up from burrows to embrace nocturnal hunts. All around, the wind rode the hills like so many snakes, and invisible clouds advanced.

Over the course of a month, Zaalouk Real Estate recruited a gaggle of real estate agents from the United Kingdom and flew them in at great expense. After being housed in various Moroccan regions, they were brought to Marrakech for a week of tutoring which was carried out via cups of coffee, cannoli, and toilet breaks. On the morning of the first day, the new recruits - who wore antique-ruby blouses, blast-off-bronze skirts, cinnamon-satin suits, and Caribbean-green neckties - were seated in the boardroom, where apart from pretending they were in an actual board meeting where their opinions mattered, they were forced to watch a short video. The ten-minute video had been prepared by Zaalouk Real Estate and concerned the art of being a real estate agent. After pressing play, Cleopatra Griffiths left the room.

"My name is Lou Baring," says the banana-mania-suited individual onscreen. (Unbeknownst to the recruits, he had lost weight and looked healthier.) "I'm a property manager, and you're going to be working with me throughout your contract."

He hops off of the table, adjusts his burlywood necktie, and stands in front of a whiteboard with the word "HUMILITY" written on it.

"Selling a property is like selling your own home. You wouldn't sell your house if the paint was peeling off the walls, the bathroom tiles were cracked, or the carpet stank. I'm gonna show you tips for getting buyers to sign on the dotted line."

> Old Uncle Lou
> Give me more, give me more, give me more
> All the girls dance on the floor
> Old Uncle Lou, they say, give me more

As music plays over the video, Lou enters the foyer of an expensive house. "Selling a nice house like this one can be a challenge. So, let's make it look nice, folks."

Removing his shoes, the camera abruptly cuts to the toilets.

"You're gonna have to clean the house from top to bottom. The best place to start is with the bathrooms. Pew!" He waves his skinny hand over his wincing aquiline nose. "If I'm not mistaken, that's the smell of salesmanship."

He gets out a sack of cleaning liquid that looks like a gallbladder.

"I like to use *Green-Clean* - a biodegradable alternative to harsh chlorine bleach, which kills the fish we love. When dissolved in water, it releases oxygen that acts as a powerful stain remover, deodorizer, and disinfectant. Best of all, it's plastic-free and it comes in compostable bags that you can seal and save for next time."

Awkwardly, the video cuts to Lou standing in the master bedroom. There are champagne-pink curtains, claret-red dressing drawers, and English-violet carpeting.

"I *believe* in sustainable bedding," says Lou. "When you prepare a house for sale, you'll be expected to dress the beds the same way that you would at home: *neatly.*"

The camera pans up and down the bed.

"Here in Morocco, we have lots of ethical bedding companies. They import my favourites, like the eucalyptus sheet set, the bamboo sateen pillowcase set, and the Tencel sleep mask, for those Sunday mornings when you want the world to go away."

Once again, the video cuts abruptly to Lou standing in the living room.

Lou is sucking on a green milkshake, and says, "Put that air-conditioning on!"

He puts the milkshake down on a cedar-wood table and allows the camera to follow him into the kitchen. There is a mixing bowl on the kitchen island that he picks up, after which he whips the contents with a metal spoon, and says, "There's nothing better than walking into someone's house and sniffing that home cooking. So, let's get cooking, and make a nice apple pie for these hard-working, potential buyers." He abruptly puts the mixing bowl down. "But let's not get carried away - after all, before God made *Accursio's*, he made the flowers in the Garden of Eden - and that's what you're gonna need when you put the finishing touches on this very special property. The Valverde Florist ships flowers across Morocco and can cater to all of your blossoming needs. I rely on Juliet Roses and Saffron Crocuses to give potential buyers the same sense of good service that they would expect in *Accursio's*."

With the music coming to its repetitive conclusion, Lou returns - by either magic or the miracles of late-night video-editing - to that same, expensive-looking foyer. "Well, it looks like you're ready to kill. So, let's get out there and sell our properties." The credits roll across the screen as Lou makes his exit through the doorway.

Two weeks later, Lou was sitting in his office with his banana-mania jacket hanging on the back of his chair, and his banana-mania trouser legs up on his desk.

Outside, the midday sun had turned the roads into rubber, and men and women walked by either with cameo-pink brollies, or wide-brimmed, deep-champagne hats. "What did they ask?" asked Lou as he massaged his much-reduced eye-bags before stirring an artificial - and in all likelihood cancer-inducing - sweetener into his coffee.

He was speaking on the phone to a new agent who had been struggling with a buyer. "No, that wasn't in the video," replied Lou as he sipped his coffee and winced at the heat. He leaned back in his chair. "There haven't been any offers on that property. Oh, you told them that? What did they say? What do you mean they don't believe you?" He watched the ripples in his coffee caused by his elevated, jigging legs. "You did the right thing saying that. No, no. No, no, no. The seller's not open to negotiation on the price. That's standard practice in Morocco." He almost choked. "More than one person owns the property so they can't possibly meet the seller. So, that's not gonna be possible." He suddenly noticed the door opening and Harry Anderson, the chief operating officer, entering the air-conditioned office, and giving him a thumbs-up and grin in greeting.

Harry was middle-aged and balding. He also wore an eggplant-purple suit, a forest-green necktie, and brown shoes. The rumour was that one of his dark-lava eyes was made of glass, and naturally that his past was altogether more interesting than the fact that he had blinded one eye playing rugby at boarding school.

Meanwhile, Lou said into the phone, "Who the hell are these people? Well, I had no idea there was a Belgian royal family. What about - did you make the apple pie?" He raised his brows and replied, "Tastes like *what*?" then hung up and turned to Harry. "Sorry about that, Harry." He mumbled something about "dumbasses". "What's up?"

Harry straightened his forest-green necktie and did his utmost to aim both eyes at his younger colleague. "We've been nominated for five prizes at this year's International Property Awards - and we need someone in London to pick them up."

"And you're not gonna send me," answered Lou satirically.

"We are - we're going to put you up in the Waldorf Hilton. You're going to be there for a week - mostly so you can send a good message at the pre-awards dinners."

"Uh."

"Yes?"

"Sorry - what are we up for?"

"They range from accolades for our website, to the suburban developments we've been representing - like the one in Errachidia."

"Uh-huh. "

"Look," interrupted Harry as he crossed his brown shoes. "We know the intended market can't afford the apartments. But we're not the first people to fail youngsters. You get contracts for buggered projects all the time - what matters is your integrity."

"Huh."

Harry coughed awkwardly.

"Nice you thought of me," added Lou. "Be good to see London sober." Lou took his banana-mania legs off of the desktop and quietly parked them beneath the desk.

"How's the not-drinking going?" asked Harry, as sweat began to appear on his balding head.

"It's hard, but I feel better."

"Shame. Some people have that weakness. They're born with it. No one in my family had it - so I guess your family's somewhat different…"

"Yea." Lou angrily slurped his half-empty cup of coffee. "Here's to London."

"Ye-hes," laughed Harry, heaving himself up from the chair, and making a beeline for the door. "You can understand," he added as he turned the door handle, "that we expect you to book your plane tickets. You ought to save us some money somehow!"

"For the Waldorf, that's fair enough," groveled Lou.

Shutting the door behind him, Harry exited the office. Lou remained in his chair. Then he jumped up and down. He danced on the spot, mouthing, "FUCK YEA". Unfortunately, his celebrations were curtailed when his smartphone started ringing. "Yes?" Lou answered, wiping his brow. "No, that wasn't in the video." Then he sat down and put his banana-mania legs back on the desk. "Did you ask the buyers what they meant by that?" He sneezed. "What do you mean they went? And the apple pie?"

Two weeks later, Lou caught the train from Marrakech to Rabat. He had never been to the capital before and walked around the terraced houses with their android-green and amaranth-pink arches and walls, and the antique-white buildings that were linked together by electric cables and bottomed out by brown-sugar tiles, umbrella-covered stalls, and potted plants containing bud-green cacti and arylide-yellow leaves.

During the French Protectorate, there had been a concerted effort to remake Morocco in a Frenchman's image, so the remodeling of Rabat and Casablanca was left to a young, French architect named Henri Prost. He had to work quickly, moreover, because Europeans were disallowed from living in old-style Medinas, which naturally caused a housing crisis.

Now, over a century later, Lou was staying overnight at Zaalouk's expense and walked along the coast of the industrial port that exported crude minerals, petroleum products from wider Africa, citrus fruits, and fine textiles. (They replaced the wheat, flax, cotton, tobacco, and saffron that Morocco had exported in the past, after the gold and silver had dried up…) The desolate browns of the rocks and the blues of the water pacified Lou as he recalled drinking in comparable countries: in the bars of Gibraltar, the clubs of Malta, and the cocktail taprooms and dinghy clubs of Bermuda…

His drooping neck cast an avian shadow as he walked under the supporting wall that held up the edge of the city, and his light-cornflower-blue eyes - which shadowed his substance and his will - stared dully at the sharp moon encircled by endless loneliness.

The next day, he flew out of Rabat-Salé Airport, arrived at Heathrow Airport, and caught the underground to Covent Garden, where he then realised he was in London.

Cigarettes.

Petrol cars, trucks, and motorbikes.

"Please, mate, give me a fiver!"

"Come on, Luv, give us a tenner!"

"You cunt! You took my fucking wallet! You cunt!"

Lou apologized to several people as he chuntered across the pavement, traversed crosswalks alongside extra-large paper cups of coffee counter-balanced by handbags, and allowed a doorman to assist him into the Waldorf Hilton where he was waited on.

A Somalian porter, wearing a bellboy suit with red piping up and down his arms, helped Lou into the elevator, and down the unusually cramped corridor to his room.

Lou tipped the porter and watched him wave goodbye as he exited the room.

The Alice-blue walls complemented the absolute-zero-blue bed frame, and the black-olive desk underneath an all-seeing mirror.

The bathroom was clean.

Lou crossed the room and looked through the window. He viewed the Indian Embassy, took a shower in the clean bathroom, and laid back on the hard bed. "Huh," said Lou, staring at the ceiling for what must have been ten minutes. Being in England after a considerable sojourn in a foreign country felt inexplicable. Perhaps all Lou could manage with regards to his work was little more than a sojourn.

The impermanence of Morocco scrubbed his brain. The impermanence of London scrubbed his simple soul.

He had no idea if the British knew where Morocco was.

Nor that Al-Mansur and Elizabeth I had made a trading agreement.

Nor that Sidi Mohammed III had made further treaties with England, Venice, France, Denmark, and Sweden.

Not even that Morocco had been the first nation to recognize the United States of America, and to give them a consulate in Morocco.

Instead, Lou was staring at the cedar-chest mini-fridge.

Cursing under his breath, he stood up and unpacked his suitcase. Then he slipped into his banana-mania suit, and the burly-wood necktie that Laura Donato had arranged for him—Donato had become such a *distant* memory.

The International Property Awards had drawn multitudes of estate agents to the Waldorf Hilton, which became a property playground for the duration of the celebrations - and the dinners leading up to the awards evening were held in the onsite *Homage Restaurant*, which featured gleaming chandeliers, supportive Roman columns, and polished wooden floors that shone under the bright cufflinks and conversations of the multinational representatives from some one-hundred active real estate agencies.

The dinners were dreary affairs.

The Malaysian agents ate too much, the English agents chain-smoked on revolving breaks, the American agents kept to themselves and only drank water, the South Korean agents got smashed, and the French agents sat together feigning fatigue. Altogether, Lou had trouble navigating the culinary excess, cigarette breaks, endless jugs of water, bespoke offers of free Chardonnay, and dismal, table-locked Frenchmen as he put on his most inquisitive face for his foreign colleagues, and chatted politely.

The Kenyans and the Nigerians, however, were good company - and Lou somehow made his way onto a table flushed with grilled meat and bottles of wine, which Alhaadi Omondi sampled periodically between stories, advice, and tittle-tattle.

Omondi was a Kenyan estate agent whose head was shaved, but whose upper lip carried a magnificent postage stamp moustache. He also wore a cyan double-breasted suit, along with a waistcoat and pocket watch. His double-laced shoes were Davy-grey.

"If I dress like him, I will make money," thought Lou.

"Do you want another story?" asked Alhaadi. The men and women around the table banged their fists, drinking their champagne. "Okay, okay, let me think…"

Lou watched as Alhaadi collected his memory.

"The following was told to me by an Afrikaner."

"Huh?" said Lou awkwardly.

The looks around the table ranged from the shocked to the downright hostile. But Alhaadi was unperturbed and explained that an Afrikaner was a white South African.

"But Kenya is *not* in South Africa!" stated Alhaadi.

Some laughter around the table restored the gentle mood.

"This Afrikaner is on holiday in Kenya. He goes to Mombasa where the crocodile farm is and after convincing the owners not to throw him in with the crocodiles - " He waved off the ensuing laughter. " - he talks to this woman who works on the farm. She tells him, 'They used to pay so well here. But now they only pay me $1.75 a day. But my husband,' she says, 'is a farmer and he's making $2.00 a day for his work.' The Afrikaner listens to this, and he starts to feel bad about his privilege. He thinks to himself: 'I'm going to make a difference in this woman's life.' He takes out his wallet and gives her a quarter. The woman takes the quarter and says, 'What's this for?' And the Afrikaner says, 'It's to even out the wage gap.'"

A burst of throaty laughter exploded from the men and women present, banging their fists on the white-sheeted tabletop, and knocking over a few drinks.

"My niece lives in London," continued Alhaadi. "She's an investigative journalist. She will want to meet all of you."

"She ought to investigate how boring the other tables are," Lou said.

Laughter ensued again.

"Lou, you're a wild man!" chuckled Alhaadi.

Then Alhaadi leaned in close, and said, "Really, Lou. She heard you were from Bermuda. She wants to meet you."

Alhaadi invited Lou to the *Kenyan Kitchen* for lunch the next day.

The property manager thanked the chuckling Kenyan, went to bed, and had nightmares about Morocco - fires and quakes destroying apartment buildings.

When he woke up the following morning, he stared in the bathroom mirror and brushed his teeth, before pulling his banana-mania trousers over his legs. Then he told himself that to fight outside control, he needed a strong persona. Soon, however, he recognized that *being Lou Baring* was harder than he had first imagined.

The *Kenyan Kitchen* was located at the base of a commercial building near Temple and boasted outdoor seating, Paris-green awnings, and a pewter-blue interior with small tables secreted around corners. It was a cramped restaurant with a constant flux of wait staff, customers, delivery men, and people enjoying cocktails.

The midday cocktail menu was popular and had won a *Blotto Magazine* award the year before, and now welcomed chutes of worker bees drowning their depressions and writing suicide notes on cocktail napkins…

Alhaadi and Lou were shown to a table that sported a vase of orchids and three sets of cutlery. Alhaadi ordered bottled Coca-Colas and looked at his gold watch.

"Is your niece coming?" Lou asked.

Alhaadi smiled as the Coca-Colas were deposited on the table. "Ah-ha!" chuckled Alhaadi as he watched the slinky waitress move away. "You're interested in her."

Lou shrugged.

Alhaadi waved the waitress back, impulsively, and ordered.

Not long after, the food arrived. The waitress put down bowls of *irio* - made with a mix of mashed potatoes, corn, peas, and greens - and *matoke* - a stew made with green bananas, tomatoes, onion, and garlic, and served with rice. Then she put down plates of grilled goat, beef, and chicken, and two smaller dishes of *sikama wiki* - made from leafy greens, garlic, onions, tomatoes, and cayenne pepper and paprika - and *kuku paka* - made with simmered-coconut-milk and charcoal-roasted chicken to make a curry. When the waitress had finished resting this enormous feast on the table, she clocked Alhaadi looking at her, and smiled pleasantly when he said, "And two coffees, please."

Lou tucked into the grilled goat. His host took the two coffees away from the waitress and smiled towards the street outside. "Here she comes…"

As Brooke Kimani strode into *Kenyan Kitchen*, she looked like some thirty-year-old doctoral graduate – when, in reality, she was a forty-three-year-old journalist. She had short hair and sharp eyebrows. She also had a large friendly mouth that was bordered by high cheekbones with well-polished skin. She was altogether gorgeous and wore a pumpkin blouse, Red-Salsa trousers, and Russian-violet heels. She carried a seal-brown handbag, that clicked when she put it on the ground.

"Uh," said Lou.

Brooke hugged her uncle and sat down. "You're Lou," said Brooke in a half-Kenyan/half-English accent.

"No, no, no - no, no - no, no, no - I'm not weird," said Lou. He noticed a large heap of grilled goat still sitting on his fork. He shoved the goat into his mouth and choked.

"Uh-oh," said Alhaadi. He beat Lou on his back for several seconds until he noticed the grilled goat travelling down Lou's esophagus.

His niece pushed Lou's Coca-Cola towards him, with a worried expression.

"Your mother never calls me," said Alhaadi to Brooke. "She needs to remember her family."

"She probably doesn't call because *I'm* with you."

"She never disowned you; you just decided to move to a galaxy far away."

"Mmm. Yea," said Brooke. She ordered a glass of water and helped herself to some of the chicken curry. She looked at Lou between mouthfuls and listened.

"I used to work in Beijing," explained Alhaadi. "There was a janitor who would tell me a new joke every morning. The first one he told me went like this: there's a married couple who go out for dinner. Suddenly, the wife jumps up, and says, 'I forgot to turn off the water faucet!' The husband looks at her and says, 'Don't worry.' And the wife says, 'Why not?' And the husband says, 'Cuz I forgot to turn off the gas cooker.'"

"That's bad," noted Brooke.

Alhaadi said, "A child goes up to his father and says, 'How much does it cost to get married?' And the father looks down and says, 'I don't know! I'm still paying!'"

"That's funny," said Lou.

The three of them spoke for a while longer.

Suddenly, Alhaadi stood up. "I must be on my way. I'll see you tomorrow night." He shook Lou's hand, kissed Brooke on the cheek, and exited the establishment.

"Where's he going?" asked Lou between mouthfuls of banana stew.

"He doesn't like paying."

"WHUUUHAHHAA!?" blurted Lou. He noticed Alhaadi's bottles of Tusker beer, and the empty plates, bowls, and glasses on the table.

"But we just - I didn't - the goats and chickens!"

Brooke laughed into her water. "I'll pay for the stuff I ate."

"MMMMWAAHHH?"

"How long have you known him?"

He gathered himself. "Two days."

Then Brooke laughed even harder.

"I've got a budget," whined Lou.

"I'll bet you do," replied Brooke.

"Jesus." He paused for a moment and looked at her. "Jesus Christ."

"I've got half-days on Fridays."

"What?"

"Today's a half-day. I'll get you a coffee. To apologise for my family."

"No, no - no, no, no - you don't have to - " He watched her impressive body ascend. " - don't pay for this, for my sake - you don't have to - some of the meals I've seen - "

"Let's get out of here," interrupted Brooke.

"That's very forward."

The journalist sniggered, ogling him with embarrassed, brown eyes. She clicked through the busy pewter-blue interior and went to pay the bill at the front desk. Brooke was served by the waitress who had served them. The waitress looked past Brooke at the fumbling property manager, with his light-cornflower-blue-eyes and his banana-mania suit, and returned her gaze to Brooke, as if to say, "Good luck with that one."

Following Brooke down the pavement like a lovesick hound, Lou cut through Londoners wearing quick-silver baseball hats, red-purple fishnet stockings, and sand-dune trousers - the desert was calling. It called him back against his better judgement. And let's face it, the universe thought, Lou's better judgement was worse than most... Brooke pointed at a café called *Chameleon Party* and he nodded and they walked inside, where Brooke bought coffees and directed him to a window seat. For ten minutes, Lou garbled his words - mostly with stories about other times he had had coffee, which could fill a small blog - but then he began to relax and set about using his light-cornflower-blue eyes to examine Brooke's high and shiny cheekbones.

"Uh," said Lou as he retreated to the foam-encrusted rim of his mug of white coffee.

"Why are you looking at me like that?" asked Brooke with a concerned smile.

"Uh?"

"Like you just got out of prison."

"Huh?"

"Like you haven't seen anyone in three years."

"Oh. Like *that*." He slouched on his barstool and drooped his head. "I've only been there a year - I'm not starved for company, you know, there are lots of people."

She winced. "You got friends?"

"There's a lot of work to do. And the people you work with become your family."

"So, it's like the mafia - "

"What do you mean?"

"I've heard rumours about Morocco." She sipped her coffee. "Just baseless claims. But the closest I got to backing them up was when I covered Muton Industries for *The Guardian*. They're a tech company that made fertilizer and they exported a lot of it to East Africa and Europe. They were bumping up the price of their fertilizer - which, of course, had been mined in Africa in the first place. I wanted to call the article 'Back to Africa', but my editor said it would alienate her readers." She laughed, licking her lips. "I reminded her that they had internet in Africa."

"But - but did they inflate the price?"

Brooke almost spat out her coffee: "Of course they did!" She sighed deeply. "I wanted the mining companies to tell me how much they sold the raw phosphate for - but they never - I mean, they didn't give me access. Which I thought was strange, because Muton was shafting them. They could have upped their prices considerably."

"You should've asked the *makhzan*," replied Lou, suddenly turning the same colour as his banana-mania suit.

"Why?"

"Because maybe - they knew about Muton Industries." Rubbing his sweaty hands, the property manager changed the topic. "You know, everyone wants to exploit Africa."

This appeased the investigative journalist. "The Italians were in Libya."

"Huh?"

"Early twentieth century. They tried to colonize Libya. The whole thing went on for decades." Then she stared directly at his aquiline nose. "Lou, what's the matter?"

"I didn't know that." He finished his coffee. "The planet's crazy."

The ensuing expression that formed on Brooke's eyebrows and her friendly mouth, signified to Lou that he had indeed said something quite imbecilic - but that she didn't care, and that, in all likelihood, he shared that opinion with most of the population.

"You want another coffee?" asked Brooke.

He agreed, and she bought two more coffees.

When she came back, she crossed her legs in a way that showed off her big thighs. "So, where do you come from again? What was it, America?"

"No, I'm from Bermuda."

"And that's American."

"No, it's British. We got a governor and everything. But she doesn't do anything because we have our own parliament and they're happy making mistakes."

"Why'd you leave? You're British! What am I saying? You can't leave because there's no difference between those islands and *these* islands."

"There was this government minister who tried to overthrow the government," explained Lou as he thought about the evacuation, his education, and his addiction. "But that was almost ten years ago - which means I've been in England for ten years."

"Apart from Morocco," clarified Brooke with a smile.

"There's not much difference."

"What about the call to prayer?"

"Huh?"

Brooke sat back and focused. Then she looked again at the sad man in his banana-mania suit and his burlywood necktie. "Do you want to be alone this afternoon?"

"Jesus - "

Brooke laughed.

"Jesus Christ." He rocked on his stool. "I'm not that interesting."

"I think you are." She ran her index-finger across her hairline. "Besides, I'm middle-aged." She stared into his light-cornflower-blue eyes. "I want to go dancing."

By the time Lou Baring and Brooke Kimani had entered the old-mauve-shaded club on the Whitefriar corner of Fleet Street, the sun had started to cast old-lavender hues, and tall buildings encroaching on the budding friendship sketched sharp shadows that chopped streets in halves and quarters as if they were squids being prepared for sushi. The club was located in the basement of one of these tall buildings and boasted a sizeable orange-peel bar that faced a thumping octagonal dancefloor.

The resident artist that night was a rhythm-and-blues singer called Yelpin' Thelonius, who gave Lou a violent thumbs-up when he noticed they were wearing the same banana-mania trousers - except Thelonius's upper half was protected by a spring-green shirt with tassels, as well as a fluttering, sizzling-sunrise cape that swished.

As the aged singer belted out his first number, the gathering crowd gesticulated to one another, and then gathered around the property manager and his unlikely date.

Shag 'em twice
Shag 'em twice

If you mess aroun' with women, boy, you make a sacrifice

Shag 'em twice

Shag 'em twice

After thrice, the asking price, is hardly paradise

So, shag 'em twice

Shag 'em twice!

By this point Brooke was laughing and dancing vigorously opposite Lou, who, at best, was putting one foot in front of the other, and waving his thin index fingers in the air. Some members of the audience who were offended by the song's content were lifted to even greater levels of rage when they realised that that had merely been the refrain.

I had a gal named Frankie Spuckus down in Dorset - goddamn!

And me and Frankie banged regardless by the faucet - and swam!

Then me and Frankie met her folks

They bought a boat: so perfect for a dumb fool's paradise!

Cut my ties, closed my eyes,

Said goodbye to Frankie's thighs.

Nought I want to colonize,

Nuh-uh!

The thumbnail silence between drumbeats was broached by Yelpin' Thelonius and his wide-faced grin, which pacified the inharmonious room for little over a second - after which the frontman, and his band, were hurled into the same, crazy refrain,

> So, shag 'em twice
> Shag 'em twice
> I'd rather have a quick sojourn than leave my love crabwise.
> Shag 'em twice
> Shag 'em twice
> After thrice, the asking price, is hardly paradise
> So, shag 'em twice!

Amidst the perspiring, well-paid, and otherwise well-coiffed audience, Brooke gripped Lou's shoulders with her hands so that they could bounce together to the crass refrain. Instead of waving his index fingers in the air, he placed them awkwardly on her waist. Enjoying this new development, the investigative journalist failed to notice the spilt rum-and-coke sliding across the dancefloor towards their feet - and how, without warning, the slowly caramelizing cocktail pulled the ground from beneath their feet and sent them flopping onto the viscous and impenetrable flooring with a *crack*. A particularly callous band of Italians stepped over the disintegrated couple, but shot Lou a glance of admiration, when he said, "WHUUUHAHHAA! Brooke, are you okay?"

"I'm sorry - I'm fine," laughed Brooke.

"Jesus - let me help you - "

"I'm okay!"

"No, no - no, no - let me - "

"Thanks - "

The self-aware couple moved out of the crowd, towards the orange-peel bar, where they asked for glasses of water from a bemused, but bored, barman. Then Lou's smartphone rang in his pocket. "I've gotta take this," said Lou over the music as Brooke smiled politely, and watched Lou step through a small doorway into the smoking zone.

Outside, the air was frigid. The property manager avoided several pairs of turtle-green shoes, after which he answered the phone, and held it up to his sweaty temple.

"They said you were in London," said Rosa "Small Nose" Baracco.

"Who's this?"

"Rosa. Casablanca."

"But I'm in London," Lou countered feebly.

"Someone got whacked the other night." Lou pressed his free hand against the reverberating concrete. *"But we left the keys in the property. The door's self-locking."*

"Jesus - "

"Yea, well, he's not helping."

Lou began to breathe heavily. Then he briefly looked inside the club. "It's not a good time, Rosa - "

"The deceased was picky, too."

"Sorry - I was - never mind - I have to get back to my hotel."

"How's the Waldorf?"

"Fine - look, once I'm there - I can get on my laptop and tell you."

"I'll time you," came the icy reply.

"Oh - hello?" He hung up and swallowed pebble-sized regrets. He paced around the smoking area, deciding if she should abandon Brooke.

"Lou?" asked Brooke as she entered the smoking zone. "What's wrong?"

"Nothing."

"It *looks* like something's wrong." She sighed, observed a necking couple wearing identical Vegas-gold trousers, and said, "It's not your girlfriend, is it?"

"I don't have anyone." He cleared his throat. "We need to go to my hotel room."

"That's the bluntest invitation I've had all year," sniggered the journalist.

"No, for my work."

"It's two in the morning!"

"I need a cab," said Lou as he ignored her protests, removed his smartphone from his pocket, and searched in vain for the spreadsheet that would allow him to stay. "I'm sorry - how about I pay for your cab?"

"I'll come with."

"You *will?*"

"Yea," stated Brooke, who spoke like a privately employed nurse. Then she and Lou fought back through the dancing crowd to the front door, where they hailed a cab.

Twenty minutes later, the taxi pulled up to the Waldorf Hilton.

Lou and Brooke were quickly swapped for Mr. Dhruv Pandit, High Commissioner of India to the United Kingdom, who told the driver to find the closest, cheapest bar.

Back at the hotel, Lou unlocked his door and ran into his room.

Brooke followed him in with a concerned expression and sat on the mattress. Parking her seal-brown handbag next to her right thigh, she waited patiently for Lou.

The property manager fished his laptop out and sat at the desk, where he turned the lamp on. He typed furiously, sometimes staring at his smartphone, and this soon became a rhythm, where his light-cornflower-blue eyes swapped screens.

Eventually, two variables seemed to match, thought Brooke, since Lou leaned back in his chair and sighed significantly. Then he dialed Rosa's number on his smartphone.

"Rosa?"

"That took a while," replied Rosa from what sounded like a busy restaurant.

"Three-eight-three-nine-five-nine-six." Her silence indicated that she was scribbling on a napkin. "Make sure you scramble the key box when you're finished."

"Idiot - "

Lou managed a sideways glance at Brooke. She was half-hunched on the mattress and had developed the semi-patient expression used by waiting staff. When Lou returned his contemplation to his smartphone, he noticed a peculiar silence. He tapped the screen and saw that Rosa had hung up. He half-tossed the phone onto the desk, leaned forward, planted his head on the hardwood surface, and breathed heavily.

Brooke removed her Russian-violet heels. "Lou?" Then she stood up and walked towards the desk, touching her hairline. "Are you okay?"

"Yea." He felt her approaching body and stiffened. "You like the hotel?"

She laughed at the strange question. "I've been here before. There was this Japanese businessman called Jack Ito, who had invented a mouth-widener. I had to interview him when I was working for *The Guardian.* They said he was a feminist..."

"Was he?"

"He asked me to stay for a drink, so I said I was married."

"I'm guessing that didn't make a difference."

"Not really - " She peered around Lou's undistinguished hair to see his face. "You're shaking, Lou, you're shaking - "

When she touched his shoulder, he stood up and stared across at the Indian Embassy. He rubbed his temples and folded his arms. "I wanted some time to myself."

"Oh, well, I can leave - "

"No, no, no - not like that - I'm sorry." He hid his eyes and waved his hand. "Time to be on my own, and - meet people - and sort of - talk to them, and - make friends."

Brooke looked concerned. "Don't you like me, Lou?"

"Yea, I like you." The property manager stared at the carpet.

"You don't think I'm too old for you?"

"No."

"Okay." Brooke tried not to laugh. "I don't want to have sex with you. Not tonight."

"Uh."

"We can do that in the future."

"Uh-huh."

"Lou," coaxed Brooke.

"Uh?"

"I do want you to kiss me - so that I can go home." She rubbed her tired eyes. Then she smiled, meandered over to Lou, and planted a French kiss under his aquiline nose.

"Thank you," whispered Lou.

CHAPTER SEVEN

On more than one occasion, Mr. Shriki explained to his students at the Regional Collège in Dakhla that the North African Gerbil - also known as *Dipodillus campestris* - is a species of small rodent found in North Africa, whose natural habitat consists of the sunset-beige earth of arable land, as well as the Windsor-tan landscape of the Western Sahara and her adjoining deserts and flatlands. Mr. Shriki knew about this particular genus of gerbil because he had purchased two siblings - a brother and sister - at the beginning of the academic year, after which he had installed "Biscuit" and "Squid" in the corner of the classroom in a reasonably large cage, featuring wild-strawberry tubes and wheels, and lots of fresh hay. He made a habit of feeding Biscuit and Squid during his lessons, and the two gerbils soon became mascots of his class groups, and representative of the collége as a whole. Little did he know, however, that Biscuit and Squid had been selectively bred by their erstwhile animal shelter to encourage knowledge retention, quantitative reasoning, visual-spatial processing, working memory, and fluid reasoning - which made Biscuit and Squid the two most intelligent beings in Morocco. Naturally, this flew over the heads of the human beings in the classroom where Mr. Shriki delivered his humanities lessons, and glanced casually at these gerbils, who enjoyed their life at Dakhla's Regional Collège.

On the first day of term, Biscuit and Squid were introduced to Mr. Shriki's new class of teenagers who observed the cage with degrees of fascination and indifference. Then Mr. Shriki - whose features were understandably alien to Biscuit and Squid - introduced himself to the class, and went around asking for everybody's name, during which he opened a pack of Spanish blueberries, and put six of them into the cage.

"Hey Squid!" squeaked Biscuit in Gerbilium. "The ape's dropping blueberries!"

Squid peered out of the little house. "*Real* ones?"

"Yea! Check them out!"

Squid hopped out of the doorway, and scrambled towards Biscuit, so that she could claim her three blueberries. She chewed the edge of one. "Man, this one's squishy."

"Here - have mine."

"Thanks, Biscuit," said Squid. The two gerbils sat on their hindquarters and happily nibbled at their giant blueberries. "Just in time for the lesson," noted Squid.

Unable to interpret the complex verb-noun combinations of Gerbilium as anything other than cute squeaking, Mr. Shriki consulted his lesson notes. "Before we jump into this week's readings - which you all should have done - I'm going to set the scene by talking about the

Western philosophical tradition," explained Mr. Shriki in Arabic. "We've got a mixture of culture in Morocco, but for all intents and purposes, we're a Western democracy, and we take part in Western operations around the world - so it's necessary to describe the very beginnings of these ideas like democracy and freedom, and, most of all, creative speculation. And before we say, 'Mr. Shriki, you're talking like a Westerner,' I want you to remember that when we use the term *Western philosophical tradition*, what we're referring to is the things that have been affected by that tradition - as opposed to the origins of that tradition. More to the point, we can't take away from that tradition - we can't remove books, films, and music - we can only add to that tradition. The origins of the Western philosophical tradition are in a city called Miletus on the western coast of Turkey. Now, back then, it wasn't Turkey: it was the Greek colony of Ionia - if you want to talk about imperialism - and the first known philosopher in this tradition was a man called Thales, who was born in 624 B.C. - which is a long bloody time ago. To give you an idea of what was happening in the East around this time, Confucius, the famous Chinese philosopher, was kicking around at roughly the same time, give or take a hundred years. As for Thales, we know that he was of Phoenician descent, which means either Lebanon or Syria. (And let's remember that in the early BCs Phoenicians were settling along the shores and islands between the Iberian peninsula, and North Africa, because it had silver, tin, and better facilities.) So,

Thales lived in Miletus, which was a pit-stop for merchant ships that travelled along the River Meander."

Biscuit and Squid were onto their second blueberries.

"This was a place where merchant ships brought spices, precious metals, and foodstuffs - but they also brought their religions and their ideas about the world. So, Thales would go talk to these sailors and ask them about the world. And they would say something like, 'Well, the fire god burnt the world into existence.' Then Thales would ask someone else the same thing, and they'd say, 'Well, the ocean spirit parted the heavens, and created the world.' And after twenty of these you'd probably give up. Because religion fails to give a cohesive picture of how the world functions. So, what Thales and his student, Anaximander, realised was that they were asking the wrong questions. They shouldn't ask, *Why* the world was created; they shouldn't ask, *Who* created the world - instead, they should ask, *What* the world was – What is the nature of the world? What are we made of? What are the stars? This means that pre-Socratic thinkers were pre-scientific scientists who speculated about nature. And with that, Thales and Anaximander quickly reached two conclusions about the world - that there was *change*, and that there was *order*. Think about crops growing. Think about the seasons. Think about the weather and the way water evaporates. Change and order."

"Don't you remember," noted Biscuit to his furry sibling, "how the elders told us about the sand-storms coming and going?"

"And the ranges in temperature in our heartlands," replied Squid.

"But let's have two specific examples of the creative speculation these thinkers were engaged in," added Mr. Shriki on the other side of the classroom, as two boys near the front drew penises onto their desks. "Thales said, for example, that 'the earth is supported by water on which it rides like a ship'. Putting to one side how we can say - as Aristotle did many centuries later - *'Then what supports the water, Thales?"*

The gerbils noted the pleasant laughter in the room. In return, they squeaked and chirruped their own laughter, and digested, before digging into their final blueberries.

"What a remarkable metaphor for explaining how the continents sit amongst the world's oceans," said Mr. Shriki. "Not to mention the fact that it predates the idea of a 'continental shift' by at least two thousand years. Not bad for a man without any digital mapping. Anaximander also said that the earth is suspended in space, is equally distant to all things, and is shaped like a drum. What's remarkable - putting to one side the wonderful analogy - is how there's no way he could have reached this conclusion through observation: that is, through empirical evidence..."

The huge black eyes of Biscuit and Squid widened. The prospect of pure imagination clarifying the mathematical building blocks of the cosmos and reaching scientific conclusions before these things called "physicists", was amazing, frightening, and bizarre - to the extent that they briefly dropped their blueberries and stared ahead.

"Anaximander's talking about space!" Mr. Shriki observed the shocked expressions around the room. "He has no concept of this, so he makes one up instead, and what he makes up is accurate. But let's move on to what these pre-scientific scientists thought were the building blocks of physical matter. For example, Thales believed that everything was made of water. Again, we can make fun of this - but put yourself in his shoes, and think like a Pre-Socratic: mammals gestate in liquid - "

Biscuit and Squid observed each other.

"Water falls from the sky and returns to it. Water makes the vegetables grow; it makes the weeds grow. Water doesn't distinguish between different types of plants. The same goes for animals - all animals drink water, they depend on water for life. Water can be a liquid, a solid, a gas - it can be something between a solid and a liquid. This is a versatile substance that is everywhere, so it's only natural that Thales would posit that everything was made of water. A later pre-Socratic, Anaximenes, thought that everything was made of air. He noticed that we breathe. But what do we breathe?"

Squid exhaled onto her last blueberry.

She watched the half-white fuzz illuminate the otherwise dark fruit. Then slowly the fuzz disappeared, and she looked at Biscuit.

"Think about watching your breath when it's cold," said Mr. Shriki. "Think about the wind. The fact that air touches everything. What we have here is simple, though often abstract, deduction." Mr. Shriki consulted his lesson notes, checked his watch, and nodded his head. "I suppose we have time. Into this group of pre-Socratic philosophers came Pythagoras, who is famous for his triangles."

There was a collective sigh in the classroom.

"Yes, we know all about those." The teacher laughed. "But he also invented what became musical theory."

Biscuit and Squid had often heard the elders squeaking Gerbilium compositions. They also remembered their mothers - from the other side of the animal shelter, and in cages quite separate from their own - and how they would sing them to sleep, when the sand-storms would rattle the animal shelter, and frighten the awkward ape guardians...

"Pythagoras led a group of mathematicians and cosmologists," explained Mr. Shriki, "who were known as Pythagoreans. They were basically a cult that abstained from eating beans, but they made great strides in mathematics and geometry. They were also interested in music, and the story goes that Pythagoras was walking through the market one day when he saw two iron-smiths - and one of them was using a large hammer, and the other, a small hammer. He noticed that the big one gave out a low note, and the small one gave out a high note. Now, they were the same note, but they were at different levels. So, Pythagoras came up with the idea of *octave* - but let's go through the ingredients: we have motion, distance, physical material, and sound. Fundamental elements of the physical world. And because Pythagoras had an abiding interest in the heavenly bodies, he applies the idea of octave to the planets. He argues that planets move in the same direction; that distant planets move slower and make a low note; that closer planets move faster and make a high note; and that as a result, there is a harmony of the spheres. In short, the cosmos becomes a musical place…"

"Have you ever been outside?" asked Squid.

"Not really," replied Biscuit.

"Sometimes, when you're asleep, I get up and look out the window. You can see the stars there. But it's not the same as being outside…"

"The planets don't make music, of course," added Mr. Shriki. "That's absurd. The music is analogous to the fact that everything is connected in some way. And, with the exception of Uranus and Venus, the planets in our solar system do move in the same direction. This means that Pythagoras got that mostly right by looking at the sky and using his imagination. Again, not bad for a man without a telescope."

The teenagers, and Biscuit and Squid, nodded.

"In sum, the pre-Socratics reach these conclusions not through experience, but through reasoning. And it's this power to reason, Karl Popper argues, that we've lost in the age of science. What we've lost is the creative power of storytelling - the power to speculate, sometimes wildly, about the world that we live in. And the connectivity of all living things that comes from this - from *thinking* in this highly creative way."

Biscuit and Squid tore into their last blueberries. The students were given pair-and-share tasks, a window was opened, and Mr. Shriki checked on Biscuit and Squid, who both waved at the generous ape and returned to their blueberries.

"All living things," said Mr. Shriki. He returned to his desk, consulted his lesson plan, and looked up when he heard shouting outside. A roar of displeasure, most probably from a cavalcade of human beings carrying banners and placards, echoed through the window and caught everybody's attention. Biscuit and Squid dropped their berries, ran onto the roof of their house, and stared through the bars of the cage and the subsequent window. Mr. Shriki got up and said, "Keep working; don't let them distract you," as he walked to the window and inhaled with worry when he saw hundreds of protestors marching on the street. They carried signs written in Arabic that said, "KILL THE FLIGHT BAN," "TWO SUMMERS R.I.P." and "IT WAS A TERRIBLE IDEA THE FIRST TIME" – then policemen in their red-orange armour, carrying AR-15s, surrounded the crowd, and ushered them down a street. And screams of derision came.

"Professeur," said a student called Malik. "What's going on?"

"More protests," replied Mr. Shriki. "You won't catch me down there," he added and returned to his desk, where he firmly bit his tongue.

"Maybe I should retire and be a gerbil," Mr. Shriki mused. The students laughed.

Observing the disappearing protestors, Biscuit and Squid were drawn back to the conclusions of the pre-Socratics:

that change and order were determinants, which affected the outcomes of their multifaceted cosmos...

Months later, on a secular module dedicated to understanding Islam that had been implemented by the Scarvaggi Regime fifty years prior, Mr. Shriki opened a pack of German strawberries and dropped two of the bulbous fruits into the gerbil sanctuary. The previous night, Squid had struggled to sleep because she had eaten too many pears during the day. That, and Biscuit had been burying the pear stems under the otherwise fresh-smelling hay which had turned their small world into a compost heap. "But that smell," complained Squid as she and Biscuit inspected the new red fruits. "Why do you have to bury the dead bits? Can't you get the ape to clean them out?"

Biscuit turned to her. "We do *not* have to rely on the ape for everything!"

"Make use of him. The little apes use him, why shouldn't we?"

"They don't *use* him," replied Biscuit.

"That's what he thinks. The little apes suck knowledge out of him."

"But he retains it, we've noticed that." Biscuit touched her velvety shoulders with his pink paws. "Don't you realise that the more we talk, the smarter we become?"

"I suppose so."

"And the same applies in here. This is like some – learning room. Where little apes talk to big apes so that they can grow."

"Not all the little apes want to," noted Squid.

"Well, that's to be expected. I don't always want to talk to you."

"Not when it's not about *food*."

Mr. Shriki could have sworn that Biscuit was putting his hands on his hips like some disappointed housewife.

"And *who*," squeaked Biscuit in Gerbilium, "ate all those pears?"

"Okay, okay…"

Mr. Shriki tore his attention from his gerbils and focused on the lesson plan underneath his stomach. "Um, uh - so today, yes - hello."

The classroom - and gerbils - blinked at him.

"Today we live in a secular country, and most of us have some understanding of Islam, but I'd like to outline the birth of Islam and how it managed to spread so quickly. Ernest Renan, the French orientalist and Semitic scholar, once said that monotheism was the natural religion of the desert. But the more romantic Arabian features of Islam were hardly part of the social factors that influenced Mohammed - and instead came in subsequent years. The word 'Islam' means 'submitting oneself - or one's person - to God'. Muslims generally dislike the term 'Mohammedism', because it suggests that Islam is centered on Mohammed in the way that

Christianity is centered on Jesus Christ. The Koran speaks to a great deal more than the spiritual life of Mohammed, but at the same time Islam presents Mohammed as the last and most significant in a series of apostles - one of whom is Jesus Christ - and delineates the message of Mohammed, as the final and unchangeable revelation of the divine will."

The overfed Squid sat on her hind legs next to Biscuit as he enjoyed a few tentative bites of German strawberry.

"It's been said that there are as many theories about Mohammed as there are biographies, and Mohammed himself was described variously as an epileptic, a socialist revolutionary, and a proto-Mormon…"

"Bit insulting," said Squid.

"What we can say with certainty," added Mr. Shriki, "is that the fundamental aspect of Mohammed is his religious mission. He's born into one of the leading families in Mecca, around 570 AD; he's orphaned, and subsequently raised by his uncle; and then he works in the caravan trade, marries a widow named Khadija, who becomes his first wife, and has four daughters. So, Mohammed is hardly some Bedouin sharing his visions with people in the desert. In reality, Mohammed's living and working in a bustling trading city, which serves Arab tribesmen and Roman officials alike. But like many places that preach prudence and self-restraint, the pagan, or pre-Islamic Mecca is a place with slavery, poverty, strong social-class barriers, and general degradation. What's noteworthy about Mecca's resistance to Mohammed is how they're more concerned about economic damage than they're concerned with theology. They're worried that his teachings are going to frighten off trading associates, and lower the quality of living, even when one of Mohammed's main targets is the pagan practice of burying children - girls in particular - as sacrifices to their pagan religion."

Biscuit and Squid acknowledged the gentle heap of hay covering the pear stems. Then their shining, black-hole eyes returned to their half-nervous instructor.

Together, they thought about Mr. Shriki's tête-à-têtes with colleagues, about the batteries that were dumped off of the coast of Dakhla. Then images of positive and negative electrodes, sulfuric acid solutions, and sea creatures blinded, and murdered, flashed through their brains, as Mr. Shriki went on with his lecture about Islam...

"After ten years, Mohammed moves his operations to Medina in 622 A.D. This is where the latent characteristics of the Muslim religion are developed. It's here that Islam reveals itself as no mere series of private religious beliefs - but rather as a self-governing community with its own aims, laws, and social institutions. It was not long before Islam conquered Western Arabia and then - after the death of Mohammed - Northern and Eastern Arabia, and parts of the Roman and Persian empires in Transjordan and Southern Iraq, respectively. After the death of Mohammed in 632 A.D., Syria and Iraq become tributaries to Medina. Egypt is absorbed into the Muslim empire - and this all happens in ten years. What enables Mohammed's successors, the Rashidun Caliphate, to control the Bedouin armies and their subsequent advantages, is a mixture of restraint and excess. Firstly, there's a balance between an intolerance of anything outside of Islam and a diversity within the Muslim community. Secondly, Islam is a coherent doctrine that can challenge the Christianity of Eastern Rome and the Zoroastrianism of the Persian Empire. Thirdly, these conquered territories - whose riches are absorbed into the Muslim empire - are first allowed to carry on with life uninterrupted: it's effectively a change of masters, and nothing more. Then a slow Islamification takes place where Hellenistic and Persian elements of these otherwise foreign cultures are molded."

There were also the solar panels, thought Biscuit and Squid. They had heard the instructing ape talk about them with colleagues, and they had received lessons in chemistry regarding the makeup and functioning of these sun-God-powered plates. Discarded solar panels were hazardous, with cadmium, arsenic, and hexavalent chromium coatings leaking chemicals into the Dakhla coastline. "They're promising to use these new ones," the gerbils recalled Mr. Shriki saying, "made from copper and indium - but it's the same rubbish: the copper and selenium are hazardous…"

Squid had suggested that more temples be built to re-birth solar panels – or, as Mr. Shriki had said, 'recycle them' - but Biscuit had reminded her that the teacher-ape's colleagues had known of only four places where such a process could be held: Accident in Maryland; Aladdin in

Wyoming; Booger Hole in West Virginia; and one other in Wankendorf, Schleswig-Holstein. The strange names of these ape-nations did little to encourage the North African gerbils.

"By 660 A.D. the Muslim capital moves from Medina to Damascus - and it's here that the subsequent Umayyad Caliphate make their centre of political operations, whilst allowing Medina to retain a focus on religious learning. Anyone who knows anything about Christianity - especially the Pauline tradition - will point out that Damascus is an incredibly significant place because it's where Saint Paul - formerly known as Saul of Tarsus - has his famous spiritual experience. So, I find it hard to imagine that their decision to move the Muslim capital to Damascus was an unconscious one, especially when we bear in mind the similarities between the Old Testament and the Koran."

Some unhappy rustling came from the gerbil cage.

"Which testament?" asked Squid.

"The one where the ape-god is really annoying," replied Biscuit, picking strawberry seeds out of his full-body moustache.

"How do we get the New Testament?"

"I guess we could buy it somewhere," Biscuit quietly burped.

Mr. Shriki held up his hands in scholastic excitement. "But the consequence of this geographical split between the *political Damascus* and the *spiritual Medina* is a split between secular and religious Muslim life, which, coupled with the grudges of non-Arab subjects and a civil war between separate Arab tribes, ends up bringing the Umayyad Caliphate to its conclusion in 750 A.D. All of this takes about a hundred years to happen, which reminds us of the timescales of history, but we should also remember what the pre-Socratics said a couple of months ago. Some of you weren't on that module, but the pre-Socratic philosophers say that the two main forces in the universe are *change* and *order*. So, we can see change and order occurring in the Muslim world, as it would anywhere else. We can sum up the general problem like this: a great spiritual teacher - like Mohammed, Christ, or the Buddha, represents the culmination of a personal spiritual process. Without their personalities, their teachings represent a new spiritual process for each of their followers, whose capacities to develop the original teachings are subjected to the same worldly tests as any other kind of doctrine - especially as the Muslim empire expands and takes under its wing the ideas of both Hellenistic and Persian cultures. Medina undergoes a huge change within a hundred years of Muslim rule. What was previously an isolated city with little learning, gradually turns into a powerhouse of prophetic tradition, lawmaking, and, through the study of history, the study of the structure, development, and interplay, between languages. These are local successes, however, and it takes the subsequent Abbasid Caliphate to apply Medina's developments to wider Muslim society after founding a new capital in Baghdad in 752 A.D. We see the blossoming of industry, commerce, and architecture - but we also see, once again, the gradual changes that pull at the roots of Islamic order. Aside from the economic success, there was an explosion of scholarship during this period, with translations of Greek, Persian, and Indian texts being written and studied. Greek medicine and mathematics are made available by Persian and Arab scholars who specialize in the fields of algebra, trigonometry, and optics; geography flourishes, focusing on foreign lands, and peoples; and all this endless reading, and writing, comes to a head in the third Islamic century when the rationalism of Greek logic and philosophy shows a secular - and almost apologetic - way of understanding the world, and how different nations are governed."

Squid scampered over to the wild-strawberry wheel, climbed aboard, and started running at a fast pace. The wheel spun faster as Squid etched a gallop in the far corner of the cage, and Biscuit half-watched her as he spoke aloud what the instructing-ape had said: that religion afforded an unapologetic view of the world, whereas rationalism and "common sense" apologized for the world - or perhaps it merely apologized for the lack of intelligent design. Enjoying the possibility that there was something silly about the universe, Squid flew off of the wheel, knocked Biscuit forward, and then whacked her snout into the bars of the cage.

"Let's remember that Plato's *Republic* - " added Mr. Shriki in a lower tone of voice since he was forbidden from breaking away from the curriculum. " - is a direct criticism of the Greek culture in which Plato lived, especially after the humiliating defeats of the Peloponnesian War. It's a meditation on the failures of Greek culture, and the hypocrisy of the Greek state. And there was every possibility that these largely secular Muslim scholars might wield their newfound rationalism, and wit, against the Caliphate, who had enabled their scholarship in the first place."

Massaging his forehead, Mr. Shriki sighed.

"This struggle between Caliphate and scholars goes on for several centuries. Eventually, the intellectual life was molded to the state's desires, and areas of scholarship, which were useful - like medicine and mathematics - were kept, whilst other areas were discarded. But what emerges out of this is no single-minded focus on theology - as some would assume - but rather a precise dedication to lawmaking: the golden thread that runs through Islamic society, protecting it from radical change. Islam's view of law as something that embraces all things - both human and divine - is equaled only by something like Judaism. If you know anything about the Old Testament - or what Jews call the Hebrew Bible - you'll be able to see the similarities between that Islamic interest in the law, and *The Book of Judges* in the Old Testament. (These are a group of ancient tribal heroes, but the comparison stands.) But Islamic Law, to conclude, is the most far-reaching and effective agent in molding the social order, and community life, of the Muslim peoples. Even in the wake of the Abbasid Caliphate collapsing in the 10th and 11th centuries, and the egos of local princes and military governors, and yet another lapse into civil war, what holds Islamic society together is the law. Even when Turkish tribesmen from Central Asia pose a serious threat to the frontiers of Muslim domains - and hopefully, we all noticed that Turkey is a largely Muslim country today, *which is no coincidence.*"

He coughed.

"Change and order," added Mr. Shriki. Biscuit and Squid watched, as the reluctant instructing-ape told the little apes that they would work in pairs, and prepare presentations, explaining why Islam had failed in Morocco...

Mr. Shriki was aware that he had engaged in thought control. That the aim of the Scarvaggis' curriculum was to illustrate why Islam had failed. But he also knew that Morocco would always be Morocco, when the rest of the Islamic world would have a stronger relationship to Islam at large. Morocco had always been a great proponent of *maslaha*: which was a permission, or interpretation, of Islamic law that allowed irregular behaviour and rules to be enacted, so long as they benefitted the Islamic community as a whole. It had justified otherwise illegal, or sacrilegious, taxes in the past, and now the Scarvaggi Family appeared to be using a similar model...

By the end of the academic year, Biscuit and Squid were not only able to distinguish Mr. Shriki as being a short man with thinning hair, wearing a quinacridone-magenta shirt, resolution-blue trousers, and half-rimmed glasses - but they were also able, by using Mr. Shriki's language, to describe one another...

Biscuit had unbleached-silk fur, tickle-me-pink hands and feet, and warm-black eyes that glistened. Whereas Squid had unbleached-silk fur, winter-sky hands and feet, and zinnwaldite-brown eyes. Amused by their new cognitive abilities and knowledge bequeathed by Mr. Shriki, the gerbils were suddenly concerned when Mr. Shriki entered the classroom for the penultimate lesson of the 2090-2091 academic year.

Mr. Shriki looked tired and removed his half-rimmed glasses so that he could pinch the bridge of his nose.

Then one of his colleagues, Mr. Kabbaj, knocked on the door and let himself in.

"Morning," said Mr. Shriki. "You cool as a cucumber?"

"Fine." Mr. Kabbaj shut the door behind him as Biscuit and Squid scurried to the edge of the cage to gather a description of Mr. Kabbaj. They surmised that he was six-foot, with thick black hair, and that he wore neon-fuchsia trousers, a non-photo-blue tie, and horn-rimmed specs. "Did you hear about the defence budget?" he asked.

"I did."

"What are we gonna do?"

"We're gonna keep on teaching," Mr. Shriki said, stroking his half-rimmed glasses.

"They cut the defence budget by fifty per cent! Out-of-work soldiers in the streets, no one defending our borders - the whole thing's a mess."

"It's always been a mess."

"No, it wasn't."

"Any country," advised Mr. Shriki, "where your own legitimacy depends on whether you can defend your city, is going to be a big mess."

"Whatever."

"The thing we've always struggled with in Morocco, is a lack of central authority. The Scarvaggis gave us one - "

"So did the French."

"Yea, and it didn't work, did it?" complained Mr. Shriki. "Just focus on your students - I don't know..."

"And do what? Tell them everything's okay?"

"They know it's not okay. But tell them that they have value."

In the cage, Squid said, "I feel helpless sometimes."

"We're not helpless," said Biscuit.

"But we're in a cage," replied Squid. "He brings us yum-food and fresh hay. That's why I feel helpless."

"But you're - you're not," repeated Biscuit, flopping on his back.

When he saw Squid laugh, he got back up, pawed her unbleached-silk fur, and smiled.

On the other side of the room, Mr. Kabbaj squinted. "Your hamsters okay?"

"North African Gerbils," corrected Mr. Shriki. "They chat to each other."

"Pfft," scoffed Mr. Kabbaj. "And by the way - stick to the course, Shriki."

"What do you mean?"

"You're gonna get us fired - *or worse.*"

Mr. Shriki looked at him with a thoughtful expression.

Suddenly, they could hear the bustle of young feet waiting outside the door, and the bell began to ring, and Mr. Kabbaj and Mr. Shriki shared a second of disagreement.

Mr. Kabbaj opened the door with a smile and let Mr. Shriki's students inside.

Mr. Shriki stood over his desk, watching his students filing into the classroom. "Morning, morning, morning - "

"Good morning, Professeur," said Malik.

"Hi Professeur," said more students, taking their seats.

"Good morning," repeated Mr. Shriki. He announced that the final lesson the following week would be spent discussing final portfolios. "In the meantime," he added, "we're going to hammer home the efficacy of green and renewable energy."

He bit his tongue.

"Both here, and elsewhere," mumbled Mr. Shriki.

Then his spirits perked up. "But we're going to start with a few words about Schopenhauer, because he had progressive views about animal rights for someone in the nineteenth century - which seems relevant."

Immediately, Biscuit and Squid perked up their sizeable ears.

"Animals?" asked Biscuit. "What are those?"

"I guess we're going to find out," noted Squid as they both sat on their hind-legs and sighed at the lack of fresh fruit in their cage.

"Arthur Schopenhauer was a German philosopher born in 1788. His father was a banker, and his mother was a novelist. Three things influenced Schopenhauer. The first was the *Upanishads*, which help to form the *Vedas*, which are the sacred scriptures of most Hindu traditions. They present a vision of a connected universe where the unifying principle is something called 'brahman'. But this diversity, 'brahman', ultimately resides in the unchanging core of the human being - which is called 'atman'.

"The second influence was the great Greek philosopher Plato, who was influenced by the Peloponnesian Wars, in which Greece was defeated by Sparta. He argued several things: in *The Republic*, for example, Plato wants to find out what justice is, and therefore if the just person is happier than the unjust person. He was the first person to argue in favour of equality between the sexes; he was the first person to argue in favour of a kind of communism; and he generally disliked democracies.

"The third and final influence on Schopenhauer, was the man whose work he developed over the course of the nineteenth century. This was Immanuel Kant, the German mathematician and philosopher, who said that metaphysical discussions about the existence of God, and what happened to the soul after death, were impossible because they reached beyond sense experience. But Kant also believed that a 'metaphysics of morals' was necessary for living an ethical life. In short, a scientific proof helps you make a choice, but it doesn't give you an understanding of duty. And this sort of culminates in Kant's 'categorical imperative' doctrine, which basically means that there are rules that people should follow no matter their circumstances, or how they feel about it. This is a well-meaning, but ultimately false, idea, in my view."

Squid twitched her snout. "Pear stems."

Biscuit smirked, or something like it, and ignored her.

"Schopenhauer's views on animals," added Mr. Shriki, "are a combination of religious, ethical, and scientific thinking."

"That word again," said Biscuit from the microcosm of the cage. "Maybe it's a type of person."

"Like Christians?" replied Squid.

Thankfully, Mr. Shriki interrupted the gerbil conference, before the prejudicial implication of their conversation could reach its conclusion.

"Schopenhauer describes the Graeco-Roman paganism that precedes Christianity as a trivial play of fantasy, cobbled together by poets from popular legends. They don't have ethical doctrines or moral doctrines, for example. But you can tell that what he's annoyed about is the fact that they don't have any rules. Whereas Christianity's success lies in its allegorical qualities. And Christianity isn't just a doctrine. If you look at both the Old Testament and the New Testament, the whole book functions as a history: it's a series of events. For Schopenhauer, the allegories and the stories in Christianity aren't allegories or symbols, so much as they are mysteries. This is Schopenhauer's problem with Christianity: you can learn something from a story, but a mystery is useless. He can't stand the cosmic question mark that comes out of Biblical interpretation, which, with Greek rationality, helps to form the entire Western philosophical tradition. So, he's taking issue with a big part of what it means to think critically in the Western tradition."

In the hay-smelling cage, Squid asked, "What about the *animals*?"

"Within Christianity, human beings are split off from the animal kingdom. Humanity is alone, and animals are little more than things. Things to be owned, things to be eaten, things to be used."

The next moment the cage seemed bigger, more expansive, more constabulary. The metal seemed colder, tougher, and more dangerous.

The hay was a distraction.

"Oh," said Biscuit and Squid, as their respective warm-black and zinnwaldite-brown eyes welled up with confusion, and helplessness, and still more bafflement.

"Schopenhauer doesn't like human beings," explained Mr. Shriki. "People are the devils of the earth, he says, and the animals are the tormented souls. He gives an example of a scientist who starved two rabbits to see if it changed the chemical composition of their brains. Schopenhauer's question is: 'Don't you wake up screaming at night?' Which is ironic because that's a very Christian question. A question about personal responsibility, and shame, and wrongdoing. It fits with the views of personal-responsibility-on-God's-earth taken by Thomas Aquinas centuries beforehand."

He stopped talking, opened a desk drawer, and opened a pack of German strawberries. He coughed lightly, smiling at his students, as he walked over to Biscuit and Squid, gave them two strawberries, and placed the package back on his desk.

Biscuit stared solemnly at the giant strawberries.

There was control, and benevolence, and kindness, and duty, in that strawberry. Maybe it was irritating to look after two creatures so helpless, small, and voiceless. Except they had loud voices. Words, sentences, and thoughts that existed, but avoided the precise ape frequency. Without words, thought Biscuit, there would be no peace between the apes and the gerbils…

Squid looked disdainfully at the strawberries. What would happen if Biscuit got sick? What would happen if Biscuit got the age sickness? Or if the instructing-ape died? He was not immortal. He was perishable, like the other apes. Time, and time again, his lessons had shown how perishable the apes were. But the instructing-ape was benevolent, and kind. Was it kindness that made the yum-foods fall from the sky? Surely kindness was a weak cousin of duty. Maybe it was a sense of duty that Biscuit and Squid shared for one another as the outrageous-orange hills, and the pale-aqua-coloured skies, lived outside, indifferent to their wild-strawberry wheel and cheap hay.

For a moment, it seemed that the whole classroom awaited the customary feeding session that otherwise defined the North African gerbils who squeaked in the corner.

But when they didn't touch their food, the human beings decided that something had changed to upset the original order...

Half-cognizant that it was expected of them, the gerbils sniffed the strawberries, nibbled them, and reclined on their hind-legs, berries in paws, looking up thoughtfully.

"What are Schopenhauer's conclusions?" asked Mr. Shriki. "He says that you have to be blind, deaf, and dumb, or completely chloroformed, to not see that animals are the same things that we are. He says that the difference lies in the accident - which is the *intellect* - and not in the substance - which is the *will*. Hundreds of years earlier we had Thomas Aquinas saying that rational thought was all that separated us from animals."

Rational thought helped them think about God, thought the gerbils.   "But now we've got Schopenhauer saying that rational thought is *an accident* - and that what really matters, is *the will*. The will is what makes us human. Which is why people who experiment on animals have forgotten that they are first and foremost human beings - and only secondly, are they scientists. The point here is that science can be as blind as religion. Focusing on renewable energy can be as blind, for example, as focusing on whether uncircumcised foreigners can become Christians, and so on…"

"The sand-storms," chorused Biscuit and Squid.

"Instead, Schopenhauer thinks that we should accept that the eternal being which lives in us, is *also* alive in animals. *Brahman* may be the diversity of the cosmos in all its beauty, but it's nothing without the *atman* - the unifying principle that connects all living things."

Mr. Shriki looked at the gerbil cage, then he returned his gaze to his students.

"It's not philosophy, but the will, which is the great equalizer."

After the real lesson about renewable energy, the students left without thanks, and Mr. Shriki stood over the North African gerbils, like an unmotivated, Egyptian deity.

Biscuit reached out his tickle-me-pink paw so that the ape-instructor could shake it.

The ape-instructor softly touched it, using his index finger.

Suddenly, the gerbils were aware that they needed to break out of their comfy cage, the Regional Collège in Dakhla, and the mutually-beneficial relation with Mr. Shriki.

CHAPTER EIGHT

The shiny spheroid of Alhaadi Omondi's head bounced through the arrivals section of Rabat-Salé Airport, with its Paris-green floors and tall windows. He spent two nights in Rabat buying wedding gifts and delicately flattering the homosexual shop assistants from whom he purchased perfumes, and gold watches. After prompting a feisty shop assistant called Ikram to fall in love with him, Alhaadi abandoned his hotel, boarded a train for Marrakech, and arrived in time to attend the marriage ceremony taking place in Lou Baring's apartment.

A notary called Meryem Zaki stood in the middle of the living room-cum-kitchen. Salvatore Yannucci and Augustu Valverde served as witnesses as Brooke Kimani and Lou Baring signed the ratifying paperwork on the battleship-grey countertop, where bottles of Wild Turkey - and not bouquets of flowers - had once languished in infamy. After doing this, the couple kissed and turned towards Alhaadi who clapped loudly and wiped snot out of his magnificent postage stamp moustache, as Salvatore and Augustu provided pecks for each of Brooke's cheeks, and then shook Lou's hand.

"The wedding day is all paid for," Salvatore whispered.

The cogs of Lou's brain struggled to chew up all this Sicilian charity.

When Salvatore saw the look on Brooke's face, he added, "Don't worry - it'll be a short Moroccan wedding."

"Only three days," said Augustu, replacing his dark-Byzantium fedora and focusing his hibernating eyes on Brooke's reaction.

The investigative journalist shot her husband a half-polite look. She was shocked that they had had anything to do with the wedding.

Brooke thanked the notary, and widened her high cheekbones, sending Meryem Zaki, Augustu and Salvatore, and her uncle, out of the apartment.

Brooke sat on the couch. "Does he get his own guest list, too?"

"I gave him yours," said Lou, sitting next to her, stroking her thigh. "He's probably got one too."

"But why," said Brooke, getting up and standing by the window, "do they have to walk us through it, like they're handing us away?"

"Because my family's fucking useless," replied Lou.

"Why do *they* have to do it?"

"What about *your* family?"

"We don't talk, you know all that."

Lou nodded as if he understood. But he didn't understand anything.

He rubbed his eyes. "We were doing so well."

"I know, I know - I'm sorry." Back on the couch, she put her legs up on Lou's legs. "When was the last time we had sex?"

"Uh. Week ago."

"That's a long time."

"Uh-huh."

"We should probably have sex."

"Uh."

Moving into the bedroom, they casually undressed and made love in two or three positions on the bed with its safety-orange bedsheets. The couple laid back and talked.

"Get a job?" asked Lou, touching her velvety head.

"I applied to a few newspapers. I want to engage with the country, but they don't want to push buttons."

"Like England," said Lou, showing off one of his rare insights, produced whenever he wanted to sound normal, or vaguely engaged. "You don't *have* to work," added Lou.

"You're right. But I want to. Funny that."

When she licked his nose, Lou said, "WUUUHHAAAA!" and almost fell out of the safety-orange bedsheets. "Don't do that!" he yelled.

"I'll get crazier if I'm stuck in this apartment all the time," warned Brooke.

"You'll find something. You'll get used to Morocco."

"I'd rather Morocco got used to me. But I know writing's not stable."

"I would have moved to London - but we've got family here," Lou assured her.

"You mean, *you've* got family here. Some family," she moaned, disappearing elsewhere for a short think. "Better than nothing, I guess."

"It's the best that I've had."

He was still talking about family, right? Either way, he seemed to have incredibly low standards, thought Brooke.

"I feel like an outsider," added Lou.

"I think you always will." She had only lived in Morocco for three months. She had made some friends – people she thought she could use – who were good at using others.

"And now the wedding," said Lou, interrupting her thoughts.

Apart from getting married, Brooke's greatest achievement had been her introduction to Meera Balakrishnan, who was the senior law consultant for Zaalouk Real Estate. She was a medium-sized woman who wore zomp-turquoise suits, veronica-purple flat-shoes, and reserved earrings. She also had long hair which she tied in a bun, and bright eyes that sometimes looked University-of-Pennsylvania-red in harsh sunlight. One day, when she had been preparing license applications for two gambling properties, Meera had been reminded by Lou Baring that his girlfriend-cum-betrothed was an experienced writer, and that she would be more than happy to check the license applications for grammatical errors. What began as a brief sojourn blossomed into intermittent contract work that saw the investigative journalist scanning through sheaves of legal paperwork, composed of clauses, licenses, and uninterrupted paragraphs. There were times when Brooke pretended that, instead of legal documents, she was scanning through *Kitah al-Ibar*, which was an ancient history of North Africa written by Ibn Khaldun, one of the greatest minds of the Middle Ages, and the father, as many believe, of economics, sociology, historiography, and demographical investigations.

But her imagination would wear off and she would be back in the woods.

"Are we colleagues, or friends?" asked Brooke in Meera's office.

Meera cleared her throat and leaned forward in her chair.

"If you need money," she answered, "you know where to come."

"Thanks," said Brooke, thinking, "If only you could tell me more."

After this, Meera introduced Brooke to the rest of her lawyer friends, as the investigative journalist slowly befriended many journalists. When the day of Brooke's *Hammam* came, the lawyers and journalists - who had attended the same universities, but who had never joined the same societies - arrived in separate limousines for the private steam bath that traditionally welcomed the new bride into married life.

The steam bath was a small chamber with lamps set into tea-green walls. These stretches were defined by attractive tiling that alternated between sugar-plum-purple, and sizzling-red, diamonds and octagons. Meanwhile, in the centre of the bath, was a fountain-like device decked in rose petals, that ebbed in the moving water. On either side of the bath were metal buckets that were situated beneath polished taps, that emptied themselves of hot water that could be poured over the new bride.

Brooke had never been treated like royalty before.

The way in which the lawyers and journalists fought to clean Brooke's hair using a special clay mixed with herbs, and then to perfume her body with lotions, made Brooke uneasy - and considered that it might provide dream-fuel for her uncle, Alhaadi…

Brooke turned to a journalist called Faiza who worked at the *Morocco Examiner*, and said, "I wish everything was more open."

"Me too," replied Faiza, availing herself of a bucket of warm water, and pouring it over Brooke's half-naked body. "My dad was an independent journalist." She picked a rose petal out of Brooke's cleavage. "He went through the meat grinder, you know?"

"How do you accept that?"

"You have to - otherwise you can't live."

(The women who had wanted to ban polygamy and raise the marriage age from 14 to 18 in the early 2000s, were hardly examples of people who had accepted their fate.)

Then Meera - wearing a salmon-pink toga, artfully drawn up below her buttocks so that Faiza would be able to covet her shapely, legal thighs - snatched the bucket away from Faiza, re-filled it with hot water from the nearby taps, and used a sponge to dab Brooke's skin in the radiant shadiness of the chamber.

"My dear," said Meera, "maybe you should come back to the office. The others are illiterate – they're real estate agents, let's face the truth – and they would love you…"

"What a waste of her talents," interrupted Faiza, trying to ignore Meera's legs, but all her brain could think of, was, *"thigh, thigh, thigh…"*

"Nothing wrong with legal work," said a grand attorney, wandering into the debate, like she was carved from roman-silver playdough.

"If that was true, you wouldn't need solicitors," replied Faiza.

The attorney touched Faiza's shoulder and said in Tamazight, "Brooke doesn't need to know our problems. She'll leave soon, anyway."

"Is it down in your calendar?" asked Faiza in French.

"I don't speak Frog."

"Oh, I'm sorry, I thought you were educated."

The *Zawiya* were leftist Moroccan intellectuals educated in France, who had returned to Morocco with a desire to work alongside the French Protectorate.

Faiza was conscious that she sounded like one of these collaborators, but simultaneously, she was happy to take part in a culture outside of her own.

Behind Faiza and the grumpy attorney, a journalist called Samira massaged lotions into Brooke's back. She had been fired from the *Not-The-Daily-Examiner*, and now lived in Marrakech with her mother, who lost her leg and sense of humour in the same week.

"Is that a pillow?" asked Brooke, feeling something against her back.

"Sorry, those are my boobs," said Samira.

"Oh," said Brooke, her hands shooting into her lap. "Thank you - the rub-down - thanks for that. But - yes – I'm looking for work – it's very hard here."

"You could monetize YouTube videos," suggested Samira, enjoying her temporary post as a bride-slave. "The Scarvaggi Family might censor it, but if people are watching outside, you can still monetize the videos."

"What, *guerrilla* reporting?"

Several attorneys narrowed their eyes nearby.

"It's better than letting men have all the fun," said Samira, adjusting her bra. "It's not like real estate and war have the monopoly on leisure."

"War?"

"Well, that's another matter. Another script in development."

A collective sigh from lawyers and journalists blew the rose-madder petals across the febrile surface of the steam bath to its edges…

The *henna* party for Brooke took place in the function room of an antique-white mosque in the centre of Marrakech. Artichoke-green banners lined the walls, and cerulean-frost tables covered with steaming hors d'oeuvres complemented the fiery-rose uniforms of the lawyers and accountants attending the party. With her green kaftan and golden robe, Brooke cut an elegant figure on her throne. The visiting henna artist was called Zahra and had plastic-spoon-shaped bags under her dark eyes, long fingernails, slippered feet, and a fuchsia robe. In preparation, she had designed a special pattern for Brooke's hands and feet: a traditional tattoo that would fade away after the celebrations - "Like my optimism," thought Brooke, as the old woman began inking Brooke's hands with white ink. "It's a sign of fertility," commented Zahra, as she looked up to smile at Brooke.

"I don't need that," replied Brooke.

Her lawyers and journalists chanted, and swirled around her, praising the impending pairing. When the other women were receiving their tattoos, Meera and Samira looked on from their fiery-rose robes, and chatted lightly.

"What's the worst intimidation you ever had?" asked Meera.

"They knocked on my door," said Samira, adjusting her bra.

"Not *too* bad."

"They said they could do a breast reduction for me." She searched for something in her cleavage. "That was for a story I wrote about the king."

"But he's been dead for half a century."

"I made arguments for reanimating him," clarified Samira.

Meera needed to be logical, but when she was faced with the absurd and unjustified elements of human existence, all she could do was nod, and remind herself that Islam was legally strong. Except Morocco was no longer strong, which suggested that they had all become heathens and idolators and that the new idols were monetary notes.

Meanwhile, Lou's *henna* party was organized to take place in another Marrakech district. The mosque was dark green, dappled with dark-turquoise tiles, and sported a darkened patch that led into the building and doubled as a kind of mason-made carpet. In the function room, Lou and various colleagues from Zaalouk Real Estate, and the wider Sicilian circuit, so-to-speak, sat together for the traditional Koran recitation.

A Koran recitation - Lou had been told - was like a song.

With Lou at the centre of a wider group of men, who either stood or sat cross-legged, the *henna* party listened attentively to the resident Imam, Hamza Rahil, for three minutes, as he chanted the essential music:

"And of His signs is that He created for you mates from among yourselves, so that you may find tranquility in them; and He planted love and compassion between you. In this are signs for people who reflect.

"And of His signs is the creation of the heavens and the earth, and the diversity of your languages and colours. In this are signs for those who know.

"And of His signs are your sleep by night and day, and your pursuit of His bounty. In this are signs for people who listen.

"And of His signs is that He shows you the lightning, causing fear and hope. And He brings down water from the sky, and with it, He revives the earth after it was dead. In this are signs for people who understand.

"And of His signs is that the heaven and the earth stand at His disposal. And then, when He calls you out of the earth, you will emerge at once.

"To Him belongs everyone in the heavens and the earth. All are submissive to Him.

"It is He who initiates creation, and then repeats it, something easy for Him. His is the highest attribute, in the heavens and the earth. He is the Almighty, the Wise..."

In his sobriety, Lou had sought spiritual guidance.

He had accepted that he was not the smartest man on the planet and that he required supervision. He saw what had happened to him without guidance, and now his brain had become a receiver for counsel, in all its spiritual forms.

"Allah, the merciful," thought Lou - and whether he deserved mercy.

"Where is the *pane ca'meusa*?" asked Salvatore in Tamazight, as the terrified Moroccan waiter sorted through the multi-coloured platters of grilled meats and puréed eggplant. Salvatore's thick forearms pointed to various platters, where his beloved soft buns with fried liver should have been balanced against one another, leaking meat juices and heavy aromas, and making the wedding guests' mouths water. "Where are they?" came the question again, full of vexation, and worry.

"I don't know, Mr. Yannucci - "

"*Know.*"

"What?"

The furious underboss slapped the waiter across his chin. "They were made at *Accursio's* this morning. They don't vanish - we don't live in some holy book - "

"I think - here they are!"

The waiter discovered four platters of *pane ca'meusa* stashed behind several dozen bottles of Marsala and Frappato wines, which had been given their own Visa, and flown in from Sicily that morning. "Here they are!" shouted the waiter. "They're warm!"

The underboss put his dark-liver arm around the waiter's shoulders. "Who put them down there?"

"I - well - I - I don't know. They shouldn't be back *there*."

"No." He held up a fat finger and used it to punctuate his words. "Think of the guests. Think of the customers. If you think of them, you'll be working at Christmas."

"Oh - *thank you*, Mr. Yannucci."

The next moment Salvatore had wandered back into the gathering wedding crowd. His extensive patio looked out on Marrakech and the Atlas Mountains beyond - and the sixty people who had come to pay homage to the marriage between Brooke Kimani and Lou Baring were sporadically distracted by the distant aero-blue skies, under which snowy peaks had been arranged like some nightmare of dentistry, their summits and ridges giving way to a blizzard-blue gloom as snow became rock, rock became landscape, and landscape grew accustomed to the wills of human beings. A reminder of the too-big-to-understand-ness that hovered over the bustling city, and the expensive Marsala and Frappato wines that flowed through the hectic wedding party.

In the middle of the room, trying to distract from the Atlas Mountains, a group of men were wearing dark-liver uniforms. They played ouds, sinters, goblet drums, and abendirs, and sang loudly as Brooke - supported by an elegant, roofed platform called an *amaria* - was carried onto the patio by Sara Privitera, Rosa "Small Nose" Baracco, Tulumeu Mascali, and Hamid "Blackish" Harrak-Costa, all wearing tight tuxedos.

Lou watched Brooke's progress from the vantage point of a decorated couch. After the platform was lowered, she stepped off, joined her husband on the couch, and touched his inner thigh as the guests applauded between slurps of expensive wine.

The same waiter who had dealt with the *pane ca'meusa* debacle now discovered that the head waiter - an ex-sommelier and quasi-savant with thirty years of experience - had fainted in the catering tent. After a short meeting with the catering crew, this particular waiter became temporary maître d', organized the waiters into mini-shifts, and began sending out the food to the already sozzled wedding guests, who had forgotten about the Atlas Mountains as much as they had forgotten about Brooke and Lou. Sheets of food rained upon the guests: bowls of humous and baba ghanouj, plates of falafel and spinach-stuffed pasty, platters lined with rolls of feta cheese and spring onion, and salvers covered with lamb, stuffed with mince meat, and pine nuts. The *pane ca'meusa* was well-received, and so was the selection of grilled chicken and lamb which was cooked on-site, plated, and then delivered to each guest.

The patio resonated with sounds of sucking and mastication and slurping. Zara Lachgar, the chief of police, enjoyed prawn cocktail, and Cleopatra Griffiths drank glasses of champagne, and Giovanni Alami-Russo and Faiz Impellizzeri stood at the edge of the crunching and slurping crowd, whispering that all this was blasphemous.

Casting his crazed eyes over the crowd, Lucio Vizzini pretended that he was on his way to chat with someone, and moved repeatedly past platters of smoked salmon and caviar, bottles of champagne, and ashtrays packed with ebbing cigars and cigarettes. But there was no one there to talk to, and Lucio began to understand and accept that he would always be alone.

Wedding guests positioned themselves around the cake. Brooke and Lou appeared - in what must have been their fifth change of clothing - wearing a cornsilk wedding dress and dark-jungle-green tuxedo, respectively, and they moved around the cake, exchanging grins, and sweet nothings, after which they cut the big gateau.

Brooke focused on wrists: brown-sugar, skinny with ganglion cysts, round and thicker than a thermos, cornflower-blue-veined and cotton-candy; black-coral watches, umpteen crucifix-bracelets, and burgundy worry-beads.

One of the dark-liver-attired band members addressed the sound system, flipped a vinyl record in his strong hands, and rested it on the raised dais. "Too Many Tomorrows" from *Sweet Charity* submerged the well-fed and -watered crowd. Lou and Brooke merged with the dance floor and moved to the music. As the property manager nested his chin on Brooke's shoulder, he spotted Nina Scarvaggi, Salvatore Yannucci, and Augustu Valverde, sitting together at one table. They were drinking wine, ignoring the fact that Salvatore was crying, and sniffling.

"Sal's crying," whispered Lou.

"*I'm* crying," replied Brooke.

"Shit, why are you crying?"

"Because I'm *happy*."

He held his wife tighter, and continued dancing, until the music played out and the crowd applauded - and Salvatore scuttled into the bathroom and looked in the mirror.

Apart from the sounds of arctic-lime articulated haulers and bud-green bucket-wheel excavators, the business-like silence of the phosphate mine in Inal was only periodically broken up by the Cantonese spoken by tired Chinese guards, finishing their shift. Beyond the artificial illumination of the mine, the surrounding desert was undistilled darkness. Along the north bank of the phosphate mine was an invisible trench, which had been dug out over the course of a month by insomniac communists under the command of Ismail. It allowed them to spy on the phosphate mine during the day - and would now enable them to do a little more than espionage.

At 11:30 p.m., Ismail lifted binoculars to his sad eyes and inspected the perimeter of the phosphate mine.

"What do you see?" asked his Defence Minister.

A sign read "Looters Beware" in Mandarin and Arabic. The Chinese were as wary of their own people as they were of the locals. Next to the sign, however, were two man-sized, brick structures, big enough to hold people.

The message was simple - work, or prepare to be roasted alive.

"Peasants," murmured Ismail.

The communist leader lowered his binoculars, lifted a battery-powered flashlight, and turned the switch on and off along the confines of the trench. Soon a black mass of two hundred soldiers had leaked out of the trench on the moonlit desert and slowly made their way toward the perimeter of the phosphate mine. There they quietly dispatched a handful of Mauritanian guards and then disconnected one of the giant spotlights that customarily watched over the nightshift, like a fatigued sun-divinity.

The head of security, Cheng Luo, motioned for his patrol to halt.

Then *all* of the spotlights covering the mine gave a pathetic flash and went black.

Cheng's eyes widened as the pilots of the articulated haulers and bucket-wheel excavators leaned out of their cabins, shining flashlights.

"These aren't looters," noted Cheng in Mandarin. The head of security loaded a flare-gun as he listened to guards prattling. He aimed the barrel above the spotlight generators and pulled the trigger. The flare soared out of the gun. It hung in the air like a cardinal blob. Then the flare plummeted past the searchlight and the generators, and marked the machines out as if they were blush-coloured insects stalking the desert.

Cheng watched the flare. It fizzled out as he prepared another.

One of his guards said, "Sir - ", but Cheng shushed him. He loaded his flare gun and raised the barrel towards the sky. He was about to pull the trigger when the spotlights returned like so many dwarf stars. Radiance flooded the mine, and half-startled guards grew terrified when they saw around them two hundred paramilitary soldiers.

The moment that Cheng realised they had been invaded came after the communist soldiers began firing their guns and pulling pilots out of the machinery.

The dark-jungle-green jumpsuits of the various guards and mine employees were swamped by the military-green uniforms of hundreds of attacking soldiers, who fired AR-15s at pre-chosen targets, such as backup generators, low-ranking personnel, and desert-worthy automobiles. There was pandemonium as the screams of Cheng's guards were drowned out by bullets ripping sand-geysers through the ground, grenades shattering communication towers, and people tripping over one another. The next moment Cheng's right knee exploded, and he collapsed face-first into the sand as his colleagues were picked off by snipers who had positioned themselves around the mine.

The gate leading to the accommodation compound exploded. Shards of metal fencing pierced the windows of container homes, vehicle tires, and plastic water tanks.

Sometimes doors opened, offering hands holding primed weapons - but no sooner had the doors opened than Ismail's soldiers picked off these vest-wearing sleepers who tumbled out of their doorways and then formed twisted shapes on their doormats. The citizen army pushed into the compound - swarming, catching, and castrating. Finally, white flags were flown, and exchanges in Arabic, Mandarin, and English were heard. Escorted by his personal guard, Ismail entered the accommodation compound and took charge of the operation. When he noticed the accounting department being frogmarched out of their container, he called to the soldiers, "Take them to the mines." The mostly bespectacled men and women were marched to the pithead.

Meanwhile, miners had emerged from the pithead. "Communists? Fine, whatever," many said in Arabic - and they subsequently pledged their allegiance to their rescuers.

There was one miner, however, who refused to join the communists.

Against a background of domestic fires and columns of frogmarched prisoners, the miner was taken to Ismail, who shook his hand, and said, "Who's this?"

"He won't join us," replied the soldier in Arabic.

"I see." Ismail stroked his new moustache. "Why not?"

"I'm a miner."

"I can see that. But you see, these people - " He gestured to Chinese and Mauritanians being marched to the pithead, and their subsequent doom. "These people are the enemy.

They'll close the mines when they're done here and move elsewhere."

"That tends to be how mines work," said the miner.

"We want you to tell people what happened here."

"Why?"

"Because you're against our movement."

"No more than I'm against the Chinese. They starved us and made us work ungodly hours. But we're not all prisoners. I'm a miner, by trade."

"Then work with us."

"No."

"Why not?"

"You want to make me political."

"Everything is political," Ismail laughed.

"If everything is political, then nothing is political."

"Power allows us to get things done. We have exercised power *here*."

"But what's the use in that?"

Ismail eyed the miner. He was clean-shaven and sported a big chin, sharp eyes, and meaty hands with delicate fingers. He looked dejected, but not without fatalistic pride.

"If we stand here, and disagree, we'll get nothing done," Ismail said.

"Fine."

A strange silence was shared, as gunfire peppered the background. They were executing people in the mines.

"You like disagreement," said Ismail.

"No."

With his heart racing, Ismail figured that his better judgement had less time-consuming exertions, like executing people who disagreed with him.

"Let him go," ordered the communist leader. The two soldiers who had been guarding the miner in due course executed the catering staff. But Ismail continued to watch the miner with a thoughtful look on his face. "Where will you go?" asked Ismail.

"Somewhere I can mine."

Ismail nodded solemnly. "Good luck."

"I would say the same to you - but communists don't need luck."

"You mean we make our own?" replied Ismail with a smile.

"You don't have any luck," said the miner, observing Ismail's infantile moustache. "It's because you have no dreams." Then he turned in his dark-jungle-green jumpsuit, walked into the darkness and up the side of the mine, and disappeared into the night.

Jing Fàn had been dragged out of her bed, and half-carried, half-dragged outside, where she was encircled by the communist soldiers and their leader. Ismail observed the Chinese manager at his feet: she was naked and covered in sand. "Shoot her," said Ismail. Jing Fàn spat blood, and cursed him in Cantonese as soldiers half-carried, half-dragged her to a wooden post. She was tied to the post using rope. Then the area was cleared, and two tiers of communist fighters formed rows before the naked, screaming mine-manager. Her fine black hair was stuck in places to her forehead, drenched in perspiration and dried blood from beatings. "Ready…" said an adjoining soldier in Arabic. The sky was no longer eerie-black and charcoal-coloured: there were cosmic-cobalt circles and shapes, and oxford-blue nets of crossing virgules. "Aim…" On top of the additional raisin-blacks, and seal-browns, was a blasphemous silence. "*Fire!*"

Jing Fàn screamed as bullets ripped into her breast. Within a second, a hole appeared in her chest, the size of a fist. Then her head flopped over.

CHAPTER NINE

The top headlines in the *Morocco Examiner* that week were:

1. *Golfing Legend Spree Curtiz Explores Tangier.*
2. *Makhzan Announces Plans to Broadcast News in Mandarin.*
3. *French President: "We Did Nothing Wrong In Morocco."*
4. *Americans Baffled By Sahara Dispute.*
5. *Algerian Ambassador Receives Parking Ticket.*

Brooke lowered the print edition and stared at Ezzine Ismaili, the editor of the *Morocco Examiner*. He had a triangular face that narrowed at the chin. He also had large white teeth, lobe-less ears, a pronounced Roman nose, and curly hair cropped short at the sides, which clashed with his otherwise spotless, thin eyebrows. He sat back and supported his rotund body by pinning his elbows to the chair arms, his almond shirt and barbie-pink necktie suffocating him.

"All you've got," complained Brooke, "are other countries talking about how wonderful you are - "

"Not France and Algeria. Same thing, if you ask me."

She smacked the paper on his desk. "The *makhzan*'s cutting the defence budget by half. They're cutting reserve soldiers like they're retail outlets."

Ezzine shrugged.

"What you need are down and dirty stories," suggested Brooke. "You'll get more traffic on your website if you cover normal people - cost of living, stuff like that."

"I like that. But that's not what Moroccans want. I've been in this place for eight years. If anything had changed, I would have noticed. Search the archives - we didn't say the king was an authoritarian when he was alive. What makes you think we'd say anything like that today?" He flashed his white teeth. "...About anyone, Brooke."

"You're cynical."

"Are the facts cynical?" Ezzine cleared his throat aggressively. "You know that before the Sicilians came, Morocco held a referendum about the monarchy. And everyone said they wanted to keep it."

"That's probably why they *killed* him," said Brooke acidly.

"You don't know our history. You're a foreigner. I don't expect you to learn, because I don't expect you to work here *at all*."

Brooke stood up and paced the office.

A black-coral desktop computer and keyboard, bitter-lemon lamps, picture-frames, and coffee mugs - carefully coordinated - and atomic-tangerine bookshelves containing blue, green, and cornflower-blue volumes. Shelves the same hue as the Sahara Desert. The books shaded like boats and ships leaving the ports - and also Brooke's husband's eyes, vague and dim, and only partially judgmental, appearing to glow along the spines of reference books...

"I'm offering to work for free," offered Brooke. "But you don't want me..."

"This is about you. It's not about the work."

"You need to explain that."

"You live to work. It gets you up in the morning."

"I thought that was menopause," Brooke half-laughed.

"But, you see, it's different here. I see my job as a way of keeping the country stable. I want things to be prosperous, safe, and affordable."

"I've seen people with broken legs begging for money - "

"And do you help those people? I bet you make YouTube dollars. You put your diatribes online - and it's *not* journalism - and make money doing that - and complain about the price of groceries from your three-bedroom apartment, when your viewers make spit - and they're watching you on their commutes to shitty jobs in offices - "

"How much money do your readers make?"

"No idea."

"Come on, how much do they make?"

"Above my pay-grade." His eyebrows quivered. "Don't write those stories."

Ezzine stared around his messy office, and in doing so re-traced his past eight years as editor. He had never had a conversation like this one. She was good-looking, too, he thought, which might come in handy with the Scarvaggi Family. But given the choice between stability and experimentation, he chose the former. "Algerian foreign correspondent," said Ezzine. "The commute is easy; the salary is good."

"Not Algeria," replied Brooke as she brushed dust off of a stack of dark-orchid books: *Collected Minutes from First Post-Monarchy Administration.* "I want to write stories about Moroccans."

"Then don't live in Morocco," came the final reply.

The streets of Casablanca toiled as Brooke put Faiza's introduction and advice behind her and walked through downtown Casablanca. The ochre signs advertising struggling shops, peach-puff walls supporting dwarfish balconies, and robin-egg-blue steps leading into neglected lobbies, filled Brooke with memories of London, with its impoverished wealth and hypocrisy. She itched her pumpkin blouse, and turned to face a small shop called *Eidabat Alkamira*, that Brooke translated as "Camera Worship".

Inside, Pierre Issawi rubbed his nose and pulled on his hairy jawline when he saw Brooke enter the shop and walk past the tripod shelves. He stepped out from behind the sales desk in his Russian-green tracksuit and sand-dine sneakers, and said, "Aha-aha! How can I help you, madame? Looking for a television - we've got good prices - or maybe you're looking for a camera?" His use of Tamazight was lost on Brooke, however, who simply shook her head, and said, "I'm sorry - my Arabic's terrible."

Pierre tongued his cheek. All foreigners thought they spoke Arabic.

"Okay," said Pierre in English. "You're looking for cameras? Something?"

"Yes, cameras. Where are they?"

He pointed to an air-conditioned corner suffused with glass cabinets.

Brooke found it hard to believe that buying a camera could be so easy when it was damn near impossible to write stories about infrastructure. She moved regardless to the glass cabinets, examined them with that cursory intensity projected by amateurs, selected one, and waited patiently as Pierre struggled with the miniature keys that had been used since time immemorial to open expensive and complex glass structures. He retrieved a spring-green camera from the display shelf, explained its basic features, and turned a vivid burgundy when Brooke said that she would purchase it.

"Microphones?" enquired Brooke. And Pierre duly selected an appropriate lavalier microphone for the camera, took them to the sales desk, and put them into the register. The owner's Russian-green tracksuit quivered with anxiety as he told her the price. "What will you be filming?" he added.

"People," replied Brooke, paying by card.

"Where?" He couldn't help but glance at the ceiling - beyond which a well-thought-out and lengthy operation to import tropical fruit into Casablanca had taken place for the past year-and-a-half: the people of Casablanca had demanded a new source of strawberries, blueberries, and fresh honeydew-melon to counter the rotten fruit brought in by the Scarvaggi *makhzan*. Mashed avocados, shattered pineapples, hugged grapefruits, crumpled lemons, and flattened papayas had plagued the city until a coalition of black-market individuals, led by Issawi, had seized the means of production and started growing lawbreaking blueberries, illicit grapefruits, and felonious papayas. What had started as a minor operation had turned into a full-blown racket, with Pierre syphoning orders through *Eidabat Alkamira*, and then posting fresh fruit and vegetables around Casablanca. "There's nothing untoward here," noted Pierre quietly.

"Well - I was actually - I was thinking of talking to gamblers."

"Oh." His athletic monobrow exercised itself when he glanced at the card machine. "Looks like it's gone through." He smiled, packed her camera and microphone into a compostable bag, and handed her the mostly-environmentally-friendly package.

"Thank you," said Brooke, looking at the ceiling.

"Grapes."

"What?"

"Nothing. Enjoy your camera. May Umm Kalthoum smile upon you."

"Who's that?"

Pierre said, "Doesn't matter," and entered a dark back room, where the spark of a cigarette lighter flashed for several seconds, and then vanished.

On the train back to Marrakech, Brooke opened the box and fiddled with her camera. She was able to charge it using the onboard plugs and then piled everything back into the compostable bag before clambering off of the train, and returning to her apartment in Marrakech.

She absorbed the silence of a home holding one spouse.

She put her compostable bag on the battleship-grey countertop in the kitchen.

Lou's things were on the coffee table, and warm-black chargers for her phone and laptop were on the floor by the plug, alongside the wild-orchid books about Morocco and Algeria, and the Windsor-tan books about communism.

Lou had complained about the latter. As if that human ability to simultaneously enquire and complain could mean anything else but anxiety about the sudden future.

After Brooke stopped worrying about her issues, she sat down with a pad and pencil and pondered over the battleship-grey counter.

6. ~~Were there drugs in your home when you were growing up?~~
7. ~~When did you start using drugs?~~
8. Did you get on with your parents?

1. ~~Where do you live?~~
2. ~~Why do you live like this, you idiot?~~
3. What did you do today?

1. ~~Why is everything in Morocco fucked up?~~
2. ~~What do you think about Morocco?~~
3. Is there any assistance you can get from the makhzan?

Brooke slammed her pencil on the countertop. She searched for "Marrakech betting shops" on her phone and wrote down their addresses and numbers on the pad. She dialed the number for *Off-Course Betting* and got her pencil and pad ready. *"Yes,"* came the answer in Arabic, *"who is this?"*

Brooke winced at the language barrier. "I'm sorry - you don't speak English by any chance? I want to place a bet."

"Yes, of course," came the reply in English. *"Horses? Camels? Dog-racing? If you're based in Casablanca, a man called Pierre is feeding fruit to gerbils, just to see who finishes first. Two died from high cholesterol, but, you know? You know, right?"*

"Who's the lucky horse this week?"

"Uh - " She could hear a shoddy collection of fictional notepads. *"Big Sal's leading. What do you want to do? You want a straight bet - or you can spread your risk with a bet to show? Doesn't matter if he comes first, second, or third."*

"A straight one. Fifty dirhams on Big Sal."

"Okay. Do you have your card ready?"

"Yes." She duly paid the amount.

"Come round to collect? You can do a bank transfer if you like?"

"I'll come round. What's your crowd like?"

A brief confusion infiltrated the otherwise business-like interaction. *"All kinds, miss, all kinds."*

As it turned out, the man from the betting shop had mixed up his notepads. Big Sal was hardly the horse that he had promised and was actually a gerbil.

The gerbil won the race, nonetheless, and was held up by its owner, whose tears stained the fur of the rodent, which was rewarded with German strawberries.

When Brooke showed up at *Off-Course Betting* in her pumpkin blouse, Red-Salsa trousers, and Russian-violet heels, the sordid men in attendance practically dropped their respective bottles, dirham-wads, scarlet fezzes, and condoms. "You've won," said the man behind the glass who had spoken to her on the telephone. He was reed-like with small hands and veiny temples. "My register is weeping today." He slipped 500 dirhams under the teller-tunnel to Brooke, who seized the money, and felt a strange warmth in her stomach, after which she shook her head free of the sensation, removed her camera, and started searching for an interview subject.

A toothless, white-haired man called Antar was the first to agree. Brooke prepared her microphone, pressed record, and filmed his wrinkled hands for privacy.

"You ready?" she asked.

"Yes, miss."

"Did you get on with your parents?"

"No, I killed them."

Brooke paused. "I think a lot of people would find that shocking."

"Not surprising."

"Can I ask why you killed them?"

"Sure."

Her eyes darted to and fro, before Antar understood the meaning of her question.

"I'm sorry. I killed my parents because they wanted to hand me over to the local captain. But that was a long time ago. My hands are now as wrinkled as theirs were." He grinned privately.

"What did you do today?" asked Brooke.

"I watched the betting."

"You didn't place a bet?" she enquired.

"No, that kills you."

"Why do you like watching betting?"

"I like watching things eat."

Brooke sighed, and asked, "Are you a wealthy man?"

"Yes, but I have no money. That's probably what you meant."

"Not necessarily."

"I don't have any money, and the state won't give me any."

"Do you think," asked the investigative journalist carefully, "that it's because you killed your parents?"

"Oh yes. That's definitely why."

"What are you going to *do*?" Brooke asked with genuine concern.

"Probably die soon. I'm old, but I don't care. Nobody here cares about old people. They used to before those nasty foreigners came. But no one cares anymore. Foreigners come through my country all the time. Then they get tired and disappear!" The next moment he fixed his fez which, in his excitement, had become unsettled on his head.

Brooke worked in this way over the course of a month: making bets, meeting owners and gambling addicts, and speaking to them. She met foreigners - Germans wearing blood-red shirts, Armenians wearing charm-pink shoes, and Englishmen donning flax-coloured Panama hats, smouldering cigars, and loose wallets - and judged from their comments that they immensely enjoyed swimming in unchartered waters, placing bets, and sometimes winning, after which they would simply fly home.

"Morocco has a varied past of state welfare provision in the form of an under-the-table social contract where the *makhzan* offers welfare to its citizens[23] in return for regime-loyalty," wrote Brooke over toast and coffee one morning as Lou pondered the loss of his smartphone charger, kissed her on the forehead, and disappeared. She performed more video-editing on her laptop, then returned to the adjacent article. "Although Morocco has attempted to improve social welfare since the transition from independent monarchy to republic in 2039, the majority of the country's social welfare remains lower than neighboring countries such as Algeria…"

"…The use of the word 'vulnerable' in this article refers to economic insecurity and whatever state of uncertainty may follow in the wake of said economic insecurity. The population of Morocco in 2079 was 32 million - half of which was made up of men[34]," wrote Brooke the following week, after an argument with Lou. She had posted two of the anonymous interviews to YouTube and had been impressed by the amount of traffic they had received. By the end of the week, they had garnered over a million views. "Research carried out by the University of Algiers on the demographic and socio-economic profile of the population showed that Moroccan and Moroccan-Sicilian men were the most vulnerable group in Morocco: low wages and high rates of incarceration in the former, and diversity quotas and gender discrimination in the latter[35]…"

"…Blacklisted studies conducted by Shriki (2081) and Kabbaj (2083) show that deprivation in Morocco - notably in the provinces of Errachidia, Dakhla, and Tangier - increases with expenditure poverty," wrote Brooke the following week. She observed her growing winnings in her online banking statement, cleaned up the grammar in the 6,000-word article, and sat on the couch considering her ethics. After shrugging off her ethics, she returned to her laptop, and changed the following: "For example, 53% of children who are expenditure poor - which Shriki defines as children below the poverty line[67] - also suffer from two additional deprivations; 62% from three deprivations, 69% from four deprivations, and a staggering 76% from five deprivations[68]…"

Tangier was situated on the northernmost tip of Morocco and boasted shipping ports, fuzzy-wuzzy leisure facilities with cooled pools and poolside cocktails, and a menagerie of taprooms, taverns, and wine-bars, that glowed at night and dulled the extremities and senses of sozzled foreign and domestic patrons during daylight hours. Beyond the city's Escher-like steps, with their cerulean-blue and bright-yellow ribbons, and the overhanging bedrooms and sitting-rooms of bone-coloured buildings whose absolute-zero shutters clattered like a hundred horseshoes, and denizens selling tapestries and rugs under black-bean electrical wires, and cigarette-smoke-suffused alleyways whose terminals held unemployed creatures, and the dilapidated squalor of Old Medina with its crackling, sandal-footed inhabitants whose rotten fruits and vegetables degenerated in the intense heat, and whose daily lives were like impoverished frames removed from an old film and posted to YouTube for foreign dignitaries and aloof novelists to examine in private, but never properly experience - beyond these things, The Republic Hotel, decked out with celadon banners and comically-large police badges for the annual Moroccan Police Convention, was an offensively misjudged idol whose sole purpose was to advance excess and finance.

Inside the hotel, police insignias and pictures of deceased officers - murdered, or probably murdered in the line of duty - lined the dark-orange hallways and corridors, where representatives from twelve Moroccan regions, retired officers, guest speakers, and ticket-buying members of the public, enjoyed long ceremonies and short dinners.

The convention's special guest was the American golfer, Spree Curtiz, who was escorted by two athletic women wearing deep-saffron dresses, and who himself wore English-red-rimmed glasses, bronze shirts, and Bermuda shorts. And so it was, that at the beginning of the final ceremony - and arseholed on methadone and tramadol to cure the excruciating back-pain from which he suffered - the famous golfer ascended the stage to intense applause to deliver his opening remarks. "Ladies and gentlemen." He adjusted his glasses to render the teleprompter readable. "It's my pleasure to be here this evening, and to represent my sport, and my nation - and to anyone who says that Morocco's closed for business, I would say, 'Then you're obviously not a golfer.'"

There followed a mixture of polite and drunken laughter from the audience.

"But let's face it, *back* - I mean, *folks*." He winced at his fiery spine. "Being a policeman is like being a golfer. We're all looking for holes. Sometimes we fill them, and sometimes we don't. Let's raise our glass to our holes, and drink to the great policemen, the good golf, and Morocco."

The female officers in the conference room - who made up sixty percent of the police force - ignored the misogyny of Spree's unusual speech, and clapped loudly as the addled golfer staggered offstage, joined his athletic handlers, and drank some gin. There followed an hour of prize-giving, with various retired officers and guest speakers announcing the prizes, handing them to their winners, and then shaking clammy palms.

After this parade of ornamental duke-blue uniforms, shining shields, and broad smiles, Lucio Vizzini ascended the stage to give the keynote address in his native Tamazight. Apart from being the caporegime of Tangier, Vizzini was also medium-sized, wore an open-necked white shirt encapsulated by a burly-wood jacket, and sported a pinched face with intense eyes that burrowed into, borrowed, and stole other gazes. "'We don't surrender - we win, or we die.' That's what Omar Mukhtar said when he was fighting the Italians in Libya…"

The two representatives from Marrakech - Zara Lachgar and Amsu Rahmouni - exchanged glances amidst the gloom of the shifting, coughing, and sniffing audience.

"The same applies to everyone attending this convention, those officers stationed around the country, and retired officers who are nonetheless bound to uphold the law. The long and short of it, my friends, is that we have been too soft on the opposition. We've been too soft on anarchists, socialists, and communists. We've been too kind to libertarians, economic liberals, and nationalists. Both sides of the political spectrum hold their threats - and both sides should be equally feared. For we serve the Moroccan Republic in a time of moral and economic distress. We are faced with calls for revolution, rebuttal, and murder - and the most the police can do is keep to those quotas we worked so hard to fabricate. And to confiscate, interrogate, and arrest. I've got news for the people in this room - and I want you to take what I say to the officers around this compromised nation and the retirees betraying our cause: what you're doing right now is not enough. You're surrendering, you're choosing to die, and you're failing to fight that spectrum with its savage colours. But those colours are not our teachers…"

His eyes blazed across the room of increasingly paranoid police officers.

"The younger generations need to understand where the power lies. The answer is that our power comes from God and that through our devout state, God is delivered with cunning, brutal accuracy. With that program of governance in mind, I hasten to add that any opposition to the ruling Green Party is dangerous, that moral depravity such as homosexuality is decadence, and that anarchists as well as libertarians must be detained. These minority groups - the sexual and political - are irrefutably equal under the law. But sometimes law must be reinterpreted so that better futures can be arrested and detained for the sake of unborn generations, and also for those still fighting today."

Vizzini welcomed Spree Curtiz back to the stage, after which he took his right hand, held it in the air for several seconds, and feigned the wiping of a solitary tear. Whistling and cheering accompanied the prolonged applause that followed. One-legged ex-officers wearing absolute-zero vests, supported by their respective wives and husbands, shouted affirmations of approval, whilst the younger generations who were actively serving stomped their feet with mad acceptance in their sorry eyes. The room was schizophrenic: ancient constabulary vows sullied by partisan politics, and the upstanding officers glued to those who were mad, bad, and dangerous to know.

Two such upstanding officers - Zara Lachgar and Amsu Rahmouni - agreed to renounce the otherwise free dinner in favour of a more private setting in Old Medina. Technically off-duty, and wearing a Spanish-violet suit and a turtle-green dress, respectively, Zara and Amsu entered a hole-in-the-wall restaurant called *Almakan Alqadim,* which literally translated to "the old place".

Inside, there were four tables covered with recyclable tablecloths, a small backlit bar with two bottles of spirits and a barista machine, and a playlist of *cha'abi* music. The officers seated themselves, ordered food and two coffees, and proceeded to hang their heads in embarrassment at what the convention had offered them. "There's a fine line between bribes and fascism," murmured Amsu in Tamazight as he stirred sugar into his coffee, "and we're about to cross it." He ground his teeth. "What the hell does Vizzini think he's doing making speeches like that in public?"

"Political parties are the new religions," replied Zara.

"But what about - "

"Keep your voice down." The Marrakech chief of police checked her watch. "They do this every year. They make a radical speech and expect the gendarmerie to fall in line. Don't sit there, wringing your hands - "

"I'm *not* wringing my hands."

Before Amsu could say anything else, the solitary waiter brought two bowls of soup, made with chickpeas, lentils, noodles, and spices, and two plates of fried sardines, stuffed with spiced tomatoes, served with lemon slices.

"Airports have been shut two summers in a row. What if they stay shut forever?" asked Amsu.

"You can't run a country like that." Zara performed open-heart surgery on one of her sardines, peeling the white flesh off of the bone. "It's not sustainable. They've started acting like second-rate *Oufkirs*," she added, referring to an infamous Head of Royal Security who had been murdered for his alleged role in the failed insurgency attempt in 1972. Then Zara swallowed her fish, and said, "This is good."

"It's called 'the old place'," said her deputy, floating into a past that he could but try to imagine. To say that the monarchy was before his time was putting it lightly. Old photographs, articles, and closed cases, which under Amsu and Zara had been re-opened, pieced together an altogether incomplete, meta-data transcript of his history. Despite the opacity of the past, Amsu found himself thinking that it would have been better if he had been born a hundred years earlier. "Not many places like this left."

"That's life," replied Zara.

Amsu finished his fried sardines. "There's something else I've been meaning to tell you. I don't know if you've been briefed."

Zara sniffed.

"Someone - "

"Who?"

"Getting there." He cracked his thick knuckles. "*Someone* is posting videos about Moroccan gamblers anonymously. They're on YouTube. They're getting a following."

The chief of police snorted. "Can they string a sentence together?"

"They're talking about business ventures, from *inside* the business ventures."

Zara relaxed the tight cloth around her turtle-green waist. "Who knows about this?"

"I'm not sure." He smiled. "I don't think Scarvaggi—"

"Don't say that name," said Zara. "Don't say that name."

"I can't imagine they're sitting around watching cat videos."

"If you're responsible for a problem, you should find the solution." She quoted a Moroccan proverb. "Any of your staff know about this?"

"Not yet. I just saw it yesterday morning. I don't wanna spread the word that there's a bunch of propaganda we can't control. Not at the annual police convention."

"There's always a way," noted Zara, finishing her soup. "Foreigner?"

"Potentially."

"Can't hurt foreigners." She raised her eyebrows. "YouTube acts like a first-world country compared to Morocco. But take my word, Amsu - they've got their own rules, and they play by those rules."

"When is Logan Paul III joining NATO?" Amsu laughed.

"That's an individual. Not a country."

"You watch; that's gonna be next."

"My point is that we shouldn't get involved. Probably this person - "

"Who, the Paul triplicate?"

"No, no – the gambler influencer. My point is that they will violate some YouTube policy, and all the videos will get removed anyway."

Amsu swiveled in his chair. "Two more coffees, please!" He looked back at his boss and prayed that she was right.

Unaware of his wife's online activity, Lou kissed her goodbye after an early supper, walked past the terra-cotta apartment blocks along the thistle-pink pavement, and entered the back door of his local mosque where a cross-section of Marrakech society was busily setting up chairs and tables, and preparing coffees, teas, and cakes.

Lou had been attending this English-language meeting of Alcoholics Anonymous for a year, and he had come to think of it as his "home-meeting". Soon the men and women were sitting on their low-backed conference chairs, and listening patiently to the introductions and calls for business so that they could make use of the sharing time, where alcoholics could share their "experience, strength and hope".

After three people had shared, Lou said, "My name is Lou, and I'm an alcoholic."

"Hi Lou," came the half-desperate, half-thrilled, collective reply.

"I'd like to thank Hamza for chairing the meeting, and everybody doing service." He reeled these things off because they were the right thing to say, and not because he believed in what he was saying. Lou had trouble deciding whether he *really was* grateful for the mechanic, the two doctors, and the schoolteacher, who had left work early so that they could serve coffee to strangers.

"I always knew I was an alcoholic," said Lou, after which he told a story familiar to everyone at that meeting: something about a black drag queen in Bermuda stroking his back and the tingling sensation he felt in his rear end; and how this made Lou doubt his sexuality, stay away from women, and drink to numb the social uncertainty he felt. Many other people shared after him, and a collection was taken for meeting expenses. Then Hamza led the group out with a prayer, and they packed up the room for the night.

Lou stepped into the night air.

The street was suffused with yellow-sunshine light from streetlights, which gave the abysses of the roads an orange tinge.

Lou adjusted his underwear through his banana-mania trousers and removed his burlywood necktie from his white shirt. He wiped the sweat away from the back of his neck and was about to make his way home when a pair of hands yanked him into a half-dimmed alleyway packed with taupe-coloured rubbish bins. Lou's heart climbed into his throat as seconds became moments, and moments ebbed. "Jesus," said Lou, as his eyes adjusted to the semi-yellow light. "Scared the shit out of me."

"Kiss my ass," said Hassan Hacimi in Tamazight. His tapered eyebrows and trimmed beard betrayed no emotion. Meanwhile, his artichoke-green, double-breasted trench-coat looked beaten up - as if it had seen too many murder investigations - and his loosened, apricot necktie seemed to be suffering from peyronie's disease.

"What?" coughed Lou.

"I said, Did you have a good meeting?"

"Yea." He had never perspired this much. "Don't tell people."

"Anonymity. I understand. It's in the name."

"I'd never think you were a detective - "

"Now, look - " He could feel the half-dissolved cake as he poked Lou's stomach. "I haven't seen anything from you in a month. You're making me *nervous*."

"Then don't call me at work." Lou was puffing as though he had run a marathon. "You're gonna make people suspicious."

"Act better," came the reply.

The property manager huffed and puffed, and walked in circles. Then he rounded on Hassan. "Look at my eyes - look at them!"

The detective was used to this.

When Hassan forced a lackey to betray their boss, it was only a short while before they panicked, and said that he was being unreasonable.

"Yea, they're red," Lou screamed in a whisper. "They're red because I can't sleep. It's like having the same fucking heart attack over and over. It's a fucking nightmare." He began to dredge excuses out of his soul: and not risible excuses used by bank clerks, which they had stolen from English pastoral novels - but more fundamental excuses, that had troubled the Western tradition since its inception on the coast of Turkey. "I'm not a miracle worker," complained Lou. "Sure, I'll get a name here, an account number there - but the whole thing is risky. It's a full-time, part-time job being a mole, and I don't know how much more I can take of this thing. I swear, I'm gonna kill myself!"

"It's funny you think you're the only one," Hassan replied.

"You mean, I'm not?"

"Would I tell you?"

"No, no - no, no, no," said Lou, walking in circles and flicking the cuticles on his index fingers, rubbing his thumbs against the displaced splints of nail, and dead skin. "No, no – no, no, no. No, no, no. When are we gonna give up trying to change stuff?"

The detective's head gleamed like some moist, mountainous rock. "The police convention was crazy. 'Let's get our tinfoil hats out. Let's tango, babies!'" He grinned wildly. "We're just touching the tip of the desert. Things are going to get worse."

"HOW COULD THINGS GET WORSE?"

The lack of any verbal reply galvanized Lou, even if Hassan's face spoke volumes, without the recent development of spoken language.

"Listen to me," whispered Lou. "You can't name anyone in this country who's innocent. You're all guilty."

"You don't understand my people."

"You think Sicilians are assholes, and you think you're innocent, that everyone here is innocent. But I'm like, What's the fucking difference?"

"There is a difference."

"You're embarrassed," said Lou, uncharacteristically shrewd.

Hassan homed in on the word. Perhaps he *was* embarrassed.

...Laura...Laura...

Embarrassed and concerned, Hassan wanted to tell Lou about how the Scarvaggi Family had blackmailed him into a contract killing.

He wanted to tell Lou about how he had played a part in Laura Donato's downfall, amidst the poles of that strong-lime-green strip club.

...Laura...Laura...

"They're cracking down on people." Hassan watched Lou in the yellow-sunshine light. "I've set a little deadline for you, and everyone else. We need to get this report to the United Nations." Then he lit a cigarette. "We need to be on the right side of history."

"We need to be on the right side of the wall when they pull the trigger," complained Lou. "I don't want to be involved."

"You live here, you *are* involved." Hassan puffed smoke towards him. "It's like in Rwanda. They sent in some troops when a massacre happened."

"Huh?"

"Yea," purred Hassan. "But you *should* be on the right side of history."

The next moment they heard footsteps and noticed a dark figure standing at the entrance of the alleyway, checking his pockets and swiveling on his noisy heels. The property manager and the detective weighed up whether he would have to be killed, packed into the boot of a car, and deposited somewhere clammy, damp, and invisible. But soon afterwards the phantom expressed a happy grunt, removed his hands from his pockets, and continued on his way to whatever late encounter had been organized.

Lou staggered to the side of the alleyway and vomited against the foundation wall. Hassan winced as Lou spat and wiped his mouth. "Next Thursday," muttered Lou.

"Where?"

"Rue El Baz."

"What will you have for me?"

The property manager aligned his back, staring unhealthily as he half-stumbled, half-walked towards the detective. "You're gonna find out."

"More about Nina. We need to prove that orders come from her directly."

Lou cursed under his breath as he wiped his ex-white shirt. "You want Moroccans? Alami-Russo, Zaki-Vaccaro, Harrak-Costa?"

"They're not Moroccan," Hassan corrected him.

Lou resented the sensation of having specks of vomit in his nasal passages as much as what Hassan had implied. "So, what are they?"

"Tourists." He flicked his cigarette butt onto the ground. "You are a tourist too, Lou, but you want to leave this country because you don't like the smell when you get up." He returned to the yellow-sunshine-hued street, stepped into his unmarked police car with one of the women from the meeting, and penciled in their next encounter.

Brooke scratched away the café-au-lait laminations from *Cardinal Doubler, 12 Pays of Christmas, Bingo Bonus,* and *Bank The Cash,* whose laminations were cadmium-green - *Black and Gold, Cashword Blocks, Dice Towers, Festive Fortune* and *Jewel Smash,* whose laminations were cameo-pink, Chinese-violet, and chartreuse - *Golden Fortune,*

Holiday Cash, Jungle Jackpot, Merry Millionairess, Lucky Drop, Money Tree Multiplier and *Sapphire Multiplier*, whose laminations were deep-sky-blue, and *Hot Money, Get Fruit, 100 Dirham Multiplier, Red Hot Numbers* and *Piggy Bank*, which offended Brooke because her face resembled the cartoon hoglets. Jumping up from the couch, she strutted into the bathroom, and observed her cheeks in the mirror.

She remembered that she hadn't won any money.

She fetched her seal-brown handbag and walked downstairs, her Russian-violet heels echoing around the dark-salmon walls, and hurting the ears of cockroaches.

A brisk walk down the street culminated in *Vizzini's V-Stop*. The bell dinged as Brook stepped inside and surveyed the frozen foods section. Except she hadn't come for food - she had come for scratch-cards.

The manager, Madame Jabal, had a Washingtonian pair of false teeth that clicked as Brooke approached the desk with a *Valverde*-brand frozen pizza.

"And a *Merry Millionairess*," said Brooke in bad Arabic.

Shuffling disconsolately towards the scratch-card rack, Madame Jabal removed the scratch-card, slapped it on the counter, and said the total.

"Thank you," said Brooke as she tapped her bank card, picked up the pizza and her scratch-card, and clicked out of the corner shop.

Someone said her name. She swung round to find her husband standing with his loosened burlywood necktie. "How you doing, babes?"

They kissed gently.

"You got off work early - where's the car?" asked Brooke.

"Garage. Air-conditioning's buggered. This weather - "
The batwing of his thumb and index finger dragged across
his mouth and chin. "Who's cooking?"

"It's not time for - " She embarrassedly checked her
watch. "Yes, it is."

"Is that dinner?" He noticed the text on the pizza. "Huh.
That's *Augustu's* name."

She managed to hide the scratch-card. She walked her
husband home, put the pizza in the oven, and went to the
bathroom. She switched on the light, ignoring her visage in
the mirror. Out came the *Merry Millionairess.* She scratched
the various laminations using her house keys, watching the
café-au-lait shavings fall onto the bathmat.

When she saw that she hadn't won anything, she threw
the card into the tub. After folding her arms, and standing
there for several moments, she fetched the scratch-card.

"You alright?" came a voice through the door.

"Yea, I'm fine."

"Remember to flush."

"Shut up," laughed Brooke. "You strange man."

"Ladies and gentlemen," said the street performer in
Tamazight. He wore a spring-frost robe, and he was holding
a traffic cone. "Let me introduce you to the Public Highway
Orchestra." He pointed to another shabby-looking man

wearing russet-brown shorts and a white undervest. He handed the traffic cone to his co-worker, and the man sat cross-legged on the cobblestones, and blew hard into the plastic tube. "The only Public Highway Orchestra in Morocco," said the robed man as he and his associate failed to persuade any of the disturbed onlookers to part with their dirhams. "Take it from the top, Yousef!" Once again, the traffic cone was hollowed out with something between a mating call, and a fire alarm.

Meanwhile, Brooke walked behind the Public Highway Orchestra. Lou had been invited to a dinner at *Accursio's*, which meant that Brooke had the evening to herself. Having persuaded herself that she ought to do more research for her journalism, she decided to visit the nearest casino, where she could slip into her subjects' shoes.

The Trinacria was a large casino with sequential royal-purple and royal-yellow lights. As the Public Highway Orchestra played another rendition of *Ode to My Mother-In-Law*, Brooke walked onto the quick-silver carpet, under the radical-red arches, and into the gleaming and beeping casino.

Brooke moved to the blackjack table.

Outside of her research, she was a novice, but she knew her way around a pack of playing cards. The fez-wearing croupier welcomed five players, including Brooke, with a description of the well-stocked bar at the far end of *The Trinacria*. Then they started.

Ten of Hearts, Six of Diamonds, Six of Cloves.

Brooke sucked her teeth and tapped her Russian-violet heels. She sipped from a plastic cup of red wine, and said, "Again."

Four of Cloves, Three of Diamonds, King of Clubs.

"Come on."

Two of Hearts, Seven of Hearts, Two of Hearts, Ten of Diamonds.

"Sorry," said Brooke in bad Arabic.

She took her neighbor's chips, flashed a winning smile at the handsome, plump-purple-suited man, and continued playing.

Her winning streak not only grabbed the attention of several pastel-pink-suited onlookers, but also a dark-liver-suited man who was watching in the security office. He zoomed the camera into the table, and watched the worrisome croupier sweating.

Brooke lost everything. Then she gained everything.

A gaggle of admirers wearing rusty-red dresses, saddle-brown jackets, and shadow-blue trousers, gathered around the blackjack table, and their presence belied Brooke's inexperience as she vaulted from affluence, to bankruptcy, and then back again.

The schizophrenic seventh heaven of winning-cum-losing warmed Brooke's stomach and told her that the other players and the croupier were complete morons.

The croupier removed his fez. He began the cycle again, but his hands froze like rusted cogs when he saw a dark-liver-hued blob approaching.

"Hello, Brooke."

Reality replaced the warmth with lukewarm confusion, not unlike accepting the wrong meal at a family-run restaurant, and Brooke recognized the voice.

She turned to find Salvatore. The grotesque lighting disguised his large stomach and lessened the blobbish effect of his overflowing neck, but otherwise, he looked healthy and distracted the crowd with his pristine white shirt and his bright white hair. He picked up her plastic cup and sniffed the boozy odour. "Frappato. Your wedding." He waved on the croupier. He took Brooke by the hand and led her away from the table.

"I was about to surrender," said Brooke.

"I'm not surprised, you know." He grinned, but his grip was firm. "It's best to get out when you're winning…"

The bar was a long affair with strawberry seats. It was manned by a bartender with a glass eye, who wore a royal-blue apron and rifle-green trousers. "Monsieur Yannucci," said the man in Arabic.

"Hello," replied Salvatore. "Show me the wine glass for Frappato."

The barman pulled out a broad glass and placed it on the counter.

"Mmm." The old man observed the glass. "For a moment, I thought it was fake."

The barman laughed. "No, Monsieur Yannucci."

Salvatore slammed the plastic cup on the counter. Wine splashed everywhere. "Then why is she drinking out of this trash?"

"She wasn't a member."

"If you give her plastic, why would she want to be?"

A moot point, thought the barman. "Please, accept my apologies."

"I don't know why you're talking to me." The old man knew full well that the barman's English was not up to snuff. "Apologise to her, in the King's English."

A race memory of a Moroccan monarch flashed through the barman's brain. Then he realised that Brooke must be British or something. "Sorry," he said in English.

"More poetry," suggested Salvatore.

"The biggest apologies, madame." The next moment he filled the empty glass with red wine, and pushed the top-heavy vessel towards her. "No need to pay money."

"It's fine - thank you," said Brooke.

Salvatore sniffed the air to make sure that the barman had poured the same wine into the glass. "That's good."

He put his hand behind Brooke's back. "Sorry about that." And the strange couple stepped past flashing fruit machines and Paris-green poker tables. "How are things?"

"They're good."

"Are you still working with Meera Balakrishnan?" Before she could answer, he said, "I think she works too hard, but lawyers are like that. Lawyers talk to other lawyers. They marry them. They have children."

"Incest."

"I'm sorry about my English," laughed Salvatore. "I should be more careful."

"It's okay. I'm actually trying to get a job at the *Morocco Examiner*."

"Really?"

"Yea, really. I got on with the editor." She disliked the lull in the conversation. "I'm hoping to start there next year."

"No."

The strange response half-irritated Brooke. "I am."

"You won't work there. There will be something else."

"Um - okay - thanks for the wine…"

They stopped walking and looked at one another. The right side of Salvatore's face was highlighted by a paradise-pink fruit machine being throttled by a drunk man.

"Does Lou know you're here?" asked Salvatore.

"He doesn't *need* to know."

"There are these young people who work for me. They tell me that women prefer to gamble online."

"Well, I'm pretty exceptional, Sal."

The white-haired underboss examined her reaction, motionless on his thick dark-liver legs, letting his huge hands hang by his sides. "Enjoy your wine." He raised his hands like a showman. "Enjoy the casino! I take an interest in it. The crown-and-anchor tables are very popular. Lou told me that the sailors like to play the game in Bermuda."

He escorted Brooke over to a table in the corner of the casino.

Apart from the croupier and several players in raw-sienna jackets, there was no one else milling about this section of the otherwise teeming carpeted floors of *The Trinacria*. Three six-sided dice - each with crowns, anchors, spades, hearts, diamonds, and clubs - were used, along with a board that also contained those symbols. The players put their bets on their favoured symbols on the board, after which the croupier would throw the dice from a rose-bonbon cup. Payoffs corresponded with the frequency of corresponding shapes. For example, when Brooke put ten dirhams on the crown, two crowns were rolled, and she subsequently received twenty dirhams back.

She learned that simplicity was dangerous. What did it matter if one went through this process five times - or twenty times - or thirty times?

By the time the rajah-coloured sun had pierced the windows, Brooke had lost everything three times. Then Salvatore hobbled back towards the table - unaffected by the inexorable passage of time - and waved on the croupier, drawing Brooke aside.

"It's bad luck," said the underboss.

"I'm sorry," said Brooke, rubbing her cheeks. "I'm sorry. There was - it was going well - but then it's like the whole table turns against you."

"I understand. Hunger is the best sauce."

"That's good. I like that."

"It's late." He retracted his dark-liver sleeve and checked his watch. "But I can give you a marker."

Casino markers were short-term, interest-free lines of credit that casinos could give to customers for gambling purposes. But Brooke had to pay it back in thirty days.

"But - I'll go to prison if I don't pay it back - "

"You won't go to prison. You're much too pretty."

"I'm looking for a quick comeback..." The implications of what she had done began to sink into her brain, like teeth into a slice of Victoria Sponge Cake.

After an hour, Brooke had used the casino marker. "Madame," said the croupier at the crown and anchor table. "I will have to ask you to leave."

"Where's your boss?"

"He went home an hour ago, madame." He rubbed his red eyes with one hand, whilst the other pressed a button. "Please, the casino will shut."

"What time do you close?" asked Brooke with desperation.

The table-games manager appeared. She was a tall woman with bright eyes, wearing a purple-pizzazz blouse, and skirt. "Madame, this way, please," said the table-games manager, as Brooke departed the crown-and-anchor table, dragging her feet.

In the security office, Salvatore sat hunched over a small screen. "Buyer beware," said the underboss, watching Brooke's blurry shape getting escorted out of the building by the Amazonian. He could hear the noise of that be-robed street performer, and his lugubrious sidekick, as they introduced the Public Highway Orchestra to the wandering Germans and Frenchmen, and all the deprived locals on their way to underpaid jobs.

In an unmarked queen-blue police car, Sergeant Fatima Ahmed and Constable Inés Harrak waited patiently for a peach-puff police wagon to park behind them. Ahmed turned her angular face to her smartphone, checking that they had the right address:

Rue El Baz. Number Seventeen.

Adjusting her hair-bun, Ahmed turned to her hijab-wearing companion. "Do you want to knock on the door?"

"You can knock, if you want to?"

"I don't; but it's good experience."

"How about you knock and I talk?"

Sergeant Ahmed sighed. They stepped out of the car and walked towards the raw-umber building, with its New-York-pink door.

Ahmed knocked.

The door opened to show a middle-aged man wearing oxblood shorts, and a pale-aqua tee shirt. He also had an afro and smelled like sandalwood.

"Yes?" asked the man, remembering the trade-off he had witnessed between two suspicious-looking men a month prior. Whereas one seemed to have been a policeman, the other looked like an accountant with his banana-mania suit and red-rimmed eyes.

"Are you Moustapha Alami?" asked Harrak in Tamazight.

"Yes?"

"I regret to inform you that you and your wife, Penelope, have been identified as agitators by the Ministry of Security. You are expected to take part in the relocation process, which will re-house you in Dakhla."

Moustapha paused open-mouthed. "But we're insurance auditors." The next moment Penelope appeared next to her husband. "What's going on?" she asked.

"I regret to inform you that you and your husband, Moustapha, have been identified as agitators by the Ministry of Security. You are expected to take part in the relocation process, which will re-house you in Dakhla," repeated Sergeant Harrak, sounding like a passive-aggressive automaton.

"That's ridiculous," replied Penelope.

Sergeant Ahmed pushed her colleague aside. "Your husband is Shia Muslim, and you're a Christian. You will be relocated to Dakhla in accordance with the Anti-Terrorism Act."

"But neither of us are practicing."

"Are you refusing to move?"

"Yes!" said Moustapha and Penelope.

Harrak walked to the police wagon, where she knocked on the side of the vehicle, and armed police stormed out of the back, securing the street and arresting the couple. Moustapha and Penelope screamed and shouted as they were dragged into the police wagon. As Ahmed and Harrak returned to their unmarked police car, a large convoy of similar police wagons made its way down the street behind them: peach-puff vehicles designed to match the dry landscape as they made their way down to Dakhla…

After weeks of digging and shifting earth in the atomic-tangerine desert, the communist revolutionaries had created a series of interconnected tunnels whose walls spritzed fulvous-orange dust onto the apricot- and beaver-brown walkways. Along these walkways were diesel-powered mining lights, kerosene lamps, and bioluminescent sticks, all of which crisscrossed colours in the otherwise dark spaces. This underworld was on the deserted edge of Dakhla, and it provided shelter during the day, and a place from which they could run night-operations.

The meeting of the revolutionary committee had been convened for the morning, and its military-green-wearing members filled a cramped study, replete with beach chairs, folding metal tables, cheap denim-coloured rugs, and kerosene lamps. They were an altogether sickly affair, with gaunt drawn faces, hollow trousers, unkempt hair in various stages of growth, or baldness, and chapped lips from the heat.

Ismail stroked his small beard as the committee members made their cases for the revolutionary army to be moved from Dakhla to the Mauritanian border. "This way," said the Energy Minister in Arabic, "we can fulfil our obligation to the Mauritanians. They sent us weapons, fuel, and food after the Algerians dropped out - and since the revolution continues in Mauritania, we need to be able to fight *alongside* them. Without the purification of Mauritania's provisional government," added the Energy Minister with pompous flare, "we may very well be setting our own operations up for disaster. Suppose, for example, that anti-revolutionary actors take over the otherwise revolutionary provisional government? Well, they certainly won't be interested in bringing the revolution to Morocco. They're going to become evil protectionists."

The Deputy Leader burped, covering his mouth. "I agree with our comrade Energy Minister. Staying outside of Dakhla is a risk. The Scarvaggis will find us."

In stepped the Information Minister. She was late for the meeting, and sat cross-legged on a denim-coloured rug. "The floor is yours," said Ismail, stroking his beard.

"The Scarvaggis are arresting minorities."

Outrage in the underground chamber.

The Defence Minister shook his head, the Energy Minister swore, and the Deputy Leader burped. The others stared into their thin laps or puffed out their chests in rejection. "Who told you this? The mole?" asked Ismail gently.

"Yes," said the Information Minister. "They started in Marrakech. But they're going to do the same thing throughout the country."

"And where are they sending them?" asked the Defence Minister.

"To Dakhla."

The others noted the development in silence, apart from the Culture Minister, who said, "Very few cinemas; only the occasional opera; a fate worse than death…"

"Dakhla doesn't have the capacity," interrupted the Defence Minister.

"But the desert does," said the Information Minister. "Cuz that's where they're going. They're going to storm the phosphate mine in Inal - return the favour…"

"Morocco doesn't own the mine," Ismail said. "They don't have mineral rights. They're going to start a war, acting like that - "

"But they have shipping rights," corrected the Information Minister. "And the Scarvaggis say that they haven't been given what they were promised. So, they're going to storm the place, pick up what they're owed, and head back to Morocco."

"The provisional government must have sanctioned it," the Energy Minister said.

"They did. The Mauritanian mine manager refused to play ball with the Scarvaggis. Now the Mauritanians are punishing him – against their own code, their own beliefs."

"What did I tell you?" interrupted the Energy Minister, staring around the cavern. "They're no better than the Scarvaggis!"

"Politicians," said the Defence Minister.

"Peasants," said Ismail.

"Although we need the weapons," said the Defence Minister, turning to face Ismail. "General Secretary, we cannot afford to alienate the Mauritanian Party of Communists. We need food, fuel, and weapons."

"Send them back," replied Ismail quietly.

An impossible wind shook the flickering kerosene flames. The multifarious ministers observed their General Secretary. "The Scarvaggis will bring supplies with the prisoners. They're going to turn Dakhla into an ordnance depot with ammo, vehicles, and food." He looked around the room. "We're going to be waiting for them."

"Lou, my nephew!" said the podgy woman, her bingo butterflies flapping around her old-lavender-patterned blouse. Her shawarma stall in the bustling *Bell Market* drew customers from across Marrakech. But her favourite customer - because he spent the most money there - was Lou Baring, who would munch on her seasoned meat and spicy-vegetable sandwiches, gulp down her lemon-flavoured olives, and drink her freshly squeezed orange juice on the extensive lunch breaks he had come to enjoy.

"Hey, auntie," replied Lou as he bumped her recycled-plastic-covered fist and looked down at the charcoaled meats, bowls of olives, and jugs of juice.

In the meantime, she noticed a big bulge over Lou's banana-mania-coloured beltline. His thighs looked larger than before, and he had more flesh around his neck.

"God forbid he ends up like Yannucci," thought the podgy woman.

"Busy morning?" asked Lou.

"It's always a good morning," replied the woman in perfect English. "There was a fight by the *Khobz* stall. But Rafiq - with the mighty moustache - he fought them off."

"Uh," said Lou.

"Now, sauce or vegetables on the shawarma?"

"Just the sauce, please."

"Okay." She squirted an old-lace line from a recycled plastic tube. "Orange juice?"

"Not today, thanks."

She beeped his card on her contactless port and served the next customer.

"Come on," whispered Lou as he struggled to zip up his pants. Through the door to the bathroom, he could see Brooke applying foundation to her glistening cheeks. "Almost - *there.*" Realising that the zipper would be damaged, Lou stopped short of securing his crotch completely, and the tag dangled precariously under an open V.

"You alright?" asked Brooke from the bathroom.

"Yea, yea, yea." He sucked in his stomach, pretending to walk as though his buttocks weren't in extreme discomfiture. The thighs were the most uncomfortable, their semi-circular girth strangled by Lou's banana-mania trouser-shackles. He tied his shoelaces in the air and tied his burlywood necktie around his collar.

"How long you gonna be in there?" asked the property manager.

"You're grumpy."

"No, *you* get grumpy when you go out for food. I know you don't like eating out; I'm gonna try to be delicate when we sit down."

"You're grumpy, Lou. You're in a rush."

"I'm not rushing. It's just - I don't - it's weird having the first-anniversary meal."

"It doesn't have to be perfect."

"But you *want* it to be perfect."

"No, I don't - "

"Yes, you do."

"Alright, alright," muttered Brooke.

"Uh," said Lou.

Sometime later, Brooke finished her makeup and walked into the bedroom. Lou sat disconsolately on a bedside chair. He watched his pithy stomach rising and falling.

"I'm sorry about the scratchcards," said Brooke.

"I don't care if you do scratchcards."

"You seem like you do," urged the investigative journalist.

"No. I'll be in the kitchen." Lou stood up and walked out of the bedroom. Brooke accepted that she had committed to worse things than scratchcards. She checked

the contents of her seal-brown handbag and stood in
the middle of the room as she thought about what had
happened over the past year, with its compromises and
adjustments, its irresponsibilities and insecurities, and
its backbones and shortcomings. She joined Lou in the
kitchen and walked downstairs to the pacific-blue taxi
which had pulled up in front of their apartment building,
blaring out loud *Qawwali* chords.

After being seated at their table in *Accursio's*, Lou and
Brooke ordered lemonades and were disturbed by the utter
lack of strangers in the swarming Sicilian restaurant. They
knew the waiters and waitresses, the occasionally visible
chefs, Meera Balakrishnan and her judicial posse, Baaqa
Bell and her Scarvaggi Family soldiers, and an assortment
of dour dentists, bankers, solicitors, and hoteliers on their
nights off.

"I see what you mean," said Lou.

"What?"

"You talk about knowing everyone. We know *all* these
people." When his wife said nothing, he added, "Do you
want a limoncello?"

"No, I'm fine."

"You can have one. I don't mind."

"Lou - " She fanned herself with the pansy-purple
menu. "I don't want one." The fact that Lou had booked
the restaurant and didn't seem to realise his hypocrisy,
added further rancour to the simmering non-exchanges that
accompanied their anniversary.

The waiter returned to take their orders and removed their menus.

The food arrived not long after. The fried eggplant with parmesan and melted mozzarella was placed in front of Lou's greedy fingers, while the golden fried calamari with whitebait and garlic aioli was positioned before Brooke's neutral gaze. A large party on the furthest edges of the new rufous-coloured carpeting were singing happy birthday, as a shiny-shamrock cake, carried by two waiters, was brought to the table and placed before the animated daughter of a Ugandan diplomat. Brooke's neutrality towards the restaurant broke new grounds of passion, and she found herself watching the little Ugandan girl enjoying the bright colours and sounds around her, subsequently resting her head against the chest of her laughing father. "…Happy birthday to you!" concluded the chorus as surround-sound applause began, clouding the bustling table.

When Brooke looked back, she found Lou staring at her.

"What's the matter?" asked the property manager with bits of eggplant in his teeth.

"You don't like those videos I do."

"I don't want to talk about that in public - " He dragged his tie over his eggplant as he leaned forward conspiratorially. "They make a lot of people I know look bad."

"Can't have that, can we?"

"What - what do - ?"

"You're a people-pleaser."

Lou laughed. "It's lucrative."

"What's funny? Nothing's funny about that - "

"I'm laughing because we can't enjoy ourselves."

"No practice. And I know why *you* don't like my videos." Lou winced as Brooke added, "It's because you think I've got a gambling problem."

"When did I say that?" asked Lou.

"Christ, you don't have to say things. You don't have to talk. It's the way you act, Lou, that's how I can see what you're thinking - "

"I know you hate me saying this." He prepared for the very worst, as the waiter removed their half-empty plates. "Try going to Al-Anon."

"Oh my God, with the fucking Al-Anon. Because they don't mind their own business - that's *why* I don't go do Al-Anon."

"Sounds like a resentment," Lou advised.

"I've got hatreds, reservations and fears, and I'm sat here eating Italian food - "

"Sicilian - "

"That doesn't matter. I'm sat here, and the country's falling apart."

"Huh?"

"Lou, listen."

But she just smiled when a waiter returned with her tender lamb rump, with balsamic and rosemary jus. And then Lou received his prawn risotto with parmesan.

At once they were both hungry, and not-hungry, maybe poised to recoil altogether.

Lou picked up a prawn, made it dance on the edge of the bowl, and looked between it and Brooke, making amazed/bemused expressions.

"Child," surmised Brooke.

"He's been training all year."

"Lou - "

"He's got awards. Look at those sugary moves."

"It's weird saying this after a year of being married. But - " She poked the lamb rump with her fork. "I didn't tell you everything about my dad."

Lou tossed the dancing prawn back into the bowl and looked at Brooke.

"He didn't *just* have a heart attack," said the investigative journalist.

"Huh?"

"He was - he drank, and - I didn't want to - you were sensitive about that stuff, and I just forgot about it - because we started taking things seriously and I didn't want - "

"Was he an alcoholic?"

Brooke nodded. "But that doesn't mean - Lou, I wanted to be with you. But I thought you knew all along - is that why you got mad?"

"No, no – no, no, no. You have to work. That's how you feel, and - "

"That's right. I want to work."

Lou slammed down his cutlery and breathed quickly. Several customers turned to face their table and the apparent racket. But Brooke ignored the clientele, shooed away an impending waitress, and returned her understanding gaze to Lou, who sighed loudly.

"Lou." She touched his hand. "You're so tense."

"It's just - that thing with Sal." Affecting a glance between anger and apology, Brooke listened to her husband's question. "Why'd you take money from him?"

"I was doing my research. I wanted to know what it was like - "

"Yea, then watch a movie. Watch a soap opera." The sound of his hissing nostrils accompanied his wary glances around the dinner table. "Jesus Christ, Brooke."

"You want to find me a sponsor?" asked Brooke, half-laughing. Except the humour was wasted on Lou, who just shook his heavy head.

"What? You wouldn't help me?" asked Brooke.

Lou passive-aggressively forked prawn risotto under his aquiline nose. "Are you saying you've got a problem?"

"No."

"Good." He forked more prawn risotto into his mouth. "Pass the salt."

She put the salt by his elbow and stared dolefully at her lamb rump. The fat had congealed on the plate. Then she looked up, and said, "Lou?"

"Uh-huh."

"This place is no good." When no reply came, she repeated herself: "This place is no good. The whole country - it's no good for us. We were happy in London - when you flew back and forth. Not because you weren't there half the time - but when you got there, you relaxed. Because here, all people care about is looking good. Plenty of people do that in London, but it's not the way of life - here, it's the gospel. This isn't just me, Lou - I've heard things. That's one of the problems with being a journalist - you hear things from normal people. They don't live in some bubble - and they're saying there are communists at the border, waiting to storm the whole country. The only thing worse than that is the bloody *makhzan* here - they're no better than the French a couple of hundred years ago. They don't belong here; they have no rights. All they do is make money out of people's suffering - I've seen it, Lou - it's horrible."

"Shut up," whispered Lou as another prawn went by the wayside.

"Just be serious for a minute - "

"No, you be serious." He put his fork down. "You're scared of all those people, but what about Moroccans? They're not saints. They beat donkeys, and they sit around kicking monkeys, and they strangle snakes!"

"Oh, so you think they're primitive?"

"You saying I'm some racist? Yee-haw, and all that shit?" Bermuda seeped back into his blood, his actions, his mid-Atlantic accent. "Shit, you ought to be grateful - "

"Is that what Sal told you?" She watched as Lou maintained the silence that he preferred by half-mouthing words and failing to make any rebuttal. "Because I know my husband's not a wanker." Gradually his face began to soften. "They're making you act like one. I'm not gonna have it. I like being married to you, but when you quit drinking, you have to fill that hole with something. That's what they tell you, isn't it?"

"You have to fill it with God."

"Why didn't you fill it with me?" Brooke hissed.

A prolonged silence poured over the table's cup and stained the rufous-coloured carpet. Then that shameful recognition began to stir the resentful minds sitting at the table, and Brooke and Lou refused to accept that the other was wrong, or vice versa, and their year of marriage had begun to crack and fracture, and all this happened whilst a birthday came to its end in the background, and a little girl fell asleep on her father.

"Can't love be God?" hissed Brooke as she privately mourned her wasted lamb rump. That, and she noticed the dark-liver-hued blob of Salvatore on the other side of the room, his eyes darting between an incorrectly cooked steak, and Brooke and Lou. "I'll be at home," said Brooke. She collected her seal-brown handbag, and said to herself, "Just be at home…" before she walked to the befogged glass door and exited. Staring at the headboard of the empty chair, Lou half-listened to the hubbub of the bustling restaurant, forking mouthfuls of prawn risotto into his mouth. The food had lost its flavour, the rufous-hued carpet had turned into a swamp, and all around the restaurant, whose lighting had been lowered to a dim-cum-romantic level, Lou searched for someone he could talk to - except they had all turned into foreigners…

The convoy of black Chevrolet suburban limousines made its way to Nina Scarvaggi's townhouse in Marrakech. One by one, the long vehicles deposited expensive-suited men and women, watched them enter the black-coral building, and drove away down the frightened boulevard. These figures hopped up the staircase, and, once inside, were protected from the oppressive heat by air-conditioning and double-glazed windows. The homely foyer's potted cacti and paintings led to the upper floors where the meeting would be held. Meanwhile, the last suburban limousine pulled up and out stepped Salvatore Yannucci in his dark-liver suit, and Augustu Valverde in his charcoal-grey suit. Augustu handed one of the young men, with their fulvous-orange trousers and white shirts, his dark-Byzantium fedora.

The underboss and the consigliere were subsequently shown to the second floor, where they were half-announced, half-thrown into the boardroom, after which they squeezed into their chairs at the table, where they enjoyed canapés, fruit, and anonymous bottled sparkling water.

At the other end, Faiz Impellizzeri sat next to Mohammed Zaki-Vaccaro. The two men lit cigarettes, taking delicate sips of sparkling water between nibbles of porchetta.

"How bad are things down there?" asked Mohammed in Tamazight.

"I don't know," replied Faiz, between mouthfuls.

Mohammed rolled his eyes.

"They come and they go. They steal things. They cut electrical wires. They like the water pipes, too. They gotta go before the convoy comes," Faiz admitted.

Mohammed rolled a slice of porchetta. "Not too bad. But if they stick around - "

"My hunch is, they're gonna run out of food."

"Old reliable," laughed Mohammed, enjoying the sensation of the porchetta sweating in his mouth. "It's a good thing it's *your* problem…"

Faiz wanted to think about everything. But he didn't know how to do that.

Elsewhere, Augustu and Salvatore were in the midst of an argument. Augustu narrowed his hibernating eyes and said, "You have *got* to hold Brooke to account. The good thing about Baaqa is that she's persuasive; not as destructive as Laura was."

"But that's Lou's *wife*," said Salvatore, cracking his thick fingers, and rocking backwards, and forwards, to make himself more comfortable.

"She needs to pay it back, with interest," stated Augustu.

"The company needs stability. If we start hurting the wives of our business partners, the whole company will fall apart."

"We're talking about one man and his wife, and she happens to owe us money."

"You're here for advice, we don't have to take it."

Augustu touched the right side of his silver skullcap of finely combed hair. He sniffed quietly, and said, "The decision sits with the boss, then."

The consigliere turned his hollow cheeks towards Nina, who was slouched at the head of the table. Her sun-cracked face had softened, but the change had aged her. The Falu-red blouse hanged, more than rested, on her frail body, and the high forehead that had once inspired wisdom and decision-making now conjured a muted presence. The exhausted brain now simply lay there, as it were, occasionally absorbing sunlight. But she noticed Augustu - and had heard their conversation - and picked up a plate of fresh cannoli, creaked forward in the high-backed chair, and passed the plate down to her squabbling underlings. The old woman relaxed back into her chair and caged her rickety fingers. She nodded at Salvatore, who plucked two cannoli from the plate, shoved them in his mouth, and sent the plate back up. Having watched this trade-off, Augustu raised his eyebrows and rested his eyes on the wilting canapés. "Hunger is the best sauce," said Nina in Sicilian, watching Salvatore's grin. "But sometimes we can eat too much." The old woman's brain evaporated again, and she creaked backwards in her high-backed chair, observing the occupied table. In particular, she watched Manfredi Mazzarrone, the caporegime of Oriental, as he clicked his fat tongue between mouthfuls of smoked salmon and boasted about his new townhouse. He wore a pullman-brown suit, suspenders, and a purple necktie, and his flat nose clashed with his pointed ears, which made him look like a resentful tapir. He laughed at someone's joke, slathered a cracker with black-olive-hued caviar, threw his head back, tossed the cracker in, and munched contentedly. Refusing to concede to unwanted food, he turned red and frowned. He clamped his hands around his throat and leapt out of his chair, his upper body corkscrewing anticlockwise in convulsions. He fell back onto the expensive burgundy carpeting, and twitched and frothed, before meeting his embarrassed maker.

Nina clapped her hands.

(The long table of caporegimes turned to look at the head of the Scarvaggi Family. Their expressions varied from the disinterested, to the terrified.)

"The food is good," said Nina in Sicilian. Her skinny jawline went to and fro. "That bug was helping Algerians to send weapons to those communists. He's been making himself a tidy sum. He bought that townhouse, didn't he? I like to pay my family, but I don't pay *that* well." She took out a small black cigar and lit the end. She puffed for a moment. "Mauritania doesn't want to help that scum. But they've got the same money-God, so they feel like they have to help those commies in the desert." She coughed. "That's why they can't find work, running shops. But - " She pointed around the room. The vein of bone-coloured smoke charted song-lines out of the cigar's tip, and they seemed to indicate a large map on the wall behind Nina: all sand, and lines. "We're going to shut the door in the desert. We're going to start with that phosphate mine."

On the floor, Manfredi Mazzarrone stared up at the ceiling, a terrible stink emanating from his once-flawless pair of pullman-brown trousers.

From the couch, Lou heard the front door open, and close. He removed his burlywood necktie and stood up from the couch as he watched Brooke enter the kitchen. Before Brooke said anything, she ran across the room and shut the window, because massive storm clouds had gathered.

"Sorry," said Lou.

The next moment a rattling rain followed the heavy thunder and hammered the windows, filling the otherwise silent kitchen with the violence of nature and weather.

"How was it?" asked Lou.

Brooke had attended another Al-Anon meeting. She had spoken with the other wives and husbands of alcoholics and had swiftly concluded that they were nuts. Then again, she figured that she was half-insane too. Maybe that's what being married to an alcoholic did to people. Maybe she had ruined her mind on her own terms, before this...

"It was okay," came the reply.

"I guess they told you to - "

"Come back, yes, they said that." She dropped her seal-brown handbag on the battleship-grey kitchen counter.

"Will you?" asked Lou against the murky backdrop of sodden city lights, brown sugar buildings, and wriggling electrical wires dancing in the half-hurricane outside.

Brooke rubbed her face, wincing with indecision, impending regret, and possible deliverance - *not joyousness*, but proper emancipation.

"Getting re-elected's really easy," said Lou, changing the subject completely. "All you have to do is fix the infrastructure. Uh-huh. Make sure the drains work well. But right now, look at it - we've had floods - "

"Come here," said Brooke, escorting the property manager to the couch. She sat down and quickly removed her Russian-violet heels. "I want to have a serious chat."

"Uh-huh."

"About Morocco, and living here."

"Uh."

"Okay-so-basically-I-hate-it. I've done a lot of research about the state of the country, its healthcare system, the amount of poverty, living wages. And it's terrible. But there's something worse, because every time I start piecing things together, something gets in the way. Something missing - some date or person - and it's finished. There's nothing else I can do. And it's frustrating because I can't understand this place, but I know you like it, and that confuses me because I'm married to you."

She cupped her mouth and stopped herself from crying. "It's such a weird country - because the people I've spoken to want things to change. But nothing's getting done about it - and they *know* that nothing's gonna change. They just, sort of, accept that - and I don't want to live like that. I don't have to - not now."

Lou stared into the distance.

He observed the Columbian-blue fridge handles, cinnamon-satin high chairs, dark-khaki suspension lamps, and battleship-grey counters and cupboards.

Old Uncle Lou
Give me more, give me more, give me more
When the girls have sex on the floor
They say Old Uncle Lou, give me more

He observed the duke-blue oven and toaster, and the dark-goldenrod cupboard-handles. The cupboards seemed to look unfinished.

"Lou?" asked Brooke, realizing that the kitchen had stolen her husband's scrutiny.

Hum it, Ham it, Hack it, Hayek
Hayek, now, baby, don't put that Keynes on me

I say, Hum it, Ham it, Hack it, Hayek
Hayek, now, baby, don't put that Keynes on me

You got me spending all this green like a clown
Just look at me

"Are you listening?" asked Brooke.

The eerie black of the storm clouds produced more thunder. Lightning struck a housing block across the street, and the room seemed to shake.

"Uh," said Lou.

"Do you remember that time in the hotel room? When we first met?" For a moment, Brooke had turned into that little girl in the restaurant whom she had envied. Then her current circumstances returned, and she aged inexorably in the clear kitchen. "There was someone who called - do you remember? I think it was a woman - but that's - that doesn't matter - and you said something about wanting to be on your own. You wanted to meet people, and talk to them, and make friends - all the normal things." She winced but realised that hurting his feelings would be inescapable. "I got the impression that everyone here used you, and that - you didn't think I would. I mean - spouses use each other - but I didn't use you, like a tool or something. Not like these people - and they don't love you, Lou - I don't have to tell you that - "

"Why are you?"

"Because if *you* can't be bothered to fix it - and *I* can't be bothered to fix it - then we're buggered. The - what we're doing - the life we have - is going to be buggered."

Lou looked down amidst another roll of thunder. "What I should be fixing?"

"The only people you see, are people at work. You get angry and have meltdowns, and now, the only thing left to do, is to leave Morocco."

"I don't enjoy the meltdowns," Lou muttered.

"I don't care - why do you do it?"

"Out of - fear - I want to be normal. I can't keep everything inside, Brooke - I'm not strong like that. Work is rough, I get tired, and everything just blows out of me - "

"But that's not good - "

Brooke stood up and covered her mouth with one hand. She pulled the curtain to one side and looked into the city and at the raging storm and its power. "B-But - " She sobbed. "I don't want you to die here. I don't w-want you to die - because that's what I've - I mean, you're g-going to die here."

Suddenly Lou was at her side by the window, and he tried in vain to calm her nerves.

"Hey," he said. "Who's saying that to you? Just tell me who said that - "

"I've g-got ideas! I've got a brain!" She pulled away from him. "I'm watching you struggle - it's awful - and the country's getting dangerous!"

"You're not scared I'll drink?" asked Lou.

"You're not in sync! You're not clued in! You're not here - right now!" She cried into her hand and clutched her forehead with the other one. "What are we doing?" She squeezed her eyes shut and felt the pressure build inside of her forehead, the heat swelling through her cheeks, and the cold observation she subsequently deployed. "Lou," stated the investigative journalist, as if she were addressing a cactus. "After consideration, I don't love you anymore." She walked away, entered the bedroom, and crept under the safety-orange bedsheets.

In the kitchen, Lou moved over to the island and opened one of the drawers. Removing two *Black and Gold* scratchcards, he plastered them on the countertop and scratched away the cameo-pink laminations.

His eyes raced around the nude squares. He saw that he hadn't won anything.

CHAPTER TEN

Whilst the Regional Collège in Dakhla had remained calm, the surrounding city had grown tense with the news that "political refugees" would soon be arriving and finding themselves jammed in prison buildings and barges offshore. The weather had also been foul, which had had a profound impact on people's moods. Vast charcoal clouds crept over the Regional Collège as Mr. Shriki put his feet up on his desk and polished his half-rimmed glasses. He cast his eyes towards the cage in the corner of the classroom, with its wild-strawberry tubes and wheels, its fresh hay smelling of the outside world, and its furry, fist-sized inhabitants.

"Hey, you there!" squeaked Biscuit, his tickle-me-pink hands holding onto the bars of the cage. "Let us out of here, you stupid ape!"

"Biscuit!" called Squid, emerging from the hut. She trained her zinnwaldite-brown eyes on her sibling and scurried towards him. "You can't talk to him like that!"

"Why not?" replied Biscuit, narrowing his warm-black eyes. "We've already agreed we're breaking out of here - "

"We need time - "

"I don't know if I can take another lecture about ape-thinking."

"Without it," cut in Squid, "we wouldn't be able to think ourselves."

Biscuit admired the distinction she had made between knowledge and intellect. It was one thing to be the two most highly developed beings in the Moroccan nation - but quite another to be able to discuss the world from some vantage point of wisdom. For without knowledge, there could be no wisdom, Biscuit admitted privately.

Meanwhile, Mr. Shriki accepted that his North African Gerbils were squeaking more than usual, which meant that they required yet another dose of blueberries. Opening a drawer on his desk, he removed a box of Spanish blueberries, walked over to the cage, and dropped four of the flavour-bombs into the hay, watching the two gerbils descend into combat about who received how many blueberries, and the like. As ever, the matter of food silenced questions about learning, knowledge and wisdom.

With the end of the second term approaching, Mr. Shriki welcomed the students into his classroom with an excited, but tired tone.

Then Faiz Impellizzeri stepped into the classroom. He locked eyes with the disgraced university-lecturer-cum-schoolteacher, taking a seat in the back row. Wearing a dark-slate-blue tracksuit, and deep-saffron sneakers, he cut a strange figure amongst the uniformed students and the balding, eccentric ex-lecturer.

Biscuit and Squid, holding their blueberries, watched the newcomer. The ape-stranger was heavyset with plump lips, cauliflower-ears, and thinning eyebrows. His eyes were dull like the horizon of his shaved head, and the grizzle on his jaw had more in common with grass allowed to grow by impartial gardeners, than any fashion. But the eyes were sad, Biscuit and Squid noticed, and belied a lack of confidence. Perhaps he had suffered in this very room. Perhaps he had once had a teacher as well…

"Teach," said Faiz in Arabic. Not knowing where they should turn their eyes, the students looked down.

"Do I have your permission?" Mr. Shriki asked.

"What?"

"Do I have your permission to teach?"

He seemed to consult his brain. "Yea."

"Thank you." He changed his tone, addressing the classroom. "We're getting to the end of term. You have hopefully turned your minds to exams. We still have a few lessons to go, and I thought it would be good to talk about the Bible in this one."

Faiz blinked dimly.

"Here's an idea I want you to think about," instructed Mr. Shriki. "It's an act of faith to declare that the world is good, because the evidence is ambivalent."

(Biscuit turned to his sibling, and said, "Ambitious.")

"When it comes to writing-from-life - as you will have to do for parts of your examination - there are some things which stretch the imagination, or rather the beliefs, of the reader. Some things are easier to believe than others. But that's why the story of the *Good Samaritan* is one of the strangest - if not *the* strangest story ever told - if you discount a couple of Japanese legends, of course."

The students chuckled politely, and the North African Gerbils squeaked.

"It is a demonstrative story - by that I mean instructive - and it addresses that difference between looking at the world with the eyes of reason, and looking at the world with the eyes of faith. These are two very different things."

He consulted his notes.

"Before we get into the actual story, which is very short, I should probably tell you what a Samaritan is: a Samaritan is someone who hailed from Samaria in the ancient world, or someone who claimed to be a descendent. The Samaritans were Jews, but they adhered to a branch of Judaism that only accepted its own ancient version of the *Pentateuch* as Holy Scripture. Now the *Pentateuch,* which is usually ascribed to Moses, is the first five books of the Old Testament: namely *Genesis, Exodus, Leviticus, Numbers,* and *Deuteronomy.* This is what the Samaritans believe in, and they were a famously hated people. Hated by Jews, who saw them as sacrilegious, and hated by other religions as well. In other words, being a Samaritan was basically like being an Irish person in the United States during the nineteenth century."

Mr. Shriki projected the story of the *Good Samaritan* on the board.

"On one occasion an expert in the law stood up to test Jesus. "Teacher," he asked, "what must I do to inherit eternal life?"

"What is written in the Law?" he replied. "How do you read it?"

He answered, "'Love the Lord, your God, with all your heart and with all your soul and with all your strength and with all your mind'; and 'Love your neighbor as yourself.'"

"You have answered correctly," Jesus replied. "Do this and you will live."

But he wanted to justify himself, so he asked Jesus, "And who is my neighbor?"

In reply, Jesus said: "A man was going down from Jerusalem to Jericho when he was attacked by robbers. They stripped him of his clothes, beat him, and went away, leaving him half-dead. A priest happened to be going down the same road, and when he saw the man, he passed by on the other side. So too, a Levite, when he came to the place and saw him, passed by on the other side. But a Samaritan, as he traveled, came where the man was; and when he saw him, he took pity on him. He went to him and bandaged his wounds, pouring on oil and wine. Then he put the man on his own donkey, brought him to an inn, and took care of him. The next day he took out two denarii and gave them to the innkeeper. 'Look after him,' he said, 'and when I return, I will reimburse you for any extra expense you may have.'

"Which of these three do you think was a neighbor to the man who fell into the hands of robbers?"

The expert in the law replied, "The one who had mercy on him."

Jesus told him, "Go and do likewise."

Picking off the remains of her Spanish blueberry, Squid cleaned her whiskers using her winter-sky paws. "I think we each love *our* neighbor," she said, blinking satirically at her sibling.

"I don't think that's what it means."

"Don't tell me you're thinking about respecting the ape?"

"That's what the story says. That's what the 'neighbor' means." Biscuit sniffed. "Maybe it's not better on the outside - "

"I never said that - "

"But what if - maybe it's *worse* out there."

Mr. Shriki proceeded to outline what had been read to the students:

"This story comes from the *Gospel of Luke*; it's part of the New Testament - and the *Good Samaritan* story is what you might call an 'inset story' - a story within a story - which is a common literary device in ancient texts. You see this in the work of Plato. And *The Golden Ass* by Apuleius. But the *Samaritan* story casts a long shadow on the most revered teaching in the Christian tradition, 'Love your neighbor'. The odd thing is that while Jesus affirms that doing merciful deeds will get you into heaven, the wording is vague. He says, 'Do this and you will live.' And what this means, I think, is that the line between life, and life-after-death, is a thin one. The suggestion here is that if you aren't merciful in this life, then you'll die a long time before your body does."

Mr. Shriki cast a short glance towards Faiz.

"There are some people - as far as Jesus is concerned - who don't live. You should recall in the Koran that Mohammed says, "Among the people are those who say, 'We believe in God and in the Last Day,' but they are not believers. They seek to deceive God and those who believe, but they deceive none but themselves, though they are not aware." This lack of awareness, I think, is what Jesus is getting at in the Samaritan story. Some people just exist. And if you're convinced of your superiority, and that's all you spend your time doing, then you're just going to be an existent. You're not going to live. That's why it's an act of faith to declare that the world is good because the evidence is ambivalent. The Samaritan who helps the homeless man is ambivalent; in other words, he doesn't want anything. He certainly doesn't want anything material. He's not trying to morally blackmail anyone, because we never see him again. He just says that he'll pay for any extra expenses when he gets back, and we can assume that he'll be true to his word."

Unbeknownst to Squid, her sibling had saved a chunk of Spanish blueberry. He tapped her on the back and presented the chunk to her. "Thank you!" squeaked Squid, as she scurried in circles, demonstrating her happiness. Naturally, the Persian-indigo juices had stained Biscuit's otherwise tickle-me-pink paws, but after receiving the chunk of blueberry, Squid gave her sibling a clump of hay and watched him clean his paws free of Persian-indigo ooze.

"Christianity, like Islam, comes after the Graeco-Roman Pagan world. I would wage that any ancient Greek who would have read the *Good Samaritan* would be shaking their head. 'What's this Samaritan doing?' they'd probably say. 'He's just thrown away his money on a complete stranger, and there's no way he'll get it back.' But that's a typical reaction because the pillar of Greek philosophy is reason. Whereas the pillar of Christian and Islamic philosophy - and monotheistic religions generally - is faith. Another word for faith could be love. So, to those who say that some stories are simply too wild to believe, or too fantastic, perhaps you're reading those stories with the eyes of reason, when you should be reading them with the eyes of love."

After which the embittered ex-lecturer delivered the innocuous and partially irresponsible lesson which the Regional Collège had instructed Mr. Shriki to teach in the first place. The tired teacher remembered the split that had occurred during the French Protectorate between Salafi Schools, which were Moroccan schools that taught Islamic-centered curricula, and *écoles des fils de notables*, whose purpose was to create a Moroccan bureaucratic class. This split, which began in the 1920s, led to a strange kind of unrest, since those Moroccans educated at the *écoles* went to France, where they became Moroccan nationalists under the tutelage of leftist French intellectuals. Mr. Shriki was different from these *Zawiyas*, however, because there was no way on Allah's great earth, that he would ever work with the Sicilians…

"Not bad," said Faiz in Arabic, after the students had gone.

"You shouldn't be on campus," said Mr. Shriki.

"I can be anywhere I like."

"Where's your pass?"

Faiz smirked, took the pass out of his pocket, and dangled it.

"Oh, you're one of those people who think lanyards are gay," said Mr. Shriki.

"You got a problem with gay people?"

"Do *you*? I've heard the *makhzan's* trying to encourage less gayness."

"What?"

"And you're not doing anything about the drainage, and the roads."

"Bu - "

"Oh, you don't get humour either?"

Truly baffled by the teacher's words - and neither understanding the insults, nor the fact that he should have been insulted by this point, Faiz said, "People are telling me you're a rabble-rouser. That you should keep your mouth shut. With all those political refugees coming down here, I wanted to tell you to keep your mouth shut."

"Yes. You've said that twice now."

Faiz creased his eyebrows. Then he turned to walk away.

"You didn't like school, I take it?" asked Mr. Shriki.

"I hated school," said the caporegime, stopping in his tracks.

"You've done well, so you can't be stupid."

"What did you say to me?" He lowered his plump lips and hunched his shoulders.

"I said, You must not be stupid. Given how *well* you've done."

"Well, yea," said the caporegime, understanding the phrase.

"Maybe you should have had better teachers."

The North African gerbils - one of them on the strawberry-coloured wheel, and the other perched on her hind-legs - discerned a deflation in the caporegime.

He shuffled across the warm, plastic tiles and stared at drawings on the wall.

Love doers of good, some idiot had written in crayon.

Giving love makes you good, another said in messy, black marker.

"What's that?" asked Faiz.

"Those?" Mr. Shriki convinced himself that they were having a conversation. "The first years wrote those." He looked back at the caporegime. "Do you want one?"

"What?"

"I said, Do you want one? You can take it home with you. Every couple of years we've got to clean out these boards. I'd feel better if they went home with people."

Mr. Shriki approached a crudely drawn donkey oasis featuring pine-green words that said, *Love doers of good*, and he took it from the wall and handed it to Faiz.

"What the fuck am I supposed to do with this?"

"You know what to do," the teacher replied.

The caporegime for Dakhla scoffed and left the room.

Except he took the drawing with him, and the North African Gerbils could only guess what he would do with it.

The next moment Mr. Kabbaj entered the room. The non-photo-blue tie was loose around his neck, and he was wet from the precipitation. "Supply teacher locked himself outside. Then the door shut behind me."

"My condolences."

"You bump into Faiz Impellizzeri?"

"He just left."

"We're in trouble," said Kabbaj, wiping rain off of his forehead.

"He told me to keep my mouth shut."

"Exactly. You won't."

"They are not our teachers," sighed Mr. Shriki.

"The way things are going - all these prisoners - we need to help the Sicilians."

Mr. Shriki, remembering his beloved lectureship, banged the desk with his hand. "Why?" he shouted. "Why do we have to? You think they'll want to spare your life?"

"Maybe - "

"Impossible, impossible, impossible!" Shriki pocketed his half-rimmed glasses. "The last time I listened to you, we left the university. That will never happen again."

"Would you rather I'd left you there?"

"Yes!"

"Fine, fuck you!"

"Fuck you!"

"Fuck you!" shouted Kabbaj, enjoying the last word. "You talk about standing up to people, but all you're doing is putting these kids in danger."

"You can't imagine an alternative?"

"I don't have to imagine anything. Either you help Faiz, or you die."

Shriki said, "I've been filling their heads with different ideas and knowledge. And by doing that, I've been loving them. Now, maybe that's a waste of time and energy. But what they do with love and knowledge is up to them. We give them a choice. If we don't love them, we don't teach anything worth knowing. We take away that choice. For God's sake, collaboration is not the answer. That is *not* the right path, Kabbaj!"

The other teacher looked at his former academic collaborator. A blackish curl had descended onto his forehead. "This is pointless," said Kabbaj, turning around, and slamming the door behind his wet rump.

Mr. Shriki replaced his half-rimmed glasses, knelt by the cage, and stared dolefully, but purposefully, at his prized North African gerbils.

Biscuit disembarked the strawberry-coloured wheel and joined Squid, who was still on her haunches and staring with her zinnwaldite-brown eyes at the unhappy ape. She thought that Shriki had realised that they were beings in their own right, but this was debunked when the teacher made kissy sounds and teased another blueberry.

"No, you don't want that?" asked Mr. Shriki, half-rhetorically.

A sweeping yacht of thunder ran aground.

"You want to be outside. I know it's raining, but I couldn't bear…" Images of gerbils threatened and executed, with chemicals, boot heels, and fists sprang to mind. "I couldn't bear that. Couldn't live with myself." He clicked his tongue and sighed. "Well, you better be on your way then. I'll find you somewhere nice. Don't worry." Then he made more kissy sounds, took out his smartphone, and searched for N'Tireft.

N'Tireft was a fishing village populated by apricot-hued buildings and overshadowed by an army of solar panels that glowered in the thunderstorm. Adjacent to the fishing village was the road into Dakhla, and then adjacent to that was a bole-brown expanse that was usually the shade of blanched almonds.

Beset by normally wizened shrubs, the land was soaked to the bone and offered swimming pools instead of parched pockets to the shrubs, and other similar plants.

Mr. Shriki parked his car outside of N'Tireft, alongside the half-flooded road, and carried the cage into the sodden, levelled landscape, as its constituents turned into soup. Inside the cage, which the teacher had covered with a bud-green towel, Biscuit and Squid swayed to and fro as they were carried into the world beyond the cadet-grey bars.

"Where's he taking us?" asked Squid.

"Maybe a different room?"

"You don't think we're - going to be *freed*?"

"Maybe," said Biscuit quietly. "Maybe I was wrong."

"About the instructing-ape?"

The next moment the cage landed with a squishy thud onto the ground. Above them, the soggy teacher removed his half-rimmed glasses, pocketed them so that his hands would be free, and pulled the bud-green towel away like a magician.

Droplets touched the unbleached-silk fur of the North African gerbils, whose hands reached up to the sky, remembering their elders in the animal shelter and what they had described about the land-kingdom from which they had originated: what appeared to be a bole-brown expanse to Mr. Shriki looked to them like a coyote-brown backyard, with knotted bumps of deep-taupe, ebony and French-bistre, with an almighty calamity stirring above them in the form of the Davy's-grey clouds.

Against the intake of their furry ears, Biscuit and Squid experienced the kind of silence that came with sonic overpopulation - noises, rackets, dins - and overstimulation. "Fresh air," said Squid, her winter-sky feet stepping across the breach. "What a wonderful smell," she added, as her paws touched the streaming dirt.

"Do you know, you're right," said Biscuit, joining her outside. "Absolutely wonderful," he added, his daydream of materiality ebbing.

Between his sobbing, Mr. Shriki wiped his face and imagined what would happen in the future - until he realised that prophecies were best left to those without educations, degrees, and prejudices. "Well, go on," complained the teacher. "What are you waiting for?" he half-shouted at the little gerbils, who stared back with their respective warm-black and zinnwaldite-brown eyes, and twitching their pink noses.

Biscuit and Squid exchanged glances. With gerbil-equivalent smiles, each took the other's paw, and they scurried at full speed into the drowning desert, avoiding puddles, swinging through the dripping branches of shrubs, and squeaking.

Mr. Shriki watched them disappear into the rain and flickering shrubs. "Biscuit and Squid," wept the teacher, sniffing. "Stupid fucking names…"

He trudged back to N'Tireft, got into his little car, turned on the radio, and cursed when Harry Nilsson's "Without You" started playing.

CHAPTER ELEVEN

own the road, around the corner from Nina Scarvaggi's townhouse, was an absolute-zero café called *Tifeo the Giant*, speckled with champagne chairs and tables, and a chestnut awning. The café had been there for over forty years and served Sicilian and Italian coffee, a selection of prepared sandwiches, and pastries made fresh every morning by Quintu Catalano, a pâtissier of great eminence who had a wide mouth, a squat nose, and brownish eyes.

Quintu had been there since the beginning and was ninety-three years old. Every morning, at 4:00 a.m., he would do ten press-ups, and go downstairs and start baking.

For his famous cannoli, he kneaded the pastry for ten minutes, then squished it through a pasta-rolling machine. He cut the pastry into ovals, wrapped them around bamboo rods, and placed them in a miniature vat of boiling oil.

"They don't heat up like metal rods," explained Quintu to the new kitchen assistant. Not that she understood a word of Sicilian - nor that Quintu could hear what she said.

Regardless of their language/hearing barriers, Quintu extracted the shells from the miniature vat and left the shells to cool. Then he started mixing the creamy filling. He used cow's milk ricotta and powdered sugar, and he sifted it to make it feathery.

"It comes out all refined," intoned Quintu to the increasingly baffled assistant. She was shown how to add chocolate buttons to the feathery filling, how to use a knife to fill both ends of the cannoli, and how to dust the cannoli with icing sugar.

"They don't keep long," warned the ancient pâtissier, pointing to the kitchen door. "Take out the old ones, and put the new batch there. You and I are going to get fat."

Smiling, and knowing somehow what he had said without speaking his language, the assistant moved into the dining area and duly replaced the cannoli in the refrigerated glass case by the cash register, which was manned by a terrified Filipino. When the assistant returned to the kitchen, Quintu was sitting in his rocking chair with crossed legs, one foot jigging pleasantly, whilst he sang under his old breath in Sicilian: "Flower, flowers, flowers all the year - the love you gave me, I give you back..."

Meanwhile, a characteristically British reporter wearing knee-high socks, khaki shorts, and a short-sleeved blue shirt with an ascot, entered *Tifeo the Giant*. He bought a filter coffee, settled into a table near the entrance, and stared into his smartphone. Nina Scarvaggi, who was sitting on the other side of the café, lowered her edition of the *Morocco Examiner*, and stared at the newcomer. She had been alerted to his presence because he had an eyepatch that half-covered a long scar on the left side of his face. The remaining copper-red eye was shrewd, and he sat in a way that suggested that he had seen it all.

"Smug," the reporter thought, watching the old woman shuffling towards his table.

"Smug, and ugly," thought Nina, as she came to stand before the reporter. "Good morning," she said in English, with her winning smile.

"Oh, hallo," he said with a Marlburian rashness, but also an Etonian bitterness, suggesting that he had been kicked out of the latter. "How can I help you?" he asked.

"I could not help noticing - "

"The eyepatch," finished the reporter. "Damned ugly thing. I said to the doctor, 'If you think I'm going to ruin people's spaghetti bolognese with some glass eye, you've got another thing coming.' I'm sorry, you're Italian. You probably take offence to that."

"I'm from Sicily."

"I say! Bit out of sorts, living in this country, aren't you?"

"I take an interest. In this place, in particular."

"Don't we all, eh?" He laughed, showing off his crooked teeth. "Bloody hell, don't we all? Tell you what, Miss - maybe you could bring those prices down?"

"You think they are high?"

"Oh, yes. I'm partial to a good espresso myself. But when I saw those prices, I thought, 'To hell with it, I'll have to shack up like a damn Yank with a filter coffee'." He took a sip and winced. "Mind you, Miss, *Britannia News* doesn't pay that well."

Nina cocked her head. "You are from a newspaper?"

"I say, terribly sorry!" He stood up as if his housemaster had called his last name. "Brumby, Miss, Elijah Brumby. War correspondent." He pointed to the eyepatch and sat down, feeling somewhat dejected, because he had lost his masculine charm. "I've covered all the major wars. I was in Moscow when the army took over. I was sent into space to cover the moon revolution. That was uncomfortable: I had to press my face to the bloody glass to see who was shooting whom on the surface. Funny thing about blood in space - shoots out like squeezing a tube of toothpaste underwater. But the worst, the one that took the proverbial cannoli, was that nuclear incident in Jakarta. That's where I lost the old peeper. Some penniless peasant took a potshot at me when the press gang was getting escorted to the hospital. Can't blame the poor savage. They took all of the potassium iodide away from the towns and cities and moved it into the hospitals. Locked the patients and the journalists inside." He coughed awkwardly. "Terribly sorry. When they started running out of potassium iodide, the patients started turning black. Never seen anything like it. You could see their skin falling off."

"So, what are you doing here?" asked Nina.

"There's a war on! Don't you know? Communists massing at the border? General discontent in the country? The only thing you're missing is a partridge in a pear tree." He peered around the docile café, with its frightened Filipinos and fresh cannoli. "That being said," added Elijah,

"I've seen more excitement in Epping Forest. There's no mistaking the effect of the cannoli. I guess I'll have to head down south." And by talking like this, by taking control of the situation, he began to share a resemblance with Harry Maclean, an exotic British officer who was stationed in Gibraltar in the nineteenth century. Who, by adopting North African culture, and speaking excellent Arabic, inveigled his way into the Moroccan Royal Court, where he was subsequently tasked with training Moulay Hassan's new Moroccan army. He came to be known as *Qaid*, and he was well-liked by his men, who enjoyed his bagpiping skills. There was another British eccentric who Brumby seemed to be invoking, and his name was Donald Mackenzie, and he was an explorer who suggested that open access to Africa could be achieved by flooding the Western Sahara. (Doubtless Brumby thought that was cool.)

"You won't go down south," stated Nina, her high forehead relaxing into a state of complete control.

"I beg your pardon?"

"You won't go down south. It's prohibited."

"*That bad*, is it?"

"No, that's not - "

"*Britannia News* waits for no man. Especially one with a solitary peeper!" He laughed again, showing his crooked teeth. "Excuse me - "

He accosted a Filipino waitress, and said, *"Dui cannoli, pi fauri,"* before he looked back at Nina, flashing the eyelashes on the aforementioned eye. "Cannoli good here?"

"The best," replied Nina. She had never met anyone like Elijah Brumby - and, unfortunately, this was as good a pretext as any for eliminating Mr. Brumby entirely. "But I have to differ with you," she said as she rested her Finn-purple behind on the chair opposite. "There is no war in this country. Two hundred wars come and go above Morocco, in Europe, but you don't write about them."

"The people in those countries do. They hear the shells."

He thanked the waitress as she deposited the cannoli.

"A lack of reportage hardly equates to peace. If it did, Morocco would be peaceful."

"We have peace," interrupted Nina.

Elijah picked up the vanilla and chocolate chip cannoli, munched half of the Persian-orange shell, and sat back, contented. "I'll bloody well find out, won't I?"

"Who seeks, finds; but who perseveres, wins."

"Which one are you, Miss?"

"I am a winner."

"So am I," replied Elijah, finishing his cannoli, and his coffee. "Where there's smoke, there's fire. Something my Sicilian fag said at Marlborough. That's why one oughtn't to pick fights with old, limey schoolboys. We're bound to know everything."

He stood up, remembering how the Indonesian government had ordered the hospital to give reporters the remaining potassium iodide, and how everyone else had died.

When he was angry, he recalled those memories. He put them out of his mind, abandoning the irritated Sicilian, and stepped outside into the heavy rain.

The Agdal Gardens consisted of several rugby-field-sized areas packed with pomegranates, apricots, and elderberries, surrounded by an ancient peach-coloured wall, which, according to Lou's smartphone, dated from the fifteenth century. Things like cultural value slipped out of the property manager's brain as the property *opposite* the Agdal Gardens - a 5,000-square-foot abandoned warehouse, with shattered windows - helped to distract him from the imminent meeting with his divorce lawyer. Not that he would be able to *see* her, since the rain - as usual - was torrential.

The drive out of the city was marked by broken pipes, overflowing drains, council repairmen wearing high-visibility jackets, and people honking at interim traffic lights.

Finally, Lou's dark-orchid Camaro pulled off of the main road opposite the Agdal Gardens and sloshed into the swamp-like parking lot of the old warehouse.

Stepping out of the car with his umbrella, Lou felt the rain on his banana-mania suit and scurried into the entrance where his American client was waiting. "Good morning," coughed Lou. "I'm sorry I'm late, the roads are falling apart."

The American golfer, Spree Curtiz, stared back. His Bermuda shorts had been drenched into another colour and his English-red-rimmed glasses had fogged over. After some prompting, Lou realised that the two athletic women wearing deep-saffron- dresses, who were forever standing at Spree's side, were actually his attorneys.

Spree approached Lou, seemingly for an embrace, and said, "Let's talk alone."

"I'm over here," said Lou.

"Oh, sorry." Spree turned around, put his arm around Lou, and walked a hundred metres away from his attorneys. "Why is it raining so much?"

"I don't know."

"Yea, but why is it raining?"

"I would've - made an apple pie, or something."

Spree ogled him. "What the hell are you talking about?"

"The property is all around us." Lou pulled at his burlywood necktie. "Will you be available to make an offer - say - by next Monday?"

"That's what I wanted to talk about."

"Well, it's simple - "

"I'm sick of the Kray Twins. They want me to turn this place into a bowling alley. Like I'm dead, or something. But I think they're *crazy!*"

"Uh-huh."

"Declaring war on queers!"

"What?"

"This damn country! Declaring war on queers! How the hell are you supposed to get anything done, when half the population's locked up?"

Lou stared back, dimly.

"Declaring war on queers," muttered Spree derisively. "I used to *be* one!" The golfer returned to his lawyers, gave Lou the middle finger, and walked outside. The property manager was not unaware of the golfer's reliance on methadone and tramadol, however, and would inform Cleopatra Griffiths that that had been responsible for the deal breaking down, the roads breaking up, the pipes bursting, the drains flooding...

> Old Uncle Lou
> Give me more, give me more, give me more
> When the girls have sex on the floor
> They say Old Uncle Lou, give me more

Lou returned to his dark-orchid Camaro, pulled out onto the main road, and waited behind some traffic lights, tapping his anxious fingers on the wheel. A massive development deal had fallen through, he knew, and he was to blame. Regardless, he fought his way back into Marrakech central and parked by *Accursio's*. Then he walked inside and met his attorney, Maria Benchekroun, and they padded across the rufous-hued carpeting to a table, where they shared bread and drank coffee.

Maria Benchekroun was a petite woman with a low forehead and round eyes. She wore a Munsell-blue pantsuit, and her nails were the colour of dark salmon. With any other client, her solicitor would have had the joy of arbitration, but since Lou was an acolyte of Salvatore Yannucci, she would have to make it more personal.

"Since you have filed a joint application with Brooke," she began, "you are going to get a copy of the application, stamped by the Moroccan Courts and Tribunals Service, an acknowledgement number, and a case number. I want you to keep these very safe. Once they process them, there will be deliberation between the respective attorneys. In this case my colleague, Rahim Fadil, and I will try and reach an equitable solution."

"It's amicable," said Lou between mouthfuls of bread.

"We like to think that," Maria breathed out, "but these things are complicated. I've worked on so many cases where the other attorney decided to make new demands. But the good news is that if we *do* escalate things, we'll get a court date much faster. And this is helpful," she added, "because it means we'll know who the presiding judge is."

"So?"

"Let's suppose that the presiding judge is a woman. Mr. Fadhil is going to argue that you were a terrible husband; that you caused her psychological harm, and so on."

"It's amicable - "

"Just stick with me. If the presiding judge is a *man*, I'll have the upper hand, because I can argue that Brooke exploited your position, put your job in peril because of her journalism, and refused to have sex with you."

"But she didn't do that."

Frustrated at her client's apparent ignorance of the law, Maria shrugged and finished her coffee. "Then we better hope that Mr. Fadhil doesn't escalate this case."

Two weeks later, Lou filled in for an estate agent who had contracted mononucleosis. It was late in the afternoon and Marrakech was gridlocked in the pouring rain. Carrot-orange office buildings, cherry-blossom-pink petrol stations, and camel-beige shops darkened in the stormy weather, their walls bleeding rainfall, and sometimes paint. The next moment his smartphone rang. *"It's Maria,"* said the steady voice. *"Can you talk?"*

"Not really." Lou squinted through the windshield. "I'm heading to a property."

"Can you meet me at Accursio's *tonight?"*

"Can do. What time?"

"I'll book a table for seven."

"Uh-huh."

Lou parked at the base of a carrot-orange office building. He stepped out, holding his umbrella, and scurried over to Herman and Lili Wagner, a German couple who wanted to open an accountancy branch in Morocco.

"Good morning," coughed Lou. "I'm sorry I'm late. Let's go inside."

He felt for the key in his banana-mania trouser leg. When the right leg failed to produce the key, he felt the left and discovered the same void.

"Uh."

"We do things better at *Wagner Wirtschaftsprüfer und Steuerberater*," said Herman in German, touching his wife's arms as if she might die from proximal stupidity.

"He couldn't even be bothered to bring the key," added Lili in German as she blinked the Moroccan rain out of her eyeballs.

"I'm sorry about this. I'll have to go back," Lou said.

"Is it true about the Jews?" asked Herman.

Suddenly, as if her husband had uttered the unsayable, Lily Wagner's mind retreated into the restructuring of companies, national and international tax planning, tax advice in inheritance, gift-tax matters in the context of succession issues, the drafting of wills and inheritance contracts from a tax perspective, tax due diligence, the preparation of business and private tax returns, the supervision of external tax audits, conducting appeals and other legal remedies, representation in fiscal court proceedings, consulting for business start-ups, company valuations, reorganization consulting, and the fact that her great-great-great grandfather had been a guard at Dachau, who had offered a cigarette to Viktor Frankl, the Austrian psychiatrist who believed that the search for the meaning of life motivated human beings in the face of paralyzing world wars, mass killings, and totally useless real estate agents - like Lou "clueless" Baring.

"Huh?" said Lou.

"We heard that Jews are being prosecuted," explained Herman, not ignorant to the fact that Morocco had traditionally been open to Jews. One great Sultan, for example, had ruled a very tolerant Morocco, where Jews and women toured widely, without questions about their presence. That same Sultan built Jewish areas with fortified gateways near the Royal Palace so that Jews could enjoy protection from the Sultan's guards. There was sometimes persecution, such as the poll tax on Jews, but during the run-up to World War Two, Moroccan nationalists stressed that Jews were members of the Moroccan nation. The Sultan went so far as to inform the Germans that he would not permit them to start arresting Jews. Inevitably, the Vichy-controlled French Protectorate restricted Jewish rations, Jewish employment, and even interned Jews in the Sahara Desert. But Herman knew that things had changed after France and Spain had left Morocco and that a number of rich Jews were advisors to later Sultans...

"Well, are they?" repeated Herman. "Are Jews getting prosecuted here?"

"I don't know, I'm not Jewish," Lou said.

Herman and Lili exchanged frowns, went to the side of the road, stuck out their sweaty thumbs, and hailed a badly driven, melon-coloured taxi.

That evening, Lou fought his way through Marrakech and parked by *Accursio's*. His banana-mania suit was soaked through, and the feeling of moisture humidifying the small of his back reminded him that Brooke had found herself an apartment. And the damper the property manager became, the more he was reminded of his solitude.

He squelched inside and met Maria Benchekroun, who directed him across the rufous-hued carpeting towards the same, legalistic table of sad dreams.

"What do you want?" asked Maria, watching Lou squidge into his high-backed chair. Maria examined the menu, looked up at Lou, and asked the same question again.

"Just coffee," answered Lou, watching the petite waitress scuttle off to procure two coffees, and a basket of bread.

Maria lowered the menu and spoke in a steady voice. "I spoke with Brooke's attorney, Mr. Fadhil, and we agreed that the case needs to be taken to court."

"Huh?"

"He wants compensation for 'psychological reasons'. Which means the case is being escalated. Which means we're going to court."

"Uh," said Lou, barely acknowledging the returning waitress. Tearing off a piece of bread, he chewed it gently, shaking his head. Then he took a sip of his white coffee and winced when the steaming liquid burned him.

"There is a more pressing issue, however," Maria said.

"There is?"

"I found out this morning the presiding judge will be Justice Lazrak."

"Is that bad?"

"Justice Lazrak has been married four times, with no success."

"Uh-huh."

"You don't understand. Believe it or not, she is a male chauvinist. She enjoys crushing male plaintiffs in divorce cases, but she also forgives male thieves."

"Aren't we both plaintiffs?"

"The divorce has gone to trial. It means that Justice Lazrak will assume that there has been some disagreement regarding the settlement."

"But you made the disagreement!" complained Lou, banging the table.

"Don't bang anything in court. We're in enough trouble already."

Moist sounds emanated from Lou's mouth as he chewed methodically, half-resembling a toddler who had been given something to eat to take away his worries. He remembered the time that Brooke had focused on the birthday party on the other side of the restaurant. An overpowering melancholy came over him, and, like a toddler who had been given some food to take away his worries, Lou did not know why he was sad.

Maria left after twenty minutes.

Alone at the table, Lou finished his coffee, looked around the restaurant, and settled his eyes on Salvatore Yannucci. The old man raised two fingers and waddled over to the property manager with two neon-fuchsia bottles of Polara.

Salvatore sat down, cracked the tops, and passed one to Lou, who sipped quietly.

"We used to drink these in the cinema," said Salvatore. "When they showed *L'attico* - with Klaus Kinski - I dropped my bottle when the first woman was killed." He noticed Lou's smartphone buzzing. "Turn off your phone when you talk to me."

Lou did so, sliding it into a banana-mania pocket.

"How are you doing?" asked Salvatore.

Lou stared into the bottle. "We have a court date. I'm gonna lose."

"One who lives within his means can be said to be rich."

"Who said that?"

"The usher boy whispered it when I was watching *Lo Squartatore Di New York*."

Lou said, "Pfft," and added, "What did *he* know?"

"He knew how to serve people," said Salvatore, shrugging.

"Well, I can't do that without money. I can't live without money."

"You are losing your wife - not your job," explained the underboss, fingering his shock-white hair. He adjusted his cultured-pearl necktie and sniffed loudly.

"She's got every right," muttered Lou. "I'm angry all the time, I work too hard, and the weather sucks."

"Rain makes the flowers grow. The land in Morocco is fertile. Did you know," he added, "that Morocco was the first country in Africa to make soil fertility maps? Then we decided to seed the soil with phosphorus. Except it didn't work."

Lou raised his head. An admission of failure was an odd thing.

"We tried to make the land better. But the sun grew hotter, and hotter. Now the rains have returned, and all we can do is shake our heads, and pray for forgiveness."

"Huh?"

"I have never apologized. That's because I have always done the right thing. But, sometimes, right and wrong can change overnight."

Whenever a customer opened the door, the Scotch mist of humidified air would blow through the restaurant, chilling the tops of their hands.

"Nina," said Salvatore, as his body tightened inside the dark-liver suit. "Once upon a time, she wanted to be the boss. But the boss - the old man - refused to hand over his life's work to a woman. So, she told me to kill him at his favourite restaurant." He raised his dark eyebrows to the high ceiling. "This place...this room...it was *here*..."

...Salvatore Yannucci examined the floorplan of *Grasso's* in his hotel room. The penultimate call to prayer resonated through the warm Marrakech air, into the window. Yannucci, strapped for time and trying to memorize the floorplan for the last time, had black, slicked-back hair, dark eyebrows, and an extremely muscular body. He was also wearing an outer-space-grey vest and undershirt, oxford-blue trousers, and brand-new tennis shoes. He folded up the floorplan, shoved it into the bin, and set it on fire. Then he tipped the ashes into the toilet, flushed them, and wiped the room of fingerprints. He made his way downstairs, ignoring the pain in his feet caused by the unusually small tennis shoes, and checked out of the hotel.

The call to prayer faded away as he stepped inside his rented Fiat, switched the engine on, and drove through Marrakech.

Later, he parked down the road from *Grasso's*. He put on a pair of rubber gloves, took a .22LR calibre Beretta pocket pistol out of the glove compartment, and wiped the weapon. He wiped down each bullet that was loaded into the clip and then threw the gloves out of the car window.

Salvatore slicked back his hair, secreted the Beretta in his beltline, and walked towards the restaurant, as large clouds polluted the early evening.

In those days, there was a separate bar.

Salvatore ordered a virgin mojito and minded his own business. Occasionally, he would glance towards a large table populated by Family Members. The Old Man was at the head of the table, poking his tender lamb rump. Salvatore knew that the Old Man had an active bladder and simply waited for him to announce that his "release valve was imminent". When this happened, Salvatore watched the Old Man saunter past sycophantic waiters and waitresses, and enter the long lavatory corridor.

Salvatore knew two things: the Old Man always used the unisex disabled toilet for privacy reasons; and the disabled toilet had *two* rooms.

The first room was a lobby-like area, with a sink and a hand dryer, and the second room, with the toilet, was hidden behind a wooden door.

Salvatore tipped the barman and walked towards the lavatories.

The disabled toilet was located around a corner from the normal toilets. As he approached the target, Salvatore applied another pair of rubber gloves and used a bank card to open the lock. He entered the lobby-like room and shut the door behind him.

"Who's that?" shouted the Old Man from behind the toilet door.

Salvatore pulled out the Beretta, aimed it at the toilet door, and fired twice.

When he heard the death rattles, he opened the toilet door using the bankcard, and found the Old Man staring at him with a pair of sad eyes.

Except she was actually an Old Woman called Claudia Grasso. In her prime, she had brought the Grasso Family to Morocco at a time of political, social, and financial upheaval. She had a round face with perfect skin, pale grey eyes, and she wore a dark-liver dress, with trim.

"Sal - "

Salvatore aimed the Beretta at Claudia's head and fired. When her body had ricocheted back onto the toilet, Salvatore checked her pulse on her wrist and throat. Convinced that she was dead, the young hitman collected the three spent cartridges, put the Beretta back under his beltline, and walked out with his hands in his pockets.

Salvatore made it back to the rented Fiat and stepped inside. He started the engine, pulled away from *Grasso's*, and drove for several blocks before pulling over. He took apart the Beretta, wiped down its constituent parts, and then drove around Marrakech, tossing individual segments of the Beretta into alleyways, gardens, and long streets.

He drove out of Marrakech, stopping by the Agdal Gardens. He sighed as he removed his tennis shoes and started unlacing them in the darkness. He threw the laces out of one window, drove for twenty minutes, and then threw the shoes out of the other window. He did the same with his gloves.

Half an hour later, he stopped on a quiet road. He took his brown shoes from under the passenger seat, put them on, and drove to the city.

A safe house in the suburbs.

Salvatore opened the garage and cleaned the car from top to bottom. The next day, he returned the car to the rental agency, claimed his cash-back reward, and reported to a young Nina Scarvaggi that what she had asked him to do, had been completed without delay...

"Nina took over and purged the family," explained Salvatore as he looked down at his profound gut, picked up his Polara, and drained it down to its fuchsia-hued dregs.

"These things have to be done to keep people safe. It's not just about people." He smiled. "We have to protect the country."

Lou spilled his Polara. The fuchsia-hued liquid dribbled over the edge of the tablecloth and stained his banana-mania legs.

"I got - we need - some time - we can have dinner," stammered Lou.

"You do that," said Salvatore, preparing to propel his immense girth. "By the way…Brooke's lawyer, Rahim Fadil, sleeps with his clients. He rapes them, actually."

The property manager stared at the rufous-coloured carpeting.

"I don't know how you can use that," admitted the underboss. "But it's good to know these things. Because everyone you look at, is also you. You can be the old man. You can be the policeman. You can be the woman kissing you. You can be the dead." He remembered the bodies he had seen throughout his career. "You can be the dead."

Outside, the rain had stopped. The roads glistened under the moon, and they reminded the city that it would rain again, and maybe with more violence.

Up and down the country, peach-puff police wagons parked by apartment blocks, mansions, and office buildings, took religious and political minorities into their peach-puff doors, and joined the clammy highway down to southern Dakhla.

The police wagons were driven by soldiers from Morocco's Republican Army, which stood at over 100,000 - including reserves - and they joined a larger convoy of armored trucks carrying ammunition and supplies on the outskirts of Guelmim, whose neatly arranged, three-story buildings were a faded variation of alizarin-pink.

Unfortunately, most of the Republican Army's soldiers had been called out to help with flood relief around the country, which meant that only a small force of two hundred were overseeing the deportation of Morocco's minorities to Dakhla, and the military operation thereafter that would invade the phosphate mine across the border.

There was a city in northern Morocco called Béni Mellal. Its streets were suffused with acid-green Peruvian peppertrees, baby-pink oleander flowers, Cambridge-blue olive trees, and emerald pomegranate trees, whilst the colourful buildings rose and fell like gentle fulvous-orange waves. In one of the city's squares, a group of soldiers was watching one of the resident communists get beat up by Khattar and Nadia Malki.

"That's enough," said a soldier with a moustache. He clicked his fingers, watched his colleagues pull the Shia Muslim couple away from the communist, who had been kicked unconscious, and watched their angry shapes get locked into neck braces inside of the vehicle. Then Durri and Salma Yassin, who were members of the Baha'i Faith, were locked opposite the Shia couple, who eyed them with a soon-to-be-doomed camaraderie. "Thy name is my healing,

O my God, and remembrance of Thee is my remedy," intoned Durri and Salma. "Nearness to Thee is my hope, and love for Thee is my companion. Thy mercy is my healing and my succor in both this world and the world to come. Thou, verily, art the All-Bountiful, the All-Knowing, the All-Wise - "

"He doesn't need your prayers," muttered Khattar, half at the Baha'i Faith couple, and half at the comatose communist, whose bloodied neck dangled in the grey brace.

"The people in this truck have been unified by God," explained Salma, her small eyes blinking in the bright red emergency lights. "How can we serve God," she enquired, "if we are constantly fighting one another?"

"By beating up the communists," replied Khattar.

"Just our luck to be locked up with heathens," added Nadia.

"Did you turn the oven off?"

"No, I thought you did - "

"Damn it, woman, I told you to turn the oven off!" Then he noticed the communist flinching as he blinked back to reality. "Welcome back, Stalin's gay nephew."

"What - makes you think - we're going back?" mumbled the communist through broken teeth and battered cheeks...

In southern Morocco, the city of Guelmim had a break from the rain. Streets were emptied of water by electric pumps

- since petrol-powered pumps had been outlawed several decades prior - and cars returned to the sodden roads. There was one police wagon whose unpunctuality had nothing to do with the weather, however, because its prisoners were simply refusing to get inside the peach-puff vehicle.

"I want to know where you're taking us, for what purpose, and how long we'll be gone," shouted Barak Schechter, a Jewish insurance broker with a short beard, cropped hair, and brown eyes, who had planted his feet against the wagon's doors.

"What about the cat!?" said his wife, Shira, another insurance broker, with a triangular face, a large mouth, and a dimpled chin. "Let us bring Mew-Mew!"

"No animals," said the soldier, pushing the Schechters into the police wagon, locking them into neck and ankle braces, and locking the doors.

"Come on - I want answers!" shouted Barak.

"Barak, please - "

"They have no right, Shira. We're just normal people who want representation."

A smug voice on the other side of the police wagon sprung up like a bad cold. "How are you gonna get *that*?"

The voice came from a woman with bruises on her square face, and holes in her jeans, which, the Schechters realised, were custom-made.

"What makes you the expert?" asked Shira.

"Well, for one thing, I'm not a religious dumbass." The interiors turned bright red with emergency lights as the police wagon lurched forward, joining the road to Dakhla. "They also don't like communists."

"You're a Leninist! It's because of you that we're in this mess," barked Barak.

"Go back to Israel where you belong. We make - "

"Look here, you commie - "

"We give you your own country, and that's not good enough?"

"We moved here because we can't stand Israel," interrupted Shira, itching the right side of her neck on the cold metal brace.

"Christ, you moved here?" laughed the communist.

A soldier sitting at the end of the wagon stood up, made his way towards the communist, and slapped her across the face. Then he returned to his seat and sniffed.

The convoy soldiered on through wet weather and prevailing high winds that shook the police wagons, their wheels sometimes screeching on the water-logged tarmac. Behind the convoy, the bending road reached into the distance, giving way to cliffs overlooking the sea which were covered with moist trees.

Behind that, the legacy of the project loomed like so many eroded cliffs and oceans: empty houses, vacant studios, unoccupied apartments, abandoned lofts, desolate duplexes, untenanted triplexes, sparsely populated high-rises, and deserted townhouses. There were also deserted dogs, forsaken cats, jilted ferrets, stranded fish, rejected gerbils, dumped tarantulas, and ditched reptiles, who helped to negate this emptiness as they made their respective howls and questioned and worried about their survival.

Lou took note of these new properties the following week. Ignorant as to the whereabouts of the tenants, Zaalouk Real Estate simply acquired them free of charge.

Dakhla was a city in the disputed territory of the Western Sahara. It rested on an arm-like archipelago that crawled out from the disputed mainland, ending in a papaya-whip-hued blob that carried consulates of Liberia, Gambia, and Djibouti, among others. Since the invasion of the Scarvaggi Family, the Saharan metropolis had morphed from a territory concerned with tourism and fishing to an economic hub that had hosted five annual meetings of the World Economic Forum, four gatherings of the United Nations Economic and Social Council, and two African Development Bank masquerade balls that had required mansion-sized tents for dining events, and custom-made gardens flown in from Errachidia and the Kirstenbosch National Botanical Garden.

At the base of the archipelago, a paradise-pink security checkpoint sat like an obscene flower amidst the parchment-coloured wilderness. A light rain prickled the semi-sloshing ground, and thick clouds zipped overhead like Payne's-grey battleships.

It had been dry when Ismail and his communists had started digging a half mile away. Over the course of ten nights, they had dug a mile-long trench parallel to the road and filled it with a mélange of military-green survivors, ex-convicts, and politicians.

"Ismail," whispered a malnourished woman of twenty-two.

She passed the binoculars to her bearded leader, watched him mount the wooden ladder with his skinny legs, and held her breath when he stared impassively at the approaching convoy of peach-puff police wagons rocking over the uneven tarmac.

"Tell the others," muttered Ismail. He lost his balance when he hopped back into the trench and was helped by the young woman towards the Defence Minister, who nodded eagerly and said, "Our people are ready - "

"I hope I haven't let you down." Ismail lifted his head weakly. "Secure the supermarkets, when we get into Dakhla."

"One thing at a time," replied the Defence Minister, wincing.

"No." Ismail furrowed his brow. "All at once."

He straightened his back and listened to the sound of guns clicking along the trench. Military-green boots shuffled in the quasi-mud, blistered fingers felt across ammunition pouches, and noses itched. Ismail achingly passed the binoculars to the Defence Minister, who ascended the wooden ladder and stared through them. He waited for the last police wagon to jostle past the security checkpoint before making his decision.

"It's time, Ismail…"

He lifted a Roman-silver whistle to his chapped lips and blew into the moist chamber. Lieutenants along the trench mirrored his action, producing a chorus of loud shrieks as a storm of shapes leapt out of the trench onto the parchment-coloured wilderness. They charged the main road and took aim at the remaining security staff.

Behind them, a party of bazooka operators, who had been stationed along the trench at strategic points, opened fire at the main road, and the security checkpoint. One of the buildings shattered into bright yellow flames and meteors of concrete, after which its supporting beams collapsed like burnt twigs, and the structure caved in.

All along the road, civilian vehicles zig-zagged across the tarmac, halted awkwardly, and then turned around. The wave of communists slithered closer, pattering the semi-moist ground with months-old ammunition, and bazooka-debris. Then another building by the security checkpoint exploded, its doors caving inwards in a detonation of chartreuse sparks, cyber-yellow flames, and crimson flares. Several policemen nipped out of the building but were gunned down by the approaching communists, who began to set up a barricade using dead bodies, vehicles, and debris.

"Ample," said the Defence Minister as columns of communist soldiers went about attending to the injured, building the barricade, and enjoying their premature success. "One garrison will remain here. No one's getting into Dakhla, and no one's getting out." The relevant soldiers re-convened with their commanding officer as the Defence

Minister and the remaining revolutionaries hot-wired police cars by the checkpoint, and police wagons in a nearby garage, which they had cleverly protected throughout.

With their new vehicles, the revolutionaries began their Dakhla campaign, and rolled down the road into a dark-salmon holiday camp. Buildings were plundered, vehicles were commandeered, and many who worked there - exhausted Moroccans who hated Faiz Impellizzeri - joined the revolutionaries on their advance. Some two hundred men and women moved down the road, blowing up numerous official buildings in a wash of fulvous-orange flames. The determined revolutionaries on the vehicles cocked rifles and handguns, and also re-loaded bazookas, general purpose machine guns, and Javelin anti-tank missile launchers, as they began their Dakhla push.

The city square in Dakhla featured deep-chestnut pavements surrounded by pale-spring-bud buildings. Odd patches of date palms, cedars, and palm trees - greeted on the ground by level blotches of *zoysia japonica* grass - were peppered around the square, as were units of local police, who awaited the convoy.

Disrupting the otherwise pleasant square was a forest-green observation tower that stretched up three hundred metres and supported a landing pad at the level summit.

Inside the observation point were two of Impellizzeri's soldiers.

Nicky had a high fringe, a well-defined nose, large lips, and a chin the size of most coffee mugs. Whereas Adil had a high forehead, a monobrow, a moustache-beard-combo, and a left ear that pointed outwards as if listening discretely for an indication of promotion. "You want a joke?" asked Adil in Arabic, as he finished the fawn-beige couscous that had been prepared by his bedridden mother. "Come on, let's have a joke."

"Yea, go on," said Nicky, his mind retreating to some desolate island, where he would be free from the risk-free comedy that was part and parcel of Adil's conduct.

"There's a Jew and a Gentile stuck in the Sahara. The Gentile's making smoke signals, he writes S.O.S. using some rocks, and now and then he looks for camels."

"Yea."

"But the Jew's just sitting there. The Gentile looks at the Jew and says, 'What are you doing?' And the Jew looks at him and says, 'Oh, I'm just waiting.'"

Nicky stroked his huge chin. His brain cells were so attuned to methods of blackmail and murder that when faced with a simple joke he couldn't respond correctly.

"I don't get it," said Nicky.

"No, but - you know it's - the point - the Jew's cocky, so he's not trying to save himself. He just assumes he's going to be alright."

"You see - isn't the point that the Jew's in his natural habitat - whereas the Gentile's not used to the desert?"

"No, but - I said the Sahara," repeated Adil.

"What the hell's a Jew doing in the Sahara?"

"I didn't think about that," sighed Adil, ignorant to the fact that it wasn't clear how Jews or Christians had managed to reach North Africa. Judaism came from the East, and the Jews had famously settled in Egypt. By the time of Islam, Judaism had spread amongst African Berber tribes. How this occurred within a population that was basically illiterate, is a great mystery. Whereas Christianity became a popular anti-Roman force in Tunisia where the church split into factions: those who followed their Roman occupiers, and those who followed Donatus, Bishop of Carthage.

But Nicky didn't care about history.

He just rolled his eyes, and looked through the window, the cyan-hued sky disguised by cultured-pearl clouds, and wheels of thunder.

"What's that?" said Nicky, pointing at the window.

"Beats me," said Adil, half-choking on his cous cous.

They watched the dark-lava dot grow in size. Then they got bored, exchanged terrible ideas, and returned their gaze to the fattening dot...

The peach-puff police wagons formed a semi-circle within the deep-chestnut square. Armored trucks with munitions and supplies joined them. People inside the pale-spring-bud buildings stared fearfully through their windows as police officers pulled Christians, Jews, Shia Muslims, members of the Baha'i Faith, and communists, out of the police wagons. The overburdened and overworked police ordered them into lines and marched them into the square, ready for processing according to fitness.

Barak Schechter, the Jewish insurance broker, moaned as his wife, Shira, was torn away from him, chained to other women, and marched to the other side of the square. Then, he was distracted by a strange, fizzing sound, which was too far away to be a drone, but too close to be a plane. When he looked through the fans of the palm trees, he saw a dark-lava arrow heading for the observation tower.

"Get down!" shouted Barak in Arabic, as the bulbous tip of the observation tower erupted in a series of orange-red bubbles that sparked and flamed. The landing pad quickly collapsed into the tower and brought down heaps of rubble into the busy square, where police officers, soldiers, and prisoners alike, were crushed.

"Charge them!" shouted Barak as he beat down an adjacent police officer. "Shira!" The prisoners lifted their chains like a fishing net, ran at their captors, and turned them into a constabulary mess. Weapons were torn away from bloody hands, keys were sought, and armored trucks were opened, as the minorities became a majority.

Khattar and Nadia Malki, the Shia Muslim couple, met each other in the middle of the square and armed themselves with Franchi SPAS-12 combat shotguns. Khattar touched the weeping Barak. "We'll look for Shira soon. But we need to organize." Then Barak took a handgun from Khattar and shot through the locks on his shackles.

Ismail's makeshift convoy of cars, trucks, and golf carts, drove into Dakhla, their anti-tank missile launchers demolishing the occasional police building. The Defence Minister's hair blew left, right, and centre, as he gestured towards six vehicles. The trucks and golf carts peeled off to secure the airport, and drove across the runway, causing all kinds of mayhem for the three departing business jets.

The rest of the communist convoy entered the city and took over monolith-like power stations surrounded by solar panels, olive-green water purification plants, and powder-blue office buildings sporting five-star catering facilities, gyms, and lodgings. Suddenly, street corners were defined by the pattering feet of communist soldiers as bullets echoed down pumpkin-orange boulevards, and raw-sienna tenements.

The Dakhla police station was a square affair with queen-blue, patterned mosaics adorning the outside walls. Several police cars were parked by the covered lobby and officers entered and exited the building in their rusty red uniforms like automatons. Inside, the caporegime, Faiz Impellizzeri, walked down a rusty red hallway in his dark slate blue tracksuit and deep-saffron sneakers. His dull eyes scanned the passing officers as he reached a large door, walked inside, and greeted the owner. The chief of police, Zowwar El Houssine, looked like a scarecrow, minus the Puritanical hat, and handed the bulky caporegime a freshly trimmed Bongani cigar. Their weekly meetings consisted of gossip, lies, and blackmail operations. Halfway through his cigar, Zowwar answered the phone on his desk. He listened blankly, dropped his cigar on the carpeted floor, and looked at Impellizzeri, who smiled back. Zowwar jumped up and looked through the window. The street was coloured by seashell-hued buildings and an obnoxious, shamrock-green, Irish-themed pub. What was more obnoxious were the military-green paramilitaries scuttling around boulevards, shooting security cameras, and aiming a bazooka at the police station.

"Where are your soldiers?" asked Zowwar.

"What?"

"Your soldiers." He turned around. "What weapons do they have?"

"What's the matter?" Faiz puffed on his cigar.

"Forget the - " Zowwar smacked the cigar out of his mouth. " - look out the window! We're getting attacked!"

He dragged the thuggish caporegime to the window, where they stared in horror at the encroaching communists and their anti-artillery weapons.

"Uh - "

"That's all you can say?" shouted Zowwar. He opened his cupboard, removed an AEK-999 machine gun, and fed it a band of ammunition.

Impellizzeri began to cry. Wiping his tears like a child, he mewled.

"Don't cry," said Zowwar.

"I don't know what to do!" cried Impellizzeri. "I want my mamma!" He slid down the wall, landing in a puddle on the carpeted floor. "I don't know what to do!"

The police chief looked at the caporegime. "Okay." Zowwar knelt. "I'm going to help you. You stay there." Then he went to his desk and picked up the AEK-999. "Don't worry. They just want hostages."

Police buildings across Dakhla were raided for weapons and ammunition by a mixture of ex-prisoners and communist soldiers. Those managers, shop-owners, and bystanders, who agreed to the revolution were recruited by Ismail and his army, whilst "the pacifists" were jailed with the same chains and manacles from the city square. Before them, a reinvigorated Ismail walked through the square, observing the gradual "re-capture" of Dakhla, and staring at those who had denied him.

"We can't declare a victory without securing the police station," said the Defence Minister. "Plus, we have reason to believe that the caporegime is there - "

"Impellizzeri?"

"Yes."

"Peasant," muttered the emaciated communist.

Burning streets, dilapidated leisure parks featuring abandoned prams, and several office buildings enjoying diplomatic immunity, witnessed a convoy of commandeered ice-cream trucks, school buses, and golf carts, making their way to the police station. They quickly surrounded the building with its queen-blue mosaics and took aim at the lobby, the available windows along the structure, and conspicuous police wagons.

Ismail hopped out of his jeep, observing the premises. His sad eyes scanned the upper floors of the police station and widened when something flickered in the sun. School-bus-yellow machine-gun fire erupted out of a closed window, blowing glass across the surrounding tarmac, as Ismail ducked behind the stationary jeep.

The communists returned fire, dappling walls with powdery slots, fractured clefts, and splintered punctures, which sent plumes of concrete plummeting to the ground.

"Cease fire!" said the tired Defence Minister.

A white flag appeared through the shattered glass.

A bloodied police officer walked outside, holding the message of surrender. He was followed by twenty officers, holding their hands behind their head and walking with a well-deserved appearance of unfaltering capitulation.

"Don't kill them," ordered Ismail in Arabic.

His soldiers appropriated the shamrock-green Irish-themed pub and then packed it with the new police prisoners.

The police station was subsequently stormed by communists, who repaired severed phone lines, re-established Wi-Fi, and rescued burnt documents out of bins.

Upstairs, Zowwar threw the AEK-999 across the room, re-lighted his cigar, and joined the shivering bulk of Faiz Impellizzeri on the carpeted floor. "It's over," said Zowwar as he put his arm around the caporegime. "Things were good for a while."

Impellizzeri shriveled, hiding his eyes from the world. He wished he could remember what his teachers had told him. "I c-can't remember."

"What's that?" Zowwar knocked ash off his cigar. "Remember what?"

Bursting into tears, Impellizzeri drove his face into his kneecaps.

"Okay." Zowwar patted the caporegime's back. "Not long now."

The next moment a body-less hand knocked on the glass door.

"Come in," said Zowwar. "Gun's on the floor."

"Don't kill me!" screamed Impellizzeri. "Don't kill me! Don't kill me!" He curled into the fetal position. "Don't kill me! Please, Allah!"

Soldiers entered the office and dragged Zowwar and Impellizzeri to their feet. They were marched downstairs and shoved into the Irish-themed pub with the others.

"Should have raided this place ages ago," noted Zowwar as he looked around the Irish-themed pub at the communist guards. "Should have raided the whole country," he added as the trembling Impellizzeri was helped into a high-backed chair. The latter relaxed when they fed him boiled eggs and dried dates. It reminded him of his school lunches: the lunches that he had stolen from other students. He recalled that provisional sense of victory that always followed the burglaries…then the crushing loneliness.

CHAPTER TWELVE

The manager of *Accursio's* had closed the restaurant early. Near the kitchen door, he prepared a table for three guests. He laid out knives, forks, and spoons, with their sweet-course counterparts, as well as Pakistan-green and pansy-purple glasses for iced water and wine, respectively. The placemats featured intricate patterns with pictorial-carmine, razzmic-berry, and Sacramento-State-green triangles, whilst greyish busts of retired Sicilian presidents, flown in from Sicily, carried Spanish vetchling flowers between ceramic fingers. The next moment the manager discerned a black Chevrolet suburban limousine humming to a halt outside the front door. He padded across the room, opened the door, and welcomed Salvatore Yannucci, Augustu Valverde, and Nina Scarvaggi inside. Shaking their coats free of rain, they exchanged pleasantries with the manager and were shown to the little table by the kitchen.

Nina rested her rake-thin body on the chair and waited for Salvatore and Augustu to seat themselves before she ordered the food.

"Three lamb rumps," she stated in Sicilian, "for three asses."

Polite laughter trickled around the table like olive oil.

"What's the cheapest bottle?" asked Nina, with as much tact as most hippopotamuses.

The manager locked eyes with Salvatore. "The Yellow Tail merlot?"

"One bottle," replied Nina. "Just in the purple glasses."

"Yes, ma'am." Later, the manager returned, pouring wine into the pansy-purple glasses. Then he returned to the galley and told the sweating chef to take a chill pill.

Augustu itched his silver skullcap of finely combed hair. He loosened his cosmic-latte necktie. "Can't tell if this is sweat or rain," he laughed bleakly.

"The air-conditioning is a luxury," replied Nina, creasing her sun-cracked face. "You spend too much time in that flower shop."

"Yes," laughed Augustu, touching the Spanish vetchling flowers, and thinking about how far they had travelled - and how far *he* had travelled.

It was Salvatore's turn to loosen his cultured-pearl necktie. Sweating into his red wine, he took a cursory sample. "Let's turn the air-conditioning on, Nina - we don't need to have a Sicilian evening."

Nina's puckered face twisted into a warm frown that, with time, lost it warmth. "Maybe too many people forget the past. And they enjoy my wine in the present."

"I'm not enjoying it - "

"Ingenuity needs a constant stream of ideas," interrupted Nina. "We know what happens to old people. They get put away - and people stop listening to what they say. But what happens when the young people run out of ideas? The world listens to them. But they've got nothing to say - so the rest of the world stops talking and it shrivels." She sipped her wine and winced. "Morocco is shriveling. The young people are finished. They're fresh out of ideas. But I'm not dead yet," she added imperiously.

The manager returned with the food.

"Anything else?" the manager queried with culinary dread.

A snort of irritation came from Nina, whose paperish hands twitched.

"My arthritis - " she whispered as she pointed at the food. "I can't - will you?"

"Of course, ma'am," replied the manager, picking up her knife and fork, and cutting up the lamb rump, mixed greens, and potatoes, into smaller bite-sized pieces.

"Thank you - that's nice."

The manager practically saluted and returned behind the bar.

"By the grace of God, I could walk in here," said Nina. "Please, eat."

The trio picked at their plates in silence for several minutes.

"What movies have you been showing?" asked Nina, after swallowing a piece of potato the size of a cereal pellet.

Salvatore wiped his neck. "We had a season of ghost movies. We showed *The Fog* last night, and next week we're going to show *The Shining* - but the television movie, not the Kubrick version with Duvall."

"Give us an old film."

The underboss breathed heavily in the heat stemming from the room and the food. He sniffed politely and said, "*Häxan* is a good one. A Swedish movie about witches. The only version you could watch for a long time had a narration by Bill Burroughs." He smiled at his own trivia. "He used to spend time in Morocco - like most faggots."

Augustu stifled a laugh and stared into his food.

Nina's puckered face twisted. "What do you know about such things?"

"Nothing," Augustu said.

"Why are you laughing about it? We don't have enough problems?" She looked to Salvatore for affirmation. "It's the end of my world, and all you boys can do is laugh."

A peculiar silence spread across the table. The pitter-patter of rain reverberated off of the windows that separated their world from the reality of their adopted country.

"Do you know how they harvest the lambs?" asked Nina.

The two men exchanged awkward glances.

"They stun the beast with a bolt. Then they shackle the beast upside down and cut the jugular and carotid arteries. They use their hand to separate the carcass and the pelt, like pulling off a plastic glove after it's been moving trash in the rain. Then they take the beast, break the leg joints, and pull the legs off, as if it's a big lobster. Then they break the atlas joint of the neck. They snap off the head, like a gingerbread man."

Salvatore snapped a breadstick in two. "Like that?"

Nina smiled and spooned more lamb into her wrinkled mouth.

Between them, Augustu laughed politely, adding, "Excuse me - "

"Wait," Nina raised a sun-dried hand. "Use the disabled toilet tonight. The others have been gutted." She nodded and added, "Salvatore doesn't like using that toilet."

"Nina - "

"You say there are ghosts. But ghosts aren't real."

Augustu looked between the *Cummari* and the underboss. Then he turned his hibernating eyes towards the bar, walked towards the toilets, and disappeared.

"Nobody needs to know that," said Salvatore.

"You need to remember," countered Nina, dabbing her cockled lips. "You need to remember how we have survived for so long. Moroccans don't understand. You and me - " She pressed her hands together. " - we are connected like the church and the state. You are the state, but I am the church. I am the pope and the bishops, and all this without knowing a word of Latin. Latin hides the stupidity of the priest. But you know that I don't speak it." She smiled. "It's much better for me to speak in other ways."

The sound of a muffled gunshot came and went.

"Nina?" asked Salvatore, creaking in his chair.

"Yes?"

"He was loyal."

"Now I know you are soft," Nina sighed.

Lucio Vizzini padded onto the restaurant floor. He wore an outer-space-grey vest and undershirt, oxford-blue trousers, and brand-new tennis shoes. The intense eyes in his pinched face focused on Nina and reported to her that what she had asked him to do, had been completed without delay.

"He was loyal," repeated Salvatore as he watched Lucio Vizzini take a seat at the bar, and stare psychotically at the countertop.

"Augustu was a mole," answered Nina. "He worked with the communists for years. He opened up hell…and you say he is innocent?"

Salvatore's dark-liver suit seemed tighter. The white shirt and the cultured-pearl necktie squeezed the life out of him. "When we first came here, he was the only one who spoke any sense. You and I were in the dark, but Augustu was a light-giver, and his advice chipped away the old regime, gave us the control we've had ever since, and taught us to respect the country. Now that he's been killed by this COCKSUCKER!" He glanced at Vizzini. "What are we going to do?"

"We are going to change," said Nina, sounding like a dying vacuum cleaner, and looking like something that had been sucked into one during a humid summer.

The Republic Courts in Marrakech were housed in a large baby-powder building featuring blue-yonder window frames, cadmium-green doors, and marble steps and floors that amplified the winds projected out of the air conditioners by retaining the low temperatures and cooling everybody's feet. The waiting chamber was a roofless well in the centre of the building that sported a central twenty-year-old cedar, potted white wormwoods, and tubbed saxaul bushes. From here, Lou and Brooke, and their respective legal teams, entered Courtroom No. 3., which was a round chamber with a roof supported by cedar-wood pillars, with blue linoleum floors, and short-backed seats with red cushions.

"All rise, please," announced the bailiff in Arabic.

Justice Lazrak entered the courtroom and sat in her high-backed chair. She was a fierce-looking woman with a bulbous nose, high cheekbones, a furrowed brow, and thin eyebrows in a permanent cast of displeasure. She wore a green ribbon on her shoulders, and a red fez was perched on her head.

"Your ladyship," said Maria Benchekroun in French, standing up in her black robe and white scarf, and aiming her round, appealing eyes in the direction of Justice Lazrak. "May I be the first to express my gratitude for having, in this difficult case, as learned a judge as there ever was - particularly in the domain of judicial separation."

"You may not, Ms. Benchekroun," grumbled Justice Lazrak. "If you do not take this time to state your case, I will ask you to leave the courtroom."

"I intend to speak quickly, Your Ladyship."

Maria Benchekroun outlined Lou's side of the case.

Then Rahim Fadil did the same for Brooke.

By the time they had finished, Justice Lazrak said, "Lunch."

The canteen was a rectangular cafeteria with plastic chairs and tables. Lou sat with Maria and watched her eat bland cous cous and doughnuts.

"I'm a bit worried," said Lou.

"What about?"

"Well, I don't think we're gonna win this. I mean - " His cornflower-blue eyes were like sad blobs of ill-applied paint. " - it was all easy before you got involved."

Maria wiped her mouth using a napkin. "You understand the law?"

"I'm not gonna rob a shop."

"And what do you think you've been doing for the past three years?"

"Huh?"

"Look, I'm not a miracle worker. If you're worried about this now, why did you apply for a divorce?"

"It was a joint application!" he complained.

"Rahim tells me she wasn't happy with that. Go to Brooke with your problems."

Lou seemed to leave the room, mentally, for a moment. When he came back, he said, "Do you have to speak French? I don't know what you're saying half the time."

"Only half the time?"

"No, no - no, no, no - all the time - it's French - you know what I mean."

"This is why lawyers were invented, Lou."

Back in Courtroom No. 3, Brooke and Lou were given earpieces to follow the court case by means of a genus of translators in the gallery.

"Some evidence of their standard of living would be appreciated," grumbled Justice Lazrak in French. "We need to perform a full review."

"I'm not sure what you're asking for, Your Ladyship," replied Maria.

"Mr. Baring fails to mention their living standards in his deposition," sighed Justice Lazrak. "Is there another record that would establish this?"

"With all due respect, Your Ladyship, I have already been through the financial affidavits about the value of their apartment in Marrakech. I noted that we had a wife who was making 120,000 dirhams a month from YouTube videos, and a husband who was making 200,000 dirhams a month from working as a property manager for Zaalouk Real Estate. Now, if he paid her 80,000 dirhams worth of alimony for the purpose of psychological compensation, Ms. Kimani would have 200,000 dirhams and Mr. Baring would have 120,000 dirhams. I needn't point out that their current situation would only be reversed, and neither client would be any wiser. Would justice really be served?"

"I will be the judge of that," protested Justice Lazrak.

The debate lasted for another hour.

Then Rahim Fadil - with a monumental upper lip, thinning hair, and white teeth - entered the fray, and furthered the topic of money in an increasingly budgetary debate.

"My client testified that Mr. Baring could earn up to 200,000 dirhams with a benefit package, Your Ladyship, but that if he went somewhere else - to London, for example - and started from the bottom, he would be making roughly 184,000 dirhams. Again, we have to add the benefit package to that." He fumbled with some documents. "I'd like to point out a couple of things," added Rahim, thumbing the warm pages. "On page five, over and over again in the affidavit, it's mentioned that Mr. Baring, during the course of the marriage, earned between 180,000 and 200,000 dirhams. Then, in the last paragraph on page ten, both my client and Mr. Baring noted that they had the present ability to earn more than they were earning as set forth in their most recent financial affidavit. Now, when they say they're both capable of earning more, it seems that that's a way of saying that they're happy with their living standards - but what that doesn't take into account, Your Ladyship, is the fact that Mr. Baring had a full-time job with a benefits package, whereas my client had a part-time job monetizing her own YouTube videos, which lacks Mr. Baring's job-security, medical insurance, and so on. The fact that Mr. Baring solicited a private barrister, whereas my client received legal assistance, is problematic, and should be taken into account when My Lady reaches her verdict."

"Thank you, Mr. Fadil," replied Justice Lazrak. She added, "Tea."

The brief recess was a kind mitigation for Maria Benchekroun, and something of a disastrous, and slow-moving Third Act for Lou, who itched his blistering testicles.

After filling up on tea and biscuits, Lou and Brooke, and their respective legal teams, re-entered Courtroom No. 3.

The bailiff announced Justice Lazrak, who entered the room and returned to her high-backed chair, watching over the blue linoleum floors.

"As officials who stand at the gates of the law in Morocco," began Justice Lazrak with a pompous, but not insincere, tone of voice, "we must remind ourselves that alimony is limited by the ability to pay. We must pay heed to the adage that an eye for an eye makes the whole world blind - whether we deal in drubbings or dirhams. What a small mercy it is, then, that this particular teaching is immaterial to this case. With that in mind, I hereby order that Lou Baring shall pay Brooke Kimani the amount of 80,000 dirhams in alimony over a period of six months, in tandem with half of Mr. Baring's entire estate - including current accounts, savings, and investments - and that these monies shall be paid to Ms. Kimani by the end of the calendar year." Then she banged her gavel, directed a violent glare at Lou, and walked out of the courtroom.

Dakhlet Nouadhibou was one of the largest natural ports on the Atlantic coast of Africa, and the only one in Mauritania. Since the revolution, the infighting, and the subsequent period of stability, the port had become a defensive hub with a not unlimited focus on exporting the revolution to other countries. As a result, a fleet of weapons-heavy barges were pulled out of Dakhlet Nouadhibou by a gaggle of tugboats towards Dakhla.

The helmsman of one tugboat, Captain Sidi Maatalla, had curly black hair, a pair of cauliflower ears, a sharp nose, and a pair of angelic lips that gleamed with spittle. He was watching the apricot-coloured coastline of the Canary Islands floating by when his first mate entered the bridge.

"There is a strange Englishman on board, Captain. He said the Cultural Minister put him on board at the very last moment," the first mate said in Arabic, as he watched the gruff captain turn his eyes towards him.

"Why wasn't I told about this?" grumbled Captain Maatalla.

"The Cultural Minister told the crew to keep it a secret. She said that the less the captain knew about the Englishman, the better it would be."

"National security threat, is he?"

"He wants to speak with you."

"I'll go down," replied Captain Maatalla, giving the wheel to the first mate, poking his sharp nose into the torrential rain outside, and entering the quarters.

"Captain Maatalla, I presume?" said a characteristically British reporter wearing knee-high socks, khaki shorts, and a short-sleeved blue shirt with an ascot. "Terribly sorry about the hush-hush. It was the only way they would let me into the country."

"Who are you?" asked the captain in English, as he sat in the cramped living quarters and stared across at the pale-skinned Englishman.

"Brumby, Captain. Elijah Brumby. War correspondent." The rehearsed words came out like a twisted Sufi poem.

"There's no war here."

"That's what they told me in Morocco," complained Brumby, wiping his damp hair to one side. "I mentioned the communist troops on the border, and they denied it. I thought I should come down and meet you chaps, and talk about the nasty weather. Now, Captain, a little bird tells me that the Moroccan communists sent back some weapons that Mauritania had given them. Something about betraying the revolution? Now, I find myself on a tugboat pushing a benighted barge packed to the rim with high explosives, artillery, and general-war-mongering-brouhaha, towards that part of Morocco which is the only place that has been brought under communist control. Now, either you're going in the wrong direction, or there's been a change of sentiment between the Moroccan Communist Party, and the Mauritanian Party of Communists."

Captain Maatalla cleared his throat, massaging a cauliflowered ear. "I don't know what's happening. I get told to push things with my boat."

He exchanged awkward stares with the war correspondent.

"When we reach Dakhla, I expect that you will be leaving us?"

Brumby smiled. "I shall get out of your pearly black hair, sir."

"In that case," said Captain Maatalla as he stood up in the damp air, "I'll return to my duties, and make sure that you get into Dakhla safely."

"Thank you - "

"And that you stay off my boat. Good morning." The captain sidled out of the cramped living quarters.

Elijah Brumby leant back in the bunk and closed his eye.

Port Dakhla was a concrete island connected to the mainland by an artichoke-green bridge. The fleet of barges from Mauritania slowly drifted into the bay and several docked alongside the concrete island whilst ten others waited for their turn. The headlamps of military vehicles glistened in the falling rain as they rolled across ramps onto the port and were driven to the mainland by Moroccan soldiers. Eland armored cars, also known as African Antelopes, had four wheels and 90 mm turrets that shone in the heavy precipitation. They formed a convoy that could access smaller roads and were excellent for metropolitan combat. Meanwhile, Olifant battle tanks, also known as African elephants, squealed and creaked onto the port, and were the heaviest military vehicle on offer. Over the hundred years that had passed since the tank had been invented by South Africans and Israelis, the African elephant had been refined into the ultimate cross-country killing machine and featured a twenty-pounder, 84 mm cannon.

Into this melee of moist metal walked Elijah Brumby, carrying his rucksack, water bottle, and camera. He was accosted by several soldiers to whom he explained his predicament, after which he was forced into a jeep, and driven towards the mainland. He noticed posters of Augustu Valverde lining the atomic-tangerine buildings, and that people - whether soldiers or bystanders - saluted these posters, as if they were rakish, religious depictions, and not poorly printed depictions of a deceased mass murderer.

"What is face wanted for, my sexy wife?" asked Elijah Brumby in poor Arabic.

"The first martyr of the revolution," replied the bearded soldier. Within seconds, he had swerved in front of a passing car carrying wheelie chairs tied together with rope. The bearded soldier and his comrades stepped out of the jeep, primed their semi-automatic rifles and handguns, and stalked towards the car, whose driver emerged like the head of a shy turtle examining its surroundings for hawks, raccoons, and coyotes.

"What are these for?" asked the bearded soldier, pointing to the wheelie chairs.

"I'll sell them," replied the driver.

"Move away from the vehicle." The bearded soldier passed the driver to his comrades as though he were a Christmas hamper and then pulled out his handgun. He shot the car six times through the windshield, returned the handgun to his holster, and waved at an African elephant tank squeaking at the other end of the rain-soaked street.

The tank came towards them and increased its speed as it ran over the car and the wheelie chairs, leaving a brown-sugar-coloured heap of metal in its wake. "Okay?" said the bearded soldier, patting the driver on the back, and telling his soldiers to stay in the jeep with Elijah Brumby. They continued driving down the boulevard.

"Why break jeep-jeep like frog legs?" asked Brumby in his execrable Arabic.

"That's what happens to looters," replied a young soldier in Tamazight.

Brumby heard the Berber dialect. He looked to the bearded soldier. "No speak Barbed wire," added Brumby, casting a winning smile in his direction. "What say you?"

"He said, That's what happens to spies," replied the bearded soldier.

Posters of Augustu Valverde rocketed past as champagne-pink and corn-coloured buildings led to the square, which had been turned into a weapons dump.

"What happen to homosexual traitor?" asked Brumby in his best Arabic.

The bearded soldier turned to him. "They join the army!"

The men and women in the jeep laughed as Brumby managed to produce a well-meaning, non-committal, English titter, and fumbled nervously with his camera. Around them, a ground invasion appeared to be in the works, with soldiers, citizens, and everything in between, working together to shift diesel, petrol, and food.

Columns of African antelopes lined the streets, being loaded with ammunition. Phalanxes of African elephants roared and belched black smoke into the dark skies.

"Oh!" thought Elijah Brumby, squinting his eye. "What a lovely war!"

Lou was sitting in his office in Marrakech, with his banana-mania jacket hanging on the back of his chair and his banana-mania trousers leading to the floor. With Brooke gone, and living in an apartment that had magically appeared on the market, the property manager wondered what Brooke would do in this situation. Maybe she would yell at him. Maybe she would ignore him. And Lou faced these options - either yelling at himself, or ignoring his innermost brain - and stared into his hot chocolate, considering leaving the country. Outside, the midday sun was blocked by a series of rosy-brown clouds, and men and women walked by with cameo-pink brollies, shielding themselves from rain. The status quo of Marrakech was not worried about the increases in food and energy prices, the extra taxes on solar panels and electric cars levied by the *makhzan*, or the communists massing at the border - if there *were* communists at the border. Brooke had been his source of undiluted news. Without her, Lou felt like a teenage blogger who had decided to write about the strange world that we lived in, but with only ten percent of the information, and only five percent of the lived experience.

Lou dialed Cleopatra Griffith's number on his smartphone and held it up to his ear. *"Hold on,"* she began. *"Right - I'm back in England. We can talk now."*

"Uh-huh," said Lou.

"I'm putting you in charge."

"Uh?"

"You've got more common sense than Krish or Harry, and you're probably more likely than the other two to keep the business running."

"Uh."

"We don't need to worry about our assets because we're just a branch of a London-based company. You don't need to worry about that."

"Uh."

"I need you to listen."

"Uh-huh," agreed Lou.

"A state of emergency can only be brought in if it safeguards an essential interest, like fighting an immanent catastrophe. If the makhzan *brings in a state of emergency, they will need to tell other countries, so that they can get their citizens back home safely. In the meantime, you've got the right to life."* She coughed down the phone line. *"Nobody has the right to enslave you. They're not allowed to torture you either. You're also exempt from the non-retroactive nature of penal laws. I'm not too sure what that last one means, but if you get into a scrape with the others, just tell the nasty people that you're exempt from the non-retroactive nature of penal laws, and they*

ought to shut up. It's been a pleasure knowing you, and I hope to see you back in England."

"Why didn't we go with you?"

"Skeleton crew." Like the tips of her blonde hair, her answer was blunt. *"When the country calms down, everyone else will come back."*

"Yea." His light-cornflower-blue eyes suddenly tensed. "No, wait - "

Cleopatra hung up.

"Hello?" The property manager shook his smartphone. "Hello?"

He threw his smartphone on the desk, walked around the office, and made himself another hot chocolate. When he wondered what Brooke would do, he rounded up Krish Patel and Harry Anderson and herded them into the central, Spanish-blue office, which was uncharacteristically empty, and sported desks without desktop computers, personal paraphernalia, potted plants, or extension cords. The rain outside struck the windows delicately and created lonely, penetrating music that depressed the three remaining men, and their semi-conscious estimates for living.

"Thanks for joining me," said Lou, sounding nothing like anything resembling a boss. "I just spoke to Cleo on the phone." He coughed. "They're not coming back."

"Bastards," muttered the middle-aged and balding Harry Anderson. He shifted uneasily in his eggplant-purple suit, forest-green necktie, and brown, squeaking shoes.

"She said they're gonna come back when the country calms down," added Lou.

"Did she say when?" asked Krish Patel, brushing the lapels of his amaranth-pink suit. "Does she have a timeframe?"

"Nope."

"Bloody cowards," interrupted Harry.

"She probably has faith in Morocco," suggested Krish.

"What absolute bollocks." Harry's prospects brightened. "Who's in charge?"

"She put me in charge," said Lou.

"She put a bloody alcoholic in charge?" exploded Harry. "But you're American!"

"I'M NOT FUCKING AMERICAN!" Lou grabbed Harry's lapels and started shaking him like a defunct container of garlic powder. "WHEN DID ANYONE SAY I WAS AMERICAN? WHAT FUCKING PLANET DO YOU LIVE ON? I'M THE PROPERTY MANAGER! I'VE GOT A BRITISH PASSPORT! WUUUHHAAAA!"

Krish separated the two men and forced them into their chairs. When everyone had calmed down, he said, "Let's be rational," and then added, "You don't *look* British…"

Ahmed Russo, the caporegime of Tangier, had empty eyebrows, a button-nose, a cropped beard that widened on his chin, and a taupe-coloured quiff that curled backwards. It was midnight when he walked out of *Ahmed's Casino*, talking quietly on his smartphone as he passed sunset buildings with strawberry-red trimming, and multifarious men and women shrouding themselves with United-Nations-blue brollies, and warm-black rain jackets.

"Seriously, I don't mind the rain," said Russo into his smartphone, his Tamazight vocabulary echoing down the tiled street, past the yelling battling felines. "I just wanted to congratulate you," said Russo, stepping into an alleyway pitted with yellow-green potted plants, sprint-frost vines, and sky-blue doors and walls that glowed in the calculated moonlight that cascaded through the canopy. "I understand, Lucio. Sorry, *Mr. Vizzini.* They can't hold Dakhla forever. I'll muster as many troops as possible for the Republican Army. I'll have to pull them from the roadworks division, but I'll get those numbers." He stopped in front of a Scarlet-coloured Porsche 911, said goodnight to the new consigliere, Lucio Vizzini, and stepped inside of his expensive, electric vehicle. He winced about Vizzini's ideas as he fished his keys out of his pocket, and keyed the ignition. The car interior turned school-bus-yellow, the windows blew out with Spanish-carmine flames, and the wheels melted into smoky-black splashes of ooze that wandered down the tiled streets in search of the evil people responsible...

Antonio Maletto's ears stuck out and his thatch of dark hair made him look like a mad professor - albeit one without a university degree or a high school diploma. He wore narrow glasses that perched unevenly on his triangular nose and his breath stank. Maletto had a landline in his terraced apartment because he liked accountability - and the landline duly rang in the early hours of the morning. The caporegime of Fez, wearing his shiny-shamrock-hued dressing gown, strutted into his kitchen, picked up the telephone, and stared out of his window at the verdant hills in the distance, the spring-green buildings on the outskirts of the city, and the flooded gardens.

"Yes?" answered Maletto in Sicilian. "Congratulations, Mr. Vizzini. I'm in my apartment. It's raining outside, but it's a beautiful morning. When will the package arrive?" He nodded in the sunlight breaking through the dark clouds. "It's a good thing you woke me up. I'll report back to you when I've received the package," concluded Maletto as he put the phone down, and began making himself some coffee.

Twenty minutes later, the doorbell rang.

Maletto entered the foyer. When he opened the door, he was faced with a young man wearing a floral-white shirt and fulvous-orange trousers. The young man emptied two rounds into Maletto's forehead and watched the caporegime fall back onto a tangerine-coloured rug. The young man dragged Maletto into the tea-green kitchen, stole Maletto's house keys, and locked the front door when he went out…

Valentina Caruso, the caporegime for Rabat, was a heavy woman with a round face. She wore tart-orange lipstick, hand-knitted sweaters, and extra-large denim jeans. Having done business out of *Caruso's Launderette* for the past decade, she started that morning like any other: she woke up at five, showered and dressed for six, and entered the laundromat with its office and low-backed chairs and slimy-green tables. She put on her horn-rimmed glasses, opened her laptop, and checked the accounts for the region as a delivery driver with a takeaway breakfast from the local café entered the laundromat, dropped off the food, and then almost tripped over the constant flow of laundry bags, compostable-plastic-wrapped suits, jackets and trousers, and shoes.

Caruso made an instant coffee with powdered milk, opened the cardboard container, and stared hungrily at the two bacon slices, the two sausages, the zinnwaldite-brown slice of black pudding, the half-tomato, the fried egg, and the cardboard container of baked beans. She worked as she ate, making notes on a pad of paper next to her laptop, and sometimes stopping to fish food out of her receding gums. One of her soldiers knocked on the glass separating the office from the laundromat. "Sorry to bother you, Valentina," he said after opening the creaky door. "But one of those towel bags doesn't have a tag. It's from the *Maxwell Hotel*, but - "

"Have you looked on the ground?" asked Caruso.

"I can't find anything."

"It's too early to be stupid," replied Caruso as she entered the laundromat.

She covered her face when a beam of volt-coloured light turned the bag into dust and the surrounding laundromat into wreckage…

Late morning shed its half-light through the half-storm as the ash-grey clouds crawled over the city of Béni Mellal like a train ordered to reduce speed prior to an accident. The acid-green Peruvian peppertrees, baby-pink oleander flowers, Cambridge-blue olive trees, and emerald pomegranate trees lined the boulevards around the brand-new Energy-from-Waste facility unveiled in one of the fulvous-orange squares. The caporegime, Sara Privitera, ascended the platform and stood before the microphone so that she could deliver her speech to the dozy mid-morning populace. She had a square jaw with thin lips, and her nose was like something from a statue. Her neck trailed into her shoulders like those long-forgotten ski slopes, and she stood with her legs apart and could feel the rainy breeze fondling her amber-hued trousers.

"Good morning, everyone," began the caporegime. "It gives me great pleasure to unveil the newest Energy-from-Waste facility in the region. For those of you that *still* don't know, these plants process non-recyclable waste to produce green electricity. Forget landfills and embrace the future of electricity. We no longer rely on natural gases piped out of our country by Algeria. Instead, we burn our waste, treat the gases released, and pump them away from our homes, our children, and our restaurants." A polite laugh came from the crowd. "Celebrate this morning, with a coffee or croissant, our new, green - " Bullets fired from a passing motorcycle penetrated the baker-miller-pink platform, the bistre-brown backdrop with its illustrations of happy Moroccan people, and Sara Privitera's chest, which exploded with brick-red detonations of blood. People standing in the front row were sprayed with blood and threw up their arms as they took cover under Peruvian peppertrees and giant bushes of oleander flowers. Meanwhile, Privitera's soldiers returned fire from their handguns, secured the area, and called the consigliere, Lucio Vizzini, and the underboss, Salvatore Yannucci, to report the crime that had been committed in front of the Energy-from-Waste facility, with its solitary, burnished-brown smokestack, its glass foyer, and its free parking lot...

Rosa "Small Nose" Baracco had, yes, a small nose, and penny-sized eyes that, when she squinted, appeared to be little more than eyeless slits. She also had dimples and a face that seemed to have been pulled down when she had been a child. But her long, curly hair - flopped handsomely over her scalp - made the brave men look. Being the caporegime of Casablanca, she thought it was her duty to smoke on her rooftop patio and to stare at the city below as if its fate were connected with her own.

Strange memories on that morning, Baracco thought. Visions between the satellite dishes, the shuttered shops with their Carolina-blue awnings, the badly parked cars stricken with parking tickets, and the melon salesmen wearing their loose *kandoras*.

"Something is wrong," thought Baracco as she took another puff on her cigarette. "Something's different," she thought again, watching her smoke float into Casablanca. She heard the door open and close behind her. When she turned around, she saw two young men wearing floral-white shirts, fulvous-orange trousers, and black gloves. Knocking over the patio table, lemonade jug, and second-hand laptop, Baracco ran up and down the patio in an attempt to shake off her attackers. She made a beeline for the closest fire escape but was dragged away by the young men to the other edge.

"Who sent you?" asked Baracco, puffing for air, and coughing. "Who's your captain?"

They threw her off the side of the building. Her small body penetrated a postal van, that rocked slightly, and then released its passenger-side airbag…

Among the ochre rooftops, patios, and nickel satellite dishes of Marrakech, there was a fresh corpse wearing a neon-green jacket and leather trousers. The pitter-patter of rain cleaned the dead flesh of makeup, smudging the eyeliner and foundation, and reducing - or elevating - the deceased woman to what she really was.

The tinkling wrist of Detective Mostafa Lazrak gripped the bar of an access ladder, pulled the rest of his body onto the rooftop, and tinkled towards the sopping corpse. Lazrak's blue-sapphire suit clashed with the otherwise brown surroundings, and his thick glasses magnified the body for which he and his officers had been called out. Officers secured the area, cordoned off any potential access points, and searched the area for evidence of murder.

"That's what we're calling it," said Lazrak dully in Tamazight as he addressed the ever-resentful Sergeant Ahmed, habitually standing as if she disliked the brief given to her by the Marrakech Police Department. "Wait a minute," said Lazrak as he knelt beside the corpse and examined the face. "That's Baaqa Bell."

"Killing caporegimes," said Ahmed. "That means it's over."

"It might just be the beginning. That's going to screw up our quota," advised the detective, wiping specks of rain off of his thick spectacles. "This damn weather..."

"It's not necessarily the work of the Scarvaggis."

"Isn't it?" exclaimed Lazrak, looking at his deputy with crazed eyes.

"It could be a foreign syndicate." She laughed at the irony. "They might have come here to stir up trouble."

Detective Lazrak waved on the coroner, yanking a yellow sheet over the body. "Another one for the shelf," decided Lazrak as he turned his gaze onto the Atlas Mountains on the horizon, their peaks capped with snow and a cold wind brewing...

Tulumeu Mascali was wearing a white shirt, pastel-pink chinos, and a Persian-orange aviator's jacket as he picked up a basket at the front of *Kamal's Market* in Errachidia and made a beeline for the deli section with its fresh food, chopped fruit, and desserts. Appearing around the corner of the cleaning section, the caporegime of Errachidia's goateed face zoomed towards the steaming potato cakes and hot broad bean soup.

The manager, Kamal, with his thick sideburns and thinning hair, slapped his flax-beige suspenders against his breasts and walked towards the dazzled Mascali. "Whenever I cut the prices in the afternoon," said the manager in Tamazight, "you drag your sorry pelt into my store."

"Yea, yea," muttered Mascali, spooning broad bean soup into a cup, picking up potato cakes with his bare hands, and stuffing them into a paper bag. "You should be happy I'm buying this half-cooked garbage," added the caporegime as he thought about his declining father in one of the nearby, patriarch-purple retirement homes.

"You own the road; you don't own the store." The little manager scratched his Eton-blue trousers and wagged his finger. "Tell me this: how's your father doing?"

Mascali looked the manager in the eye.

"Honestly, how's he doing?"

"He's fine."

"Fine? Come on, we all know he's dying. The old man is dying. That's what happens when you screw people in the butthole. You end up in a godless home."

Mascali placed the potato cakes and the soup in his basket, turned to face the outspoken supermarket manager, and rubbed his shoe on Kamal's shining sneakers.

"Is that the best you can do?" muttered Kamal.

"I'm going to take him his soup and his potato cakes. And then I'm gonna come back here, and we're going to - "

"You're going to buy more? Great. Good for you."

"Listen... *Who* do you think you are?"

The manager leaned in, and said, "Your time is finished. I run a supermarket; I know these things. You came, and you raped my country, and now you are finished." He tapped the caporegime on the shoulder, and added, "The boats are ready for you."

Mascali walked towards the check-out, paid for his potato cakes and soup, and walked through the sliding glass doors into the moderate rain.

Elsewhere, Kamal brushed his hands together, looking forward to sitting in his air-conditioned office, when he heard a series of gunshots. The cashiers screamed their heads off and Kamal jogged down to the front of the store, where he found them pointing at the sliding doors.

Stepping outside, Kamal found the body of Tulumeu Mascali on the ground, his arms and legs like crosswords, and his soup seeping into the wet tarmac. The supermarket manager looked up at the sky, smiling, and said, "Thank you, friend..."

Hamid "Blackish" Harrak-Costa, the caporegime for Agadir, owned a penthouse on the promenade and enjoyed watching the bobbing, multi-coloured yachts, and the warbling waves whose navy-, non-photo-, and star-command-blues, puzzled the eye. He rarely travelled outside of his province and preferred his rigorous evening schedule, during which he inspected hotels, casinos, betting shops, and restaurants, so that he could check their accounts, prescribe remedies where necessary, and reward loyal people. Before he left the penthouse that evening, he cooked himself a light supper of Moroccan spiced fish with ginger mash. He was halfway through his meal, accompanied by a glass of Tyrian-purple juice when his nauseating doorbell rang. Throwing down his napkin, Harrak-Costa walked down two flights of stairs and answered the door.

"Thank God," said his fellow caporegime, Giovanni Alami-Russo.

"Why aren't you in Guelmim?"

"The shit has hit the fan. I need to come in - "

"You're not coming in," replied Harrak-Costa in Sicilian. "It's probably safer if we speak Sicilian out here."

"Not tonight," replied Alami-Russo in Arabic.

"You're giving me a headache; what do you want?"

"They're whacking capos up and down the country. They're doing a purge, like the old days, and we're on the fucking menu. We're getting replaced with looney-toons!"

Harrak-Costa gave a sideways glance at the passing cars on the promenade. "Listen," he said, squinting at his colleague. "In half an hour, I have to do my inspections. I have to make sure the waitresses are safe, that nobody's stealing money, and that the food is well-cooked. I can't do that with you spitting conspiracy theories on my doorstep - " He cut off Alami-Russo. " - when you *know* that I've got enough trouble in the Scarvaggi Family. I don't need more problems. Now, leave me alone."

"What do you mean, you've got enough trouble?"

"What - look - you see this?" He pointed at his skin colour. "I can't change this. And there are people in the Scarvaggi Family who take offence to my shade."

"Oh, come on - "

"Don't - listen, you cocksucker - we had that racist joke thing between us? Remember? Then you started putting on makeup, trying to make yourself lighter."

"What the hell are you talking about?" complained Alami-Russo.

"Look at yourself! You look like a reject from an olive oil commercial!"

"We need to get out of Agadir, we need to get out of the country."

"Those goombahs in Marrakech have been trying to kill me for years! They didn't manage it back then, and they're not gonna manage it *now*!"

Suddenly, a venetian-red Ford Fiesta sprayed unmellow-yellow sparks out of its passenger window, pricking the vanilla steps of the building with surges of ultra-heated dust, and riddling the two caporegimes with erupted, scarlet punctures. Alami-Russo fell across one of the lions guarding the staircase, whilst Harrak-Costa clumped his limbs against the stairs, and then plummeted down them onto the pavement...

The smouldering remains of an opal Fiat 500 crackled and sparked in the tempestuous fighting that had erupted in the streets of Laayoune. The bodies of the two hitmen - their fulvous-orange trousers turning oxblood-red in the intense flames - arched and curled as outrageous-orange fires licked their progressively scabby bodies.

Around the Fiat 500, the expansive streets of Laayoune snapped with gunfire, small explosions, and the shouts of communist soldiers, as Republican Army soldiers either laid into them with machine-gun rounds or ran awkwardly in the opposite direction. Also, windows in peach buildings blew their glass onto the roads below, and African elephants gurgled across the tarmac, their twenty-pounder 84 mm cannons obliterating enemy tanks, jeeps, and soldiers alike. More than anything, the smell of diesel, burning rubber, and human hair, filled the cloudy skies with terrible stenches.

During the battle, Mohammed Zaki-Vaccaro, the local caporegime, suffered a heart attack in his office and collapsed over his desk, muttering, "Nina - gonna be angry." His colleagues draped a white flag outside of his window and put their hands on their heads as communist soldiers flooded the building. To their astonishment, when the Scarvaggi soldiers explained who the dead man was, the communist soldiers set about carrying the body to the nearest bathroom, where they carefully washed the corpse. Ismail, well-fed and -watered, entered the building. "Bring the linen cloth," he said, watching his soldiers bring specially made wrappings for burials into the bathroom. They enshrouded Mohammed Zaki-Vaccaro in the linen cloth and drove the body - past smouldering Scarvaggi tanks and deceased Republican Army soldiers - to the local cemetery. Ismail, his Defence Minister, and a gathering band of soldiers, separated themselves into rows of men, and rows of women. Then the men recited, "Allahu Akbar," as they raised their hands up to their earlobes and placed their right hands over their left hands. "I seek refuge in Allah from the accursed Shaitan," they added, after which they said, "In the name of Allah, the Entirely Merciful, the Especially Merciful. All praise is due to Allah, Lord of the worlds - The Entirely Merciful, the Especially Merciful, Sovereign of the Day of Recompense.

"It is You we worship, and You we ask for help. Guide us to the straight path - The path of those upon whom You have bestowed favour, not of those who have evoked Your anger or of those who are astray."

They remained where they were, repeating, "Allahu Akbar," after which they said, "O Allah, let Your Peace come upon Muhammad and the family of Muhammad, as you have brought peace to Ibrahim and his family.

"Truly, You are Praiseworthy and Glorious. Allah, bless Muhammad and the family of Muhammad, as you have blessed Ibrahim and his family. Truly, You are Praiseworthy and Glorious."

They remained where they were, repeating, "Allahu Akbar," after which they said, "O Allah, forgive our living and our dead, those present and those absent, our young and our old, our males and our females.

"O Allah, whom among us You keep alive, then let such a life be upon Islam, and whom among us You take unto Yourself, then let such a death be upon faith. O Allah, do not deprive us of his reward and do not let us stray after him."

They remained where they were, repeating, "Allahu Akbar."

As the clouds above darkened and shed their precipitation on the mourners, more of whom came by the minute, the funeral by the half-destroyed city went on unfazed.

"Assalaamu 'alaykum wa rahmat-Allaah," said the mourners, turning their heads to the right.

Then, positioning Mohammed-Zaki-Vaccaro so that his body would face Mecca, he was buried.

CHAPTER THIRTEEN

It was a freezing dawn in Marrakech when Lou stared into the mirror to find a man who was older, thinner, and altogether less handsome. The aquiline nose seemed heavier, the hairs poking out of his nostrils were less controlled, the bags under his yellowed, light-cornflower-blue eyes had become engorged, and his drooped neck was painful, especially since he had hardly slept. The squally meteorological conditions returned his brain to the problem at hand. He considered what Brooke would do. She would probably go through with it. "Madness," thought Lou, checking his watch and remembering that he was naked. "Bonkers," mused the property manager as he dressed in his banana-mania suit. "But she would yell at me forever," he decided, stuffing his passports into his jacket pocket. It was not a case of multiple personalities. It was more about Lou trying to figure out which personality people wanted.

There was no winning combination, he realised. In this world of polarities, you were either pretty, or ugly - rich, or poor - safe, or doomed.

Downstairs, Lou stepped into his dark-orchid Camaro and drove to Krish Patel's apartment several blocks over.

The streets were quiet below the old-mauve apartment block. Krish appeared, and scurried into the car, saying, "Did you bring a suitcase?"

"Nuh-uh," said Lou, pulling away from the pavement and slinking towards Harry Anderson's apartment building.

"Harry has a suitcase." Rain pelted the windscreen. "Is that alright?"

"Uh-huh."

"You should take this thing to the garage." The idiocy of the statement sunk into Patel's little bear eyes. "Otherwise, the car still looks great. Drive on, old chap."

Harry Anderson dragged his brown shoes through the building's front yard, watching the dark-orchid Camaro pulling alongside the curb. He waved at Lou in the window, put his suitcase in the boot, and lodged himself in the back seat. "Straight to the airport," ordered Harry as he wiped the rain off of his balding head.

"No," replied Lou.

Harry frowned. "Fine. Kill us all. See if I care. You stupid, American-weirdo prat."

The Camaro hissed through the half-dark boulevards and turned onto Rue El Baz. Parking his car at an awkward angle, Lou got out, knocked on the door, and was surprised when a woman wearing a hijab answered the damp door. "Banana-mania," said the woman in English. "That must mean that I can trust you." She smiled and offered to show Lou inside, but the property manager cut her off, "Thanks, but I've got to be on my way - somewhere else - I just - the woman who used to live in this house - Brooke Kimani - does that name - the name probably doesn't mean anything to you."

"She moved out. It doesn't surprise me, with all these new apartments on the market. The *makhzan* must have introduced a bill or something."

"When was that?"

"Couple of weeks ago."

"She was one of my clients, you see - I need to follow up on something."

"Then you need to call England."

"You mean - she moved to England?"

"Yea."

"Thank you. That's very helpful," said Lou, quietly relieved, as he stepped into the Camaro, and drove to the long-term parking area of Marrakech Menara Airport.

"No flights grounded," observed Harry in the backseat, as his colleagues stared at the old-lace monument to modernist architecture looming outside.

The entrance, which was the size of most university sports halls, glowered in the thundery conditions, casting shadows over the tiled floor beneath the covered area, the bleak roars of airplanes hurling themselves into the clouds vibrating the car.

"Did you bring cash?" asked Krish, knowing debit cards were risky.

"Uh-huh," said Lou, searching his pockets, and frowning as nothing made itself known in his banana-mania pockets. "Wait a minute…"

"What?" muttered Harry.

"I left the cash in my bedroom."

"Sweet bloody Christ," said Harry, unbuckling his leisurely stomach, opening the door, and retrieving his suitcase from the boot. The others took it as a signal that they were proceeding with "Operation Yellowbelly," and walked with Harry to the check-in gate, where they showed their passports and bought economy-class tickets for what they described as "an urgent business venture to the land of Sunday Roasts".

The journey on foot towards the departure lounge was like travelling through a honeycomb, smiling at the female worker bees, nodding seriously at the male drone bees, and wishing to God that there was some Queen Bee who would save the country.

"It's not popular," said Krish, "but I'm a royalist through and through."

"Will you shut up?" whispered Harry.

"Case and point," sighed Krish, finishing off a small tub of peppermint ice cream, whose sole purpose was to supplement the waste surplus destroying the world. Meanwhile, Lou's brain returned to boarding school; he made a fiction to remain alive. He could see Brooke making it out of Morocco. He could picture her shacking up with a strapping Englishman with a bear-cock. Like, the biggest dick Lou had ever seen. He envisioned Brooke buying a house in Cornwall and having amazing sex all the time. "Why Cornwall?" thought Lou, searching for logic. "Safe, remote, and filled with second-home-owners," his subconscious answered.

Old Uncle Lou
Gonna die, gonna die, gonna die
When the girls have sex on the floor
They step on Uncle Lou, like a fly

The song, or versions of it, bubbled through the property manager's consciousness as the plane landed in Seville. The scorching city was in southern Spain, which had been conquered by Muslims in 711 A.D., after which it became a cultural and commercial centre under the Abbādid Dynasty, and then the Almohad and Almoravid confederations. Muslim control of the city was curtailed in 1248 by Spanish Christians under Ferdinand III, a major figure of the *Reconquista* that re-established Catholic authority in Spain. Ironically, Lou, Krish, and Harry sweated their way through an arrivals section, that had more in common with the Moscow Metro than any Catholic house of God. Collectively, they exhaled when they made it through security and approached a Naples-yellow stall selling SIM cards, cold drinks, candy bars, and news magazines. The woman sitting at the stall was wearing a low-cut, neon-blue top, an outer-space necklace suspending a wedding ring, and khaki shorts with grease stains. Her dark hair was tied back in a ponytail, her hooped earrings dangled perilously, and her girth was such that it was hard to tell where the stall ended, and where she began. Harry Anderson pushed ahead with his suitcase, smiling at the woman in the stall. "Hola - SIM cards - SIM - for the phone?" he said in English, sliding his finger over his phone.

"These are the phone cases I've got," replied the woman in Spanish, and gestured to the persimmon-hued, pewter-blue, and pink-lavender smartphone cases.

"No, no - gracias," replied Harry. "No, the - I want - this - " He slid his finger up and down the phone again. "The bloody - SIM - the SIM card - for the smartphone."

The woman pulled out a bunch of SIM cards, and said in fast Spanish, *"What-SIM-cards-would-you-like-a-monthly-plan-or-pay-as-you-go?"*

Krish pushed Harry to one side. "Cuanta. Cuanto. Cuanta. Cuanto?"

Harry watched the unfolding scene, as if he was a mental health nurse.

"Cuanta? Cuanto-Cuanta? Aquí?" added Krish, and the woman beamed a tolerant smile at the Englishmen and held up six fingers.

"Cientos?" Krish asked.

"How much?" interrupted Harry. "How much for the bloody things?"

Lou pushed the two men out of the way. "Tres. Gracias."

The woman rang up the price on her Naples-yellow tablet and received a crumpled Euro that Krish had discovered in his leather wallet.

Half an hour later, the Zaalouk delegation arrived at the Hilton Garden Inn. The puce-coloured buildings looked like a congregation of shining tombstones, and the hotel desk in the lobby was covered by three dangling Portland-orange lights.

The concierge was a limp man wearing a razzmic-berry three-piece suit, who pursed his lips between queries, and whose back seemed to be permanently vertical. "I'm sorry, gentlemen, but you'll be lucky to find a room during the holiday season."

"Can I just - ask you - what month it is?" asked Lou.

The concierge looked at Lou, then at the two other men.

"It's December," said the concierge. Then he looked at the screen beneath him. "The best I can do, right now, is a suite with one bed."

"We can do that," said Krish.

"No," said Harry with a calm tone. "No, Krish - we can't do that."

"Okay," said the concierge. "We happen to have a golfer staying with us. He gave us his express wishes that the settees should be removed from his penthouse suite; the settees are in storage, adjacent to the gym. Now, I could work those into your room?"

"It's not Spree Curtiz?" asked Lou.

"You know him?"

"I do - I mean - I met him - I did some work for him."

The concierge said, "And you *don't* want to share the bed?"

"We'll take the settees," Harry cut in.

The honorary British consul in Seville was named Dame Cressida Whatley. She was a heavyset woman in her fifties with square teeth, large cheeks, and a stubby nose. She was wearing a white tee shirt and a queen-blue suit as she walked into her office. She greeted a bearded man wearing a rajah suit, shook his hand, and sat down. "Your name's Brumby-Curzon," said Whatley, as if it were an accusation. "You're not related to that Elijah Brumby, by any chance, are you? That grim, one-eyed war correspondent? When he was in Moscow, your lot set a raven on him. He didn't take the offer too kindly, apparently, and threatened to phone the consulate in the middle of a mutiny."

"I honestly couldn't say," said Brumby-Curzon.

"Alright," said Whatley, picking up a paper file from her desk, and thumbing the pages as though it were a long novel of dubious quality. "Give me all the juicy details," she added, locating the first page. "Anything odd about Mr. Baring's upbringing?"

"Born in Bermuda. Mother's artistic. Father's a raconteur."

"That's the official description, I take it?"

"Parents divorced when Baring was six. Mother lives with her family; father vanishes, presumed dead. Baring stays in Bermuda for schooling until he's sixteen."

"Run-of-the-mill upbringing…Where does he go after that?"

"His aunt pays for him to go to Stowe School."

"Prospero reaches the island. How does he get off, Brumby-Curzon?"

"Studies for his B.A. in property management at Coventry University. He starts an internship in London at Acton Properties. Then things go off the rails a bit."

"Gap in his résumé the size of Acton - and such a good, boring start."

"He was there for about a month. They didn't appreciate his drinking."

"Prospero and his bottle." Whatley pulled the neck of her shirt. "Except Zaalouk Real Estate couldn't give a monkey's - but they care enough to ship him to Morocco."

"Yes, ma'am. He gets on quite well at the Marrakech branch."

"Because he's bone idle. But then he meets one of our people?"

"We try sending a raven, who works for the Marrakech police department. He's been on our books for several years now, and we figure that Lou might be an avenue. The raven tries blackmailing Lou. They wanted him to gather some intelligence. Get the fool working for us. Regrettably, about this time, the country starts falling apart - "

"And not because of us, I take it?"

"The country becomes politically more volatile."

"The raven's a throwaway," decided Whatley.

"We don't know where he is."

"Bloody sloppy." Whatley squinted her piggy eyes and tightened her mouth. "What happened to the swallow in London?"

"Baring sobers up. This is something he does well. He receives awards on behalf of Zaalouk Real Estate at the International Property Awards - "

"Happy-clappy, multicultural bollocks - "

"The swallow makes contact, ends up dating him, and marrying him."

"And how on earth did *that* happen?"

"She weighed up the risk and she married him. Baring was still in contact with our raven, but our swallow tries to make better use of Baring as a floater - someone we can use. But she was already a provocateur in her own right, and the YouTube provocation which she produced, ended up depreciating her attempts to make Lou a better floater."

"She divorces him," said Whatley, readjusting herself in the creaking chair, and looking expectantly at Brumby-Curzon for details.

"She was called back by her case officer."

"So much for Miranda - or was she meant to be Ariel, I wonder?" Whatley shut the file and walked around the office, which was adorned with British flags, potted cacti, several portraits of Prime Ministers and monarchs, and a royal-yellow globe. "One: Lou gets pulled in by a throwaway agent, who we can presume is deceased. Two: Lou tries to please the raven, but to no avail, because things are heating up. Three: Lou gets seduced by a swallow, marries the girl, but he can't focus on his wife because now he's a workaholic, instead of an alcoholic, and her own provocation operations destroy what could have been a perfect chance to turn him into a more effective floater. Four: all hell breaks loose in the Western Sahara, the communists invade Dakhla, Lou's company leaves him and two others in the dust because they're a bunch of property wankers, and Lou and his colleagues disobey the central office."

Brumby-Curzon raised his eyebrows.

"That's a turn-up for the books," declared Whatley, her flat shoes padding across the raw-umber carpeting. "They catch a plane to Seville at the last minute, they take Spree Curtiz's settees, and now I have to clean up this whole bloody mess."

Brumby-Curzon shifted in his rajah suit. "I don't think it would be advisable to send him back to Morocco."

"He'd be shot on sight," remarked Whatley, rather hyperbolically, since the Scarvaggi Regime had nothing but good things to say about Lou Baring; that was, until the communists invaded northern Morocco, and the whole country changed regime.

"And all we have to show for it is chicken feed," added Brumby-Curzon.

"If only we could get our hands on someone from the belly of the beast. Seduce them. Bring them over to the West. Put them through our exciting interview process."

"We have to wait a while. We could possibly do a prisoner exchange."

"Doable?"

"I don't see why not."

"Good morning, then," said Whatley, sitting back at her desk.

The agent collected the paper file from Whatley's desk and stalked out of the office.

Double-checking that he had left the room, Whatley pressed the intercom on her desk and told her secretary to allow Lou Baring into the office. The hardwood door on the other side of the room opened, and in walked the sweating property manager. "Good morning," said Lou, shaking hands with the British consul and sitting down. "I'm from - Bermuda - but the accent's not American - I have a British passport – like, for real."

"Mr. Baring, I've seen your passport."

"Uh-huh, but - "

"I believe you, when you say you're British," said Whatley, folding her hands over her desk. "So, you managed to escape Maghreb?"

"No, Morocco."

"Never mind." Clearly cultural history was not his strength. "First of all, welcome to Seville, and secondly, it's good to see people from Britain. It does get lonely here."

"The mafia's running Morocco," interrupted Lou. "And the communists - they're worse, you know - they're going around the country killing people! Wait a minute." His face hardened. "You said something, like, I managed to get out of Morocco?"

"I beg your pardon?"

"Like you're expecting me to come here?"

Whatley loosened the collar of her queen-blue jacket around her neck. "People in London have been monitoring intelligence coming out of Morocco for years. It shouldn't be surprising that we're watching who goes in, and who's coming out - especially with the communists, as you say, and the current *makhzan* as it stands."

"Huh?"

"Sir, you *are* aware that countries spy on one another, I take it?"

"Really?" He panted and licked his lips. "Why?"

"You've never wondered what your neighbors were doing in your apartment block? It's perfectly natural. Same idea, different application."

"How do you know - I live in a flat?"

"I don't - do you own a house?"

"No - I lived in a flat," replied Lou, staring into an imaginary horizon.

"Mr. Baring," interjected Whatley, rapping the desk with her knuckles. "Do you know a man named Kossi Bundhoo?"

"Nuh-uh."

"Are you aware that you are wanted for the murder of Kossi Bundhoo?"

"I DIDN'T DO IT!" shouted Lou, across the desk.

"The Mauritanian Party of Communists have charged you with the crime. This is complicated by the fact that Bundhoo was murdered when his party was on the fringe, but now that they control Mauritania, there are retroactive laws holding you accountable."

"Says who?"

"There's the Mauritanian Party of Communists, who recently had a re-shuffle; there is also the Moroccan Communist Party, who are working their way up Morocco, as well as damning reports in the *Dakhla Worker* and the *Choum Female Engineer*. The Mauritanians want to arrest you. The Moroccans want to arrest you, too. The second avenue is politically less damaging, but when the Moroccan Communist Party seizes power, which will be in the near future, they will establish the same penalties."

"You don't think the commies have a chance?"

Whatley laughed and said, "The commies, as you call them, have a tendency to make their own luck, and to export it with devastating efficiency to other countries."

"We've gotta stop this!"

"Correct me if I'm wrong, Mr. Baring, but you said that the mafia ran Morocco?"

"The mafia's running Morocco," repeated Lou. "And the communists - they're worse, you know - they're going around the country killing people! They're worse!" Like a *Commie Bastards* album looped to play perpetually, Lou repeated the same arguments via the same concerns.

"Why shouldn't there be a revolution?" asked Whatley, understanding the ex-property manager as a living argument against free will.

Lou had no answer to this simple question.

"As one British national to another," said Whatley, creaking in her chair. "Leave Seville and return to England. Take your colleagues with you. You must know, this is only the beginning. An Englishman caught between three cultures is better off fighting his case in England than in South-Western Europe. And stay away from journalists."

The weather in the British Overseas Territory of Gibraltar, near the southern tip of the Iberian Peninsula, was very warm, and cirrus clouds peppered the otherwise clear pale-aqua sky, that yawned over the rocky headland like a sinful whale. The old-lace tower blocks loomed over the Persian-plum-topped dwellings and failed to cast any shadows in the all-encompassing sun. An observation tower that straddled the mainland and the man-made dock which extended across the harbour began to "whoop-whoop" with odd nautical alarms. The officers behind the glass notified the marine section of the Royal Gibraltar Police that a small inbound vessel had been spotted floating aimlessly in the local port.

"Looks unmanned," said the chipper English accent into the radio; "and the engines seem to be off as well; it looks as though the tides are bringing the vessel closer. We're meant to be receiving two general purpose tankers in the next half-hour. One of them's captained by that Pole, Jagoda, and I don't want to get on his bad side. You dig, Simon?"

Inspector Simon Webb, and constables Dirk Burton and Alice Chapman, boarded the quick-silver-hulled interceptor, with its plump-purple and process-yellow bands, and swiftly rode out to the middle of the harbour, where they caught the foreign boat.

"Small cabin cruiser," said Inspector Webb from behind the wheel of his interceptor. He was a middle-aged man with a clipped, white moustache, arched eyebrows, and a beakish nose with reddish veins pricking the end. He circled the cabin cruiser, switched on the loudspeaker, and picked up the mouthpiece. "I would like to remind you that it is lawful for any immigration officer, without a warrant, to enter any vessel, where there is reason to believe that non-Gibraltarians may be harbored, or concealed contrary to the provisions of this Act, and to search for and to take into custody such non-Gibraltarians to be dealt with according to law." He lowered the mouthpiece, looking expectantly at Constable Chapman, who squinted.

"Do you want to board her?" asked the young constable.

"Looks like we'll have to," replied Inspector Webb.

The interceptor pulled alongside the cabin cruiser as guns were unholstered, ropes secured, and the interceptor's engines neutralized.

"Hello?" intoned Inspector Webb as he kept his hand on his holster and jumped onboard the cabin cruiser. The floor was covered with rotting melon rinds, an assortment of rich-black and rose-ebony wrappers, two empty bottles of rosso-corsa fizzy drinks, and what looked like an empty, scarlet-hued wine-box. "You're in Gibraltar," said Inspector Webb, wincing at his discovery. "We're police."

Over the bobbing of the two boats in the water and the squawks of seagulls below the cirrus clouds, there was an ever-present thudding noise - like a decrepit, old man knocking senselessly, and slowly, upon a door that would never open in his unhappy lifetime.

"It's the cabin door; it's unlocked," said Constable Burton.

Inspector Webb removed his handgun. He opened the door as far as it would go and watched his companions duck to avoid possible danger.

But nothing came.

Only the putrid stench of dead flesh.

"Oh, Christ," said Inspector Webb, peering into the cabin below.

The sideboard had been smashed open, the bolts holding the table onto the floor had been ripped apart, and the body of a man with a shaved head, a trimmed beard, and what must have been very expressive eyebrows, was laid back on the cushions. The body was wearing an artichoke-green, double-breasted trench coat, a white shirt with a loosened apricot necktie, black shoes, and Crayola-coloured socks. The man's attire had seen better days, however, and depressed indents from blunt instruments ran up and down the body, like the rolling hills of Celtic states.

Outside, Constable Chapman inspected the empty fuel tank.

"Must have been out here for several days," said Inspector Webb.

"Then he must have been going in circles," said Constable Chapman. "Supposing he came from Tangier, for example, he couldn't have burnt through that much fuel."

Inspector Webb pulled out a surgical mask from his pocket, slapped it over his face, and searched the pockets of the dead man.

Constable Burton searched beneath the sideboard. "There's a hidden safe, sir."

"He's a Moroccan policeman," interrupted the inspector, with several damaged forms of identification flapping in his palms. "There's a note as well." He passed it to Constable Burton beneath him. "Might want to try the code - right *there*," he added, indicating a five-digit code to the officer as he restrained his already unhappy tummy.

When they opened the safe, they found a plastic bag filled with memory sticks. They were of various sizes and descriptions and looked as though they had been compiled over a long period of time. "He did a good enough job hiding these things," said Inspector Webb, as he and Constable Burton joined Constable Chapman outside. "His name was Hassan Hacimi," added the sad Webb. "He was an inspector, like me."

CHAPTER FOURTEEN

The boardroom in Nina Scarvaggi's townhouse glimmered with rain-addled sunlight that shone through the window, brightening the long table. As per usual in business meetings, the table was covered in canapés, ashtrays, bowls of fruits, and anonymous bottled sparkling water. There were only four bottles laid out, however, and as the door was opened by a youth wearing fulvous-orange trousers, it was clear that it was going to be a small meeting of like-minded people. The Spanish prime minister and the Algerian president were shown into the boardroom, with their advisors, and they took their seats at the long table.

The Spanish prime minister, Diego Delgado, had a long nose, wide eyes, plump lips, and delicate hands. He was also wearing a big-dip-o'ruby suit, with a blue tie, and black shoes.

The Algerian president, Eleanor Zidane, had bright red lips, a wide nose with a dimple on its tip, and curly hair tightened back into a bun. She was also wearing a pinstripe suit with blush- and bronze bands, a cadmium-orange shirt, and carmine heels.

On the other side of the room, the sliding doors opened, and Nina Scarvaggi was wheeled into the boardroom, and seated at the head of the table. Her Falu-red blouse hung on her body as if she were a coat-hanger and her Finn-purple dress was a cloud. She looked tired - but the chance of meeting these political leaders awakened her and the brain within her high forehead was soon taking in their body language.

Behind her, the new consigliere, Lucio Vizzini, walked into the room wearing his open-necked white shirt and his burlywood jacket. His intense eyes hummed amidst his pinched features, as he stared coldly at his esteemed company.

"Will you be seated?" asked Delgado in English, flashing one of his winning smiles.

"No," replied Vizzini.

The Spanish prime minister's smile faded away.

"All here," interrupted Nina, continuing the conversation in English. "Perhaps you can tell me why you refuse to support a democratic *makhzan* in Morocco?" She looked directly at the Spanish prime minister, who crossed his be-socked ankles.

"You can't expect Spain to give you weapons when she, Morocco, and Algeria, are members of NATO. The region has been destabilized."

"That depends on what you mean by destabilization."

"Your *makhzan* is facing mass flooding destroying your infrastructure and you have communists charging through southern Morocco."

"That is not Morocco's fault," replied Nina. "We might as well have a ground invasion coming from Mauritania."

"But you don't - you have Moroccan communists, with Mauritanian weapons, fighting their fellow Moroccans." He sighed. "You have a civil war on your hands."

Lucio Vizzini stepped closer and said, "There are two parts of the North Atlantic Treaty Organisation. There are political priorities and military priorities. We cannot define the communists as a military power in their own right, because that would imply a foreign power's influence over the Moroccan nation. If we follow that line, we will do great harm to North Africa, and we simply cannot commit to such a line. Therefore, Morocco is faced with a political uprising forged in a neighboring country. Our intelligence shows us that their leader - the man called Ismail - broke out of a Mauritanian mine, staffed partly by a Mauritanian prison - and that is proof enough of the foreign minds working together to destroy the Moroccan nation. But they are nothing more than a political rabble. We don't hold Mauritania, and her government, responsible for unemployed fools who decide to cause trouble for other countries."

The Algerian president clicked her carmine heels under the table. "You've been causing trouble for long enough," she said, thinking about the boy Sultan, Abdul Aziz, who had signed "the act of Algeciras" in 1906, formally placing Morocco's administration, system of customs, national bank, and police force, under French/European control. Unable to collect taxes, the *makhzan*'s control over Morocco had collapsed. "You have no right to be here. The country you occupy is turning against you."

Nina pursed her thin lips. "Why do you keep all that French architecture? Why don't you destroy it?"

"They're good buildings."

"They are *symbols*."

"The English tore down all their political statues. Now they have footballers, comedians, and T.V. presenters lining their streets. The result is that children don't know who they are, because they worship their screens and sleep all the time. There's no chance, as long as I am alive, of the same thing happening in Algeria. There's no chance that I will lie to my people and start destroying their history." She glared defiantly at the old *Cummari* and clarified, "You have been in power for too long."

"I am sorry that we used up the natural gas you wanted," said Nina.

"We need a political solution," interrupted Vizzini. "That's why we are sitting in this room. We need a healthy solution, from our best allies."

"But people are joining these communists," said Delgado, flapping his hands and shifting in his chair as though someone had told him a particularly good Spanish joke. "The whole thing might turn into a bloodless revolution - "

"The blood is there," complained Nina. "They are killing my people!"

"*Your* people?"

"The Moroccans are my people." She squinted and pointed at the Spaniard. "You have Basques, you have Jews, you have Armenians, and Turks. When people start killing them on your soil, do you watch them die? Do they belong to someone else?"

Eleanor Zidane rolled her eyes.

"And *you*," added Nina, pointing at the Algerian president. "You have Arabs, you have Christians, and you have Mozabites - and Mozabites have their own language!"

"You put your minorities in trucks," replied Zidane, brushing away a curl of hair. "Was that a political, or a military, priority?"

"You are the president of your country. You make hard decisions."

"I will not give you weapons to kill Moroccans!" She stood up, joined her advisors, and was shown out of Scarvaggi's townhouse.

The Spaniard flashed another winning smile. The grin vanished when he noticed how dissonantly Nina and her pit bull were staring at him.

"Do you miss owning my father's country?" asked Vizzini, reminding the Spanish president of how the Spanish Crown of Aragon had once ruled the Sicilian Island. There was also an invocation of the Spanish protectorate in Morocco: a northern strip along the Mediterranean, and a southern strip touching the then-titled Spanish Sahara. The Spanish had left Morocco in 1956, apart from small enclaves along the Mediterranean.

Delgado simmered in his big-dip-o'ruby suit and rubbed his delicate hands against one another. "It could have been avoided," noted the Spaniard. "But you cannot change the past." He stood up, joined his advisors, and was shown out of the Scarvaggi townhouse.

Vizzini scoffed in the boardroom. He tossed an olive in his mouth, put his hands into his burlywood pockets, and strutted around the room like a cockerel. "Spics and sand-niggers," muttered the consigliere. "Might as well ignore most of the continent. They're not making strides in green energy, building materials, or politics. They should be thankful we came here. Get on their hands and knees and start praying."

"Lucio," hissed Nina, her arthritic fingers gripping the edge of the cold table. Her eyes bulged out of their sockets as she caught the demented consigliere's attention. "Call Dr. Zaki - bring him here - I can see the face - the Old Boss, the stupid woman!" Nina began convulsing, coughing, and slapping invisible shapes, as Vizzini rushed to her side and called for the fulvous-orange-trouser-wearing men to apprehend Dr. Zaki.

Opposite the Charles River in Boston, Massachusetts, the Pagan Rock Club opened its doors to crowds of American-flag-waving men and women, and everything in between, who stormed the music venue. The performance space inside had a low ceiling, a burnished-brown bar in the corner of the dance floor, cherry-blossom-pink and chili-red lights that swooped across the room at intervals, and unisex toilets protected by French-blue swinging doors, covered in a decade's worth of fingerprints.

Several hundred men and women, and everything in between, packed the venue, ordering drinks from an increasingly stressed part-time barman, and formed a seething mass of expectant youngsters, clapping their hands and stomping their booted feet. Suddenly, the curtains parted and out walked the American golfer, Spree Curtiz: still wearing his Bermuda shorts, his bronze shirt, and his English-red-rimmed glasses; still arseholed on methadone and tramadol in an attempt to cure his terrible back pain.

"Friends of Morocco!" announced Curtiz, waving his hands around the packed room. He was greeted with a thundering applause, which shook the building's foundations. "Welcome to the first Morocco Charity Concert!" Once again, he was greeted with loud applause and several people in the front row shouting, "Uh-huh! Yass Spree!" Then a gloom came over the famous golfer as he held up his hands in supplication. "But there's a bigger reason I'm here tonight. You know, folks, when you're on the third hole, and the weather has started to turn, life can throw things in your direction. As some of you may know, I was in Morocco several months ago. I was shocked by the homophobia and came to hate Morocco very passionately. But then one of my personal assistants had the guts to sort out my background on descent.com - and thank God she did - because - I've discovered, to my delight - that I'm two per cent Moroccan." People started clapping wildly, shouting loudly, and stomping furiously. "And I realised that my hatred of Morocco's homophobia was a calling on my part.

A calling for me to start this wonderful organisation, so that the good people of Boston could return Morocco to the state of grace that once flowed through its veins." The men and women (and everything in between) of Boston applauded irresponsibly. "Before we start our amazing line-up tonight, I'd like to introduce you to someone." At this moment Curtiz went offstage and fetched a man-sized effigy of Lou Baring. He returned with the effigy and tied the papier-mâché body to a sacrificial wheelie chair. The audience - all of whom followed the Morocco Communist Party on Twitter, and who had been educated about Lou and his well-known murder of Kossi Bundhoo - booed the effigy and tossed drinks at the stage. Some of them passed out from hatred.

"Should we teach him a lesson?" Curtiz asked the audience.

"Uh-huh!"

"Yass Spree!"

"Kill all real estate!"

Curtiz took out a box of matches, struck one against the box and held the flame to the effigy's feet which quickly caught fire and set the rest of the body ablaze.

The stage filled with smoke as the first music act of the night approached their instruments. The musicians sported French-raspberry mullets and forest-green trousers, the lead singer smoking a cigar, as he approached the microphone with malice. "Our next song - " He kicked the fiery effigy away from him. "Get away from me!" There was general applause. "Our next song is about a beautiful man who was a leading advocate of the *gay market*." He flicked his cigar into the crowd, picked up his bass guitar, and played the first three, happy-go-lucky notes of that chic composition,

Hum it, Ham it, Hack it, Hayek
Hayek, now, baby, don't put that Keynes on me

I say, Hum it, Ham it, Hack it, Hayek
Hayek, now, baby, don't put that Keynes on me

You got me spending all this green like a clown
Just look at me

Several days later in London, Lou was sitting in the Zaalouk Real Estate headquarters. He was working in a shared office with exposed ducts, dangling Eton-blue lights, and two rows of deep-space-sparkle tables where people worked on laptops. Sandalwood shelves carried potted money trees, snake plants, and Boston ferns, and panes of glass separated the shared office space from executives sitting in solo offices.

"Huh," thought Lou with all the heartache that our technological strides had to offer. To his right was a man named Orlando Willoughby, who had forgone university in favour of sitting inside, talking to property moguls about London, and sniffing loudly. To his left was a woman named Tallulah Forbes-Dempsey, who split her time between the office, an accessible cocktail bar, and her parents' terraced mansion.

"Huh," thought Lou with that damaging sense of dissatisfaction and low self-esteem. His smartphone buzzed on his desk and he winced when he saw the name. Scurrying into the shared hallway, he answered the phone. "Are you okay, Brooke?"

"What's that question for?"

"I wasn't expecting you to call me. You're not hurt or anything?"

"I'm fine."

"Uh."

"Yea."

"Uh," repeated Lou.

"Do you have Twitter?"

"I don't know."

That familiar, almost wife-like pause, stifled the phone line:

"What do you mean you don't know?"

"My job has Twitter. But I don't have a personal account - "

"Okay, fine," interrupted Brooke. *"That's okay - someone put it on YouTube, so I'll send you the link that way."*

Rubbing the end of his aquiline nose, Lou squinted in the dodger-blue hallway under the fluorescent lights. He panted through seconds of deliberation. "Brooke, don't you think - I don't know - like - we shouldn't be talking like this. Don't you think - the way, like - as if we're - you know, it sounds like I'm married - "

"You need to know what I'm telling you. They're burning effigies of you."

"Who is?" He pulled at his beltline and nodded to himself. "What's an effigy?"

"It's a big doll that's meant to look like you."

"Fair enough."

"No, but they're burning it."

"Oh yea." He took a deep breath. "Why does it look like me?"

"They really got the nose right."

"Why'd you take so long to call me? It's like the first time in months, and you're talking about people burning me. It sounds like a terrible prank. Are you pranking me?"

"Lou, listen - "

"But - hold up - you're gonna say that I already said we shouldn't be talking, because we're divorced and shit, and I wanted to get in there first and say that you should've called me months ago. You could've asked about the alimony money - that would've been nice - just to have someone to talk to - someone who was just normal."

"Lou, I - "

"I've never heard of an effigy," said Lou, hanging up, and walking back into the office.

When Lou returned to his shared desk, Orlando Willoughby was sitting with his legs crossed, and staring at Lou as though he had tried to blackmail the Royal Family.

"The boss is annoyed with you," he said, hissing between his words. "You don't have Twitter, do you? If you had Twitter, you'd catch up with everything. Really quickly."

"Huh?"

"The thing on Twitter."

"It's really bad," added Tallulah Forbes-Dempsey. "It's like, so bad. It's, like, literally, the worst thing I've ever seen in my life. Honest to God, it's the worst - "

"Top ten worst things," said Orlando, levitating his hands in the air. "It's like, here, right? - but then Lou's, like, down here, right? - and everything else is, like - "

"Uh-huh," said Lou.

"Do they have effigies in America?" asked Orlando.

Without warning, Lou put his hand out and pushed Orlando gently. But there was something in Baring's light-cornflower-blue eyes that spoke to wars, and holocausts.

Cleopatra Griffiths leaned out of her glass case. She called the ex-property manager into her glass case, shut the door, and frowned.

Everyone could see them talking.

"We didn't have to give you a job when you came back. You didn't listen to us, you came back on your own volition, and the boss chickened out, and made me the boss. They said that I needed to start cutting back," she said, straining her high cheekbones. "But I kept you on, Lou, because you didn't have anyone else. But now you're repaying me tenfold for that mistake, aren't you?" She strutted around in her carrot-orange pantsuit, plunging her knife-thin high heels into the desert-sand carpet. "Twitter's exploding, and the sparks, and flames, have got your stupid mug on them." She turned her desktop monitor around and pressed a button on her keyboard. Lou leaned in, watching Spree Curtiz dragging out an effigy of Lou, and setting it aflame.

"They really got the nose right," said Lou.

"That's all you have to say?"

"You see the guy burning me? That guy used to be gay. Told me so himself."

"Lou - I need you - to offer me - your resignation."

The knees in Lou's banana-mania trousers buckled. His aquiline nose twitched, the bags under his eyes lengthened, and his shoulders melted.

Tears tickled the English-red corners of his exhausted eyes, as his dry lips formed invisible words that described his innermost desires, neuroses, and phobias.

"Why are you doing this?" asked Lou.

"You'll find it easier to find work if you resign. Getting fired is a black mark."

"But I cleaned up, Cleo - I cleaned up and got everything right - and - I'm sorry we came back from Morocco - but - I was scared, and there - nothing was working."

"That's not an excuse for abandoning your post."

"But the post was stupid!" screamed Lou. "What's wrong with me?"

"Nothing - "

"Why don't you hate the people in the video!? Why don't you hate Spree Curtiz!? You think they're brave because they're on Twitter!?"

"I don't think - "

"Yes, you do, you fucking idiot!" Tears streamed down his face. "I just want to be normal! Why can't I be normal? You think Spree Curtiz is normal? The guy's a fucking junkie!" He lunged across the desk and started shaking Cleopatra Griffith's lapels, shouting for help from a cosmic being who had, so far, been helpful. "What's the matter with you, Cleo? You're some peroxide devil woman from Venus! Let the Venusians take you back, Cleo! Let the fucking saucers come and take you! WUUUHHAAAA!"

Orlando Willoughby and Tallulah Forbes-Dempsey rushed inside the office and pulled Lou away from their distressed boss, who was yelling and shuddering.

The ex-property manager was dragged out of the office and forced into the dodger-blue hallway. For a long time, Orlando shouted, "Fascist!" through the glass. But Lou had lost all of his senses as he was half-carried, half-dragged out of the building, onto the streets of Richmond, by two security guards who secretly hated real estate agents.

Richmond Green had once boasted several Common Limes, London Planes, and Norway Maples, but they had been cut down to make room for a merry-go-round, whose heat-wave-orange and lawn-green lights shone through the windows of surrounding terraced houses, expensive cafés, and time-honored, energetic pubs. Gone were the liver-coloured fallen leaves, and their pleasant smell of rotting matter. The tarmac, the pavements, and the medium-carmine of the bricked terraced houses, were more apparent than before, and the way the Green had lived had sadly changed.

On the corner of Richmond Green was a pub called *The Cocksure Feline*. Its front was livened with maximum-yellow-red lettering against a midnight-blue background, and it was into this pub that Lou Baring wandered after being fired for having an effigy of him burned on Twitter. With his arrival, the weather had darkened and frozen over, and it had begun to snow clumps of mint-cream snowflakes populating the air, and Richmond Green was on its way to becoming the winter wonderland promised by the obnoxious merry-go-round, its bright colours, and its Santa-Claus-suit-wearing owner.

Lou sat at the bar in his banana-mania suit, removed his burlywood necktie and ordered a double Wild Turkey. The black barman had a goatee, bags under his eyes, and small ears that were on their way somewhere. He gave the drink to Lou, who sat drinking the burnt-orange liquid with a half-nervous expression in his light-cornflower-blue eyes. Thoughts of Brooke flashed through his mind. When he finished the drink, he ordered another double Wild Turkey, and looked around *The Cocksure Feline*.

The room was full of men wearing Mountbatten-pink suits and trousers, and women wearing malachite-green dresses and blouses. Most of them spoke amongst themselves, whilst others were watching the violent rugby match on the television.

"Thanks," said Lou, nodding politely at the barman.

When he drank the burnt-orange-hued fluid, he felt more assured of himself. Gone were the doubts, like the trees in Richmond Green, that had polluted his levity. "I can drink like the rest of London," thought Lou. "I can drink like the rest of the world," he added, chucking the rest of the clinking, ice-filled glass down his desperate gullet.

Not that desperation had entered his Kobi-pink brain. Desperation was for other people. "This is levity," thought Lou, catching the attention of the barman, who privately rolled his eyes, fetched Lou another drink, and feigned humour.

Old Uncle Lou
Give me more, give me more, give me more
When the girls have sex on the floor
They say Old Uncle Lou, give me more

Gunmetal-coloured pints of Guinness, Japanese-carmine bottles of Château de London Thames, and the kelly-green shots of chartreuse, had sucked the colour out of the room. Gone were the Mountbatten-pink suits and trousers, the malachite-green dresses and blouses, the KSU-purple rugby jerseys, and the laser-lemon chairs. "Bring them back," thought Lou, removing his jacket, and fanning his sweat patches. Everything was blurred and terrible as the lemon-meringue luminescence forced shining glares into Lou's vision, making the world brighter, but hiding it, all the same.

He turned to look at what he thought was the goateed barman, and said, "They're never gonna understand us. Britain's an island, but they don't seem to like islanders."

"I'm from Croydon," said the barman, with a mixture of irritation and detachment.

"Bermuda," said Lou.

"What?"

"That's me. In my blood - "

"Well, it's probably dead now with everything you've had to drink."

Lou stared at the barman in bemused drunken confusion as to what to say next, and who to say it to, and what to say in return to the inevitable refusal of advances. He picked up his glass of Château de London Thames and tried standing up. Like a man whose legs had miraculously grown back after a history of risk-taking, the ex-property manager - and now ex-real estate agent - shuffled through the crowded throng of people, all of whom ignored him with commendable remoteness. But had they taken their attention away from their navels, they would have noticed that the man wearing the banana-mania trousers and carrying the banana-mania jacket, was heading for the loud television screen in the corner, showing Morocco.

"Our first story is the revolution in Morocco," said the ugly presenter on the television. "Our correspondent, Elijah Brumby, has this report."

"The region of Souss-Massa in Morocco is known for many things." The voice of Elijah Brumby was accompanied by bright-yellow landscapes, blanched-almond dunes, burlywood sand, and dark-salmon canyons. It was clearly stock footage, however, because there was a distinct lack of rain and flooding. "The national park is home to many endangered species, and the Massa River basins hold agricultural industries, such as the processing of seafood, and ornate silverwork. But the latest addition to Souss-Massa might determine the future of the country." There were shots of African Antelopes blasting houses with their 90 mm turrets, and African Elephants leveling whole streets as communist soldiers waved on traffic. "The local government - the *makhzan* - has surrendered to the Moroccan Communist Party, who began to reclaim the region several days ago, after a military campaign in the south of the country."

"Reclaim?" mumbled Lou.

"The local governor, who only recently took the post, has negotiated with the communists, and has committed to restoring agricultural and tourist economies."

"Big teeth!" shouted Lou as he watched footage of an African Elephant's 84 mm cannon taking aim at retreating Republican Army soldiers and blasting them away.

"Elijah Brumby, Britannia News," signed off the war correspondent.

"What a bunch of carrot-stained fucking bullshit," complained Lou.

"Shut up, mate," said a man behind him. He had a boulder-shaped head, small ears, a bulbous nose, and jowls that jiggled when he spoke. "It's their country, innit?"

"You don't - don't you - don't you, bloody - you don't – cracker boy."

"Get it out, mate!" laughed the heavy man. He jeered at Lou, sipping his pint of lager, and pointing leisurely at the muddled fellow before him. "He's lost the plot."

"Haven't you - got chickens to fuck?"

"WHAT?"

"So go fuck 'em – on Venus – fuck 'em in the Martian canal, Captain Boswell."

"VENUS?"

The goateed barman spoke over the quiet crowd. "If you and he want to double down on your beliefs, can you take it outside, please?"

The lemon-meringue luminescence battered Lou's sight, returning him to the booze-induced caverns of outlines, shadows, and cosmic blurs. The dark world was brighter, and the angry people less confused. "Going now," thought Lou, finishing his Château de London Thames and navigating his way out of the establishment.

When he stumbled into the cold air, he immediately thought about Morocco's climate. But the rains had come and washed his world away. They had destroyed his Morocco. England had more in common with the country that he had evacuated, and yet, as their meteorological conditions aligned, his sense of alienation deepened. England was a damp country, and her people were damp, with dark-lava mold. Despite the heavy snow and the hidden landscape of metal and concrete, Lou found his semi-native homeland to be as damp and as isolated from his own desires as ever. "What does England know about what I want?" thought Lou, as he fell into the snow.

Allied Chemicals, a British company, sent their delegate to the Canary Islands. She then hopped onto a Boeing CH-47 Chinook and landed in Dakhla. Germaine Sharpton had premature grey hair, a narrow nose, large cheeks, and a downturned mouth with the vestiges of a smile at the furthest edges. She was also wearing a livid-blue pantsuit, Indian-red heels, and a gold necklace. She was shown by men and women wearing military-green overalls through the city square, across the deep-chestnut pavements, and past the pale-spring-bud buildings. Despite the recent acquisition of Dakhla, Sharpton was impressed by the clean roads and the ordered lines in front of the supply offices. The soldiers escorted Sharpton to a small building that had once been a city hall. Despite the general disrepair of the building, the cleanliness improved the deeper they moved into the building.

An iceberg staircase, with kobicha-brown banisters, welcomed the delegate into a large meeting chamber, which looked over Dakhla. There was an imperial-red rug that stretched towards a high-backed chair, behind which tall banners boasting Lincoln-green pentagons flapped nonchalantly. Apart from these things, and the mardis-gras-purple floor, the chamber was barren.

The doors behind Germaine Swallow creaked shut and she noticed how sunny the weather was, despite her company forecasting rain.

Without warning, a door on the other side of the chamber opened. Out walked two men wearing magnolia robes, with mango bands. They were also wearing imperial-red fezzes, but their presentation could hardly be said to be "communistic". Whereas one sat on the throne, the other moved towards Germaine with a white scroll. When he was several metres away from her, he stopped, unfurled the scroll, and said in French: "Sharif, great king; Emir-of-Emirs; Moroccan king; king of all Maghreb, we send greetings. Sharif, the eternal hero of Moroccan history; the founder of the greatest monarchy in Africa; the great freedom-giver of the world; the worthy son of mankind, we send greetings. Sharif, we have gathered here today to tell you: sleep in peace, because we are awake, and we will always be awake to look after our inheritance." Then the man rolled up the scroll, held out his hand, and added, "You may approach."

Germaine walked up the imperial-red rug, squinting towards the imperial-red chair.

The man in the chair was the so-called communist, Ismail. He had trimmed his monobrow, shaved off his beard, and cut his unruly hair.

"What do you want with my inheritance?" Ismail asked.

Germaine looked first to the consort and then back at Ismail.

"I'm sorry, what do I call you?"

"Sharif, great king; Sultan-of-Sultans," replied the consort.

"I know someone called Moulay Ismail. He was a Sharif. But he was Sultan in the 16th Century. This isn't the same man, I take it?" Germaine attempted to clarify.

"You came this far to be funny?" asked the consort. "Moulay Ismail ruled for fifty years. He brought control to Maghreb, and great prosperity. The great builder of cities, organizer of armies, economist of commerce." Then he bowed, adding, "*This* is the true heir to Sharif, Emir-of-Emirs."

"Your Majesty," said Germaine. "Allied Chemicals, and His Majesty's Government, wish to extend our services to aid in your holy mission."

"How generous," replied Ismail.

"You have charged Lou Baring with the murder of Kossi Bundhoo?"

"The Mauritanians charged him with murder. But we follow the same ideals, and so we are willing to re-affirm the charge - for the time being. I'm afraid that you will have had a wasted trip. If your concern is with Mauritania, we would like to know why you should like to speak with us, when your concerns are with them, and their nation."

There was a prolonged silence.

"As you know," Germaine said, "there was a period of instability in Mauritania. Some of those dangerous elements persist. We find it easier to speak with your regime."

"We are a popular crown prince," laughed Ismail. "Your king is like a distant cousin to us. But even he would admit that popularity is flimsy."

"Then let us help you, Your Majesty," replied Germaine, increasing her smile. "Together, we can look for more phosphate prospects in the Western Sahara. The Inal mine has been prodigious, but with a steady hand, everything could be yours. Morocco is an impressive, ancient nation, Your Majesty. If you put Lou Baring on trial, the people will see your power - and, in return, the phosphate will give you great wealth."

In the face of her rhetoric, the crown prince creaked forward.

"A band of foreigners raided our country, murdered our great-grandfather, enslaved our people, and destroyed our land. And you think that that is impressive?" asked Ismail, with a frankness that would have leveled even the proudest monarchs. "You want to bring stability, when it was stability that killed Morocco. We can only offer our inheritance; not just of Morocco, but of greater Maghreb. We shall be its Sharif - Sultan-of-Sultans, Emir-of-Emirs. Bring us Lou Baring, and we shall give you a souvenir of all that we have suffered. But make no mistake. You are sleeping - and we are awake."

Germaine bowed in her livid-blue pantsuit. She was escorted by the consort down the imperial-red rug and shown out of the temporary royal chamber. Then she walked down the staircase and stood outside. The sun brightened her gold necklace, and she smiled because she had made a deal with a member of the royal family. "So, that's why the commies and the royals get on so well," thought the glib delegate.

CHAPTER FIFTEEN

Lou's apartment in Richmond had Isabelline-grey paint on every surface, and featured ivory-hued cabinets, cupboards, and work surfaces. The bedroom was the same size as the kitchenette. There was a rusty radiator on the lower wall facing the roadside, a grim pair of lavender-blush cabinet doors, and linen carpeting whose scuffs and stains made McDonalds look hygienic. The same safety-orange bedsheets covered the squeaky mattress, and the double-glazed windows barely disguised the noise of constant traffic.

It had been a rough morning after his debacle in *The Cocksure Feline*.

He woke up on the linen carpeting in his bedroom. Then he stood up, shuffled into his dismal kitchenette, and made himself a cup of instant coffee. He checked his mail by the door. When he ripped one envelope open, and read the letter, he felt his banana-mania knees go weak. The Home Office explained that Mauritania wanted him for murder and that sanctions would be launched because he was now considered a threat to national security.

"Uh," said Lou.

He would only be allowed to leave his apartment between 10:00 a.m. and 11:00 a.m., and he would be under twenty-four-hour surveillance.

"Uh," said Lou, gripping the bridge of his nose, and thinking about what Brooke would do in this situation. "Need a lawyer," he decided.

Under the circumstances, Darcie Baba had forgone her usual solicitor and had decided to speak with the injured party personally. She was a Moroccan-British lawyer whose parents had fled Morocco when the Scarvaggi Family had taken over. Now she specialized in human rights and rejoiced in taking on high-profile cases like Lou's. She had liver-coloured eyes, thick eyebrows, and a prominent nose. She wore liseran-purple lipstick on her plump lips and had fat cheeks, as if she had never grown up. She wore a medium-blue turtleneck sweater, which barely disguised her large breasts, and her short hair was the same colour as her maximum-green trousers and her shoes.

"This isn't going to be fun," said Darcie, sipping a store-bought Americano and staring at the still-hungover Lou, as he fumbled with a sandy Alka-Seltzer packet. "They want to indict you for being a threat to England's security. The best thing to do is to let them get away with this; then we can appeal the verdict."

"Me and Hassan Hacimi - this guy - we did some stuff."

"They found his body in Gibraltar."

"Huh?"

"They didn't find anything else...Should they have?"

"Nuh-uh. I just thought - maybe he could defend me."

"They found his body," said Darcie, dumbstruck. "He's *dead*."

"Uh."

"You should distance yourself from him. Because you can't prove you helped to collect information without implicating yourself in the murder."

Lou rubbed his temples, sipping his Alka-Seltzer.

"The British Government wants to deport you. Now, a foreign national can be deported as per section 3(5)(a) of the Immigration Act of 1971. But you're a British citizen, so they can't invoke this legislation. You're also a dual citizen."

"I am?"

"You're aware that Bermuda went independent last year? And that you now have both Bermudian and British passports? You're aware of holding these passports, yes?"

"Oh, that."

"Yes."

"Sal told me to do it," said Lou, watching his breath in the cold kitchenette. "But they found out where I was and they revoked it." He paused. "Shitty place, anyway." The loss of his original national identity was little more than a diplomatic speckling.

"In that case, the British Government may revoke your British passport on the grounds of your being a threat to national security, or even on the grounds of fraud," explained Darcie.

"But you said - I was - I'm supposed to be a threat?"

"Yes."

"What's that about fraud?"

"They can swap the charge against you. They do that sometimes."

"But - my passport?" asked Lou, wincing in the freezing kitchenette.

"If they revoke your passport, you will be given written notice, and you'll be given the right to appeal." She finished her store-bought Americano and explained, "National security cases are held by the Special Immigration Appeals Commission, whereas the First-Tier Tribunals do everything else. The trouble with the commission is that they withhold sensitive evidence from appellants and lawyers and then they appoint special advocates to represent the appellants."

"What's an appellant?"

"That's you. I'm going to argue that your case has nothing to do with national security - because then they won't be able to give you an advocate."

Lou prepared another Alka-Seltzer.

"We can also demand that the Home Office withdraw your passport, instead of revoking it."

"Huh?"

"If they withdraw your passport, you're still a British citizen, but you can't travel. The problem with withdrawing your passport is that the appeal option disappears."

"But that's, like, what *we're* doing."

"Yes," laughed Darcie, flicking her hair. "We're going to apply for an appeal at the First-Tier Tribunal. I'm going to say that you took part in fraud on foreign soil, but that this fraud never threatened, or continues to threaten, the United Kingdom. I'm also going to say that the fact that Zaalouk Real Estate is a British company is completely irrelevant because it profited from foreign assets more than British ones."

"I didn't do fraud," said Lou.

"Are you sure?"

"I don't know - maybe."

Replacing the copious amount of copy - with which she had attempted to explain to Lou the intricacies of the British legal system - back inside of her briefcase, she retrieved her empty paper cup and sized up the ex-Bermudian with a doubtful stare. "I'll be in touch with you soon - and if you could start telling the truth," she added, "that would make my job easier."

But what Darcie Baba soon realised in her email chains and conversations with Lou Baring was that he was a principled man. There would be no mistruth in Lou Baring, and whatever misdemeanors he had accrued, were merely the results of his attempts to please, gratify, and satisfy, his controllers. There was no life for him without a controller, and this was something he understood, even though the ways in which he could forge some kind of freedom were totally beyond his understanding.

In Marrakech, African Elephants cleansed barricaded streets of Scarvaggi strongholds as African Antelopes swerved through parks, and neighborhoods, protecting locals. Gamboge-coloured buildings were felled so that the tanks had better access, and military-green soldiers spread word of communist victories amongst the urban sprawls. The thundering granite-grey clouds subsided as golden-yellow sunshine flooded fiery boulevards, shattered avenues, incandescent crescents, and bare, disfigured highways.

The people of Marrakech began to show their support of the invading communists, shouting, "Long live the revolution!" in Tamazight out of their doorways, windows, and backyards, as tanks, jeeps, and armored trucks flourished. Teenagers and children trailed Ismail's personal jeep as he inspected the impressive remains of the subsumed city, and waved at Morocco's fate.

From the safety of a truck driven by military escort, Elijah Brumby snapped photographs of Morocco's new leader, Ismail, as he shook hands, smiled, and saluted. Although the communists had yet to storm the nation's authentic capital, they had, for all intents and purposes, conquered Morocco's political centre of operations, and had secured the crown jewels of the Scarvaggi Family, and their varied western associates.

Ismail returned to his seat in the jolting jeep, his sad eyes tracing the charred walls and streets of Marrakech. Meanwhile, his Defence Minister whispered in Arabic. "Sharif, great king; Emir-of-Emirs; Moroccan king; king of all Maghreb, we send greetings. Sharif, the eternal hero of Moroccan history; the founder of the greatest monarchy in Africa; the great freedom-giver of the world; the worthy son of mankind, we send greetings. Sharif, we have gathered here today to tell you: sleep in peace, because we are awake, and we will always be awake to look after our inheritance…!"

The sky in Richmond was ghost-white and shavings of snow descended upon the international-orange brick buildings, the granite-grey roads, and the unhurried buses. Through his window, Lou watched people walking to work wearing goldenrod-hued jackets, ankle-length coats, and macaroni-and-cheese-coloured snow boots. The colours reminded the ex-property manager and ex-real estate agent of Morocco, with its open spaces, and fresh air. Whereas London was a grim metropolis whose squat terraced buildings sat, huddled amongst the cold, refusing to speak to one another. Putting this out of his mind and thinking about what Brooke - and Darcie Baba - would do, he opened an ivory-coloured cabinet and withdrew some instant coffee and powdered milk. He was wearing a white shirt and his banana-mania-coloured trousers: the last of his wardrobe. Then, having made his coffee, the door-buzzer screamed. He answered the door, let Darcie Baba inside, and watched her wince in the kitchen.

"Oh, Lou," said Darcie, brushing snow off of her maximum-green trousers, removing her winter hat, and looking around the dismal apartment…

Aluminium pie containers dotted countertops, their interiors marked by metallic-sunburst crusts, and dehydrated condiments. Then, there were the transparent takeaway containers, whose once-mode-beige sauces had transmogrified into moss-green crusts, with misty-rose-colored rice on the edges.

The mature smell of day-old takeaway containers filled the room with a banal dread, and Darcie ignored the odd stenches, remembering her own failings.

"I couldn't be more embarrassed," she said, blinking her liver-hued eyes.

"Huh?"

"You don't watch the news, do you?" She had meant to sound casual, but the words came out as an accusation of Lou's green masculinity.

"They had the effigy thing…so, I stopped watching."

"I don't know who found this," said Darcie, pushing an unwashed plate away so that she could lean against the counter. "But there must be private forces at work."

"Uh-huh."

She sighed. "When I was at Cambridge University, I dressed up as Joseph Stalin for a Christmas party. I'm not proud of it. Young people do stupid things all the time. But Britannia News are running photographs of me, as Stalin, and telling the world that Lou Baring, the awful murderer, has hired an anti-communist fool to defend him."

"Who's Joseph Stalin?"

Stifling the urge to roll her eyes, Darcie took a deep breath:

"Stalin was a communist dictator, who killed millions of people."

"What, like, *personally?*"

"That doesn't matter," interrupted Darcie. "The pictures make me look like I don't take communists seriously. You see the issue, right?"

"What do we do?" asked Lou, sipping his disgusting coffee.

"I'm sorry, Lou, but you'll have to find someone else." She creased her thick eyebrows and pressed her bosoms against Lou. "I'm so sorry. This is such a mess you're in, and I'm sorry you're in the middle of it."

"Darcie?"

"I'm sorry," she said, pulling away, and replacing her winter hat. Then she walked into the corridor and let herself out of the apartment.

Lou moved towards the corridor, but then he turned around. He walked past the ivory-hued cupboards and stood in front of the window that overlooked the sink. Ghost-white shavings of snow disguised the otherwise obvious policemen downstairs.

Darcie appeared on the patterned pavement and waved at Lou in the glass.

"Darcie!" shouted Lou.

She walked down the flaky street and disappeared around the corner.

Lou banged the windows, raving like a madman. "DARCIE!"

A voice upstairs shouted, "Will you shut up?" and banged on the floor.

Lou stood picking his aquiline nose, trying to preserve some kind of grooming, as the vibrations turned into paranoia, and his paranoia grew limbs.

"Why do I live in this world?" thought Lou, shuffling between his bedroom and his kitchen, and trying to find a noiseless point where he could think, however dimly. The notion that people had betrayed him was never considered. Things like that happened in movies with buxom blondes and strapping males, like *The Brain Suckers*, but it just wasn't within the bounds of possibility in a world bereft of brain-sucking aliens.

The Clinique Internationale De Marrakech was an antique-brass building surrounded by deep-jungle-green trees. The ground was dry, the weather hot, and sticks and twigs snapped on the tarmac as a convoy of military-green limousines pulled alongside the entrance, deposited Ismail and his bodyguards, and watched them go inside the glass doors. They were greeted by several doctors who escorted the communist-cum-crown-prince to the top floor on which glass-walled gangways connected different sides of the dark-electric-blue chamber. Ismail was shown into a room with a dark-magenta couch, English-lavender curtains, a coffee table, a television, and an Eton-blue medical bed carrying a feeble Nina Scarvaggi. The old *Cummari* had been stripped of her Falu-red blouse, Finn-purple dress, and unpretentious flat shoes, in favour of a denim-blue hospital gown with flower motifs. Her eyes were shut, her vital signs were passable, and her mouth was a slit, her sun-cracked face mummified in the overcast lighting.

"Peasant," muttered Ismail.

Dr. Zaki appeared behind him, introduced himself, and checked on Nina. He was wearing a bedazzled-blue suit with a blanched-almond waistcoat.

"How long does she have?" asked Ismail in Arabic.

"I can't say."

"Will she make it to court?"

"It's a shame she didn't tell me sooner," noted Dr. Zaki, ignoring the powerful man standing behind him. Then again, one tried to look powerful in the face of death. "The cancer has metastasized, and if it spreads to her liver, she's going to turn yellow. But she may cough herself into a stupor first, and expire like an ancient, English princess."

The clicking of guns patterned the room, like soldiers' footprints in snow.

"Dr. Zaki," murmured Ismail. "I don't think you understand me."

The good doctor straightened his back, turned around, and pointed his sharp nose towards one of those debatable next-of-kins that he had met throughout his practice. "If you let me do my job, and give her oxygen therapy, she will live to fight another day."

"Good," replied the crown prince, and walked out of the room.

Dr. Zaki ran his hands through his curly black hair. There were touches of grey, here and there. He had lost some over the past months. But the barber-esque pantomime was merely an attempt to ignore the ailing Scarvaggi. She had put his children through Western universities, she had given him good work, and now she lay expiring under the distorted patronage of a new regime - a new world - a new... *something*.

It was not Dr. Zaki's prerogative to ask "why". But, as he stared through the tips of the deep-jungle-green trees around the antique-brass building, he couldn't help asking "why". He couldn't help shaking his mind's fist at all this divine silence.

"Sharif, great king!" The Tamazight words echoed around the hospital, the exterior grounds, and the roads that returned to the city. The words were overwhelming, nationalistic, and important. "Emir-of-Emirs; Moroccan king; king of all Maghreb, we send greetings. Sharif, the eternal hero of Moroccan history; the founder of the greatest monarchy in Africa; the great freedom-giver of the world; the worthy son of mankind, we send greetings. Sharif, we have gathered here today to tell you: sleep in peace, because we are awake, and we will always be awake to look after our inheritance...!"

Dr. Zaki turned the same shade as his blanched-almond waistcoat.

On the morning of his deportation, Lou removed his banana-mania trousers and white shirt for the last time, changed into an orange jumpsuit, and stepped inside the dark-liver van. His light-cornflower-blue eyes ached in the wintry air, and he watched his breath flit between two members of London's Metropolitan police.

The van drove onto a highway and entered Heathrow Airport. They braved banks of snow and sleet as they drove straight onto one of the runways. Then they parked next to a flimsy metal staircase that led into a Poseidon MRA1: an old-silver maritime aircraft used exclusively for rescue missions. The policemen marched Lou into the orange-soda morning - avoiding specks of heavy snow descending from the outer-space atmosphere - and handed him over to the olive-drab fellows of His Majesty's Royal Airforce.

Handcuffing Lou's ankles and wrists, the soldiers pushed him up the flimsy metal staircase into the congested aircraft's interiors. There were high-backed chairs, and a large, safety-orange chair with straps that was intended for prisoners. After he was strapped into the latter chair, the soldiers fed him bottled water and crackers and took their seats for takeoff. The plane taxied onto the runway and sped up, lifting into the outer-space clouds, and cutting through fibrous sheets of falling snow.

Lou shivered. What Brooke might do in this situation had evaporated completely. Suddenly, a quotation from the Koran came to mind.   "He said, 'I am the servant of God. He has given me the Scripture, and made me a prophet.

"And has made me blessed wherever I may be; and has enjoined on me prayer and charity, so long as I live.

"And kind to my mother, and He did not make me a disobedient rebel.

"So, Peace is upon me the day I was born, and the day I die, and the Day I get resurrected alive.'"

"That is Jesus' son of Mary—the Word of truth about which they doubt."

All of the crew had brown hair, aquiline noses, and pleasant smiles. One of them stuck his face into Lou's, and said, "Are you alright, sir?"

"Huh?"

"Are you alright, sir?"

"Uh-huh."

The soldier nodded kindly and returned to his post by the window. There, he sat through the rising and falling of temperature and time.

After several hours, the radio crackled to life in the cockpit. The captain was wearing a headset around his cauliflowered ears and his shrewd eyes darted around the various flight displays, direction finders, altitude indicators, and systems information displays. The unpopulated airspace was barren and he could almost see the wind striking the surface area of the windshield as they progressed.

"Good morning, this is MRA1 rescue craft - Mike, Romeo, Alpha, One - en route to Romeo, Alpha, Kilo. Is that received? Over." He coughed quietly, waiting for the reply.

"That is received," replied the radio in a thick Moroccan accent. "You have flight clearance as far as Mike, Mike Alpha."

"Copy that, air control," replied the captain, turning to his navigators. "They're playing games, Charlie, wake up."

"Yes, captain?" answered the navigator, replacing his thermos in the cupholder.

"Mike, Mike, Alpha - what's he referring to?"

"Marrakech Menara Airport. Due north, about 190 kilometres."

"Jolly good," replied the captain.

In the cabin, the same friendly soldier approached Lou Baring.

"Hello, sir - would you like to look out the window, or anything?"

"Sure," replied Lou.

The ant-sized geography of Morocco was full of Payne's-grays, periwinkle-purples, and paradise-pinks. The whole country was like something out of a movie. Then they noticed Portland-orange flames blazing under clouds of thick, black smoke.

"Burning solar panels, apparently. All that green tech. All for the chop, I'm afraid," explained the soldier to the increasingly worried Lou, who panted heavily in his chair.

"Damn shame, really. On the right track for the longest time. We can only hope the new regime's thinking on the same page," added the soldier, in the face of clear evidence that Ismail's Moroccan kingdom had no interest in renewable energies.

Heaps of smouldering electric vehicles, mountains of crispy solar panels, jumbles of flickering wind turbines, and the remnants of whatever recycling had been started: base chemicals and chemical feedstocks that had been derived from used-up plastics, retroactive oil that had been extracted from otherwise un-recyclable plastics, and styrene that had been acquired from polystyrene through a process of cracking long polymer molecules into monomer building blocks, starting the whole process again…

The more the plane descended, the more apparent the smouldering stockpiles became. Lou mumbled, "Uh," but kept silent, and wheezing, for the remaining trip.

The plane touched down at Marrakech Menara Airport amongst a throng of military vehicles. The old-silver maritime aircraft pulled alongside an air-bridge, decompressed its cabin, and opened its heavy, pressurized door. The crew of the plane - apart from the captain, who stood like a Roman statue by the door - stood in a straight line, and saluted, as Lou Baring was carried out of the aircraft by Moroccan soldiers. The rush of fresh air relaxed Lou's airways, but he continued to hyperventilate as he was half-carried, half-escorted through the fluorescent lighting of the brief air-bridge.

Arriving in the pistachio-green arrivals lounge, Lou spotted another escort party. These soldiers were heavily armed and they seemed anxious to offload their cargo…

"Shit," muttered Lou, as he noticed Salvatore Yannucci in a wheelchair. His dark eyebrows had turned bright white, his thick forearms had atrophied into flabby tubes, his chubby stomach had slimmed, and his tree-trunk legs had degenerated into corpulent noodles. Below the trouser legs of the safety-orange jumpsuit, there were two feet whose soles had been removed. There was bandaging, but a gangrenous stench persisted.

Salvatore coughed, and said, "Lou!"

"Bastard!"

"I didn't know! I didn't know!"

"Bastard!" shouted Lou, his aggressive escorts shoving him forward.

"I didn't know! They don't tell me anything!" Salvatore was wheeled towards the air-bridge. "No! No! Don't take me! I want to be with Lou!"

"Bastard!"

"Take me back to him!" pleaded Salvatore, as he was wheeled down the air-bridge. "Take me back to my son! Take me back to my family!"

"I'm not your fucking son!" screamed Lou.

He closed his eyes, imagining that he was in his freezing Richmond apartment, eating Chinese takeaways, drinking coffee, and masturbating to pictures of Brooke.

When he opened his eyes, the Poseidon MRA1 had taken off.

Lou's new property was a jail cell in the converted Republic Theatre in Marrakech. "Do what you like," the guards told him. Regardless of the language barrier, Lou began turning the pine-tree-coloured hole into a home.

On one side of the room, he placed his Daily Reflections book. On the other side, he placed his Koran. In the middle, he rolled up his safety-orange jumpsuit, and set it down. The heat was excruciating at times, so he ended up dozing in the nude.

Apart from the constant fluorescent blaze, there was no light.

"It's not the sun," Lou reminded himself, picking up the Koran.

"Among the people are those who say, 'We believe in God and in the Last Day,' but they are not believers.

"They seek to deceive God and those who believe, but they deceive none but themselves, though they are not aware.

"In their hearts is sickness, and God has increased their sickness. They will have a painful punishment because of their denial.

"And when it is said to them, 'Do not make trouble on earth,' they say, 'We are only reformers.'

"In fact, they are the troublemakers, but they are not aware.

"And when it is said to them, 'Believe as the people have believed,' they say, 'Shall we believe as the fools have believed?' In fact, it is they who are the fools, but they do not know.

"And when they come across those who believe, they say, 'We believe'; but when they are alone with their devils, they say, "We are with you; we were only ridiculing.'

"It is God who ridicules them, and leaves them bewildered in their transgression."

The concrete floor was really amazing when one studied it relentlessly. There was Russian-violet, salmon-pink, tart-orange, Venetian-red, and blips of Van-Dyke brown. Sand from the Western Sahara made this study more difficult, because it obscured the colours with its own Navajo-white and peach-puff-coloured particles, but Lou used the opportunity to write down everyone he had met during his tenure in Morocco. Names of deceased caporegimes made linguistic valleys of the prison cell's dunes, as did titles of ex-colleagues from Zaalouk Real Estate, and the faces of other dead people. The face of Kossi Bundhoo, which was one of the first faces that Lou ever saw in Morocco, flickered intemperately through Lou's cerebral matter, culling the senses, and stirring the erring sections of the Bermudian's brain, with their penchants for indifference. Over many months, Lou's capacity for guilt widened, and he found himself weeding his brain, second after second, searching for possible misdeeds, but finding nothing. Because the guilt of his wasted life - his directionless life - was meteoric in comparison to whatever fleeting misconduct he may have committed amidst the purposeless days. But there was nothing that Lou could see that might improve him. Nothing except Brooke, of course. "She and the rest have gone," thought Lou, drawing in the sand, and probing for forms that echoed her face, without making any serious artistic attempts.

When they took the bag off of his head, Lou realised that they were at the base of the Atlas Mountains and standing in front of Lake Lalla Takerkoust. The Munsell-blue water ebbed and flowed against the pebbled shores, and atomic-tangerine shrubs - the same colour as the rocky hills in the distance - bobbed in the gentle wind. His companions were two soldiers wearing azure-blue caps with tassels, camelian-red uniforms held together by golden buttons, and white cotton gloves that cascaded brightness upon their black combat boots, which had been shined to hell and back.

Alongside their uniforms, they had the postures of the royal guard.

The cigarette burns on Lou's face stung in the harsh sunlight, and his red-rimmed, light-cornflower-blue eyes winced against the weather, the company, and the circumstance. Instead of shaving himself with the water provided, he had swallowed the bucket, and now felt queasy on top of the adrenalin. The unadulterated horror. One of the royal guards said, "On your knees, please," in English, and watched as Lou lowered his bruised and battered legs onto the pebbled, rather uncomfortable, ground.

The Bermudian took a deep breath.

When nothing happened, he took another deep breath.

"Broo - "

He was shot in the back of his head, and his flaccid body collapsed onto the quasi-sandy beach, and the waves laughed, back and forth.

THE END

ACKNOWLEDGMENTS

I would like to thank Charlie Franco, Rick Febre, Amit Dey, and the Montag Press team for helping to publish this book. I would also like to thank my partner, Ellie, and my mother for both supporting me. But the biggest "acknowledgement" during this whole process was that *Morocconomics* was about my native Bermuda, something that I had been running away from for most of my career. Now, there are rich Bermudians and there are poor ones. But when I realized that Lou Baring was one of the rich Bermudians, the novel made sense; and the kaleidoscope of individuals I had known in Bermuda - the ones who had bumbled through life making large sums of money and seemingly avoiding tragedy and death - suddenly took shape in all their absurdity in my creative mind. More importantly, Brian Burland helped me to understand my people: a forgotten Bermudian writer, acknowledged as a genius by foreigners, but sadly ignored, or downright avoided, in his native Bermuda. When I studied novels like *Surprise*, *The Sailor and the Fox*, and *Love Is A Durable Fire*, I realized that writing about Bermuda and Bermudians could be every bit as exciting as Baldwin's New Yorkers, Joyce's Dubliners,

Lovecraft's New Englanders, or Dostoyevsky's Russians; and that what connects these wonderful characters and stories is the common chemical of people. If Bermuda cannot recognize that she is full of people, then little can be done to save her. Bermudian writers like Khalid A. Wasi, Jonathan Starling, Gernel Darrell, and Angela Barry understand this. Hopefully, by writing *Morocconomics*, I now understand this. That is why I have dedicated this book to uncertainty and the morons who try avoiding it. *Morocconomics*, and Bermuda by extension, is filled with them, and they would do well to surrender to God.

AUTHOR BIO

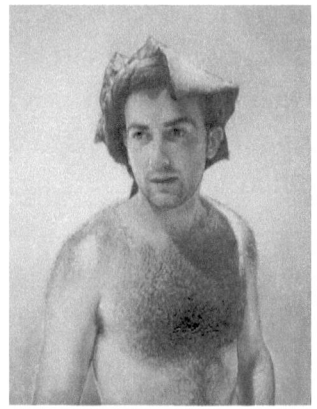

Dr. Walker Zupp is a Bermudian author. He received his Ph.D. in Creative Writing from the University of Exeter. He currently lives in Cornwall, where he is a member of the Cornish Writers association and the British Wittgenstein Society. He really isn't that busy – not by choice, of course – and would love to be invited to book festivals, universities, and schools to talk about writing and life. He can be reached via his email: walkerspurlingzupp@gmail.com

OTHER NOVELS BY WALKER ZUPP

Martha

"A freewheelingly scabrous, energetic, and darkly funny tale, pinpricked with pathos and sympathy, all concealing a strange sort of seriousness. Probably the strangest and most scatologically unbridled book you'll read this year, and that's a recommendation."

—George Green, author of *Hawk*

Nakadai

"One can picture Walker Zupp's sly grin as he composes Nakadai, an absurdist fantasy narrated by a grad student where a philosophical genius is empowered and enslaved by an inter-dimensional being called the Great Word who plots to invade the world. Written with breath-taking pace, language, academics, and eastern and western civilization are skewered by Zupp's rapier wit. Zupp captures the pathos and absurdity of contemporary life as his prose propels the reader into a parallel world that often feels eerily like our own."

—Stephen Scott Whitaker, National Book Critics Circle

Fibber

"A transmutation of Kotlovan, ringing close to the Aki Kaurismaki adaptation of Crime and Punishment. An important piece of modern proletariat story-telling with style."

—Connor de Bruler,
author of *Hell, South Carolina*

www.ingramcontent.com/pod-product-compliance
Lightning Source LLC
Chambersburg PA
CBHW020635020726
47494CB00001B/200